For Nancy,
And for Andrew and Lisa, Christine and Tim, Katherine and Rachel,
Sara, Saurin, Sarina, and Priya,
Rachel, Chad, Makayla, Lexie, and Josie

DANCING

WITH

BEARS

"My soul is moved to tell of bodies changed into different forms; you gods, who made the changes, help me."

—Ovid

WHAT A BEAR DOES IN THE WOODS

They walk on the entire foot, as does man.
—*A Field Guide to the Mammals*

Antenna thrust before him like a wiry erection, Lyle Gustafson jumps downed trees, flails brambles, and leaps a snarl of brush. We're trying to keep up—the young guy with the video camera, the woman with her long blond hair peeking from her cap, and I with my gimpy leg. The forest drips from the recent cold rain, and our boots skid in the soggy burgundy and ochre leaves. Lyle's yelling, *Rudy! Rudy!*

Lyle's in the clearing, dancing with Rudy, the black bear he raised from a cub. Rudy's on his hind legs, moving in little steps, beating a rhythm with his feet, and Lyle mimics the steps, he does a kind of bear jig, and they wave their arms as if they're trying to hug each other but are shy, and I wish I could hear the music they're dancing to.

The young guy from the TV station is loaded with equipment, bags slung over both shoulders, bandoliers criss-crossing his chest. He shoots some long shots—Get the woods, the context, the woman says—then he moves in closer, but now Rudy and Lyle seem tired of dancing. Rudy's on all fours rummaging around and Lyle's squatting nearby talking to him, telling him how much he's missed him and he's a hell of a good bear and how's he been making out, did he find enough grubs and acorns and berries?

The guy with the camera pulls a can of beer from his new Banana Republic safari jacket. The can pops and sprays all over. He's sucking up the foam that's fizzing out of the can when he sees Rudy coming for him. Rudy's nostrils are crinkling and he's making little whuffing noises. "Don't run," Lyle advises, but it's too late. Rudy lunges. The guy back pedals, Doc Martens sliding in the wet leaves, arms flapping as if he's trying to fly out of here. He loses the camera. He loses the can of beer. He loses his Tilley hat. He lands on his back in the mud.

Rudy plants his paws on the guy's shoulders. The guy's the color of the white larvae Rudy's been licking out of rotting logs, and the guy looks as if he's going to cry. Rudy studies the guy's face, Rudy's muzzle an inch from the fellow's lips. Now the guy is crying. The woman has picked up the camera, and the camera's rolling.

Rudy's making little noises, or maybe it's the guy, I'm not sure, little gargles in the throat, and the beer is making a sparkly sound as it flows from the can, making a little yellow pool in the leaves. Rudy heads for the fizzy sound, leaving the guy on the ground, paw prints on the shoulders of the new safari jacket. Rudy starts licking up the beer. The woman's on one knee, taping Rudy, and Lyle's chuckling quietly. Rudy laps the leaves dry, then grabs the can in his front paws, sits back, and pours the rest of the beer into his mouth. After awhile he lies on his back and sucks on the can, like a baby sucking on a bottle.

The woman producer's found the Tilley hat and she wants to put it on Rudy's head, but Lyle says, No, Rudy's not a circus animal, he's not even a tame animal, despite all appearances, and bears don't like to be touched, he says, as she's putting out her hand to pet Rudy. She lets her hand hang in the air, petting empty space, or maybe imagining Rudy's there anyway. He'd look cute, she says. That's the trouble, Lyle says. So she hands the muddy hat back to the camera guy. He puts it on. He doesn't look cute.

"I've tried petting them," Lyle says, "but they see it as an infringement on their personal space. A mother touches her cubs, and they touch when they mate, of course, and young ones will play with each other, wrestle and roll around, but otherwise they think you're out of line if you try to touch them."

She stands beside Lyle, who's hunkered near the ground. His head is beside her knees, her right muddy boot near his left muddy boot. She looks wistfully at Rudy, who's found some fat white grubs under a rotting log and is chewing them up. "Would he bite me if I tried to pet him?" she asks.

"He'd probably just move away from you. At the worst he'd slap you. But he wouldn't hurt you. Black bears are not aggressive."

She raises her hand a little. It's a nice hand, shapely, earnest, nails trimmed, no nail polish, no rings.

"Petting a bear," Lyle goes on, a sly irony in his mellow voice, "would be like me putting my hand between your legs."

She doesn't move her hand.

"Without an invitation," Lyle adds.

She looks at Rudy, not at Lyle.

"A breach of etiquette," Lyle says.

The guy's scrambled to his feet. He grabs the camera, but the tape has run out. He's still shaking so he drops the new cassette in the mud, then the old one, but Lyle says don't worry, we're going to take Rudy home with us so Rudy doesn't get shot because bear hunting season starts tomorrow, and I'll give him a bottle of Sam Adams Double Bock and you can videotape that. Won't he get drunk? the woman asks. Sure, Lyle says, we all will.

WHAT WE DO IN THE WOODS

...female black bears regulate urine flow, painting a scent to cover over their territories.
—*The Great American Bear*

Lyle's lost.

I assumed Lyle had a sixth sense about direction, that he knew these woods as if they were his home town, but he's off loping on a route we will later discover to be parallel to the unseen road, which all the time is only a hundred yards away from us. My gimpy leg starts hurting, and I fall behind, and I'm afraid they'll forget about me and I'll be left alone to starve, freeze, and die in the woods, but after awhile Lyle remembers me and pauses until I catch up. The camera guy's limping too, he must have bruised himself in one of his tumbles, so Lyle carries the guy's equipment. Besides keeping his eye on me and shouldering the guy's equipment, Lyle has to keep track of Rudy, who keeps wandering off, overturning old logs and pawing up rocks, searching for the fat white grubs he likes so much. So maybe that's why Lyle has trouble getting his bearings, because he has so much to keep track of, because he has so many distractions.

Like the woman producer, who keeps up with Lyle pretty well but then disappears, and we think we've lost her, but Rudy finds her, and Lyle's following Rudy, and the woman's trying to find a little privacy in the woods, squatting beside a tree taking a leak.

Rudy's very interested. The woman can't move. Lyle comes crashing through the brush. *Rudy! Rudy!* he calls, then sees her, then says, *Rudy, leave her alone,* but Rudy finds the splashing sound and the aroma extremely compelling.

She smacks Rudy on the nose.

Rudy gives a snort, as if to clear his nostrils, and waddles away, back to Lyle, pretending he hadn't been interested after all. The woman pulls up her jeans—there's a brief flash of white skin—and strides toward us as she buttons up. The camera guy appears through the brush and looks around, wondering why there's a certain vacuum in the psychic *Zeitgeist*. Lyle's been watching her all the time, without embarrassment or apology, as if as a Forestry employee it's his duty to keep an eye on everything that happens in the woods.

Finally we stumble onto the dirt road. "You stay here," Lyle says. "I'll get my truck, and I'll come get you. You look pretty bushed." He looks up and down the narrow road, which curves in both directions, so we can't see his pickup from here. "I think we're that way," he says, jogging off.

Rudy's lying in the ditch beside the road, lazily pawing at some fast food wrappers.

"You watch Rudy," he yells back. He disappears around the curve in the muddy road.

I look around to locate the camera guy and the woman, because I'm sure Lyle can't mean me. How would I stop Rudy from wandering off?

But they're not paying any attention. The camera guy's kneeling in the grass, his Tilley hat muddy and askew, trying to clean his equipment. She's found a rock to sit on and stares blankly into space the way you do when you're beat and you're ticked off and it's getting dark.

Rudy clambers out of the ditch. He ambles across the road, heading for the trees. He pads within a few feet of the woman, but she doesn't seem to give a hot damn whether Rudy gets shot by hunters or not. He plunges into the woods.

Hey! I yell. *Hey, Rudy!* I try to sound authoritative, like Lyle, but Rudy keeps trucking. "Rudy, Rudy," I croon, trying Lyle's friendly approach. Rudy keeps going, faster now.

I look around for help. They're paying no attention. "We've got to keep Rudy here," I explain, as rationally as I can. But the camera guy's busy with his equipment, and the woman looks at me as if to ask, Haven't you caused enough trouble already? So I run-limp-skip after Rudy.

Then she's striding ahead of me. She cuts off Rudy. She waves her arms. He gallomps past me back to the road.

As we reach the road again, Lyle jogs past, going the other way, smiling ruefully, saying the truck must be the other way. Rudy runs along with Lyle until they're out of sight. A minute later we hear a horn honk.

Rudy rides with Lyle. The rest of us sprawl in the bed of the pick-up. Lyle says Rudy got used to riding as a cub. All he needs to do, Lyle says, is see an open door, and you can't keep him out of a car.

CHEZ LYLE

> What shall we sing about now, which tale shall we lilt?
> We'll sing about this, and we'll lilt this tale
> of that Northland feast, those revels of the godly.
> —*Kalevala*

Lyle's invited us to spend the night, me and the TV documentary team who're doing the story on Lyle and his research, even though I'm not part of the TV documentary team. I'm only a free-lance scribbler who heard about Lyle's forays into bear companionship and how people could join him on certain weekends to "Bond with the Bears." I've never had a particular interest in bears, but I thought a change of pace from my lackluster existence might snap me out of the middle-aged doldrums that have seduced me lately. Lyle's an easy-going fellow with a wry sense of humor and a knack for making you feel at home. I feel a little out of place, but I feel that way anywhere.

There's plenty of room in the old log lodge Lyle uses as his research station, he says, and he has extra sleeping bags and cots, and he's pulling venison out of the freezer while the camera guy follows him with the camera. He's a young guy, the camera guy, new to the job, I think, and he's imagining he's Robert Altman or Martin Scorcese at the beginning of their careers and he's going to be them someday. It's going to be an hour-long documentary, for Northern Lakes Public Television.

The woman producer, who's older than the TV guy but not so old, follows Lyle around asking him questions, holding the mike, and she's taken off her cap, a forest green cap with the station logo, a yellow walleye standing on its tail and winking, on the front, and her blonde hair is braided and wrapped around her head so I guess when it's down it's long. She wears jeans and high black boots and a green plaid shirt, as if she's trying to look outdoorsy, but she isn't fooling Lyle, who has a little smile behind his bushy beard that's streaked with gray. His brown hair's streaked with gray, too, and he wipes it out of his eyes with a boyish gesture as he throws the chunks of frozen venison into the Dutch oven. The meat sizzles madly, and he talks about how sometimes you can't tell who's human and who's a bear.

"Native cultures all over the world have stories of people turning into bears and bears turning into people. You skin a bear, the carcass looks like a human. Indian shamans become bears to heal the sick. Dozens of tribes have bear clans, put on bear skins, bear masks, bear paws on their hands and feet. Bear ceremonies begin the year, regenerate vegetation in the spring, make strong the weak, straighten the lame, speak to the spirits."

Lyle talks to the woman—I think her name's Diane—while he uncorks several bottles of wine and the guy circles them with the camera. She tells the guy to stay still, for chrisake, it's a documentary not a Kenneth Branagh film, so the guy makes one more circle, like a kid who wants to assert himself, and then he stays planted while Lyle talks to her.

"There are hundreds of bear stories," Lyle says. "There are stories about women who marry bears, and then the bears kill her brothers. Or in other stories her brothers kill her bear husband. Sometimes the woman gives birth to a half-bear, half-human baby, and he's the beginning of the tribe."

A cork pops, as if some deep dark trouble had finally been overcome, and Lyle goes on, warming to his lecture, and looking closely at the woman, as if this part is especially for her. "There are stories about a bear who becomes a woman and she wants to marry the fellow, only secretly she's still wild, you see, still untamed. She has teeth in her vagina, and she wants the fellow to fuck her. *Fuck me,* she keeps saying. *Fuck me.*"

The woman glances at the camera guy, but he's taping away, so she just holds the mike, and I can tell she's editing all of this in her head, trying to decide whether to beep or cut the whole story.

Lyle continues, "But his grandmother, who knows the score, says, *Watch out, Grandson.* So he makes a clay pecker, and the next night, when the bear in the form of a woman says, *Fuck me, fuck me*"—by now we all know she's not going to use this but the guy still tapes and she still holds the mike— "he sticks that clay pecker in her instead of his

William Borden

own. She grinds that clay pecker into dust." Lyle's twisting the cork-screw into the next bottle, working his wrist back and forth, grinding the steel into the cork, until he grips the bottle between his thighs and gives a jerk, and the bottle of Syrah ejaculates the cork with a sonorous kiss of satisfaction.

"The next night she's hot for him again. But this night, with his grandmother's advice, he makes a stone pecker, and he gives it to her with the stone pecker. The stone pecker breaks off all her teeth, so she has to become a normal woman. She can't be a bear anymore. He tames the wildness of woman."

Lyle looks slyly at the woman producer, whose blond hair has un-raveled, and wisps like strands of spun honey fall across her face. She lets her arm drop, as if it's tired. The mike points to the floor. "It's a fear that goes back millennia," he says. "The notion that women have teeth in their vaginas."

"I never knew that," the young guy says.

She smiles. She shows her white teeth between her red lips.

"Most myths have some basis in fact," Lyle says.

She darts her pink tongue along the edges of her incisors.

"Little teeth," Lyle says, "like on a northern pike, each sharp as a razor."

"Jesus shit," the camera guy says, quivering in a strange sort of fear-ful anticipation.

Diane says, "Women have powers men have never imagined."

"I know that," Lyle says. "Now watch me conjure up some bis-cuits."

Lyle hauls a quart-size crock out of the refrigerator. "This sour-dough starter," he says, as the woman producer, whose name for sure is Diane, follows him, glass in her hand, "is over a hundred years old. It was taken to Alaska with the gold rush, and later returned in the company of an Inuit shaman who married the widow of a miner who died mysteriously after the shaman and the wife fell headlong into love. They lived not far from here, just over the lakes in Canada, for several years, then disappeared, never to be heard from again."

Lyle pours half of the sourdough, which has a wild, pungent odor, into a large ceramic bowl with strange totemic figures painted on it. "For years after, two bears were seen, always together, which is unusual, because bears are loners." Diane stares at the sourdough bubbling, giv-ing off a heady aroma, the aroma of—well, the aroma of semen.

EATING AND DRINKING WITH BEARS

> Autumn...is the period of hyperphagia, excessive eating,
> necessary to lay on enough fat to survive the winter...
> —*The Great American Bear*

Lyle's stashed an extensive collection of wine in the lodge's root cellar, which he has remodeled into a state-of-the-art wine repository, and he has half a dozen bottles breathing on the table. He likes a California Barbera with the venison, but he's uncorked a couple of Medocs and an Australian Shiraz, as well as a California Syrah, to taste the difference, and a Muscadet to drink with dessert, which will be the lemon soufflé he's whipping up now.

The camera guy is taping the creation of the soufflé, but Diane is telling him the documentary isn't for the Julia Child show, for chrisake, but the camera guy—is his name Ted?—thinks he's Frederick Wiseman or Maurice Ophuls and he's got to capture every fly on the wall—now he's focusing on my snifter of single malt—Lyle's drinking Lagavulin, which is too smoky for me—we had a little taste test—so I've got the Cragganmore, and Diane is drinking the Talisker, drinking it maybe a little too fast on an empty stomach because she's unbraided her hair. Her hair cascades like finely spun gold down to her ass. Her hair flows like a sun-blazed mountain stream. It bounces insolently down her back as if it had been restrained by those tight braids so long it's become a wild beast let loose to roam. I know these metaphors are mixed but that's what her hair does to me, and I'll have another touch of that Cragganmore, which Lyle explains is twelve years old and is distilled in Speyside, Scotland, where the river Spey meets the Avon and Livet, and aged in oak barrels that previously held bourbon or sherry.

Diane takes another swig of her Talisker—the only single malt made on the Isle of Skye, Lyle informs us, on the shores of Loch Harport, the smokiness absorbed by the sprouting barley (the bear-grain) drying over a peat fire. Robert Louis Stevenson, he adds, favored Talisker.

Diane grabs the camera from the camera guy, tells him to sit down, damn it, drink his Sam Adams Autumn Wheat, she's taking over, and she pans the room, taking us all in—the bubbling stew, the breathing wine, the paintings and photos of bears on the walls, the moose head above the mantle, the snifters of single malt, the fire leaping in the stone fireplace, Lyle ladling the venison stew into hand crafted pottery bowls, I dressing the salad, Lyle hauling the golden fluffy biscuits from the oven—she's on her knees on the brightly hued rag rug pointing the camera at Lyle's crotch.

We relish the flavors in awed silence. The venison, redolent of arcane herbs and imported spices, surrenders to my molars the way logic hands itself over to beauty. Bites of root vegetables float in the stew—slivers of pert carrot, pebbles of moon-yellow Yukon potatoes, tendrils of slyly sweet yams, crescents of translucent onions, clitoral bulbs of garlic, tokens of humble parsnips. Thick slabs of real butter melt into the languorous dream biscuits like desire soaking into the quick surprise of life. Esoteric salad greens tease and titillate my palate.

The camera guy, mouth stuffed like a squirrel's, asks what bear meat tastes like.

An iron silence snaps down like a saw-toothed trap on a predator's neck.

Lyle glances disappointedly at the questioner. He sighs a woeful exhalation. He says quietly, "Eating bear meat would be to me like carving up my own brother, who is a drug enforcement agent in Texas, and my own sister, who runs a second-hand clothing store in Eugene, Oregon, and cooking them, and eating them."

For awhile everybody eats in silence. It's as if a rock has been dropped into the ocean and it takes the rock a long time to find its way to the bottom of the sea.

Lyle pours everybody more wine. He tells us how he found Rudy one day in the spring. "I was tromping through the brush when I heard a rifle shot. By the time I got there all I saw were tire tracks in the muddy road and a trail of blood. Some bastard in his pickup, driving along, saw Cary, Rudy's mom, still sleepy, and maybe she was too trusting of humans because she was accustomed to me. He must've slammed on his brakes, grabbed his rifle, and drilled her, lounging there by the roadside, expecting maybe an apple or at least a kind word. Hauled her into the back of the pickup and cut off her radio collar. It was Ben Creswell, I'm sure of that. He poaches deer, elk, bear, lives in a shack back in the woods, turned feral in Vietnam, killed one game warden, got off claiming it was an accident. More stew? Biscuits?"

We pass the plates. Lyle resumes.

"So there I stood, surveying the scene of the crime, the leather collar heavy in my hand, when I heard a whimper up above. The little fellow had climbed a tree and was still up there, dismayed and abandoned and alone in the world. I sat down on the ground, leaned against the tree, and waited quietly for awhile so he'd get used to me. I happened to have a peanut butter sandwich in my coat pocket—crunchy peanut butter from the Co-op, so there's no sugar and no preservatives—secured between slices of my home-made whole-wheat-oatmeal-bran bread with its nice crackly crust. After awhile I pulled out the sandwich and took a bite, so the flavor would waft up to him.

"When he climbed down, sliding and scrabbling, he scampered right up to me and gobbled up the sandwich, and I gathered him up and fitted him inside my coat, next to my flannel shirt, next to my heart, and brought him home. I wasn't going to make a pet of him. He's a wild bear. As wild as he can be, anyway. Trouble is, he imprinted on me. He thinks I'm his mother. He thinks we're all bears. So it's a problem during hunting season. According to the rules, the Division of Forestry rules, which, as a Forestry Researcher, I'm obliged to adhere to, Rudy has to stay out in the woods and take his chances like every other bear. But the rules don't cover every contingency. That's the trouble with rules. So, during hunting season, Rudy lives with me. Here, we better finish this Medoc."

NOT SHOOTING AT BEARS

The Koyukon say that a woman threatened
by a bear should expose her genitals to it.
—Giving Voice to Bear

We're all pretty happy now. We're outside, under the stars, nothing but National Forest all around us, and Lyle has lined up the empty wine bottles and the empty single malt bottles on the fence a hundred feet away, and he's put a candle in each bottle and lit the candles so we can see where the bottles are, and he's loading his deer rifle, and we're going to take turns trying to shoot the bottles. If you miss, you have to take off an article of clothing.

Rudy is in the pen Lyle built for him next to the lodge, eating the rest of the venison stew. We ate all of the soufflé, but Lyle says Rudy doesn't need sweets. Diane was surprised that Rudy would eat venison, she thought bears were vegetarians, but Lyle says, Hell no, each spring he finds pieces of fawn in the bear scat he collects, bits of fur. Bears, Lyle says, are omnivores, like us.

Rudy makes little grunting noises as he eats. He seems to like the stew a lot. One of the bottles of Cabernet wasn't quite finished—it was half full, actually—but Lyle wanted the bottle, so he poured the rest of the Cab into the stew before he gave the stew to Rudy. He poured another bottle into the stew as it was cooking.

Lyle says he's writing a gourmet cookbook. The cookbook's going to be called *Wild Cooking*. He already has an advance from a major publisher. He also has a contract for a book on bears, *Bear with Me*. And he's been approached by one of the cable networks about hosting a TV show. He won't say which network, it's too early in the negotiations, everything's very delicate at this point, but, Lyle says, it would be a deconstruction of the old Frank Buck *Bring 'Em Back Alive* series, which only Lyle and I are old enough to remember. Lyle says the theme would be one world, we're all in it together, let's get used to it. Maybe he'd have a Native American sidekick—but it wouldn't be a Lone Ranger and Tonto thing, he assures Diane, who has missed the bottles for the third time and seems to prefer to remove her shirt and bra and belt rather than her boots, I guess because the ground is cold—I took off my shoes and socks after missing four times.

No one has hit any bottles and the candles are burning down as the little flames dance in the soft autumn air. We heard a wolf howl awhile ago and we howled back, but it must have known we weren't real wolves because it never answered. I don't know how authentic our howls were because we're pretty drunk which is probably why we're having such trouble hitting the bottles and why—what's his name?—Ed?—is down to his under shorts but he insists he'll hit the next one and he hangs on to the rifle and shoots again. Lyle hasn't shot at all and has all his clothes on but no one has mentioned that, I guess because he's the host and he's letting his guests have all the fun.

Ed has a small circumcised penis and blond pubic hair, but no one is paying much attention. Ed is hopping around trying to get warm, but Lyle says Ed can't put his clothes on, it's against the Lumberjacks' Rules as laid down in legendary time by Paul Bunyan, the Father of all Lumberjacks, which Ed seems to believe. Lyle is helping Diane take aim, talking in her ear, fitting the stock of the rifle into the hollow of her bare shoulder and arranging her hands on the rifle and putting his big hand into the small of her back, into her hair flowing like dark honey full of danger and mystery down her naked back, and his other hand is positioning her elbow and accidentally—I'm sure—brushing her breast, which is firm and round like a ripe melon, and her nipples are small and pink and erect. She misses again.

Ed hops faster, his penis flopping, but Lyle says real woodsmen bear the cold without complaint, and I think now Diane's going to take off a boot, which she does, but she takes off the other boot, too, which she is not required to do, even by the mythic rules set down in time immemorial by Mr. Bunyan, but apparently she removed her boots only to slip off her jeans, because now she pulls her boots back on.

She's standing in the light thrown weakly from the windows of the lodge, illuminated sufficiently that I can see enough to get excited but shadowed enough that everything is still pretty much a wonderful mystery. She stands at ease, with her weight on her left leg, her right leg slightly bent, her boots hugging her sturdy naked calves, her nipples pointing into the cool night air and her lush honey hair undulating down her lithe back and her black bikini panties an oracular bandit's mask. She wants to shoot again.

Lyle starts to help her once more, but she shrugs him off. She snuggles the rifle into her shoulder and squeezes off a round as if she's done this every night of her sweet life. The Talisker bottle explodes. The candle falls to the earth. She puts her bra on.

What are you doing? Lyle asks.

Paul Bunyan rules, Diane answers. When you hit, you get to put something back on.

Lyle starts to argue, but Ed, suddenly seeing some hope for his hypothermia, grabs the rifle and starts shooting. We can't stop him until the rifle's empty, and still he's naked. Ed gives up and heads inside, his clothes wadded in his arms, dancing over the cold earth and sharp pebbles, fuck the Paul Bunyan rules.

Now Lyle gets down to business. He wants to wind this up before Diane puts all her clothes back on. He loads the rifle, aims, and hits a bottle. He hits another. Another. He's deadeye Lyle. He seems to have forgotten about me. He doesn't care whether I take off my clothes or not.

There are three bottles left, and he has to reload. When he does, Diane takes the rifle. She aims. She fires. She snuffs out a candle—leaving the bottle untouched, although it wobbles a little.

She takes off her bra.

She picks up the rifle and shoots out the second candle.

She slips off her black bikini panties.

Now I realize what's she's doing. She's showing Lyle she can hit any damn thing she pleases, and she pleases to take her clothes off.

She's naked, except for her boots. And her wild honey hair.

She hugs the stock of the rifle into her shoulder once more. She closes one eye. She sights. She takes a little longer this time. The crack of the rifle splits the cool silence. The last candle flickers, then dies.

It's dark. There's no light from the cabin. Ed must have turned off the lights. I can't see Diane. I can't see Lyle. All I hear is Rudy snoring.

I think it's Rudy snoring—little *whuffs* and *whoofs* and then some slurping sounds as if he's licking his lips.

STARRY NIGHT

Our universe may be lost somewhere among the millions of possible universes that have been found in string theory.

—Michio Kaku, *Hyperspace*

The Big Dipper perches overhead, and the Little Dipper hangs nearby, as if they were ready to scoop up that river of cream pouring through the cold abyss that is the night sky. I'm in the pen with Rudy. The lights are out in the lodge. I've put my shoes and socks back on, and I've put my coat on, too. Rudy's making *whiffing* noises and pacing.

I think maybe the *whuffs* and *whoofs* and *slurps* I heard earlier were not Rudy, after all. After the *slurps* and *whuffs* and *whoofs*, I heard a drawn-out groan as if somebody were in great but delectable distress, and then I heard the door to the lodge open and close.

Infinity reaches beyond the stars, beyond the galaxies. Astronomers say there's a spatial end of the universe, that it stops where the farthest stars are racing, hurtling still from the Big Bang. But if we say the universe ends, we have to ask, in the next breath, what's beyond? There has to be something beyond. Even Nothing is Something.

We can't imagine infinity.

We can't imagine no infinity.

Time and space are one, they say. Time began with the Big Bang. That's the only way to look at it, they say. But of course we don't look at it like that. Time stretches forever in both directions. What was before the Big Bang? Cosmologists say we can't ask that question. But what other question is there? When did it begin? And what was before that? And before that?

It goes on forever.

How can that be?

Maybe Time has three dimensions!

Does that explain precognition?

Why do we remember only the past? Why not the future?

Or is Time a treadmill? We imagine we're getting somewhere, but after we're breathless and sweating, it's the same damn scenery.

The most recent and careful calculations by cosmologists conclude that the stars are older than the universe. Doesn't that worry anyone?

And where is the missing mass in the universe? What's that all about? Ninety per cent of the universe is missing?

Where the hell is it?

It's in our minds. The missing mass is our thoughts. All the thinking of the ages—it grows heavy. The darkness between the stars. The emptiness we throw ourselves into: The Future.

Physicists advise that there may be tiny black holes, microscopic little vacuum cleaners, whizzing through the universe, sucking wee things into their pinpoints of infinite gravity. This hypothesis comforts me. These itty bitty gulps roaming the universe, flinging themselves through town and forest and shopping mall, through my skull, explain my forgetfulness. Tiny black holes pass through my brain, and they suck up my memories.

Rudy comes over to me. I haven't been afraid of Rudy, so long as Lyle was around. But now Lyle isn't here. Lyle's inside, fucking Diane. Lyle keeps saying, Remember, despite appearances, Rudy is a wild bear.

There are all these bear stories about how you can't trust appearances—what you think is a bear is a human, what you think is a human is a bear, what's wild is your brother, what's familiar can explode into chaos. Rudy's eyes gleam like two amber stars. Does he think I'm a bear? A friend? A dinner? Rudy makes little *whups* and *wheeps*. Are they random noise, or are they bear language?

He's on his hind feet. He puts his paws on my shoulders. His paws are solid and heavy and not to be argued with. He opens his mouth. Lyle says bears recognize you by smelling your breath. I open my mouth. We breathe each other's breath, Rudy and I. His breath doesn't smell bad—venison, garlic, wine. Like my breath.

Rudy's moving his feet. His paws on my shoulders seem lighter, seem cajoling. I think I hear music. Maybe it's Rudy making the music, breathing and snuffling and shuffling in a bear rhythm, a sonorous wistful purr as from a distant viola. I take little steps, side to side, in the starlight, breathing Rudy's breath as he's breathing mine, bear air billowing in my lungs, bear molecules sighing in my heart, bear longings surging in my arteries, little bear steps, Rudy leading, back and forth, one two, one two—*dip*.

RECIPE FOR VENISON STEW À LA LYLE

Chunks of venison, garlic, onions
Potatoes, carrots, other root vegetables such as parsnips, rutabagas, yams
Thyme, basil, parsley, red pepper flakes, a bay leaf, a juniper berry or two
Tabasco sauce, Worcestershire sauce
Olive oil, a little flour, some bouillon
Fresh cilantro, chopped tomatoes
A little brown sugar
A robust red wine, one you can't easily forget

Pour yourself a glass of wine.

Heat a dollop of olive oil in a big Dutch oven. Dredge the venison in flour that's been mixed with thyme, basil, salt, and pepper, then throw the floured chunks into the sizzling olive oil and let the venison brown. Sauté a handful of chopped garlic, chopped onions, and carrots. Add the bouillon. (I use chicken bouillon—it soothes the venison's natural arrogance.) Add the bay leaf, a few pepper flakes, a dash of Tabasco sauce, a few shakes of Worcestershire sauce, and a juniper berry or two.

Pour yourself another glass of wine.

After awhile, add chunks of potatoes and any other root vegetables you have handy. Throw in the chopped tomatoes, the brown sugar, and more garlic, whole cloves this time, so those little nuggets of earthy insouciance will surprise you now and then, the way the unexpected touch of a lover can spring a shiver from your tailbone.

Pour yourself another glass of wine.

Pour the rest of the wine into the pot. Open another bottle of wine. When everything is tender, ladle the stew into hand-crafted pottery bowls, garnish with a flurry of fresh cilantro, and eat.

This venison stew goes nicely with a crusty, hearty, home-made bread. If you don't have time to make bread, sourdough biscuits make an excellent complement. Balance things out with a light salad, say of watercress, arugula, and other greens, a splatter of goat cheese, and a dispersion of kalamata olives. Dress with walnut oil and rice vinegar.

DIANE: HER STORY

> Bears do not make love like other quadrupeds but
> can embrace each other mutually, like human beings.
> —Vincent of Beauvais, 13th century

Lyle makes love slowly. It's the second time. I rushed the first one, but I was cold.

It had been years since I had practiced with my dad, his old 30/30 kicking my shoulder until I learned a kind of Zen thing, like the archery, where I could slide my mind into a different place where everything is in slow motion. The candles were a last-minute thought. It seemed so fucking cool, and Lyle, bless his heart, didn't know what to think. He thought he was so sharp, with his stupid version of strip poker.

I laid him there on the ground, jerked his pants to his ankles so he couldn't get away. I had to work to get him ready, what with the cold and all he'd drunk, but once there he stayed the course, and I got on top and rode him to the finish line. Then we stumbled inside to his big bedroom and his big bed and another woman's clothes in the closet, which I opened out of curiosity, expecting as much, I'm not sure why, woman's intuition.

I don't know what happened to the other guy, so quiet, taking everything in, but nice enough, a beard like Lyle's, a writer, I think, maybe writing it all down.

THE STORY OF THE THREE BEARS

You know the story. An open door. Supper on the table.

Goldilocks (Honey-Hair) settles into a chair, stretches out on a bed, goes through the mail, weighs herself on the scales, investigates the medicine cabinet, tries out the bubble bath, brushes her teeth, sprays perfume, looks in drawers and closets.

What is she looking for, that blonde bombshell? A home? A family? Unconditional love? Or did she hope to discover her animal nature, repressed by civilization's decorum? Celebrate her natural savagery, wild and woolly and with sharp teeth, that peeks from the folds in our clothes and the gaffes in our manners?

The stories say she found Little Bear's chair, bed, venison stew just right, but in the real story, the Ur-story, that's denned up in the dark depths of our collective unconscious, Honeyhair doesn't give a hot damn about Little Bear's stuff. When the bears come home, Honeyhair is slipping into Momma Bear's pajamas.

LYLE'S WIFE'S LETTER

Saskatoon, Saskatchewan

Dear Lyle,

I don't need the clothes right now. I'll stay the winter with Mother. Besides, she's forgetful sometimes. I know this is when I usually come home, when hunting season's over and hibernation begins, but you won't miss me. If I came back it would be like last winter, I out in the cold even as I stood cooking in the warm kitchen and you shadowed by your amateur bear watchers, basking in the warmth of female adulation in the snow-whipped woods. I notice the looks on the women when they see me, Lyle's poor wife, a nonentity or, worse, a chain around your leg. Well, don't let me put a cramp in your style, not that I ever have.

Not even when I was your student and you were teaching animal management at the University. Back then no one had heard of sexual harassment. Back then faculty-student affairs were part of the curriculum, like finals and dissertations. I didn't feel taken advantage of, not even that first time, when we were in the woods following Number 24, back before you started naming the bears and the other Forestry people disapproved. But you always were a rebel.

My job was to pick up 24's scat and put it in a plastic bag and record where and when I found it. Later, back at the lab, I'd weigh it and examine it, to see if she'd eaten berries or beetles or whatever. Not a glamorous job, but that's science for you.

It was a hot summer day. You took off your shirt. You don't have a great physique, but you're lean and muscular. Your skin was white except for the bronze of your hands and the reddish copper of your face up to where your cap came. It reminded me of my father, a farmer in Saskatchewan, wheat and mint, when he'd come in at night all dusty and sweaty and take off his cap and shirt to wash up for supper, and his white chest, set off by the burnished brown of his face and hands, always had a strange effect on me. I felt as if I shouldn't be watching him. I felt as if I was seeing him totally naked. Yet I couldn't take my eyes off him. He'd ask for the towel and I'd hand it to him. I'd watch him dry himself. He looked smaller than he should have. It was the only time he looked as if things could hurt him.

I wasn't thinking about my father when you took off your shirt. I was scooping up bear shit. When I stood up, you were bare-chested, wiping the sweat from your face with your wadded-up shirt. There must have been sweat in my eyes, too. You know how it is sometimes on hot days—you see things that aren't there, and I was thinking about bears all the time—so when I looked up, I thought the bear was there, the bear we'd been following, and the white was the white some young bears have on their chests, and the wadded-up shirt was the bear's head, and you had walked off and the bear was there instead, and I felt guilty because I was stealing her shit. I know, the bear didn't want it anymore, she'd left that behind like yesterday's faint regrets. But you get odd thoughts on a hot afternoon when you're not really thinking straight and you haven't been quite human yourself, sleeping on the ground with rocks gnawing your back and eating trail mix and deer jerky and smelling like sweat, bug repellent, and tenacity, and you and I never talked in the woods because we didn't want to apprise the bear of our presence in case she was near, and, besides, you had this Indian thing about being in the woods, you didn't talk, you tried to blend in, you "become what you're looking for," you'd say, which I took to mean I should become a bear not I should become bear shit.

A flirtatious breeze wafted through the branches of the trees, riffling the leaves into a coquettish whisper. Sunlight freckled the mossy earth. Petulant odors of earth and grass and a hundred organic entities swarmed in the air. Insects buzzed their private symphonies.

You fell to the earth. Like a bear you charged. Like most black bear charges, it was a bluff, because black bears are pretty harmless, running like crazy right up to you then stomping their front paws and giving a loud *Whoof*, which scares the bejeesus out of you if you're not expecting it.

I kneeled. You smiled. Since then, I've seen bears smile like that. It's a subtle smile, but it's there if you look for it. We breathed each other's breath, the way bears do to recognize each other. Your breath smelled like summer and danger and like the aspen leaves you'd been

William Borden

chewing and like the wild raspberries we'd eaten, the few the bear had left. I could smell my breath, too, coming back, salty and raisiny, mixed with your breath, and I smelled flowers somewhere, piquant prairie roses and lusty wild orchids. Your brown hair hung over your forehead. I put the palms of my hands on your stubbly jaws, as if I were holding a head in a lab for inspection. I looked into your blue eyes. I felt as if I were diving into a cool cerulean mountain pool, sinking thankfully into another world I'd never have to leave. Your chest was so white it needed to be protected. I pulled it next to my heart, wrapping my arms around you, and you held me as if you knew you needed that refuge, and after awhile you leaned back and I let go to see if I was holding you too tight, was trying to protect you too much, but you were leaning back so you could unbutton my shirt so I could be a bear too and you did and I was.

Before I left this time we talked about a separation. I'm not sure if this is it or not. We can see how things are in the spring. Things look better in the spring. Then again, some springs you think the snow will never melt. Or it melts all in one day, and everything's mud, black and gritty and implacable.

Your wife

THE GIRL WHO MARRIED THE BEAR

—From the *Tlingit*

Once a girl went picking berries with her mother and sisters. They saw some bear droppings. Girls are supposed to walk around bear droppings, but this girl didn't care, she jumped over the droppings and kicked the droppings. They picked lots of berries, berries so ripe the berries dissolved like raindrops on their tongues. On the way home, the girl saw some more berries. She stopped to pick them. Her mother and sisters went on ahead.

The girl dropped some berries on the ground. When she looked up, she saw a handsome young man. He said, "Those berries are dirty. I'll show you some good berries up ahead. You don't have to be afraid." They walked ahead and they picked more berries. After awhile he said, "You must be hungry." He cooked them some meat, and they ate. Then he said, "It's too late to go home now. We'll go home tomorrow." So they slept there. He said, "Don't lift your head in the morning and look at me, even if you wake up before I do."

The next day the girl wanted to go home. "Don't worry," he said, "I'm going home with you." He slapped her on the top of the head, and he put a circle around the girl's head the way the sun goes. She forgot about going home. All summer they traveled. Finally it was autumn. "It's time to make a home," he said. He started digging a den. She knew he was a bear then. When the man was digging he looked like a bear. The rest of the time he seemed like a human being. The girl didn't know how else to stay alive, so she stayed with him as long as he was good to her.

William Borden

A SECOND LETTER FROM LYLE'S WIFE

Saskatoon, settled in 1882 by teetotalers

Dear Lyle,

I bought three cassettes of oldies romantic music. It was one of those TV deals, where they play the music as the titles scroll by, and the one they're playing is highlighted. Those songs used to seem so meaningful, didn't they, when we were young, as if the singer knew what we were thinking right then when the song was playing on the radio. Why don't those synchronicities happen anymore? Is it because they don't play those songs anymore? Or is it because we've lost our innocence? Babies are born now, it seems, having read Camus and having witnessed, watching some tiny flickering uterine TV, wars and atrocities and ten years of Geraldo.

Sometimes I miss you, but I'm learning to live without you, and it's not much different than living with you, because you're gone so much, and even when you're home you seem away, mentally, I mean.

I feel stronger alone than when I'm with you. I don't understand that.

I'm sorry to hear about the investigation. I'm sure nothing will come of it. After all, that was your money, those advances, and to say that it belongs to the Division of Forestry because you work for the Division of Forestry and the books are based on your research with them, well, that's ridiculous.

I know you've encouraged me to get involved with research again now that the kids are grown, but, Lyle, you're the bear expert, where would I fit in there?

I don't think I ever really wanted to be an animal researcher.

But I took your course at the University, and you were just a fresh instructor yourself and didn't know what you were talking about half the time, I realize that now, but then I thought the only way I could have you was to become a researcher.

Oh, I could do my own research now—a lot needs to be done with salamanders, we don't know beans about them, not to mention flying squirrels, green herons, or bats, and I'd be contributing to science—I used to feel I was contributing to science by cooking your breakfast, Lyle, and I was, and everything in philosophy is merely a footnote to Xanthippe's moussaka, hot and spicy and mouth-watering whenever old Socrates wandered home from his gabfests—but I'm getting off the track, I guess it's the Jack Daniels Black I'm sipping.

Actually, when I got pregnant the first time, I felt relieved that I didn't have to study anything, I could just be a mother, which, it turned out, was a full-time study in itself. I didn't mind writing all those articles for you, both technical and popular, because I knew that your heart and mind were really in the field work, and I could organize your fragments of half articulate scribblings and your stream-of-consciousness audio tapes into coherent and even sometimes entertaining articles. And I didn't mind putting your name under the title of each one, because I knew that's how a reputation is made, and I don't expect you now to go out and tell everybody it was I who wrote everything. I just wish—I don't know what I wish.

Do you know what I really wanted to be? I simply wanted to be in the woods. You can be alone in the woods, that's the only place, really. Sure, there are billions of microbes and spores and plants and insects, and even the rocks have a presence, so you're not really alone, but in spite of all that buzzing and grubbing and the psychic pressure of a million trees thinking their slow fibrous thoughts, nobody's bothering you.

There are the mosquitoes, that's true. And in the spring the gnats. And the ticks. And later the deer flies. But they only bite and suck your blood, a common enough habit among many organisms, some vertebrate.

I used to pretend I was Wonder Woman. I had this rope coiled up to be my magic rope which I hung in the barn and swung on, to swing from my automatic-pilot plane onto the ground, and I wore these boots and blue shorts, and I stole this thing from my mother's drawer which was like that thing Wonder Woman wore on top—I guess we'd call it a bustier but I can't believe that's what my mother would've had, a farm wife on the dusty plains of Saskatchewan. Wonder Woman was probably a lesbian, come to think of it, but you don't think those things as a kid, which is probably just as well because life is confusing enough when you're young, but I don't think that's why I liked Wonder Woman—although Eleanor Baer was my best friend all through high school and she wanted us to go to the prom together because all the boys were disgusting; but she was always troubled, her father drank and beat her, and she drove her car too fast on the ice the next winter and the car flipped over and she tried to walk to shelter but froze to death.

Mother walks every day, icy sidewalks or not. She says it keeps her blood thick. I tell her blood is the same density outdoors or in, in Saskatoon or Tahiti, but she has her own views on hematology. Sometimes she gets lost, but so far she's found her way home.

What was I looking for, out there in the woods?

HOW TO MAKE A DOCUMENTARY

> He sleeps through the winter
> and his dreams are very sweet.
> —*Sami Bear Song*

Snow is falling in large lumps, drifting from a gray sky like lazy thoughts on a Sunday afternoon. Rudy's sacked out in a hole under some logs. Ed positions his video camera and light, and Lyle crawls in, takes a blood sample, slips a thermometer up Rudy's ass, counts Rudy's breaths per minute, and squiggles back out.

Diane crawls in to say hello. Earlier Diane seemed very familiar with where things are in Lyle's log lodge—silverware in the drawer by the stove, coffee cups in the cabinet to the left, pepper grinder behind the olive oil—and in the bathroom a silver tube of rosy lipstick by the sink and a second toothbrush in the hand-made ceramic toothbrush holder. I wonder if that was her black lingerie peeking from the drawer in Lyle's bedroom, and her soft slippers by the bed.

When it's my turn Rudy seems a little cranky, his eyes squinty and edgy, his breath stale and gravelly, while I lie before him, my head and torso in the hole and my legs and feet out in the cold and getting colder. Rudy doesn't seem interested in me. He puts one paw over his nose and closes his eyes, and, after a big sigh, his breathing slows down. It's warm in the den, partly from the video light but also from Rudy's body. I reach out my hand. I touch Rudy, touch his black fur. It's coarse. It's alive. It's wild.

When I scoot out, Ed is trying to slip a new tape into his camera without taking off his stiff new Eddie Bauer Arctic gloves. Finally he pulls off the gloves, but, as he does, he drops the tape into the snow. As he reaches into the snow for the tape, he drops his gloves.

Lyle and Diane are standing off a few yards, standing close together, not talking, just looking around as if they were wishing Ed and I weren't here, but that may be my imagination.

Now Ed's squared away, even though there's snow inside his gloves, and the camera is running, and he's turning slowly in a circle, getting what he calls his establishing shot. Then he shoots Lyle riding off alone on his snowcat, as if Lyle were the only one here. Then Lyle comes back on his snowcat, and they'll use that shot as if Lyle were just arriving at the den, sort of from the den's point of view, or POV, as they say in the movies. In the documentary it'll be just Lyle and Rudy, and Diane and Ed and I will not exist.

On the way back to Lyle's lodge—it's a few miles through snow-drifted, uncharted forest—Ed's driving the snowmobile again and I'm holding on again. Lyle's up ahead on another snowmobile. Diane's on that snowmobile. She's holding onto Lyle. Ed's never driven one of these snowmobiles before, but he didn't tell Lyle that. We're bouncing all over the place, Lyle and Diane have vanished, and I wonder if I'm going to be bucked from this untamed bronco—Ed's whooping and yipping, pretending he's a Brahma bull buster, my life's cheap—and I'll die here in the woods in the snow and the cold, forgotten, alone, and unmourned.

BERSERK

> I arrived and saw what they call there the "happy life"...with men gorging themselves twice a day and never sleeping alone at night...
>
> —Plato, *Seventh Epistle*

My shoulder's a wreck from flying off the snowmobile when Ed hit a log, but Lyle moved my arm around with the aplomb of a seasoned physical therapist and pronounced no serious injury, advising a cold pack to keep down the swelling. It's a wonder I wasn't killed. Ed shows no remorse, more concerned with playing back his tape to see if what he got is okay or do we have to go back tomorrow and do it all over again. He didn't even know I'd been thrown off, just kept going, the roar of the engine drowning my cries of outrage. If Lyle and Diane, noticing my absence from Ed's snowmobile, hadn't come back, I'd be a TV dinner for turkey buzzards by now. It was tight, the three of us on Lyle's snowmobile, Diane's hair in my face and her perfume in my olfactory receptors and my arms around her fur coat. The pain in my shoulder seems to be going away—I popped five of Diane's Midol—so maybe my injury is less serious than I thought. Maybe I'll test my shoulder by bringing in more logs for the fire.

The air is an icy wall that crackles in my throat and stings my skin as I crash slowly through the twilight. It's as if I've stepped onto a different planet where the atmosphere is prickly and rude and I'm not wanted.

I hear Lyle and Diane talking. They're side by side in the wooden swing a few yards from the lodge, although they can't swing with snow piled up to the seat. Diane's wearing furry mukluks and mittens and a brown stocking cap and a fancy fur coat that looks as if it belongs on

Fifth Avenue, and Lyle's wearing his old beat-up parka with a fur-lined hood, Air Force surplus, regulation Arctic survival gear. They haven't seen me so I step back behind the woodpile. I feel a little bad about eavesdropping but not much. After all, I didn't come out explicitly to eavesdrop. It just happened, the way most things just happen.

Diane is saying urgently, "I want to fuck in the woods. I want to fuck in the woods in my fur coat in the snow. I want us to fuck like bears." Lyle's saying bears don't fuck in the winter they sleep in the winter, but Diane doesn't seem to care that much for zoological accuracy because she's leading Lyle into the trees.

I'm just taking a walk, following their footsteps because it's easier stepping in the holes their boots made in the knee-high snow than stomping out a new path, a lot of wasted energy, and it's quieter, too, so they don't hear me, there in the clearing where she's on her back in the snow wearing her mink or whatever and Lyle's on top, his parka, which the Air Force perhaps did not design for every Arctic emergency, unzipped, and she wraps her coat around them both so it looks like one big furry animal in the snow under the black leafless trees with snow gently falling, one big furry animal moving in jerks with snow accumulating on the fur, and the animal is making throaty noises from deep inside the fur, deep inside the animal's needs and desires.

When I return to the lodge, Ed is eager for Lyle to come back because Ed's got a surprise for Lyle, only I'm not sure how Lyle will like it. "Look, look," Ed says, dragging me over to the station's van, with the call letters and the yellow winking walleye on the side. They must have given a higher priority to the documentary once they saw his tape from a few weeks ago, or maybe they don't need the van this weekend. I see Diane's driven here by herself, because her Volvo is nosing the rear of Lyle's pickup as if their two vehicles were intimate. Ed's pulling something furry out of the van. "I got this bearskin," Ed says, "at a second-hand store, one of those stores in small towns that has everything. I saw it on my way up here. I'm going to put it on and jump out at Lyle. Where is he?"

I say I think he's out in the woods.

"He's a real scientist, isn't he! He must be measuring stuff, or looking for signs of other bears hibernating. Maybe I should get my camera."

I say it's too dark for his camera. I say I think sometimes Lyle likes to be alone. Then Ed thinks of Diane and wonders where she is. I say I think maybe Lyle's showing her something about bears.

Then we see them coming out of the woods, and Ed hides, and Lyle and Diane walk toward the lodge, lifting their feet high the way you walk in the snow and planting their boots down before they throw their weight forward until they get to where the snow has been packed down and suddenly a bear jumps out on its hind legs yowling and swinging its paws.

Lyle and Diane stand and watch.

The bear jumps up and down and yowls louder. The bear's trying to scare them. Lyle and Diane watch Ed in the bearskin for a moment, without expression, without interest, even without much surprise, and then Lyle opens the lodge door and they go inside and close the door behind them.

Ed the bear stares at the closed door. Suddenly, with a great roar, the bearskin turns in a circle, it lumbers across the yard, it flails into the dark twiggy woods, it lunges into the gathering glacial gloom. It crashes through the brush. It yowls, over and over again, its howls and wails fading the farther into the woods it thrashes. Then I don't hear anything.

I go inside. Lyle and Diane are sitting on the big oval multicolored rag rug in front of the fire, putting their stockinged feet to the warm bricks. They're sipping sherry. Lyle asks if I'd like some. I say, even though he tried to kill me and left me to freeze and die, I'm worried about Ed.

"Ned," Diane says.

"Ned?" I say.

"Ned's his name," she says.

"I thought it was Ed," I say.

"Ned," she says.

"Well," I say, "I'm worried about him. He went into the woods."

"He went berserk," Lyle says.

"Yes, I guess," I say. "Sort of."

"No sort of," Lyle says. "Berserk. The real thing."

"Should we go get him?" I ask.

"He'll get tired," Diane says.

"He'll get lost," I say.

"He can follow his tracks back," she says. "We followed ours."

"And yours," Lyle adds, looking at his sherry.

"But it's dark," I say. I look at them, but they're looking at the fire. They're sipping their sherry, a *fino*.

I hesitate a moment, almost lulled by Lyle's equanimity, but then

I ask, "Where's a flashlight?"

"You'll get lost," Lyle says.

"You'll freeze," Diane says.

"But Ned!" I yell.

"Ned's gone berserk," Lyle says. "The real McCoy berserk."

Lyle coats the walleye fillets in a crust of sesame seeds, blue corn-meal, and fresh basil (snipped from the plant growing from the pot above the sink), fries the walleye quickly, then douses them with a splash of ouzo. He throws on some Greek olives, crumbles feta cheese over the ensemble, and scoops the works onto handmade pottery plates, thrown by a potter friend of his in Albuquerque. He's made potato pancakes from shredded potatoes, onion, garlic, green peppers, and wild rice soaked in Bombay gin, and he's topped the potato pancakes with sour cream mixed with yogurt and a touch of cumin. Diane's put together a salad of mixed greens, some with names I've never encountered before, tossed with a dressing of hazelnut oil and raspberry vinegar. We begin with a Pinot Grigio to accompany the salad. Oh, yes, and there are fresh asparagus spears draped with aioli and toasted bread crumbs. Diane brought the fresh asparagus from Byerly's in Minneapolis, imported from below the equator. Ned is still missing.

Lyle has set only three places.

"I can't eat," I say.

"You don't like it?" Lyle asks.

"Ned," I say. "He's been out there over an hour. He's freezing to death."

Lyle fills our glasses. The Pinot Grigio glistens like a skittish hint of spring. "I can't do anything for him," Lyle says. "He's in the hands of the god."

"What god?" I ask.

"The bear god," Lyle says. "Sit down. I'll tell you about it."

I look at Lyle. I look at Diane. I look at the door. They look at me, glasses poised at their lips. I smell the walleye, the spices, the sweet aroma of piquant wood smoke, the nuances of intimacy. The logs crackle in the fieldstone fireplace. The candles on the table flicker flirtatiously. Suddenly everything is clear. Lyle and Diane are in love. They're inviting me to share a moment of repose and communion with them. They will love me if I let them, if I'll stop blathering about Ned.

I sit down. I taste the Pinot Grigio's crystalline bravura. I sample the verdant ribaldry of the asparagus, the aioli's gusty finesse, the bread crumbs' spunky modesty. I'll look for Ned in a moment.

"The berserkers were a tribe of warriors in northern Europe," Lyle explains. "They wore bear skins. *Berserk* means *bear skin. Ber* means *bear, serk* means *skin.* To run berserk is to run in a bear skin." His features melt and flow in the firelight and candlelight. "The berserkers were possessed by the bear god. They thought the bearskin protected them from arrows and knives and spears and swords. They were fearless in battle. They ravaged and raged, rampaged and pillaged. They were hell on wheels."

Lyle removes the asparagus plates—clay dishes molded by a friend of his in Quebec—and brings out the walleye, which has been warming in the oven, "breathing the ouzo," he says, and pours a Bordeaux into the artistically irregular glasses blown by a glassblower friend of his in Seattle, and places the potato and wild rice pancakes on the plates beside the walleye. "If the bear god enters you," Lyle says, "you think you're invincible. And maybe you are."

There's a pounding on the door, like battering rams. Lyle picks up his fork and sections himself a bite of the walleye. The lodge shakes with the pounding.

I open the door. A bear staggers inside, a bear with Ned's face sticking out of the bear's throat, as if the bear had eaten Ned and Ned had managed to peep out on the way down. Ice hangs from Ned's nose and lips and eyelashes, and the bear's head is nodding Hello to me, snow shaking from the black head like dreams off cold reality. He collapses onto the floor.

We let him sleep on the kaleidoscopic rag rug in front of the fire. We leave him in the bearskin. We finish our dinner. Lyle fixes a plate for him to eat later. Diane's made chocolate brownies for dessert. We eat the brownies, the interior dotted with chocolate chunks the way life sometimes—but all too rarely—is filled with moments of unexpected richness, and topped with fresh whipped cream flavored with Tahitian vanilla, and she's put marijuana, that a friend of Lyle in California grows, into the brownies, with which we drink espresso, and then we sip Courvoisier VSOP.

DANCING WITH BEARS

I was a bear
And I was boppin'
Yeah I was boppin'
Boppin' in my bear feet
—Nine Big Dogs

I wonder if this is the way it is for Rudy when he's hibernating—off in some indeterminate space, bathed in warmth, his body tingling all over, his head feeling a lot larger than it should but he's able to see the neurons in his brain firing and exchanging messages.

Maybe not.

Lyle and Diane are dancing, and Ned is on the hearth in front of the fire. He's still a bear, still berserk, but sleeping. I'm on the couch watching the fire lick the logs, fingers of flames massaging the wood. I realize, in a gradient of dawning certainty, that the solidity of my body is merely a convenient illusion. I am in essence nothing but the empty space in the atoms that compose my bones and muscles and organs. I am the void between the electrons and the protons, I am the eternal uncertainty of tachyons and leptons, I am the elusive charms of quarks and the mysterious weavings of strings, but I don't mind my quivery dissolution because there's music seeping into the empty spaces.

Lyle and Diane are slow dancing in their heavy wool socks, the way we did in high school. Nat King Cole is singing that he loves us beaucoup. I'd like to dance, but there's no one for me to dance with.

That's the way it was in high school.

I stare at the flames. Gobs of self-pity ooze into the empty spaces in my body, clog my airy insights, muddy my quarky euphoria.

Diane stands before me. Chance with me? she's asking. She extends her hands. She's wearing a ring I've never seen before. "Dance with me."

Dance! Of course she said *dance!* Has she thrown off Lyle? Is she in love with me?

Her warm breath nuzzles my cheek. Her honey hair tickles my nose. Her perfume balloons my brain. Her thighs press against mine, as if her legs are tired and need support. We shuffle back and forth to Nat's velvety croon. I get an erection.

Lyle's in the corner, playing a viola. He's playing along with Nat. Lyle's in white, transformed, an angel, a halo shimmering around his head.

Lyle's wearing his long underwear. A lamp blazes behind his head.

Nat stops singing. We continue to dance. We don't need music, Diane and I. Our stockinged feet slide along the polished wood floor like desire after satisfaction, like hope after charity, like the faint arc of music slipping into the maw of silence. We're cocooned in the eternal present, the unbending moment. We suck the breast milk of possibility.

Lyle materializes beside us. He's put another record on the turntable. The three of us are dancing, dancing to Pachelbel's *Canon in D.* Diane's auroral hair singes my cheek, her sagey scent sizzles my nostrils and starches my socks. When I close my eyes all hundred and eighty colors in the long Crayola box eddy across my eyelids. We dance under water, in slow motion. Diane kisses Lyle. Tongues flicker like little pink snakes. Diane turns to me. She's going to say she can't kiss me because Lyle is her true love. I understand, it doesn't matter.

Full wet honeylips pressing into mine, she loves me after all, and the little snake is licking nectar on my tongue. She sucks my breath, my reason, my soul. She takes up residence in my brain, she pulls off her boots and puts her feet on the hassock of my unconscious, she curls around my hippocampus and drips honey over my corpus collosum, my pituitary gland flashes red like a fire engine, my eyes are closed because I can see better that way, her lips depart, lips come back firmer, I look to see Lyle's azure eyes, his lips pressing mine...

My gimpy leg gives out. Lyle and Diane catch me. It seems no exertion for them to hold me up. We dance on, embodiments of the lazy fugues. We fade dreamily into the music. We dissolve into time's warm arms.

By the time Ned wakes up the fire has crumbled to red coals, the

William Borden

candles have been put out, and the door to Lyle's bedroom is closed. I don't remember when we stopped dancing, or when I sat back on the couch, or when I fell asleep.

Ned stands, leaving the bearskin on the floor. He doesn't seem to know where he is, yet he seems to know everything he needs to know. I tell him Lyle's kept a plate for him, but he ignores me. He drinks what's left in the wine glasses on the table, then he pulls on his Eddie Bauer down parka, and he pulls on his gloves and puts on his Russian fur hat and he pulls the ear flaps down over his ears, and he goes out the door. I hear his van engine start. He lets it warm up a minute, then I hear him drive off.

I never see Ned again. Later, when I inquire, Diane tells me he stayed on at the station for a week or two but couldn't seem to get his mind on his work, and he was let go.

After the sound of Ned's van dies away, I throw a few logs on the fire, and the flames leap up, and I realize I'm sitting on Ned's bearskin feeling the heat lap at my face. I think of Rudy in his den and I wonder if he's cold and if he'd rather be here in front of this fire. But then I think, Rudy's a bear, he's doing what a bear is supposed to do, and I'm me, in front of the fire getting warm, as I'm supposed to do, although I'm a little lonely as I remember where Lyle and Diane are and what they're doing or they've done it and now they're sleeping, their legs and arms intertwined, each body warming the other.

I'm warm now so I take my clothes off and I sit naked in front of the fire, and it's like being licked all over by warm dry tongues. When the fire dies down, I grab the edges of the bearskin and pull it around me until I'm warm and my skin is next to the bear's skin, and I rub my hand over my furry head with its nose and sharp teeth.

The next morning I awake to Lyle placing fresh logs on the fire. He's wearing a woolly robe and fur-lined moccasins. His legs are hairy and white below the robe. He ignores me and goes into the kitchen.

Diane comes out of the bedroom. Her hair's a mess and sleep creases her pretty face and she's wearing one of Lyle's flannel shirts and fuzzy white slippers with a bear face for toes. She looks surprised to see me. "I thought you were Ned," she says.

"I'm me," I say.

Lyle speaks from the kitchen. "Ned left during the night. I heard the van."

I stand up. I gather the bearskin around my shoulders and try to close it as Diane gives a glance down there and I realize I'm still naked.

I ask Lyle why didn't I go berserk?

Lyle hands me a glass of fresh-squeezed orange juice, flakes of pulp swimming in the current. "Everybody's different," Lyle says. "Like bears." I drink the orange juice. My taste buds run berserk.

DIANE'S RECIPE FOR PACHELBEL BROWNIES

1 3/4 cup boiling water
1 cup oatmeal
1 cup packed brown sugar
1 cup white sugar
1/4 lb butter at room temperature
2 eggs
1 3/4 cup flour
1 tsp baking soda
1/2 tsp salt
1 Tbsp cocoa
3/4 cup chopped nuts (optional)
12 oz. chocolate chips
1 to 4 Tbsp you know what—use your judgment

Pour water over oatmeal and let stand 10 minutes. Add sugar and butter to the oatmeal and stir until butter is melted. Add eggs and mix. Add dry ingredients and mix. Add half of the chocolate chips. Pour into a greased 9 X 13 glass pan and sprinkle with the remaining chips and the nuts. Bake at 350 for 35-40 minutes. Do not over bake.

LYLE'S WIFE HAS A DREAM

Saskatoon, where *La Troupe du Jour*
is presenting *La Sin d'un Amour*

Dear Lyle,

I suppose it was bound to happen after such long abstinence, the erotic dream I had last night, the first, my goodness, I think since college, before you and me. It was a bear.

I was on my back in the woods and naked and he put his paws on my palms, and he was winking at me like we both knew this was a big joke. The bear reminded me of John Kennedy, the smile I guess it was. Anyway, JFK the Bear stuck his tongue in my mouth and I got turned on and I started to play with myself. But the bear said, "I'll take care of that, if you don't mind," like we both knew it was pretty funny, me and a bear, but there we were, we might as well have fun, seemed to be the mood we were in.

He was licking my ears, and you know how I am about my ears. Then he was inside me, but it wasn't big or pushy. It was thin and long and darting around. It was like nothing I had ever experienced before, and I wonder if it really is like that with a bear. I would never want to, you know, in reality, but in the dream it was an ethereal, poignant, juicy—not exactly a climax—maybe more of a *denouement*.

Do you know what I mean?

Probably not.

I'm not sure why I'm telling you this. You know I'm a pretty demure gal and don't write smut, don't read it, not usually, although I admit some of those videos we watched together, well, I'd rather not think about them, not because I'm embarrassed but because I'm getting wet again.

I'm writing this to remind you of me and what we did together, so you won't forget me or the way I could look, dressed in certain things you liked to buy me, although, in all honesty, they turned you on more than they did me, but I guess that was the point, wasn't it?

But JFK the Bear didn't care that I wasn't wearing the garters and stockings. He liked me naked. He liked to slip and slide inside me. I know the common wisdom is that animals simply do it, there's not much pleasure, for the female, anyway, no foreplay to speak of, it's all estrus and nerve endings and in and out, find the next sow, and no indication that the male hangs around to ask if it was good for her, too. But who knows?

Sure, you've made videos of bears doing it, and they seem less than romantic in those videos, but don't you wonder if it isn't like when they make videos of humans doing it, like the ones we watched, where there doesn't look like much romance there, either? Those people do it like the bears in your video, a lot of ramming and grunting, and it's all fake, anyway, unlike the bears, who are real, and there's no, Take Two, Get it up again, Mr. Bruin.

What I'm getting at here, Lyle, is, is there a Heisenberg effect going on? When the bears are watched by humans, do they simply want to get it over with because somebody's watching? Whereas in the privacy of their own daffodil-carpeted clearing in the lush woods, with the scent of wild flowers and the pungent aroma of earth and fungus in the air, do the bears get romantic and nuzzle and lick slowly all those places you like to lick and I like to lick?

I think there's research to be done here.

I remember now, I saw a documentary about John Kennedy, no, it was about Jackie, but Lyle was in it, too, of course, so that must be why he was in my unconscious, lying there in wait.

Well I glanced up and saw that Mr. Freudian slip and slide, which I'm going to leave. My mind and heart and everything is an open book to you, Mr. Lyle.

You know who

STILL LIFE WITH BEARS

> The worst solitude is to be
> destitute of sincere friendship.
> —Francis Bacon

I've surprised Lyle, coming unannounced, and he seems uncharacteristically down. It's late morning, but he's having breakfast. "Porridge?" Lyle asks. It's a creamy, viscous concoction that makes a sexual sound as it plops into my bowl, a generous brown earthenware vessel crafted, Lyle confides, by a blind ex-hippie on Kauai who lives in concupiscent harmony with three Hawaiian sisters. Lyle sighs wistfully.

Lyle's alone. No sign of the Volvo. It's a cloud-ridden, gloomy, dull winter day. He stands on the rag rug, an apparent companion to the rag rug in the living room, this one an oval of dark hues and bursts of surprise, bits of orange and red, white and green, blue and yellow, a braided kaleidoscope stained by food and grease. He scrapes the pan with the wooden spoon. "It's my own recipe," he says.

I take a seat.

"Careful of that chair," he says. "One of the legs is broken. I haven't had a chance to fix it." I take another chair. Each chair is wooden, heavy with age and character. They don't match, yet there's a common sensibility to them.

He passes me a hand-built pitcher, full-bellied and glazed the color of ocean depths. "It's cream," he says. "I know it's hell on the arteries, but, god damn it, we have to have some richness in our lives, don't we? What do you want to die of? Too much, or too little?"

The cream circles the perimeter of my cereal like a lazy seduction, then it swerves into the center, as if seeking some irreducible answer. I pour a little more, to see what new configuration it might make, carving rivulets with my spoon, making dams and destroying channels.

Lyle passes me a pot of honey. I make a spiral with the honey, starting from the outside and working in to the center. It oozes into the cream in some places, and in others it rests like a jetty atop the cereal. I slide the honey pot back to Lyle. He ladles the honey onto his cereal. He gazes at his bowl a moment, as if looking for some omen, then he stirs everything together vigorously, maybe even impatiently. I don't stir mine. I like to keep my sensations separate. I slip my spoon into the hot cereal so that I also get some cream, to cool the porridge, and some honey, to sweeten it. I'm careful to get the right amount of each.

Lyle pours us coffee. It's French roast, Harrar Ethiopian, a robust, slightly angry bean, Lyle says, to jump start us on a dreary morning. He uses a cone and filter; he doesn't trust the automatic coffee makers. If the water's boiling, it releases undesirable flavors into the beverage. "You want a temperature that'll leave the acidity behind," he says, "just as love that's too hot or too cool leaves a bad taste in the mouth and wet goop to dispose of."

I say he seems a little melancholic.

He doesn't reply. Nor does he ask me why I'm here. He doesn't even seem surprised to see me.

I tell Lyle I'm thinking of writing something about him and his bears.

"There've been a few articles," he acknowledges, as if not too impressed by my plans. "Either dry and academic, or slick and superficial. Which are you interested in?"

"I was thinking of something more personal," I say.

Lyle stares out the window.

I gaze out the window.

Several small out-buildings, relics of the place's incarnation as a resort, are scattered about the yard, including a sauna that had fallen into disrepair but that Lyle restored, putting in an electric heating unit, a shower, and a small changing area. The snow falls thick and heavy, the ponderous gray sky releasing its hoarded softness. Time lumbers clumsily past.

"I'd better go," I say.

"You'll never make it," Lyle says. "Your car will slide into the ditch. Snow will cover it. You won't be found till spring."

Outside, the snow piles up, higher and higher, like man's unwitting history.

"You'll die."

It's quiet in the cabin. Large windows admit the grudging afternoon light. It seems to be getting darker by the second, as if someone were pulling a shade down all over the world.   Lyle straps on snowshoes—made the old way, he says, by an Ojibway friend—and heads out to take readings of wind, snow depth, temperature, and, he implies, other esoteric phenomena—but my guess is he just wants to be alone. He says to make myself at home.

I scan the bookshelves, packed and overflowing, that line one wall of the main room: everything ever written about bears, it looks like. I peer in filing cabinets, crammed with photographs and field notes, articles and magazines, journals and clippings. Video tapes are scattered helter skelter.

The silence and the solitude pile on one another, heavy as the memories of what you were afraid to do. The air is thick, truculent, hostile. I search Lyle's modest collection of old 33's and newer cassettes, an eclectic (what else?) mélange of Sinatra, Leadbelly, whale songs, and sound effects for stage and screen. I paw through filing cabinets. I find letters to Lyle from women detailing the things they want to do with Lyle and what they want Lyle to do with them. These folders are stuffed haphazardly among the folders that contain letters from other bear researchers and articles about the evolution of bears and how they and wolves branched off from the same line of mammals and a folder of black and white photographs of a woman without clothes on in the woods doing various things with a man wearing a mask, perhaps it's the Lone Ranger without his clothes or six-guns.

Lyle opens the door and tells me to come out and try the snowshoes. He kneels before me, strapping them on my shoes. I take a step. I pitch forward. Lyle hauls me upright. "Try again," he says. I shake my head. I remove the snowshoes. My left leg's weak, I tell him, from polio when I was a boy.

So we come inside, and Lyle sits at his vintage roll top desk and records some data in a notebook, and then he enters something into his computer, and then he goes into his bedroom and closes the door, and I can hear him talking on the telephone, but I can't tell what he's saying. He stays in his bedroom a long time.

I find a letter on Lyle's desk:

> My dear wife,
> I miss you as the earth longs for the sun at the winter solstice.
> You stay away like the sun. I'm holed up here in my den, nothing
> to do, no one to talk to. I might as well sleep all winter. Yesterday

I walked out into the woods, where we

It stops there. The pen lies across the paper, a page torn jaggedly from a notebook.

The electricity's out. Lyle lights candles. The fire in the fireplace roars bravely. Outside, the snow falls like destiny. We sip Talisker. I ask him—delicately, I hope—if he's worried, now that the Division of Forestry investigation has broadened to inquire into allegations that he made sexual overtures to some of the female volunteers who helped him track and observe the bears these last few years.

He looks closely at the Talisker, holding the snifter up to his eyes, letting the flames flicker behind the golden whiskey, as if he's looking for the answer there in the single malt. "Things happen in the woods," he says. "It's a different world. You know that."

I nod. I sip.

"In captivity," he continues, "bears are different. There are a couple of bear preserves, where folks keep bears who are no longer acclimated to the wild. The bears don't hibernate, because hibernation is a response to the absence of a food supply. And these domesticated bears, because they don't have much to do in the way of hunting and gathering, spend their days and nights playing with each other, the way people do when they have time on their hands." He sips his single malt, and I'm not sure if he's changed the subject or answered my question.

Lyle rigs up a grill in the fireplace and roasts a couple of moose steaks he's dug out of the freezer. "Nothing fancy tonight, jocko," he says, sprinkling the steaks with a mixture of olive oil, soy sauce, hoisin sauce, lime juice, and crushed garlic and covering the steaks with strips of thickly sliced bacon.

I remember, "Today's ground-hog day."

"So it is." He wraps a pair of potatoes in foil and hides them in the coals. "In Europe, in the old days, it was a bear, not a ground hog, that came out of his den to be a harbinger of spring. But Americans can't face the real wildness in their lives, so they substitute a little guy they can pick up with one hand and is no danger to them."

We sit in front of the fireplace, on the big rag rug, concentric ovals of thick braids, a swoop of creamy wool looping around a dusky scarlet like dried blood, a silky black corralling a dizzy magenta. "The business of the shadow," Lyle says, "well, the shadow is your soul. When you die, your shadow leaves you. The bear's hibernation is a death. If the bear comes up on February second and sees his shadow, that means he hasn't died. He has to go back down and spend another six weeks in the underworld. He has to really die, so that he can really be re-born. Then he can come out, spring can come, the flowers can bloom and the bees buzz. The bear's hibernating is like Persephone going to the underworld." Lyle flips the charred moose steaks over. "Febru-ary second is six weeks after the winter solstice, halfway to the spring equinox." He pokes at the potatoes. "Up here in Minnesota, of course, February two is the middle of winter. We see no hope for another two months."

We eat by the light of the flames, our plates balanced on our knees, and by our toes glasses of a somewhat truculent Barolo from the village of Serralunga d'Alba in the northern Apennines. Lyle wishes he'd left the Barolo laid down for another couple of years, but sometimes, he says, he gets impatient for something and he goes after it before it's ready. The moose is a little tough, because he threw it on the flames while it was still frozen, and the raw center has a fervid unpredictabil-ity.

"We're not the end of evolution, you know," Lyle says, gnawing at his steak, a gift, he confides, from an old Anishinabe friend purported to have unusual spiritual powers as well as a sharp eye with a rifle. "We're an accident. You think about all the species that went extinct. It wasn't because they were slower or dumber than the ones that went on to evolve further. They were unlucky. Food source dried up, ice age wandered in, continent shifted—shit happens."

Lyle's poured melted butter speckled with Provencal herbs and red pepper flakes over the baked potatoes, which got a little dry. Before hand, to round out our essential vitamins and minerals, we ate raw carrots dipped in a satay sauce and raw celery with the hollow stems filled with organic chunky peanut butter mixed with fresh cilantro and cream sherry. Nothing fancy, Lyle keeps saying, adding that sometimes simplicity seems elegant.

"We'd like to think the human species is exactly the thing that amoeba was dying to be, a billion years ago. We assume, without a tic of a doubt, that all the Big Bang wanted was to culminate in a planet overrun by psychotic bipeds, creatures who can't decide if they belong in a herd or are doomed to solitude. But is that likely? Or another case of runaway egotism careening out of control?"

Lyle uncorks a bottle of Port to soothe any worries we might have about evolution's fickleness. "No, we're hardly the end-point," he continues. "We're an anomaly, a switching track on the great railroad of evolution, a sidebar in Darwin's Daily News, a temporary miscalculation, a dead-end, a bad guess, a slime mold with an attitude."

"You sound pessimistic," I say. The Port has a musky, uncompromising authority caressed by a velvety coquettishness.

"Au contraire, mon frère. If I thought we were the ultimate goal of the universe, then I'd be disheartened. Then I'd doubt Nature's crazy wisdom. Then I'd think the universe, or God, or Ultimate Meaninglessness was a sorry, useless son of a bitch, or else plain mean. But to realize that we confused primates are a mere misstep, a punk band in the great symphony of the galaxies, why, that fills me with joy and affirmation. To think something better than us might come along restores my faith in the splendid munificence of Universal Spontaneity."

Lyle refills our glasses. "God bless Chaos," he says. "Sure, there's Order, too, there are things we can count on, in the short run, anyway, like winter and the phases of the moon and the pettiness of certain state officials; but in the long run there's unpredictability, mutation, dandelions, even love, things without rhyme or reason, wonderful in their impetuosity."

He takes a sip, allowing the ruby essence to permeate the membranes of his mouth, the tiny molecules of impetuosity to frolic in the playground of his brain. "Evolution's another name for craps," he concludes after swallowing. "There's a lot of dice to be thrown yet. Evolution's patient. Evolution has a helluva bankroll and nowhere to go in the morning."

Darkness hangs like a shaggy tent from the roof beam of the lodge. The darkness smells vaguely rank, like wet things drying by a fire, but that may be only the lingering bouquet of charred moose.

I wonder if Lyle has any bear claw necklaces like Indians wear or bearskins that they wear in their bear rituals. "I'm not an Indian," he says. "They have ceremonies to ask the bear's forgiveness. Our culture doesn't. I wouldn't know how to ask for forgiveness."

Lyle lends me thick wool socks and fur-lined moccasins. I lay his sleeping bag on the floor. I finish off the Martell VSOP. The fire is roaring—Lyle put more logs on, to last the night. Outside, it's still snowing, and I wonder where it can all come from, Nature's Bounty.

Lyle appears in the doorway to his bedroom. He's wearing pajamas. It's difficult to see in the flickering light from the fireplace, but they look like little teddy bears all over his pajamas. I read that the teddy bear arose as a cultural phenomenon and a commercial bonanza when Teddy Roosevelt, out hunting in the Badlands of North Dakota, refused to shoot a bear cub. All those fuzzy teddy bears in all those beds, in all those arms, all over the world, are the bear that the first President Roosevelt, the Rough Rider, who was weak as a kid and had asthma, saved. The teddy bear proliferated, like a benign virus, embodying the notions of kindness, salvation, and cuddliness.

"That floor's hard," Lyle says. I say I'll be all right. "Listen," he says finally, "you want to sleep in the bed with me? I'm not suggesting anything except comfort."

In the big bed with Lyle I'm reminded of Boy Scout camp, where I slept in the pup tent with Bill Reid and we talked about sex and girls and tried to figure out how it was done but couldn't, except Lyle's snoring, and I can't figure out how I suddenly got outdoors, because I'm looking up at the night sky, at the stars glittering in their certain configurations, the Big Dipper and Cassiopeia and the Milky Way.

The ceiling is arrayed with tiny sparkles, each carefully positioned to create, as in a planetarium, an accurate representation of the night sky. The stars shine after the lights go out.

LYLE'S RECIPE FOR PORRIDGE

I like to mix up a big batch ahead of time, for the whole winter, but that might be too much for the average person, so here's a scaled-downed approach.

4 cups oatmeal

2 cups steel-cut oats

2 cups oat bran

2 cups wheat bran

2 cups farina

If you find other grains that beckon to your taste buds, add them, too. Mix well. When you're ready for that stick-to-the-ribs breakfast, but you're by yourself and not very hungry, heat 2 cups of milk to scalding, then add about 1 cup of the dry mixture. Cook over a low heat 15 minutes or so, until the grains and oats have surrendered their abrasive independence and agreed to commingle peaceably, or until the porridge can pretty much stand on its own, like a teenager who thinks he knows everything but of course doesn't.

Now at this point you can get a feel for the kind of day you think it's going to be; or, if you're the sort who makes their own luck, you can decide what kind of day it's going to be, never mind what the random universe and Fickle Fate's surprises have in store for you. So, depending on your mood or expectation, you can add chopped walnuts, pecans, sesame seeds, sliced banana, apple, peach, raisins, prunes if you're in need of greater regularity, chocolate chips, cinnamon. Arrange these additions artistically over the surface of the steaming porridge. Add a sweetener—raw sugar, brown sugar, maple syrup, or honey—although honey is really the preferred sweetener here. Don't be afraid to go for a wilder flavor, a honey that's been made by bees foraging in fields of wildflowers, fruit blossoms, and herbs, the outlaw kind of honey you might find at a farm house on a back road with a hand-lettered sign out front that says HoneY FOr sALE, not that wimpy commercial honey in those squeeze bottles in the shape of an animal we should have more respect for. Add milk, half and half, or cream, depending on your mood and your arteries. I go for either skim milk or heavy cream, one or the other, because halfway measures are the fall-back positions of cowards and bureaucrats. Add cream if you're feeling reckless, or despairing, or nostalgic. Add skim milk if you're timid, ascetic, fidgety, an existentialist, or under a doctor's profit-seeking care. As you add your sweetener, take an aesthetic pleasure in the patterns you create. The sprinkle of the sugar, for example, might mimic the constellations at night, if you have a steady hand and a memory for astronomy charts. The dribble of syrup or honey might trace the labyrinth on the floor of the Cathedral of Chartres or the ground plan of the palace of King Minos on Crete, and a close meditation on these figures can lead, according to some, to a greater clarity of mind, if not to a brief glimpse of the inner workings of the Mind of God. Likewise the pouring of the cream or milk should not be hasty or random but an attempt to resonate with the Natural Order of Things. Follow the spread of the liquid. Notice the designs it makes. Does it seep beneath the apple slice but creep over the fragment of walnut? Does it cozy up to the swirl of honey or run away from it, like a frightened lover? These configurations have been used by some shamanic cultures to predict the weather and the fates of young marrieds, and these forecasts have scored better on the scale of probability than the prognostications of astrologers or the Minnesota Multiphasic Personality Inventory. Tibetan monks, when deprived of sand for their Tantric sand mandalas, have used this porridge and the patterns made by the honey and cream as meditation aids, and these monks have sat all day in deep meditation, staring at the three-dimensional multi-hued patterns, their minds drawn ever deeper into the ultimate secrets of the universe.

I was visited once by three Tibetan Buddhist monks, world-class chanters who sang three notes at the same time and experts in the behavior of the Himalayan bear (*Selenarctos thibetanus*), which is the only other black bear found on the earth, who weren't even cold in their thin saffron robes as they trod lightly in their green Sorel boots through the snow on their way to visit a hibernating American black bear (*Ursus americanus*), the morning after one of the monks spent the day meditating on his breakfast porridge. Finally, at midnight, having taken the essence of the porridge (it was sprinkled, as I recall, with walnuts, apples, tangerine wedges, raisins, sesame seeds, and chunks of comb honey) into his mind and meditated on it there, he got this big grin on his small beardless face, he shook his smooth head, the way you do when you've discovered something and it's even weirder and better than you'd imagined, and he grabbed his spoon and ate the porridge, shoveled it in, gobbled it down, put it away, looked at me (the other monks had gone to bed), belched, and said he had just eaten the ten thousand Buddhas and the hundred thousand devas and, in effect, I guess, the Meaning of Everything.

I didn't know exactly what he meant, but it seemed like a significant recommendation for my porridge. He went on to tell me that he thought I was the reincarnation of some mad monk of the thirteenth century whose name I can't remember now and couldn't pronounce then, but this monk was known for living a wild life (wine, women, song), even though (or because?) he was very highly evolved, and he had a habit after that of reincarnating as a bear.

And so when the Tibetan people would see a bear acting crazy, sucking milk from yaks' tits and seducing women when their husbands were out herding goats, everybody figured it was old what's his name, who had attained enlightenment and was now permitted to enjoy himself. A few decades later he'd be back again, maybe as a monk this time (whenever a wild, wacky monk turned up, they knew it was him), or maybe as a woman who loved bears.

And sometimes a woman left beer out for the bear, to draw him near, and then she'd get intimate with the bear, because he was such a good lover, and it was thought being intimate with the Buddhabear, as he was called, would give the gal a boost toward her own Buddhahood. So the bear, through the centuries, was quite popular, and he was drunk a lot of the time. So he was called Beer Guzzler, Yak Milk Sucker, Honey-Thief, Beer Smelling Furry Guy, Woman-Crazy Snuffler, Honey-Pot-Licker, and Surprise-Fucker-from-Behind (all these names according to my friend the monk's translation).

There were a few narrow-minded monks who said the bear wasn't really the reincarnation of the enlightened monk of the thirteenth century, but the villagers and herders ignored those monks, deeming them petty and jealous and not very evolved, because when Honey Breath (as they also called him) showed up, a person felt something indescribable, a tingling, my monk said, at the base of their skull. (He touched me at the base of my skull, and I swear an electric current shot up my medulla oblongata and uncombed my hair, and a white light like electric cream splashed across my brain. It lasted for an instant then was gone, but my skin tingled for hours after, and for weeks I needed less food and sleep and didn't care for alcohol, and when I did sleep, I had dreams full of vivid colors where I was flying. Gradually these phenomena petered out, but I've never forgotten that snowy explosion in my brain, and I wish that monk would come back and do it again, but a few months later he was killed in an automobile accident on the New Jersey Turnpike, and I still wonder if he had any second thoughts or stirrings of prophecy before he climbed into the passenger seat of that van as that freezing rain began to fall.) The peasants, he said, felt the tingling when the bear came around—in fact, they could tell when the Buddhabear was nearby, even when they couldn't see him, because they would feel that electricity slither up their spines. And if the bear looked at you, you might hit the enlightenment jackpot right there. Some of those people the Buddhabear eyed went off afterwards to become monks and lamas, and some went crazy.

Well, I've wandered a little far afield from my porridge recipe, but everything's connected, at least that's what the monk told me, and I don't know where else to put this—I guess my monk friend would call it—this bit of dharma.

The three monks stayed three days, and I learned about Tibetan bears and Buddhabears, and they learned about American black bears, and we had porridge every morning. That winter Rudy was denned up in an old ice fishing house I'd dragged into the woods. A tree limb had knocked in the roof of the ice fishing house, so it was like a cave inside, and there wasn't a lot of room in the den, but the monks crawled in one after the other and squeezed next to Rudy—who was waking up and getting irritated by this intrusion, whoofing his I'm-gonna-be-cranky-very-quickly whoof—when the monks started chanting their three-notes-at-once prayer.

They started low and soft, like the rumble of an earthquake. At first Rudy seemed disconcerted by the sound. He scratched nervously at the earth, opened his mouth, showed his teeth. I was afraid things might get out of hand, the monks not tune in to Rudy's warning signs.

The low rumble got louder. The monks sang higher, their rough voices rising up the scale, the syllables sounding like *Oyyyy Oyyyy Oyyyy Royyy Royyy Royyy Boyyy Boyyy Boyyy.*

Rudy settled down. He closed his eyes. He breathed with the long vibrating syllables. He wasn't asleep. He was listening.

I slipped outside because it was so crowded in there. After a few moments it seemed like that old fishing house itself was singing. Then it seemed like the woods were singing, the chant droning out of the dark trees, the snow singing three tones at once, the clouded sky humming, the earth moaning a bass deeper than the bedrock far below.

Then there was another voice. I thought at first one of the monks was hitting a fourth note, had achieved a new resonance. But that wasn't it. It was Rudy chanting with the monks.

All afternoon I listened to Rudy and the monks praying.

Finally the monks were scrabbling out of the ice fishing house and smiling and picking dead leaves and twigs off their robes, and they weren't singing anymore, but the praying was still ringing in my ears, and it was going on in my head as we walked back to my lodge and I was still hearing it all through supper.

The monks wanted meat for supper. I thought they were vegetarians, and they said they usually were—the one monk said, actually, because the other two didn't speak any English—but tonight they were going to eat meat. It seemed to be some kind of religious thing. So, since I didn't have any yak meat in the freezer, I hauled out some ruffed grouse I'd nailed in the woods and baked the grouse with a Dijon-mustard-pineapple glaze, stuffed them with a pumpkin-acorn dressing, steamed up Basmati rice, decorated the rice, fluffy and aromatic as the first rose of summer, with roasted red pepper, zucchini, and tomatoes, and we all had a sip of a pertinent Gewurztraminer, which handled the grouse better than I thought it would. For dessert we had a tea the monks had brought with them from a far corner of the globe and a box of fortune cookies I had bought at Mel's Supermarket in town.

We spent the evening opening all of the fortune cookies and comparing our fortunes. The monk who was flipped out of this incarnation and into his next one in the car accident did not get a slip of paper that said *Do not get into a van on a rainy night in New Jersey.* Nor did I get one that said *A woman will leave you.* However, I did get one I like, which I taped to the lamp over my desk. It says *On earth there is no heaven, but there are slices of it.*

After the monks left, the lodge smelled of incense for a long time. They burned incense every day, and I got so that I didn't notice it, until they left. Weeks later, I'd come into the lodge from being outdoors all day, and I'd sniff the fragrance of Tibetan concentration, and I'd think, *The monks are back,* and I'd be happy. But then I'd walk through the dark and empty rooms, my boots clunking on the wooden floors, and I'd realize it was only the fading scent of memory clinging to the forgotten places of the house. It was as if they had left little pieces of themselves in the air, to remind me of them. Eventually, the scent of the incense faded, the way memories do, the way love, sometimes, does.

That spring Rudy came out of hibernation early and wouldn't go back, even though there was nothing for him to eat. He was alert and raring to go, but he was thin and hungry and there was no food yet in the forest. No willows had budded, no grubs had slithered up from the earth, the earth hadn't even thawed or the snow melted. So I bought frozen berries from Cal Simonson who drives the Schwann's truck. The pale yellow Schwann's freezer trucks are ubiquitous in Minnesota, making deliveries to homes like the mailman does and then parking for a spell on a street corner downtown for folks to stop and buy frozen delicacies like Sliced Peaches in Brandy and Thai Chicken Pizza with Peanuts. I thawed the berries for Rudy, and I fed him fresh vegetables, and apples, and pears, and peanuts, and scraps from the table. What he liked best, though, was the porridge. He loved the porridge. He ate it every day, and he got fat and strong. And when the forest greened up, he headed out again, eating bear things again.

William Borden

LYLE'S WIFE REMEMBERS

Dreamy Saskatoon

Dear Lyle,

When I was pregnant the first time, I had a lot of strange dreams. We'd been married only a year, and I'd just passed my oral defense of my dissertation on *The Diet of the Black Bear in a Northern Minnesota Forest and the Long-Range Impact of Resorts, Clear Cutting, and Other Unnatural Development on the Ecological Vitality of the Area.* In one dream I gave birth to a cute bear cub, but the doctor was angry, like I'd done something wrong, and the doctor was going to kill the baby bear, but you were there and you said, No, so the doctor gave me the baby bear, and I cuddled her—it was a girl cub—and she sucked at my breast.

The doctor in that dream was Bud Ostrum, the mailman. He was a lanky, randy fellow back then, remember, always flirting with me—but I may not have told you that, how he some days brought the mail right to the door, and I'd invite him in for a cup of java because he was lonely, his wife had left him, and I thought he was merely being friendly to a front-heavy lass, until he wanted to take photos of me naked. He had a particular fascination, it seemed, with pregnant women, and he said there were magazines that would publish the photos, and I could make some money. Well, we needed the money, that's for sure, but I couldn't see doing that, so I was rather firm with him, which may have been unkind and detrimental to his self-esteem, for which I have felt slightly guilty, but I don't think I can take full responsibility for his present corpulence, which he refers to as "mature huskiness," or for his arrest that time for bothering Fran Makosky's unmarried niece when she came up from the Cities to have her twins in secrecy.

Another time I was in labor, and the doctor—it was the real doctor this time, Dr. Gupta—looked in my vagina and asked, How did a bear get in there? I didn't know how to explain. But it didn't seem unusual to me.

When I finally had Bernadette, for a moment there in the delivery room, when I saw that black hair all wet and swirled over her head, I thought, My god, it's true, she's a bear! How will I explain this? Then she cried, but sometimes, you know, baby bears and baby humans are hard to tell apart when they cry. But then the doctor held her up.

I was relieved, of course. And yet, for an instant, I was disappointed. Because that would've been interesting, wouldn't it? To have given birth to a baby bear?

During my second and third pregnancies, with Babette and Bjorn, I didn't have those dreams. I was relieved. But I missed them, too.

Your dream wife

HOW BEARS NEGOTIATE

> There is no feast without cruelty.
> —Friedrich Nietzsche

We're in New York City in an expensive restaurant that's pretending it's in New Orleans or someplace else in the South before Sherman rampaged through. Pastel-colored gauze is draped everywhere, and I'm sitting in a swing, and across the table from me Lyle and Diane are wafting back and forth in another swing, like a porch swing, and the lights are so low I can't tell if that's okra in my bisque or something that once moved of its own volition. We're meeting with Sidney Renard, who flew us here (not first class, however), and who I assume is picking up the check. Sid is sitting on my left, in a normal chair. He loved the documentary on PBS last week, hailed as "a post-post-modern exposé of inter-species bacchanalia."

Sid waves away his soup, which he hasn't touched because he's been talking, while Lyle and Diane and I have finished ours, because we've been listening, and the waiter refills our wine glasses and brings another bottle when Lyle gives him a nod. Sid is an independent producer with, he assures us, close ties to HBO, Ted Turner, and Showtime, and he thinks a dramatic feature on bears, with Lyle and Rudy in the woods, scripted by yours truly and directed by Diane, would make us all a lot of money, and he has a contract right here for us to sign before dessert because if we don't sign now, Sid says, he can't pitch this idea to HBO and Ted and Showtime—and who knows? Maybe Jane, Mrs. Turner, would want to be in it!

The waiter brings our salads of esoteric greens sautéed with bacon bits and mushrooms from foreign countries with balsamic vinegar dribbled over the greenery. Lyle and Diane swing rhythmically back and forth in their gauze-wrapped white swing. Lyle asks the waiter if the recipe for this salad might be available. Diane says to Sid she would need to consult her attorney before she, or Lyle, signed anything. Sid says I would write the script for sure if I sign now, but later, well, who knows what Ted might say, maybe Jane will want to write it. The waiter says all recipes are the property of the chef and highly guarded secrets—although a cookbook is available for purchase.

Sid has a question about one particular shot in *Lyle's Bears*, a close-up of Rudy from the rear. Sid says he didn't see any, well, any male appendages on Rudy. Is Rudy really a guy bear? Lyle quaffs his wine and smiles. He explains that the male black bear retracts his testicles in late summer, after the mating season—and his fun—are over, and they stay hidden until spring, when everything wakes up again. "It's not so strange," Lyle observes, "when you think about it. A fella goes out in the cold, he shrivels up. A bear goes a little farther, that's all. Well, if you don't need them, why let them swing out there, vulnerable to accident, mayhem, and wanton attack?"

Sid is very tan. He spends a lot of time in L.A.—by the pool, apparently—taking meetings. His dark hair is slicked back and gives off a glossy, one might say greasy, sheen. His brown eyes have a predatory glint. He doesn't eat his salad, either.

"It's a typical example of evolutionary back-tracking," Lyle continues, "Mom Nature making sperm that can't survive at body temperature, then making a little bag to hang outside the body so the little fellas can cool their heels until the time is ripe to go forth on their little hero's journey. Evolution is a mad inventor, a Rube Goldberg juggling DNA with his eyes closed. Well, a fella's sperm is like a fine wine. A good vintage needs the right temperature." Lyle motions for another bottle of wine.

When the entrees are served, Sid suggests we might include in the film a hunting sequence. Lyle could hunt a bear.

Lyle stops the gentle rocking of the swing he and Diane are sharing. He stares at his plate a moment. He ordered the Creole shrimp.

Sid asks if the shrimp is okay.

The waiter is sure the shrimp is okay and doesn't stay for the answer.

Diane shifts a little in her seat, as if she knows something is coming and she doesn't want to be in Lyle's way. Lyle takes a deep breath. It's a sad breath, more than anything, a sigh of disheartenment, fatigue, and incoming disaster. "I know hunting's necessary," Lyle says, sipping the impudently seductive Graves. "I simply wish they gave the bears half a chance. They don't *hunt* bears. They *ambush* them."

Lyle seems to decide that's all he's going to say. He seems to want to enjoy his meal. But Sid is not sharply attuned to Lyle's moods, as Diane and I are. Sid blurts out, "Well, you'll show us how they hunt. We need some drama in a film for the commercial channels. You know, the usual—the chase, the sex, the kill, the climax." Sid turns to me. He pats my hand. He says, "But you know all about that. You're the writer."

Lyle tries to eat. He tries to ignore Sid. But Sid persists. "How do they hunt bears, Lyle?" Sid inquires.

Lyle bites off the flesh of a shrimp, setting the tail aside. He chews. He takes a bite of rice. (Little red things in the rice. Grilled red bell pepper? Pimento? Tomato?) He takes a bite of sweet potato. (Whipped, with brown sugar and walnuts and a splash of bourbon?) He washes it down with the Graves, then suggests to the waiter that a burly but agile Chardonnay might be the perfect sparring partner for our entrees. The waiter compliments Lyle on his oenological acumen.

Sid's a nervous guy. Some part of his body is always moving, usually his eyes, darting here and there as if scouting a nasty surprise, or as if wondering if somebody's going to find out something he's tried hard to keep secret. He's about forty, and he wears a sport shirt, even though all the other men here are wearing ties, even Lyle. Lyle wears a plaid tie that's about three inches narrower than this year's fashion, and his best red flannel shirt, a button-down shirt. Who says Lyle is not sartorially with it? Diane is dressed very stylishly in something long, something multicolored in earth tones, something in diaphanous layers that caresses her ankles and sometimes generously reveals a long stockinged leg.

Sid called her the day after the documentary aired on PBS. Could she and Lyle fly to New York and discuss a deal? They had a possible writer? Bring him along! Sid would have plane tickets waiting.

There was a guy at LaGuardia wearing a crumpled chauffeur's cap holding a smudged cardboard with "BEARS" scrawled on it. Instead of a limo, however, the guy, who didn't seem to understand much English, was driving a beat-up Buick, and there was stuff in the trunk so we had to hold our suitcases on our laps, and as near as I could make out the guy was saying that the limo broke down and Mr. Renard was sorry.

It turned out it was not the Waldorf as Sid had promised or the

Dancing with Bears   *61*

St. Regis which had been his second choice—they were unexpectedly full, the driver—his name was either Mohammed or Bob, I couldn't tell which—said, pulling up in front of a hotel on Eighth Avenue. At one remove from the hotel's revolving door was a movie marquee announcing TRIPLE FEATURE BOBBIE'S BACK DOOR SWEAT AND LEATHER WET LACE and adjacent to the hotel on the other side was another marquee featuring HOT BOYS and STUD SATURDAY NIGHT while across the street bright lights flashed LIVE SEX LIVE GIRLS TOTALLY NUDE 24 HOURS. Lyle was looking rather interested in all of this, but Diane told Bob, or Mohammed, or maybe it was Ahmed or Hobbit, to take us to the Waldorf.

"But Mr. Sid said," Ahmed protested.

"Move your sorry ass," Diane said, and Ahmed understood her.

The Waldorf had lots of rooms, but Diane had to put ours—one for me and one for her and Lyle—on her credit card because she couldn't reach Sid right then—actually it was the public television station credit card. She mentioned the hotel mix-up to Sid when we arrived at the restaurant. Sid blamed everything on his secretary and said he'd straighten out the room charges first thing in the morning, and of course we did the right thing, and he'd fire Habib, too, for good measure.

Lyle lays down his fork and looks at Sid. "You know how they so-call *hunt* bears?" he says. "*Before* hunting season starts—*two weeks* before the season *starts*—they can put out bait. They build themselves a stand. Hell, they construct a god damn clubhouse in a tree. They might have a portable television, watch football, eat popcorn, haul in a sofa. And then a few feet away they set out some sweet enticement. They might set out bait twenty different places until the bears find one, then they build their tree clubhouse with their TV and lazyboy. They keep putting out the bait until the bears come around for those treats every day. As if that's not stacking the deck, you've got your high-tech assassins who set up photo-electric timers, so even when they're at home they know to the minute *when* the bear stops by for his dinner."

The waiter brings the Chardonnay, but Lyle pays no attention, so Diane gives the nod to the label and tastes the wine and motions for the waiter to fill the new glasses, while Lyle picks up steam, and Sid is beginning to eat his blackened snapper.

"Then hunting season opens. By now the bears are used to the football game and the cigar smoke and the beer. Like people, they get used to things, and they gallumph up to the sweet mess—maybe it's bacon smeared in maple syrup with a few apples mashed in, or a bag of leftovers from Dunkin Donuts—only now it's bear hunting season. Nobody's told the bears bear hunting season's begun. They don't know. They're there for dinner, the way you're there now, stuffing your mouth with that overpriced snapper that's too spiced up for you to taste the natural flavors. So the bears are eating, and the so-called *hunters* are choosing the biggest and best-looking bears—the prime genetic specimens, who should be saved to perpetuate the best of the species— and they knock them off like ducks in a shooting gallery."

Lyle downs his Chardonnay. The waiter's there to refill his glass. Lyle goes on, working up a sweat. "Suppose you stayed here in this ante-bellum seraglio for two weeks, and I gave you a hell of a good meal every evening, and you got used to it. And then one evening, while you were sucking up those red beans and rice, you looked up, and here I was across the table pointing a big old gun at you"—Lyle points an imaginary rifle at Sid— "which doesn't alarm you because I've been holding it every evening for the past two weeks, you think that's merely the way I look—but *this* evening"—Lyle pauses— "*this evening*"—he leans over the table, his face in Sid's face, Lyle's lapis eyes fixing Sid's squinty shiftiness in a hypnotic paralysis— "*I blow you fucking away.*" Lyle's finger squeezes the invisible trigger.

"Excuse me," Sid says, and heads for the gentlemen's lounge.

We polish off the desserts—pecan pie soaked in bourbon for Lyle, sherbet for Diane, and I have the "Dream the Impossible Dream Dessert," a chocolate orgasm with a whipped cream topping—and sip the cognac and the coffee with chicory, but we're still bereft of Sid's company. We wonder if Sid is ill. So I check the gentlemen's lounge, but there's no Sid. When Lyle leads us into the kitchen—despite the waiter's protests, Lyle insists on personally complimenting the chef, who, it turns out, is a small Jamaican woman wearing many gold rings on her delicate fingers—she says it's been a real parade back there, the man with the sport shirt and the beady eyes passed through earlier and rushed out the rear exit without a word.

LYLE'S WIFE, FILM CRITIC

> Saskatoon, where they buried Prime
> Minister Diefenbaker, often called
> "The Chief"

Dear Lyle,

I was watching TV and it was Hollywood stars pretending to be circus people, and this woman was snapping her whip at some poor tigers, making them jump on and off things and acting like it was a big deal, and I remembered years ago when we took the kids to the circus in Winnipeg. They had bears they dressed in clothes and the bears rode bicycles and rolled balls around, and, Lyle, you looked so sad.

You got up and left, and after the twenty clowns spilled out of the Volkswagen and after the family walked on the tight wire, everybody on somebody's shoulders, and after the women in their white bodies that looked so cold rode around on the elephants, after everybody left and the kids were asking where you were, we found you out back by the bears' cages talking to the bears. You were telling them life wasn't always fair and even if you let them out they'd be captured again or, worse, killed. It was like when a person sees orphans starving on the TV news, and you can't bring them home with you, they're left to their fate and the whims of politicians. So buck up, you were saying to the bears. At least they knew somebody understood, and you gave them caramel apples you had bought on the way out.

That's the way I feel now, Lyle, except I'm both you and the bears. I'm talking to myself (but not out loud, like Mother, and not answering myself, like Mother) telling myself I understand how it is being in a situation I don't like, but I don't know how to get out of it.

Get out of what? maybe you're asking. Life? I'm not suicidal, I have a lust for life, like Van Gogh (woops—just remembered: he looked for that starry sky inside his head once too often), but really what I'm getting at is I thought the documentary Babette taped and sent to me made you bigger than life, and those shots of people in our living room getting drunk and the stew bubbling—was that supposed to be Fellini or something? Babette said some people thought it wasn't really a documentary on bears but a puff piece on you. That's why I feel like those circus bears. I ride a bike in circles while you're there at the center of things. And after the show is over I'm in a cage out behind the big top smelling the elephant poop.

It's too bad New York didn't work out the way you wanted but how nice you got to stay at the Waldorf. It was a nice post card, and I only want to bask in your reflected glory.

Well, I apologize for the sarcasm. It slipped out, despite my better nature and my great reservoirs of inner goodness and inexhaustible forgiveness.

Your, so far, loving wife

DIANE: SOFT BEARS

> Oh let me be
> Your teddy bear
> —Elvis Presley

Since he's become famous, people send Lyle bear things. He's got bear cookie jars, bear wrist watches, magic bear amulets, bears carved out of logs with a chainsaw, pasta shaped like tiny bears, and stuffed bears. It's a tribute to Lyle's soft, feminine side that he keeps these stuffed bears on the king-size bed, and we have to move them off when we go to sleep at night or make love in the afternoon. The stuffed bears are white, brown, black, tan, beige, and olive-drab, and there's even a blue bear. One of the bears wears a railroad engineer's cap. One wears a vest. One wears a cowboy hat. There's a fireman bear, an Indian bear, a pirate bear, and a sailor bear. There's a Green Beret bear, with ammunition bandoliers and a machine gun. We also received a bear in a tux, and a mohair bear designed by Annette Funicello herself.

Lyle's out checking his hibernating bears, who are snoring under the snow. I'm not much for the outdoors myself. My lips get chapped, my skin gets dry, my toes freeze. The only reason I came to Minnesota was this job with Northern Lakes Public Television. I wanted to escape the frenzy of commercial TV, where I worked before. I want to make money—who doesn't?—but I want to do something meaningful, too. Public Television, of course, doesn't know diddly about marketing. They think anything successful smacks of selling out. I think we all sell out. It's a just a question of how much we get.

I don't think getting suspended by the Division of Forestry has hurt Lyle's popularity. *Lyle's Bears* is available at Blockbuster and the other video stores, and it does very well for a documentary. The cable

William Borden

company is backing off from the one-world-Wild-Kingdom idea, however, afraid of the scandal, although I assure them that scandal only makes an audience more interested. But they want to present a wholesome image, untainted by moral ambiguity or intellectual complexity.

As for *Bear with Me*, Lyle's book on bears, the articles he's written over the years are so diverse in style and approach that they hardly make a coherent whole. I ask Lyle if he couldn't revise them to give them continuity. It shouldn't be hard, I say, since he wrote them in the first place. But he says the research comes first. Maybe we can persuade the writer to do something with them.

He comes and goes with some regularity now, the writer. He always brings something when he comes—a bottle of a hard-to-find vintage for Lyle or a bouquet for me. He's a comforting, soft-spoken man, about Lyle's age, but lacking Lyle's charisma. He usually leaves when I come, as he did yesterday, to give Lyle and me our privacy, I assume.

Sometimes, here at Lyle's lodge, where the only clamor is the muted sigh of the snow falling on the log pile and the only screaming is from the blue jay—or from me, when Lyle does that certain something—I don't call it my G spot, we call it my L spot—out here, surrounded by the naked trees and unnerved by this gaping stillness, I discover empty places in my mind, like forgotten and abandoned rooms in my psyche that the noise of urban living filled up. Like all post-modern urbanites, I need noise, clamor, anger, frustration, confusion. When I lived in New York it was always noisy, and now, in my apartment in Minneapolis, I hear sirens and fire trucks, while here the hungry silence gobbles up thought and ambition. No wonder somebody developed Chaos Theory. What else could explain our lives?

Well, I bring mystery novels. I snuggle into Lyle's old easy chair that smells like Lyle or stretch out on our bed amidst the rainbow of teddy bears. I like the novels by women best. Sometimes I think of writing a mystery novel. There would be a murder at a public television station. The detective would be a strong, sexy woman producer. The murderer, she would discover, is an evil, litigious station manager with thick glasses and a blond beard and a fat stomach, given to wearing loud ties and squeaky loafers, although I might have to change some things to preclude another lawsuit. Maybe the victim would be a famous host of a nationally syndicated weekly radio variety show who tells stories about a fictional Minnesota town full of elderly Norwegian bachelor farmers. And when the woman detective was horny she would grab a man, the way men do women, and satisfy herself.

I thought Lyle would keep me company, but he says he's behind with his record-keeping, and, besides, he has to go to these hearings. How can they accuse him of mistreating the bears? Sure, he put Dolly out of her misery without getting permission, when her leg was gangrenous and her body swarming with bacteria, but should he have let her wail and moan while the paper-pushers in St. Paul took their sweet time?

And he endangered people because he wouldn't use tranquilizers on the bears who were pawing at kitchen doors? Who's been hurt?

Well, the old lady over at Fancy Creek Lake shouldn't have left her garbage out and shouldn't have been hitting that bear with a frying pan.

So, left alone, I knock around this big old cabin, once a lodge for a resort, with its high wooden ceiling and shiny log walls. I open cabinets and look in drawers. I shuffle Lyle's mail, some unopened for weeks but resist opening it myself. I check my weight on his scales which need recalibration, reading as they do ten pounds too much. I might brush my teeth with Lyle's toothbrush but I don't tell him. I might soak in a steamy bath until my fingertips are wrinkled, sampling first one then another of Lyle's wife's bath oils. I like the eucalyptus best. I inspect the medicine cabinet, noting that Lyle's wife abandoned her mascara and a piquantly musky perfume, which I spray—I don't know why—on me after my bath. I enter the walk-in closet, full of his wife's clothes. Sometimes, as I'm fingering her skirts and dresses and blouses, I sniff the faint fragrance of her absence.

I try on Lyle's wife's clothes. She likes brighter colors than I do. Should I wear brighter colors for Lyle? Or does he like me better because I don't wear bright colors? There's a drawer in the back of the closet. It's full of bustiers and bras with holes for the nipples and panties with slits in the crotch and garter belts and nightgowns you can see through and high heels and black stockings and white stockings and lavender stockings and pink stockings. In the bottom of the drawer there are photos of her wearing these things. She looks very good in them.

I imagine wearing one of these outfits for Lyle. But to wear her clothes—that seems wrong; incestuous; weird. Besides, I don't think Lyle would like it.

But to wear them, as I'm wearing them now, for myself—the panties with the slit, the bra that shoves my breasts up and exposes my nipples, the white garter belt, the white stockings, the heels—I feel oddly excited.

What if she were to walk in now? Catch me here in front of the full-length mirror admiring my tits? Get the hell out of my Frederick's of Hollywood, she'd say. Or would she find me sexy, and worthy of Lyle?

When I wake up, Lyle is staring at me as if something has gone awry in the order of things. I sit up and say, Lyle, what's wrong? Then I realize, oh shit, I've still got the wife's lingerie on and I've fallen asleep with the teddy bears.

I thought you were..., he says.

I was curious..., I say.

Lyle nods. He understands curiosity.

I think I wanted to be her. For awhile. You never talk about her. Do you want to talk about her?

He shakes his head, *No.*

I remove the gauzy lingerie. I fold the panties with the slit in the crotch and the bra that shoves my boobs forward and the garter belt that flatters my hips and the stockings that compliment my legs, and I position them in the drawer more neatly than they were before. Lyle watches the way he watches a bear do something new, as if he's trying to figure out what's going on in the bear brain, because the bear can't tell him. I'm standing there naked. I know I shouldn't have been doing what I was doing.

"Do you want me to get you some things like that?" he asks, as if he were asking if I'd like cream in my coffee.

I say, "Yes."

That's when I realize I want to replace his wife.

Saskatoon, where there are bear
hunting seasons spring and fall, and
in the spring hunters kill mother
bears, leaving the cubs to starve

Dear Lyle,

Babette said she visited you (She's changing majors again, did she
tell you? First nursing, then dental hygiene, then civil engineering, and
now medieval literature—wide interests are fine, but I'm afraid she's
losing her way. Why is it always I who worries about our children? You
say you have confidence they can work everything out, and mostly they
have, once Bjorn went into treatment, and he seems pretty satisfied
working at the food co-op in St. Paul although it has no future but at
least he's eating healthy foods.) Anyway, Babette said you have a bunch
of stuffed bears on our bed.

You always hated stuffed bears.

You never let the children have stuffed bears. Stuffed rabbits, dogs,
cats, giraffes, pterodactyls, anything else was all right, but you thought
it was humiliating to bears, or to your work, or something. I never really understood, but I went along with you because I felt that parental
unity in these matters is important so children aren't confused.

I'm confused.

Babette said there was a writer there when she visited. Are you
going to be famous? I mean more famous? I hope the writer wasn't in
connection with the investigation. Why would those women who were
helping you, they were volunteers, after all, accuse you of harassment?
For sure you have a wandering eye, and other parts of your body wander, too, but it's not in your nature to force yourself on anybody, and if
women can't take a pat on the fanny I think we've gone way overboard
on this sexual harassment thing, and I wish my friend Lois in Bemidji

would stop sending me those clippings about the investigation. She acts like she's doing me a favor, but she's always been jealous because you picked me not her to be your assistant that summer so long ago and three children later. Lois was always hot for you and now she's on her fourth marriage. This one owns a hardware store. He gave her a wrench set for Xmas and an ice auger for her birthday.

Monday Mother was in the bathroom screaming. She wanted to know why they'd put her in jail, and why was I there, too, was it for robbing that bank or was it mistaken identity? Okay, I said, we won't watch any more cop shows on television.

Anyway, Lyle, explain to me the stuffed bears on our bed.

Your curious wife

LYLE'S HEARING

> Do not weep; do not wax indignant. Understand.
>
> —Baruch Spinoza

We're in the small town that's the nearest thing to civilization in this federally and state protected vast wonderland of forest and lakes and wildlife, some thirty miles from Lyle's cabin. The town's a jumping-off spot for the canoers and backpackers and, in the winter, the cross-country skiers who venture into the wilderness where the government doesn't allow cars or snowmobiles or anything driven by internal combustion. There are outfitters' stores on either side of the street and a couple of restaurants, three churches, several bars, a bakery, and a grocery store. We go into Inga's Bakery. Lyle orders four old-fashioned sourdough doughnuts. I get a cinnamon roll. Diane asks for a bear claw.

We sit in the cab of Lyle's pickup, the engine running, the heater struggling, our breaths visible, eating our pastries and sipping our coffee from Lyle's thermos (Tanzanian, French roast). We're packed pretty tightly, with Diane in the middle, our thighs pressed together and our elbows knocking so we have to be careful with the coffee. We're sharing the metal cup that screws off of Lyle's thermos. I believe I can taste Diane's lips on the cup, a sugary muskiness, with a hint of the pale lipstick she's wearing. I look down at the white waxed sack that held her bear claw, and I read on the sack that rests in her lap, *Sweet Delights*.

I'll bet.

When it's time for the hearing—this is about the allegations of unlawful receipt of outside payments, unapproved travel, wrongful appropriation of funds, taking unauthorized sick leave, improper filing of reports, failure to file reports, improper bear management, use of a government vehicle for unofficial business, failure to keep adequate records, lack of cooperation, and meeting the public out of uniform—or, as Lyle puts it, "bad bookkeeping and illegal independence of mind"—and thus whether Lyle should continue his bear research or should he give slide shows to tourists and collect camping fees. The sex thing is being handled by another department, and anyway one of the women who filed a complaint has moved to Hong Kong to work in the zoo there, and one of the other accusing women is undergoing hypnotic regressions to recover memories of alien abductions she has experienced since she was three years old, and she thinks the aliens have used her to incubate half-alien, half-human embryos, and her story might be in a book that's coming out soon—Lyle steps out of the cab and saunters over the packed snow into the regional office where the hearing is supposed to take place, brushing crumbs off as he goes. A Canada jay swoops down to jab at the crumbs.

Diane and I are alone in the cab. She doesn't move away, even though she has room now. I assume she's too absorbed in Lyle's troubles to notice my thigh tight against hers and the fact that I'm breathing her perfume, and it must contain a powerful pheromone because I need to keep my hands casually in my lap as I stare at her Sweet Delights.

Diane watches Lyle enter the log building, watches the door close behind him like Dire Destiny, and then stares at the Canada jay hopping in Lyle's footsteps. She munches a crumb of bear claw and sips her cold coffee. She crumples the Sweet Delights bag and drops it on the floor, already littered with debris. Suddenly her hand presses my thigh, a mere inch from my own burgeoning Sweet Delight.

"I'm quitting my job," she says. "They've suspended me anyway. I should hang in and pursue my appeal, but I can't take this uncertainty." Her hand squeezes my thigh, as if my thigh were an extension of her thinking, as if it were there to record each step in her logic. "If I quit now, I'll lose my back pay and, probably, my appeal." She looks me in the eyes. Her honey hair falls down the buttoned front of her coat, over her breasts that I remember from the night she shot out the candles. "But if I quit"—her fingers tighten around my thigh, and I'm thinking she's going to say quitting will give her time to devote herself to me because she's had it with Lyle— "I can devote myself to Lyle"—of course, of course that's what she was going to say— "and pursue a myriad of business opportunities for him, so he'll be recognized as the multi-talented man that he is. Don't you think that's what I should do?"

I place my hand on hers. I want to say—I don't know what I want to say. Yes, I do know what I want to say, but I don't think I should say it. Besides, I've forgotten how to speak. I'm suffering some breakdown in my brainstem. "Don't you?" she asks again, gripping my hand, the heat from her hand surging up my arm, down into my chest, a reverse cardiac attack.

Her lips are inches away. They're full and sensual, although cracked at the moment from the cold, and small fragments of lipstick cling to them. I want to flick my tongue and salvage those tiny rosy fragments. Her pliant lips part, her breath, sugary, coffee-flavored, slightly leathery, wafts between us. Her tongue peeks between her teeth. I open my mouth. To lick? To kiss?

The door pops open. Lyle's face appears. He climbs into the cab. "Hearing's postponed," Lyle says, jerking the gearshift into first. "The guy from the main office who's supposed to conduct the hearing can't make it. There's a bear of a blizzard between here and St. Paul."

So we drive back to Lyle's, relieved but uneasy. That's life in Minnesota in the winter.

William Borden

LYLE'S WIFE WRITES OF THINGS THAT BREAK

Icy Saskatoon

Dear Lyle,

Thank goodness Mother broke her arm not her hip. At least she can still walk. She has a plastic elbow now. She calls herself the bionic grandmother.

I told her to stay inside when it's so icy, but she said she's been taking her daily walk for years, in rain, through snow, on ice, she might as well get a job as a mail carrier. But, I said, you're old and your bones are brittle. I'm young as Sonia Henie, she said, and slid out the door.

She is pretty nimble for an old lady, and, as I watched her from the window, returning from her walk—she wasn't gone long, it was thirty below Celsius—she was doing okay, until she reached the stretch of ice where kids have been sliding and have worn the ice to a saucy sheen that bounced the sun like a mirror. Maybe the glare blinded her, or confused her, or sent her into another reality, but she put her right foot out, spread her arms, pushed off, and glided, on her galoshes, smooth as Sonia Henie, and she was doing all right until she whipped herself around to skate backwards.

Who did you think you were, Sonia Henie? I asked, picking her up and trying not to fall—I hadn't even put my coat or boots on, so I was shivering and sliding out there myself—and she said, "I know perfectly well who I am. Do you know who you are?" Which I didn't know whether to take as a motherly reprimand or an existential accusation. So I ignored her and grabbed her elbow to steady her, and she started to cry. I asked her if she was sad. "No," she said, "I broke my arm."

She spent the night in the hospital after they nailed her arm together, and I was alone for the first time in a long time. I dreamed I was skating in the Olympics. I was executing impossible leaps and twirls. I was hell on skates, until my skate broke, and I slid across the ice to the judge's box, and there you were, you were the judge, and you said, Too bad, you lose, and I said, *But I did everything perfectly, until the very end, isn't that what counts? Besides, it was the skate that broke, not me. I tried to get the skate off to show you, but when I looked up you had vanished.*

Then I heard a crack. I thought it was the ice that was cracking, but the cracking was coming from my chest. My heart was cracking into little pieces. My heart was falling apart.

It's the human heart alone that is resilient enough to take shocks and loneliness and cold and keep on beating, but how long can a heart beat if it's frozen, because it hasn't been warmed by love?

Dreams are strange, aren't they? But you always wake from dreams.

Except that last dream, the one we call Life. That hibernation with no green-up.

And when we wake from that years-long wandering in the universe's sleep, what do we find?

William Borden

INTO THE WOODS

If you go down to the woods today
you'd better not go alone...
—"The Teddy Bears' Picnic"

Lyle's edgy, maybe because Diane's in L.A. meeting with television producers to explore various opportunities. Or it may be the winter, long even by Minnesota standards. I feel a little testy myself, no doubt from weeks of deprivation of sunlight to the pineal gland. Lyle confides that he and Diane had their first fight, something about long distance phone calls to Canada and Hong Kong, and his giving private tutorials to female students from the community college, which all seem pretty innocent to me; but I suppose the relentless cold and cloud cover has put her biochemicals in arrears, too. We're all victims of meteorological implacability.

Lyle divulges that he's been suspended and isn't supposed to do any research until the investigation has been completed, "but," he asks, "am I supposed to let science wither? Hibernation is not merely a long doze so you don't have to bother with galoshes and earmuffs. No sir. Take your ground squirrel. When your ground squirrel is bopping about in the summer, finding food, fucking, chattering, his little old heart beats five or six hundred times a minute." He gives me a hard look, to be sure I appreciate that coronary machine-gun. "We can't even think that fast, jocko. But when the ground squirrel hibernates, his heart shifts down to 25 beats a minute, in only a day or two, and his temperature drops to near freezing, sometimes below freezing. How does he do that?"

"I don't know."

"I don't either. But your ground squirrel wakes up every week or so—heart rate revs, temperature rises—so he can get up and pee and shit. Then he curls up and cools down again. Why am I telling you this?"

"I don't—"

"I'll tell you why I'm telling you this. Because a bear doesn't piss or shit all winter. Now you and me, if we don't pee, we get uremic poisoning, and we die. But the bear utilizes that urea, changes it into protein and things, all the fucking winter. The bear is the only animal who knows how to do that. If we can figure out how he does it, and we can figure out how we can do it, too—hell, jocko, think of the advances in medicine, think what that would mean for deep space travel. Already this research has allowed doctors to lengthen the time between some people's dialysis. But there's still a lot we don't know. What if you and I, when we got lost in the woods, say, could learn how to hunker down and slow everything and even recycle our urine? Wouldn't that be a pisser?"

He throws me an old coat and a fur hat and leads me outside. "I've got important data on hibernation. If I don't do any more testing this winter, everything I've done so far is down the drain. Will the bears keep snoozing as long as it stays cold, or will they get stressed from the long winter and get mad and leave their dens, like some people I know?"

His two snowmobiles crouch before us. "I've got eight bears I'm monitoring. We'll do three today—one for you and two for me. Each saddle bag has pencils, notebook, hypodermic syringes, needles, alcohol swabs, vials, thermometer, blood pressure cuff, stethoscope, flashlight. You've seen what we do. I'll check on Barry and Larry, they're off to the east. You monitor Holly, she's north of here."

"But—"

"Holly has three cubs. We need to get their weight and length. You've got a set of scales in your saddle bag to weigh the little fellas and a tape measure. If she gets nervous, back away until she gets used to you. There's a flask in there, too, for a sample of her milk."

"Milk?"

"Thirty per cent fat. Talk about your cholesterol! Your mom and mine, the cow down the road, give up only three per cent fat. Of course, those cubs need that cream. Just run your fingers through Holly's fur, grab a tit, give a few squeezes. You've grabbed a gal's tit before, haven't you?"

"Sure, but—"

"There's a little pump in the pack, but I use my hand. Wait till the cubs are nursing, sneak your paw in there. She won't notice anything, if you're careful."

"How can I be careful, squeezing her—?"

"Some researchers drug the poor gal, haul her out, do their measurements. But who wants that dope in her veins, interfering with Nature's pure harmony? It takes a little patience and empathy to do it without drugs, that's all. She'll probably be a little restless, you being a stranger. But that coat and hat smells like me, so you might pass inspection."

I sniff the sleeve of the coat. It has a fierce, raw odor, part animal, part earth, part wood smoke, part rank mystery. "Some people think I'm out here playing games," he says, "following these fellas and gals around, picking up their shit, getting television crews to immortalize me and writers to hang on my every word. Well, fame's fine, and if it lasts thirty minutes instead of fifteen, that's okay, too, but, bottom line, I'm doing science here. You think this is fun going out in the middle of winter, crawling into bear dens and sticking a thermometer up a bear's ass?"

"You mean I have to—"

"Yeah," he admits, "it is fun." He straddles the snowcat. "I hope you'll have fun, too, jocko." He puts his gloved fingers on the starter rope. "Don't forget to put a little Vaseline on the thermometer."

"Wait!" I cry.

"Fear," he says patiently, "is useful only in moments of danger. And," he adds, "not always then."

"Where?" I cry.

"Where what?"

"Where's the bear?"

A grin slowly spreads around his teeth. He shakes his head. "Look at me," he says ruefully. "I'm so excited I forgot to tell you where. What would you have done?" He rips a sheet from my notebook. He draws me a map.

"Here we are," Lyle says, handing me the map. "Here's the road. Follow the—"

"A road?"

"Not a real road."

"Then how will I know it's a—?"

He's getting impatient. "Because there aren't any trees in the middle of it." He narrows his eyes, assessing the depth of my arboreal incompetence. He resumes, speaking more slowly and more deliberately than necessary, needling me with his backwoods irony. "Stay on the area between the trees that might resemble a road if you think about it for, oh, maybe a mile. You'll see a big red pine on your right, and next to it a birch that's fallen over. You take a left there."

"Left to where?" I ask, never mind that I don't know a red pine from a black oak, and every few yards around here there's a birch that's fallen over.

"Into the woods, jocko. From there it's easy." He grips the handlebars. Panic runs in my eyes. "It hasn't snowed since I was out there last. Just follow my track."

"Track?"

"The track of my snowcat." His machine rears forward, his head snaps back—Newton's law at work—and he speeds away. I watch him disappear into the trees. His engine whines into the brittle air, then fades, swallowed by the silent, unforgiving forest.

I miss the damn red pine. I'm trying to keep from breaking my neck as the huge machine rears and jumps, and my shoulders are sore the way I have to hold the handlebars, and I have to watch out for rocks and downed limbs but everything's covered with snow. And why the hell didn't I tell Lyle, Do your own bear monitoring?

I quiet myself down. I take my time. I tell myself, This Is An Experience. I Can Use This. I can write a novel, maybe, A Real Novel, quit cobbling together these oddball free-lance assignments ("Maple Sugaring on a Lesbian Commune," *Sapphic Wilderness*; "Innovations in Overalls: Do We Need Those Brass Buttons?" *Garment Weekly*; "Breasts and Overalls: A Possible Carcinogen?" *Medical Supply Bulletin*; "Overall Art: The Latest Craze?" *Threads*; "Big Boobs Bounce Better in Overalls," *Busts and Butts*; and a paperback, *Overall Babes Do It All Over*, Slippery Tongue Press) under various *noms de plumes*.

But after awhile I realize I've been bouncing along for a long time. The wind's picking up, my hands are getting cold, and my butt's numb. I stop the machine and stretch my legs. The snowmobile track I'm following now is different than the one I started out following. This one is smooth, without the familiar tread.

I get on the machine and head back the way I came. Eventually I see a large straight pine and, beside it, a downed birch tree. I make out a trail winding between trees and around logs. Rattling over the rough terrain, I follow the trail. I forget to worry about how I'm going to crawl into the den and find—what was her name, anyway?

I think it will really help me to remember the bear's name. She's probably a smart bear, and she won't be fooled by me wearing Lyle's coat and hat. Telling her her name will, I hope, soothe her anxiety. What better proof of love and devotion than uttering the beloved's name?

Maybe, when I greet this bear, I could mumble, and end the mumble with a "—y."

I wonder if a bear's rectal temperature is really that important.

As for the bear milk, maybe I could find a little half and half in Lyle's frig, pour it into the flask.

No, I berate myself, Lyle has entrusted me with a scientific duty. He has confidence in me. If he didn't, would he send me out here alone?

Lyle, I remind myself, likes to play jokes.

I stop the snowmobile. The track stops a few yards ahead—trees and brush all around, nowhere farther to go—but something's wrong.

The snow's been packed down. Sure, I think, it's packed down because Lyle was here a few weeks ago. But there's a silence in the black bare trees, an emptiness that seems to pull back, to deposit a brooding anguish here in this clearing. Logs splay here and there in an unnatural configuration. Darkness splashes the snow.

The darkness is blood.

I take a step toward the scattered logs. My boot slips. I've stepped on something small, frozen, dead. I've stepped on a bear cub.

Back at the lodge I wait for Lyle's snowmobile to return. When Lyle hops off his machine, he's grinning, his eyes bright, his cheeks rosy from the cold. I can tell how much he loves this work, plunging into the cold, into research, into the dens of these bears. He's on a razor edge of science, an astrophysicist peering into the embers of the big bang, a neurosurgeon spotting the brain's dark den of the soul. He looks excitedly at me, like a kid, hoping I've had as much fun as he has.

> ...punishment overtakes the transgressor
> who sins against the soul of a bear...
> —Sir James Frazier, *The Golden Bough*

The other two cubs are in the den, frozen. Lyle buries the tiny bodies under rocks and logs. He sweeps his flashlight beam across the muddled blood-soaked snow. Footprints come and go. "He followed my trail to the den." He picks up a bullet casing. He takes a deep breath rattling with pain. "I led him to her."

Our headlight bouncing over the crusted snow, we follow the ribbon of snow smoothed by the sled carrying the murdered Holly. We reach the highway. The trail continues beside the highway for a few miles, then angles into the woods and disappears.

Lyle shuts off the engine. A menacing wind keens through the trees. "Cold front's moving in," Lyle says. "I'll take you back to the lodge."

"No." I climb off the Arctic Cat.

"It'll be thirty below soon."

I don't move.

"Hurry up, damn it."

I've spent too much of my life left behind, a scribe of second-hand life.

"He could kill us both, you know."

It's pitch black. Lyle is only a voice from the abyss.

He says, "Creswell doesn't give a shit about you or me."

"Let's go."

Lyle's boots crunch in the snow. I follow the sound.

"Creswell doesn't think, Gee, if I shoot these two fellas, I might get arrested." Lyle's voice drifts away. "Creswell's a loner, lives in his own world."

I hop-skip to catch up.

"He doesn't even think about what's lawful."

I stumble.

"For Creswell, it's kill or be killed."

I'm on all fours in the snow.

"He's a simple man in a simple world."

The wind wails.

"Are you there, jocko?"

My icy breath wheezes. He helps me up. He brushes off the snow. "You'd better think about what you're doing."

I'm too cold to think.

Lyle adjusts the rifle on his shoulder. He walks more slowly, so I can keep up. He says, "If he does kill us, there might be more of a cry for justice if two of us get it than if it's only me, famous though I am."

I follow the crack and squeak of Lyle's boots in the snow. I don't know how Lyle can see where to go, but he does.

The steady crunch of the snow is a mantra. I'm in another dimension, beyond space and time. I stay there, I don't know how long, not thinking, not worrying, my mind a smooth track on the cold slope of eternity.

I slam into Lyle. A lighted window flickers through the trees. Wood smoke drifts on the wind.

The bolt of his rifle glides, clicks.

This is crazy, why didn't I let Lyle take me back, I could have gone for the sheriff.

A headless body swings from a tree limb.

Somebody else came calling?

It's Holly, skinned.

Lyle whips open the door, rifle swinging right to left, ready to fire.

My quest for experience has been a mad mistake.

Lyle yanks me inside.

My whole life has been a map of wrong turns. A collection of errors. A syllogism of confusion. A muddle of illogic. A farrago of folly.

A grease-crusted skillet sits atop a wood stove. An unmade bed nudges the wall. A kerosene lamp hangs from a wall. Books and magazines, creased and thumbed over, some picturing soldiers and guns, others chess pieces, clog a stack of orange crates. The fetid air reeks of smoke and solitude, anger and obsession, nightmares and madness.

A bear crouches in the corner.

My bones are made of ice. I shake uncontrollably. Lyle enfolds me in Holly's fur. Her head, a heavy totem, rests above my eyes. I inhale her ferine breath.

I have to urinate. Go, Lyle says. Be careful.

I clasp Holly to my chest, her arms swinging, her legs striding through the air. I dart outside. I lean against a wall, tug off a glove, unzip with stiff fingers, pull out, let go. Nothing comes. Everything is suspended in the glacial night—the naked carcass, the groan of branches, the confidence of gravity, the vacuity of fear, the peril of courage, danger's sudden hunger, the future's surprising eruption.

A dribble. An ache. A hole widens in the snow. I close my eyes, gripped by a grand mal of relief, oblivious to everything.

I shake, stow, zip, tug on the glove.

I peer around the corner. A path worn in the snow between the outhouse and the door at the rear of the shack. I'd better tell Lyle about the rear door.

I look in the window.

A man has a rifle pressed against the back of Lyle's head. The man leans Lyle's rifle against the wall. The man wears a thick black fur coat and a black fur hat and is smaller than I had imagined.

I ease the rear door open and step into a dark entryway. A vertical crack of light signals the inner door. I nudge the door until I see the man's back, see him holding the rifle to Lyle's head.

The man's not saying anything. I'm afraid he's going to kill Lyle now, immediately, without talk, the way he must have killed Holly and all the other things he has killed. I think he's probably not used to talking, living as he does alone.

I think if I rush him, if I hit him from behind, Lyle can grab the man's rifle.

Or, I'll cause the man to pull the trigger, and he'll blow Lyle's head off. And then mine.

No, I need to draw the man's attention to me. Distract him. Then Lyle can get the rifle. Before the man shoots me. I hope.

I inch the door open. Can I grab Lyle's rifle leaning against the wall before the man sees me? Get the drop on him?

A long step, and I might be able to grab the rifle before he sees me, might—

William Borden

—trip—
—*The fucking bear's back?*—
—explosion—
Wet gritty stuff on the floor.
Lyle?
Cauliflower in tomato sauce splattered everywhere.
Lyle pulls me up.
Where's Ben Creswell's head?

AFTER THE FALL

...the Lapps...strip themselves of the garments
they had worn in killing the bear....
—Sir James Frazier, *The Golden Bough*

By the time we get to the snowmobile, snow is piling up like the eternal silence that follows Armageddon. Our tracks are gone. It's as if we were never there.

Back in Lyle's yard, Lyle peels off his gloves, coat, hat, boots, sweater, trousers, socks, wool shirt, and long underwear and, naked to the cold, throws everything into a charred oil drum. He pours on gasoline. Flames *whoosh* into the darkness.

I strip off my clothes and throw them onto the fire.

Snow peppers my skin like ashes from a nightmare.

An owl hoots a hollow tremolo.

Lyle says, "The Indians would say that's Ben's spirit."

I begin to shake. There's a muffled flutter as the owl, or Ben's soul, wings away, swallowed by the night's icy mystery.

We stand under the hot shower to wash away the dried blood and to warm our bodies while the sauna heats up.

In the sauna I can't stop shaking. Lyle holds me, his body cool and bony. I cry, heaving sobs and gasps, as if some panicked animal were trying to escape from my chest. Lyle holds me tight, keeps the animal from bursting out, until the sobbing and the shaking abate, and he lets go, and we sit side by side, looking forward, silent.

It takes a long time before we sweat.

Lyle goes outside. He comes back carrying a handful of long, black, whip-like branches. He hands them to me. He turns his back, red from the heat, his backbone curved and knobby. I remember Ingmar Bergman's *The Virgin Spring*. I brush his back with short, hesitant strokes, but I can tell it's no good, so I put a little more into it, and his back straightens up, he leans into the blows, and I put my shoulder behind it now, I give it all I've got, and I feel a surge of energy and excitement, whipping Lyle's back until it's scored and purged.

I hand him the branches. I turn my back to him. He lays into me, and it stings and burns, and it feels good. After awhile, it hurts in a bad way, and I move away. We sit on the bench, drinking water and ladling water onto the hot stones. We stay until we can't stand the heat any longer, then we stay a few minutes longer. We stagger out, legs wobbly, bones jellied, strangely giddy. In the shower we lather up good. We scour each other's back. We rinse quickly, because the hot water's running out. There's only one towel, so we share it.

We stumble naked through the snow to the lodge. I don't feel the cold.

I stagger to Lyle's bedroom. I fall into the bed.

My dreams explode in blood and flesh.

LYLE'S WIFE DREAMS OF BEARS

Dream-splashed Saskatoon

Dear Lyle,

In the dream I had last night you were in a dark woods, and snow was whipping around, and you were walking with a bear. I know, you walk with bears all the time. But this bear was walking upright, like a man, and he had a limp, as if maybe he'd caught his leg in a trap when he was a cub, and I felt you and the bear were in danger.

I woke up, sweating and afraid. I almost called to be sure you were all right. But I thought, if you're not all right, you won't be there to answer the phone, and then I'll really worry. And if you're all right, I'll wake you up and piss you off. And besides, if something has happened to you, eventually somebody will notify me.

Do you remember, Lyle, the time I was sure I heard you call me—you sounded as if you were right next to me in the kitchen—but you had actually fallen in the woods and, you thought, broken your ankle? Fortunately that volunteer assistant from Denmark, the tall thin girl with the boy's haircut and the gold stud in one nostril was nearby and was able to ease your fears and help you to a car and it was only a sprain. So I wondered if last night the dream was psychic like that.

Yesterday Mother was in my room weeping. She thought her father was punishing her by locking her in her room. Did Grandpa often punish you? I asked. When he drank too much, she said. I guess we never know what turmoils our parents have gone through, do we? We can't imagine them young, with parents of their own. We're forever innocent, in some ways—at least until Life stops by with a smack or two aside the head.

Are derailments possible in Life's runaway rush down the infinitely

William Borden

parallel tracks of Determinism as we hurtle clickety-clack toward Grim Destiny? Can those quirky quarks, in their fickle unpredictability, avalanche into molecular, even cellular, surprises? Is our Future certain, waiting patiently, knitting and tapping its toe until we arrive, eyebrows raised, mouth agape, surprised at what was in the cards all along? Or is our future iffy, haphazard, a roll of the dice, a spin of the wheel, a book yet to be written, spontaneity's slippery spectacle? Was Spinoza's fervid determinism the consequence of the predictability of Amsterdam's genever? And Hume's bouncy uncertainty the happenstance of a night drowned in Talisker?

Philosophical Me

LYLE: GREEN-UP

> It is not worth the while to let our
> imperfections disturb us always.
> —Henry David Thoreau

The morning after Ben's fateful quietus, the snow falls gently like a mother's soft hand soothing a troubled spirit. Jocko sleeps. It's a tormented sleep, with yelps of fright, howls of terror, like poor Molly's wails when she was caught in that saw-tooth trap a few years back—Ben Creswell's trap—who else would've set it?—and her leg so mangled, there wasn't anything to do but shoot her, except I never carry my rifle so I had to trek back to the truck, then drive home and get my rifle, and by the time I got back she had expired, entering her bear bardo in a froth of torment and anguish.

I'm up early, moving around, like I've got gnats in my long johns. I strap on skis and head out, leaving the writer to his nightmares—I'd squeeze into his vertiginous purgatory if I could, and help him out, but only shamans can do that. I'm only a bear researcher and bon vivant.

I ski like a sprinter over the white snow, into the woods. My muscles cry for action, gobble up the miles, plunge into the crisp air. Regret? Whatever clings to my moral dipstick is cleansed by the warming air, getting balmier as I glide over earth's pristine duvet. Guilt? A terrible thing, surely, a man's brains sticking to the ceiling, but it's an end to the senseless murders of innocent animals, not to mention the forest ranger a few years back, or the likelihood that if it hadn't been him it would've been me, and jocko. Sure, if we hadn't gone back there, nothing would've happened. Not last night. But someday?

Ben sowed, he reaped. And I? What seeds am I spilling from the holes in my karmic soul, skiing more slowly now, my adrenaline fading, my muscles cramping, still a couple of miles from home? I'm not usually so ruminative, but, I have to say, an act of violence and an adhesion of culpability set the moral engine in gear, and a fella has to give some thought to his standing in the scales of accountability. I did say, at one point, to my fellow wayfarer, "You saved my life," whereupon he said, "I killed him," and I answered, "He killed himself," and he, "But we—" and I, "It was him or us, jocko," and he sighed, "I guess you're right" but didn't sound convinced. In the wild, though, you realize that life, if not cheap, is on a bargain table, a Crazy Days Sidewalk Sale, from swatting a mosquito to a bear's chewing up a hapless fawn, or even a boar grabbing his own cub for dinner. Did we kill Creswell, or the U.S. Green Berets, training all of the compassion out of him and sending him into meaningless carnage?

When I get home, wrung to grateful fatigue and mental oblivion, I stagger into the bedroom, ready to share a snooze with my matey, but he's gone. We come and go, wordless, quarks popping in and out of existence, supernovae blasting then sucking themselves into the heavy nothingness of black holes, angels dropping by to give a hand then slipping away before you can say Thanks or Will I see you next Monday then?

A day later a warm front heaves in and slams the door on winter. Snow melts. It takes a week to see grass, three weeks for the drifts to ooze into the ground. The nights still hang close to freezing, but during the days the sun blesses everything. Frank Running Bear and his family are in the woods, tapping the maple trees. They're not supposed to be in the state woods here, but I don't say anything, never have. Hell, they're their trees, and sugaring doesn't hurt the trees, and the maple syrup they give me lasts all year and is rich and strong and full of vigor, with a hint of the wood smoke from the fire they build in the woods to boil down the sap. Frank's close to eighty years old and spry as a wildcat. He's outlived four wives and may outlive this new one, even if she is only twenty-three. She's out there with the rest of them, chopping wood and hauling sap, and being seven months pregnant doesn't slow her down a bit.

And then, like an alarm going off before you expect it, everything is greening up, and it's that beautiful moment after the ice goes out on the lakes when the leaves pop out on the trees but the mosquitoes haven't hatched yet. The eagles are nesting, and the loons are making feathery love, and huge arrowheads of geese skim the sky's blue skin, shooting farther north, their raucous honking bouncing off the treetops. And throughout the woods, from caves and brush and hollows, skinny and shaggy and snuffly, amble the bears, blinking from their primeval dreams, their empty stomachs growly, sniffing for buds, for grubs, for summer, for love.

DIANE: ANOTHER DOCUMENTARY?

> Animals come when their names are
> called. Just like human beings.
> —Ludwig Wittgenstein

I always thought those garter belts and heels looked silly, but when Lyle gave me that box and I felt the silk between my fingers, I couldn't wait to get out of that restaurant and back to the hotel and slip on those filmy unmentionables. Nor could I wait to make love under the eye of the video camera and watch us afterwards on the TV, as if we were stars on a very special program. And then to make love while watching us making love on the TV, as if our ecstasy were being doubled with every thrust and spasm. And then to video us making love as we watched ourselves making love, the watchers watched. And then to make love watching us making love as we're watching ourselves make love...

I don't know why Lyle erased the tape.

One afternoon I was knocking around the empty lodge feeling lonely and restless, not knowing what to do with my hands, and I put the tape in the VCR, but the tape was blank. I know it was the right tape because I had put a little "xxx #4" in red ink on a tiny stick-on thing, since I didn't want a big label on it, "Diane and Lyle Fuck Like Crazy in the Marriott." When I asked Lyle about it, he said he needed the tape for the bears. But he has plenty of blank tapes because I brought a whole bunch with me from the station when I resigned. I was really disturbed, because I'd been looking forward to limitless replays of those videos. I'd even thought of editing them into a "Best of" tape—for our eyes only, of course. It seemed like an invasion of trust, somehow, Lyle erasing our concupiscent shenanigans without asking my permission, some very special and unique moments lost to the whims of magnetic scattering. Who does he think would see the tapes besides him and me?

But what do you know, here comes the writer, driving up in his old rusty green 1972 Malibu. Why am I glad to see him? And why am I surprised that I'm glad to see him?

LYLE'S WIFE'S MOTHER MAKES A DECISION

Same old place, on the banks of
the South Saskatchewan River

Dear Lyle,

Mother's agreed that Marigold Manor is the place for her. I've
arranged to move her in as soon as a room opens up, which means
whenever somebody there dies, but that's life, isn't it? We die to
make room for the next generation of crazy people.

Mother's taking it in stride. What convinced me finally was her
wandering off Friday and getting lost a block away. I thought of a
radio collar, but those collars are big and heavy, and I'd have to roam
the neighborhood holding a big antenna.

Marigold Manor is run by the Ursulines. The Ursulines began
in sixteenth century Italy devoted to the education of girls, but here
in Saskatoon, when their school for girls closed because of low en-
rollment, like many enterprises these days they diversified and tran-
substantiated the school into a nursing home, the classrooms into
rooms with beds and televisions and the gym into an area for physical
therapy and weekly wheelchair square dancing. Mother abandoned
Catholicism when she married Dad, but I didn't tell the Admittance
Clerk that. When the clerk asked me what religion Mother was, I
said, "I think she's still searching." The clerk raised an eyebrow, as if
she thought we should all make up our minds by the time we're old,
but isn't that precisely when we should start questioning anew, after
we've seen what life can dish out but before we're too daft to think
things through? It may be too late for Mother to do the latter, but in
her own way she seems to be re-evaluating things, like where she is
and who I am and what's that funny smell. The Ursulines don't push

religion too much, merely the optional mass and the picture of Jesus on the wall, the one where he looks like a rock star.

Same Old Me, I Think

William Borden

POST-MODERN BEARS

 All criticism...is a volatile mixture
of Rube Goldberg and Piranesi.
—Harold Bloom

I'm going through the videotapes Lyle made of bears to see if there's any footage we can use for *Lyle's Bears Part Two*. Diane wants to call it *Rudy's Rude*, but that puts Rudy in a bad light. I suggested Wild About Rudy, but she wasn't wild about that. So we left the title up in the air while she flies off to Pequod, Maine, where Hot Skillet Press has its home office, to clear up some misunderstandings about recipe copyrights and the relevance of kitchen testing, then to New York and L.A. to pitch *Rudy Redux* (or whatever we wind up calling it).

Some of the tapes aren't labeled, so I'm never sure what I'm going to be watching. I start one tape which is a black-and-white French movie about a boy who was raised by wild animals and then was captured, and this doctor is trying to civilize the boy, teach him to speak and wear clothes and use a fork, but the wild boy isn't behaving very well. I'm beginning to wonder if the French doctor is doing this for science or his own ego when the tape jumps to color and a good-looking woman with lush red hair is holding a bear cub in her arms and feeding it from a bottle. Her face is the same as the one in the photo that had been on Lyle's desk the first night I was here but is now in a drawer in Lyle's bedroom, beneath his boxer shorts which are in various colors and patterns, some quite gay and fanciful.

I freeze the frame and look at her face, which has freckles under the eyes. I get the feeling she's not altogether comfortable in front of the camera. I suspect that she prefers privacy to disclosure, and that she's only doing this—appearing on camera, feeding the bear cub, putting up with Lyle–because Lyle's asked her to, and because she loves Lyle. Her eyes have a wary look to them, as if she's not sure of the permanence or reliability of this moment or of any moment, and she's not sure what the next moment might bring–it might be okay but then again it might not be. I think they're eyes that have been disappointed and wish they hadn't been.

When I unfreeze the frame, the bear cub wriggles like a furry fish to get out of her arms, so she bends over to set the little fellow on the floor–they're in the kitchen–I recognize the rag rug–and as she bends over, her tank top hangs loose and her breasts swing free. I rewind and slo-mo forward, to get the graceful movement of her breasts. Then the camera looks down at the feet of the cameraman as the cub tries to climb up the pants of the cameraman. The cub is standing on Lyle's shoes, and I think the cub is Rudy.

I rewind, and I notice that the woman is wearing a wedding ring, and that it's identical to the wedding ring Lyle used to wear. I zoom in on the freckles that splash provocatively down her breasts. I'm disappointed that the camera is more interested in the bear cub than in the woman's breasts, and I wonder if this little moment might not say a lot about why the woman isn't here anymore in Lyle's kitchen.

The French movie never comes back. I don't know if the wild boy winds up running for mayor or rips off his tie and heads back to the woods. The tape goes blank, a jumble of pixels and white noise. I notice its mesmerizing effect and wonder if it might be a meditative device, something to focus on to clear the mind, like *Om*, and could I sell an article to *Meditators' Monthly* and maybe *Video Buddhism*, when there's color again, and it's the yard behind Lyle's lodge, where we shot at candles it seems so long ago but it's been only a few months, not even a year, even though blood has been spilled, and on the tape Diane is sitting on the riding lawn mower, and she's cutting the spring grass, so this segment must have been shot recently. She's wearing a cap to keep the sun out of her eyes. All she's wearing is the cap.

I wonder if Lyle is experimenting with a post-modern thing here, intercutting the story of a boy raised in the wild and the attempt to civilize him with the story of a bear raised in the home and the attempt to make him wild, and if Diane riding the Lawn Boy naked like that is a dadaistic image using a Levi Strauss trope (I think of the book by Marx–Leo, not Karl: *The Machine in the Garden*)–a naked, or nearly naked, woman cutting grass, nature undoing nature, the machine tamed by nakedness, the nakedness a symbol of Innocence in the Garden of

Eden, and the cap an ironic commentary, an icon symbolizing work (and a gesture toward Marx—Karl, not Leo) but at the same time making the nudity more sexual by the incongruity of cap and nakedness. I zoom in on the cap, which is forest green, or maybe one would call it heather, with a logo on the front. The logo has a pine tree in the middle with a loon on one side of the pine tree and a bear on the other, confirming that the cap is an official Division of Forestry cap. The bill of the cap is rolled, giving it a masculine, worked-in, well-handled look. A humorous juxtaposition? A *Venus de Minnesota* wearing a macho cap? An *homage* to that greatest Marx of all, the true revolutionary, *Groucho?*

Wait a minute! What's wrong with me? She's not wearing nothing but the official Division of Forestry cap! She's wearing work boots, as well. Which makes sense, when one is manipulating dangerous machinery like that.

I wonder if I should congratulate Lyle on putting together this post-modern, avant-garde, Straussian neo-Marxist feature. Or did Diane put it together? Or was it, in true post-modernist fashion, only an accident, and I should not be seeing Diane's tanned thighs straddling the roaring engine, as the Lawn Boy, ejaculating shorn grass in a spume of emerald froth, rolls across the greensward, bouncing Diane's pert breasts?

I decide to keep the tape in my own collection for the time being. It'll be safe that way.

LYLE'S WIFE WATCHES BRYANT GUMBEL PET A BEAR

Saskatoon, named after the berry

Dear Lyle,

Imagine my surprise this morning when I saw you on TV handing Bryant Gumbel that stuffed bear. Is there really a "Lyle Bear" now? Will it be sold everywhere or only in select upscale outlets? The so-called Lyle Bear is cute, I have to admit, wearing that green cap like yours, but doesn't that contradict, Lyle, everything you've ever stood for? Bryant cuddled and petted the Lyle Bear and wasn't embarrassed to show affection for a dumb stuffed animal, whereas you looked awkward giving it to him, like maybe you aren't completely comfortable with all the hoopla that's surrounding you. Mother said she saw "that bear man" on TV, but she doesn't seem to remember that you and I are married. Well, you don't either, so far as that goes.

What did you think of Bryant's new hair-do, with the part on the side? I thought it looked strange at first, but I've gotten used to it. I notice, also, that Katie Couric is wearing more make-up than she used to. I liked her natural look better. Is change for the sake of change the order of the day?

I appreciate the regularity with which you send the checks. Is it love or guilt that prompts the movement of your pen? The exchange rate is in my favor, so I'm able to stretch the money more than I thought. I've thought about getting a job, but checking groceries doesn't seem like a self-actualizing use of my time, although I suppose an experienced Zen Buddhist could enter fully into each moment, and if I were really evolved I could find satori in a scanner.

So I'm reading Spinoza's *Ethics* instead. I liked geometry in high school, Euclid, the theorems and proofs and the inevitability of it all.

But the ruthlessness of logic depends on the suppositions one begins with, doesn't it. Axioms and postulates we take for granted. Take on faith. I've taken you on faith, Lyle. Does that mean I've taken you for granted? Or you, me? Non-Euclidean geometry proves that we can't take even poor old Euclid for granted. Axioms are arbitrary. We use them if they work. Do any axioms work for us anymore? Or are we adrift on Life's roiling sea, strangers, all of us, touching momentarily then floating on, trees uprooted like those ocean-soaked logs we saw that summer we spent on the Oregon coast when you were giving a seminar at the university on "Bears, Bees, Birds and Beetles: The Tao of Wildwife Management" (as it was misprinted—accidentally?—in the bulletin) and having an affair with that willowy ornithologist who stopped taking her lithium and wound up building a nest on the cliff where we were staying and you talked her into the ambulance by flapping your arms, pretending to be a condor. Those logs must have come all the way from Japan.

I saw a recipe in a magazine for Margaritas made with tequila and Grand Marnier and lime juice and sugar, and they're pretty damn good.

No longer shackled by the superstitions of religion or the promises of science, tossed about by the winds of human fickleness, dizzied by the vagaries of our body's chemicals and assaulted by the hounds of industrial pollution, carcinogens in our food and rips in the earth's protective gown of ozone—can we rely on anything? Should we? Or should we simply be happy, happy to be free, Nietzschean supergals and guys at last, dancing on the froth of the waves until gravity pulls us to our certain breathless destination?

Have you ever tried tequila, lime juice, honey, and Jack Daniels?

If there had been a Mrs. Fritz Nietzsche, wouldn't she have taken Fred down a peg or two? Could he have climbed beyond good and evil if he'd had to take into account Mrs. Freddy's PMS? Aren't these philosophies, abstract and abstruse, merely the consequence of those fellows not finding a good woman to keep them down to earth? Was any important philosopher married? Plato? No. Hobbes? No. Descartes? Spinoza? Kant? Locke? Leibniz? Hume? No. No. No. No. No. No. Schopenhauer? Kierkegaard? Santayana? Sartre? Wittgenstein? Nos again. What does that tell us about philosophy? About marriage?

Why haven't there been any great women philosophers?

Because we know better.

Or tequila, lime juice, brown sugar, vodka, Cognac, and Saska-toonberry juice? It shows Platonic Ideas to be mere Shadows of the Realities of our Transitory Urges.

THE CHARGE

He has lived well who has lived secretly.
—Ovid

Lyle's left me in charge, although what I'm in charge of is uncertain, since he's still on indefinite suspension, yet the Division of Forestry hasn't replaced him, because the state legislature cut their funds and the federal government eliminated their grants for wildlife research, so there's no one to do even the ordinary things he did, like issue fire permits and identify poisonous mushrooms for random hikers.

The Division of Forestry wants Lyle to move out of the lodge. They say it belongs to them, never mind that Lyle has increased the value of the property tenfold. Fortunately the judge who goes ice fishing with Lyle was quick to issue the restraining order, so he's safe until the fall, it looks like.

Diane, too, has left me in charge, while they continue their whirlwind tour of Lyle's cooking demonstrations, cookbook signings, and Diane's power lunches to round up financing for her latest idea, a sitcom called *The Bare Facts*, about a nudist bear researcher in the north woods, his bear, and his girl friend, who is an outwardly prudish but repressedly libidinous forest ranger. It didn't take me long to write the pilot, but my heart wasn't in it, because I think sitcoms are a meretricious insult to the intelligence of any minimally sophisticated viewer, an egregious falsification of reality, and a soporific opiate that trivializes honest tragedy and oversimplifies the truly complex, paradoxical, and ironic in human affairs. (I'll never understand why I couldn't get an agent for my pilot, *Chief Detective Zen Master Zaki*, set in San Francisco, in which Zaki, a combination of Peter Falk and D. T. Suzuki, catches criminals using a meld of mysterious mental powers and aikido.)

The basic idea for the sitcom was Diane's. She and I were standing behind the cameras while Lyle was shooting the pilot for his cooking show. We were shooting in a Minneapolis suburb, at the studios of the singer who is now a symbol—like a character in a classic novel, Raskolnikov or Madame Bovary—and Diane mused aloud, "We could produce a sitcom," and I suggested that the bear researcher be a nudist, and she liked the idea. Later that night, back in my hotel room, I whipped out a pilot. Diane says Bochco's people are interested but want total creative control, which we're refusing absolutely.

I don't mind the solitude here alone in Lyle's house. I don't mind being in charge, either, even if my charge is ambiguous. After all, isn't that life? We feel as if we've been left in charge—of something, no one's told us what—and we're trying to figure out what our responsibilities and benefices are? On the other hand, there are plenty of people—parents, spouses, clergy, state highway patrolmen, and editors—telling us we're not in charge of any damn thing after all.

The mail carrier advised me, *sotto voce*, the other day when he delivered the mail, to keep the envelopes from Saskatchewan separate for Lyle. The mail carrier—Bud Ostrum is his name—said he'd heard I was out here "holding down the fort." Bud winked as he furtively handed me the letters. Bud's in his fifties and bald and wears wide red suspenders with flying ducks on them. He says he's going to retire soon and open a taxidermy business. He says there's lots of potential there, even if Fran Makosky currently has a full nelson on the business. He's heard that some of her customers get impatient at how long it takes her to get their animals and fish stuffed or freeze dried, she's so busy in her back room—at which Bud gives me a wink and a nudge.

He's been taking a taxidermy correspondence course, but it's hard to learn the fine points, he says, because the porcupine he's been working on, salvaged from a road kill, isn't turning out as lifelike as he would like. Or maybe he'll go into cabinet making. Or, he muses, with a far-away glaze in his eyes, photography, a hobby he used to pursue with considerable enthusiasm until, he adds darkly, he encountered completely unjustified hostility from the community and Sheriff Irv Nyquist—don't I agree that the naked female form big with child is the most beautiful shape the Good Lord ever put on this Green Earth? I ask Bud if I can postpone a definitive judgment on that point. Bud gives me a long careful look, then says he'll drop by some photos for my appraisal.

William Borden

Now a lady has called, hysterical, because a bear has climbed into her van and won't get out, a bear with a radio color and a green kerchief around his neck, so it's Rudy, and I have to go drive her van back here, and then he'll get out, and I'll give him the left-over shrimp in tomatoes and garlic and feta and capers and retsina on basmati rice I had last night, a little experiment of my own, Lyle's not the only gourmet chef in the world, and then I'll drive the van back to the lady. I'll wear Lyle's Division of Forestry cap, so the lady will think I'm in charge.

LYLE'S WIFE, FASHION CONSULTANT

Saskatoon, from misaskwatomin,
Cree for the delicious dark
red berries that grow here

Dear Lyle,

I'm watching the videotape that Lois, my friend in Bemidji, sent me because she gets the new cooking channel, and, Lyle, why are you wearing *overalls?* You *hate* overalls. And that silly Smoky the Bear hat? Who is your fashion consultant?

I had a funny feeling watching Lyle's Bears that the woman with the long blonde hair chewing her venison with sharp white teeth and drinking her wine with abandon was looking at you in a more than professional manner. It's odd that you've told me about the cameraman who went berserk and the writer who keeps prying into things, but you never mention the woman.

Mother's settled at Marigold Manor and doesn't cry and doesn't call me a bad daughter every time I visit. I don't know if she's really accepted her residence there or if it's the anti-depressants. It's all chemicals anyway, isn't it, what goes on in our brains, and even if her euphoria is chemically induced, surely it's better for Mother not to cry and better for her not to blame me. Could I give you a chemical, Lyle, that would make things the way they used to be?

But what is "the way they used to be"? Was there a moment when everything was perfect? There were many such moments. The trouble is, they didn't last. How could they? Life goes on. Your blood sugar goes down, bills come in, the car needs repair, the dentist finds a cavity—nothing stays the same, not even love.

Because you seem different in that video. Oh, the cerulean eyes are the same and the beard (who trimmed it so nicely? some expensive

New York City *coiffeur?*) and your hands as you pour shitake mushrooms (you thought a shitake was an oriental religion before you met me) into a frying pan—I'm rewinding, not because I want the recipe, who gives a shit about creamed chestnut, winter squash, and shitake soup, I just noticed that you weren't wearing your wedding ring. Our wedding ring, which I'm still wearing.

So far.

LYLE'S WIFE, FASHION CONSULTANT, PART TWO

Saskatoon, Home of the
Homespun Craft Emporium and
Dr. Doolittle's Fun Farm

Dear Lyle,

You were asked to remove your wedding ring because it reflected the light?

And because you didn't want to get food on it?

My goodness, Lyle, the pressures and arcane demands of the modern entertainment industry! We folks out in television land have no idea, do we, of the sacrifices famous people must make.

Well, at least in your second show you traded in the Smoky hat for a bare-headed look (whose idea was the pony tail? Isn't that a little *too* trendy?) and exchanged the overalls (which did suggest Mr. Greenjeans of Captain Kangaroo fame) for a plaid flannel shirt and paisley tie. (Are you *trying* to look ridiculous? I know, you'll say both the shirt and the tie have red and blue and green in them and so they go together, but there's more to an ensemble than the colors in a small Crayola box.) But you didn't need a *focus group* to tell you the Smoky hat and the overalls were all wrong, all you had to do was ask me, but of course what do I know about *television*? I'm just

Your so-called wife

P.S. I wonder, Lyle, homeostatic organisms that we are, if we ever adjusted to each other? Or is adjustment the betrayal of some inner beingness that we would realize if we didn't have to adjust ourselves to live with somebody?

William Borden

But we have to live with people, don't we?

Are we fated, then, to compromise our essential being? To grow truncated and warped, like a sapling shaded by tall pines and wrapped by vines, seeking sunlight but winding up gnarled and stunted? Do we, as Jung thought, have a Self that is constantly seeking to realize its *telos* (as Aristotle would put it)? Or, as the Buddhists propose, is the self an illusion, and the real thing is to live in the moment and be compassionate? Or, on the third hand, are we mere machines, as Skinner thought?

Whatever.

LYLE'S WIFE HELPS A TROUBLED TEENAGER

Still here

Lyle,

I don't know why after all these years you bring up Lionel Running Bear and the fact that he was only eighteen while I was, well, the mother of pubescent and prepubescent children, and it did not go on for months. Well, not that many months.

Besides, I think I can say it was I who turned Lionel's life around. He quit drinking and he quit smoking marijuana and he quit stealing (although I suppose the time in the pen helped there), and now he's a spiritual leader who conducts sweat lodge ceremonies and is entrusted with a sacred pipe, and he has a full-time job with the county as a road maintenance worker, and he's married and has four children and gives talks about sobriety. So I think that in my own way I helped him on his way back to the straight and narrow, the Red Road, as he would say, helped him recover some self-esteem and pride in his heritage. Is that so bad?

Mother wandered away yesterday. They found her coming out of the adult movie theater. She said she was waiting for the Gene Kelly movie to come on, the one where he dances in the puddles. I asked her what she thought she was watching. She said she supposed it was some sort of sex education movie but it went on for a long time. Then she smiled this funny smile, like she knew what kind of movie it was but she was going to pretend she didn't because that's what we expected of an old crazy woman like her. For a second there she seemed fully cognizant.

I wonder if we go crazy so we can do the things our culturally and parentally imposed inhibitions won't let us do. What do you think?

You never seemed to have that much trouble with inhibitions, did you?

What if we lived like animals, without inhibitions? That's the difference between civilization and the wild, isn't it? The urbanity of wars versus the savagery of rooting around for grubs and fucking when you feel like it.

I remember when Rudy kept smelling my crotch until I smacked him on the nose a few times. I inhibited him.

Maybe everybody needs a little smack now and then.

You know whom

LYLE'S WIFE TENDS HER GARDEN

Dear, Etc.

Lionel? Oh, well, Lionel.

Remember? He was cutting the grass and helping remodel the lodge and make something of the root cellar. He showed me how to put in the wiring because he had learned some electrical skills from his father who helped build houses on the reservation. He and I would be down there putting up paneling and wiring the lights and constructing wine racks. The kids were off at various camps—Bernadette riding horses and learning from her tent-mate how to masturbate, Bjorn becoming an Eagle Scout and learning to smoke, and Babette at the language camp learning swear words in Finnish and other languages.

Lionel seemed older than he was. I thought he was 24. Twenty-two, at least. He was watering the garden. He was holding the hose, spraying the water back and forth. I was weeding a few feet away. He asked if I was hot. I said I was. I forgot for a moment his sense of humor. All of a sudden that cold spray hit me. I screamed, the way women do when they're caught unawares.

It was feeling good, cold water spraying all over me.

I could see my breasts and nipples through the wet cotton. I grabbed the hose out of his hand, the tomato vines nipping at my dripping legs. I wet him down good, so his jeans clung to his legs. "You're all wet," I said.

"So are you," he said.

I have to admit, I had been thinking about Lionel—his shy grin, his muscular shoulders, his soulful eyes, irises like rich coffee. I would watch him out the window guiding the power mower, his smooth skin shiny from sweat. For lunch I made the sandwiches he liked, fried egg on white bread with mayonnaise and a thick slice of onion, and glasses of cold milk, the glasses sweating, like us.

It was a dry summer, and the bears weren't finding their usual food, so they were rummaging through people's garbage. You were off trapping them—the bears, not the people, although you always said you ought to be trapping the people in those big boxes with the sliding doors, baiting them with Big Macs, and removing the people instead of the bears—so as I looked at Lionel, wet and dripping and his black hair plastered down, I said, "You're wet," again, and he said, "So are you," again, and we knew we really wanted to say something else, but maybe the metamorphosis of a feeling into words is impossible, like expecting a bear to question the efficacy of the categorical imperative.

My heart was beating fast. I said, "I guess you better take your clothes off." He said, "You better take yours off, too." We said it like it was a joke, only we weren't joking. I was trying to figure out how I could get back to the joking, but Lionel, bless his heart, lifted my tee shirt up over my head, and I let him peel it off.

He seemed to suck on my breasts with his eyes, even though my breasts were kind of droopy—three kids pulling on them, and gravity, but they still had, and still have, if I do say so, a resilience, and a fullness—and it seemed the only way to make him stop staring at my naked breasts was to unsnap his jeans.

Quite legitimately he retaliated by unsnapping my shorts. There was nothing for me to do then but unzip his zipper. It was like peeling an orange, pulling his wet jeans down his bronze thighs. My shorts, on the other hand, cascaded down my legs, his fingertips brushing my skin like butterflies all the way to my ankles.

He fell on his knees. Maybe he lost his balance because his jeans were wadded around his work boots, but he had never had trouble keeping his balance before, so I prefer to think it was to worship, as his hands tenderly tugged my panties to my feet, his calluses like mice nibbling my legs, hungry for something neither of us could name.

Afterwards, we hosed the mud off each other, and I told you that a bear had rolled in the garden, that was why the tomato plants and other things were smashed. I felt guilty, yes, but I felt happy, too, and I was surprised at how I could feel both things at once, and I felt young again.

I felt like a girl all summer, until Lionel got caught breaking into that liquor store that night, led astray by those two other boys. Even though Lionel was only sitting in the car, the police said he was as guilty as they were.

Lionel is the only man I've made love with, besides you, since that hot day in the woods tracking Mrs. 24.

So far.

Your devoted, and so forth

LYLE'S WIFE WRITES TO SET THE RECORD STRAIGHT

Home of the Saskatoonberry pie, mm-mmm!

Mr. Lyle,

Now that you've brought up Lionel Running Bear, I realize I might have made my relationship with him seem nothing more than a sweat-soaked grappling in mud and radishes. Of course when you and I were married—will you look at that little slip! We *are* still married—aren't we?—when we were *together*, then, I didn't want to go into my thing with Lionel, partly because I was, I admit, a little embarrassed (but not ashamed).

The next day, Lionel and I were in the root cellar to get cool—although by then it was the wine cellar, even if the three hundred or so cavities were still empty, their hungry maws waiting to be filled with vintages and varietals from the many vineyards of the world—and we were pretending there was still some carpentry work to finish down there, but we never discovered what it was. Later, as we lay in the darkness, redolent of freshly sawed wood and unrepressed desire, I understood that Lionel was not a contingent lunge in the mud, not the one-time aberration of a bored housewife, but a serious fling, a daily hunger, a memorable experience of a lifetime. Not the only memorable experience of my life, I hope, but true and meaningful nonetheless.

Now, however, from this distance, geographically, chronologically, and, let's face it, emotionally, I believe it's appropriate for me to explain myself further, even though you haven't asked for further explanations, and probably you don't want further—well, not "explanations," really, but rather a "sharing," as they say in this group I'm going to, a support group for people who are going through changes in their lives.

I went to it because I was feeling overwhelmed by Mother. I went not expecting to like it because I've always been pretty private, especially when it comes to blabbing my guts to strangers. I know, compared to you, I'm Oprah Winfrey or the *National Inquirer*, or so you think, but, really, I don't talk much about myself, not the personal things. But in this group—the leader, an older woman psychologist, wide in the hips, empathic and accepting—everybody was talking about the problems they were having with their husbands or boy friends—there was one guy there, but he was having problems with *his* boy friend, so we were all in the same boat—I forgot about the problems I was having with Mother, and I started talking about you. I hope you don't mind.

Even if you do mind, Lyle, too bad. You don't know these people and never will, and, really, I don't just bad-mouth you. In fact, some of the ladies wonder why I'd ever leave such an interesting and charismatic man as you. One woman even wanted to come live with you, you sounded so exciting. She said she wouldn't care if you had other women because that was part of your charm. I thought she was getting carried away, and she seems a little unstable, like when she told us she liked to pee in public, which made me wonder if that meant she was going to do it right there on the carpet, but she didn't. She was going on so about how fascinating you sounded that I got, I admit, a teeny bit mad, and I told her to go ahead and live with you if she thought you were so damn fascinating, and I gave her our address. But she was back in group the next week and didn't say anything more about it. Her name is Pepper. In case she does show up. Short for Peppermint. Volkensky.

Me

ANOTHER CHARGE

In a war among the races, I would side with the bears.
—John Muir

The Division of Forestry, plagued by bothersome bear complaints and with most of their staff searching for the lost Amazon Scouts, a group of women over forty who learn to survive in the wilderness but haven't been heard from for days, is suddenly worried about their image in the public perception, and they have miraculously found some discretionary funds with which to hire a part-time, temporary Bear Control Officer who will be in charge of removing, one way or another, "nuisance bears" (as they're called) in the area. So now I have my own, really official, D of F cap, the bill of which I'm bending and scuffing so it won't look new, so I won't look new, so I'll look as if I know what I'm doing. I'm entitled to wear the other official headgear, a hat sometimes referred to as a "Smoky" hat, which makes me look like a fire prevention animal, but I don't wear it when Lyle or Diane are around, because they laugh at me, so I wear it only when I'm off on my own. I don't think it fits properly, is what I think is the problem.

Diane and Lyle are looking for the lost Amazons. She thinks it would be prime publicity for Lyle if he found the Amazons, especially since one of the Amazons is the wife of a U.S. Senator. Although the Senator and the Senator's wife have been separated since he was seen with a *Playboy* centerfold (whom he says is only a friend of his daughter), the Senator (but not the centerfold) has joined the search as well. Diane and Lyle are blazing their own trail, so to speak, not participating in the organized search ("Why be lost in the crowd?" she asks) but hiring their own helicopter and engaging the services of Sandra Flies Far, the sister of Frank Running Bear, who came by the other day with a few jugs of maple syrup. Sandra Flies Far has a reputation for psychically finding lost things.

Sandra Flies Far is about seventy years of age, a plump soft woman with raven hair streaked with gray, a sly smile, and a faraway look in the eye that looks to the side, while the other eye looks straight at you. They say that look-away eye is the eye she uses to find lost things—Frank's keys to his van, which he's always losing; Beatrice Snowbird's ninety-year-old father, when he wandered away a few summers ago and was picked up for indecent exposure in a case of mistaken identity; Placid Hardhead's great-grandfather's right arm, amputated after the massacre at Wounded Knee in 1889, frozen and wrapped in a sacred deerskin and hidden under rocks (the ground too frozen to bury it) but discovered by an archeologist and eventually displayed at the Museum of Natural History in New York City, leading Placid to initiate a years-long lawsuit to recover the arm and give it proper burial, the Museum finally acquiescing after Placid and other tribal members drummed and sang before the exhibited arm, interrupting Museum tours and arousing public support for the rightful return of the arm; a rare bottle of Medoc Lyle was searching for, which Sandra located by running her finger down a list of wine merchants and stopping at a small distributor in Lyons, France; assorted knickknacks, mementoes, money, and runaway children on the reservation and its environs; and, many years ago, the body of her husband, Casper "Baby" Flies Far, who was killed by unknown persons during the occupation of Wounded Knee in 1973, when Caspar was a member of AIM.

Back here at home base, when a call comes in, I grab my hat, or cap, depending on my mood, and call Bud Ostrum, whom I've hired as my assistant, and he comes over as soon as he's through delivering the mail. We hitch the big live box to the pickup and drive to wherever the nuisance bear is a nuisance—usually somebody's garbage can or a camper's fresh fish. I put some porridge and honey in the box, and then we come back the next day and pick up the box and the bear and cart them away. I put a few capsules of Valium in the porridge, so the bear's pretty relaxed and lets me put the radio collar on him, and I do the Lyle things, like measure his teeth with the calipers and stick a thermometer up his ass and make a lot of notes and videotape the bear. Bud's still scared of the bears, but I'm getting to be an old hand, recognizing when a *Whoof* means *bluff* and a *Whaaf* means *business*. I Whoof back, and that usually puts the bear in his place. If he *Whaafs*, then I give him some room, the way you would a cranky drunk in a bar.

If the bear already has a collar, I look him, or her, up in Lyle's book and call her by name and chat with her awhile, try to be Lyle, in other words. Later I plot the site of capture, and site of release, on the big map Lyle keeps on which he traces the bears' romances and peregrinations.

Occasionally I capture a bear with a medical problem. Abercrombie, for instance, a large cinnamon boar with old scars on his head, had a festering wound in one paw, so I trucked him over to Joe Manello, the large-animal vet. Joe put Abercrombie under with an experimental psychotropic drug, cleaned the wound, smeared salve on it, and pumped Abercrombie full of antibiotics and vitamins.

I agreed to keep a special notebook on Ab, to see if the psychotropic had a lasting effect. What should I look for? I asked Joe. Joe, a good-looking former wrestler and Harley Davidson enthusiast, assured me that the drug would not change Abercrombie; it would only release in Abercrombie his unfulfilled potential. I wondered if that was necessarily a good thing. "Isn't that what we all long for," Joe asked, amazed at my obtuseness, "the full and unrestrained flowering of our true selves, so often pruned by society's prudery and stunted by the misguided shadows of parental projections? Who are we," he asked, his bellowing voice rising, "if we're not ourselves?"

"On second thought," Joe said, eyeing the snoring Abercrombie, whose paws were twitching in dreamy pursuit of something and whose male member was extending, the drug apparently eliciting an erotic fancy, "I'll keep an eye on him here for a few days, then release him."

I said okay and drove off to collect the bear that was alarming the guests at Emma's We Won't Tell Travel Lodge, a string of rustic cabins shaded by pines and oaks out of sight of the highway where, according to the guest register, all the couples who have ever stayed there are named Mr. and Mrs. John Smith.

It was Towley clawing the screen off the back door of cabin five, aroused by the menstrual odors from the lady within, her companion having fled by himself in his car, leaving the poor woman alone, with only her screams to alert Emma that something was amiss. Towley can be pretty edgy under any circumstance, never mind his present agitation, so, reluctant to approach him with my usual aplomb, I opted instead to haul out the tranquilizer rifle and let him have a dart of sedative. He stumbled around for a bit and seemed to lose his bearings. That gave me a chance to get into the cabin by the front door. The woman was still screaming and weeping and unaware, apparently, of her nakedness, so I gave her a shot of tranquilizer, too, and only then, when she had calmed down and I got her dressed, did I realize that she was Eunice Nyquist, Sheriff Irv Nyquist's wife. I drove her to Mel's Supermarket in town, where she had left her car.

The bears are making nuisances of themselves this summer because we had a lot of rain and then it was dry and the berries didn't do well, so the bears don't have their usual food sources.

AMAZONS

> Diana was not merely a patroness of wild beasts...
> she...heard the prayers of women in travail.
> —Sir James Frazier, *The Golden Bough*

Lyle and Diane found the Amazon Scouts. Sandra Flies Far took them straight to the temporary lean-to where the women were gathered around the Senator's wife, who had broken her leg. She had taken a nasty fall out of a tree she had been climbing, hoping to recapture her youth as a tomboy. The women were practicing psychic healing, in which one of the women was proficient. Another woman, an MD, had set the leg, but she was a dermatologist, not expert in orthopedics. The dermatologist didn't believe in psychic healing, so she didn't participate in the group meditation, although, in spite of the fact that the leg was the group's focus, the dermatologist's adult acne cleared up for the first time in years.

I say Sandra Flies Far took them straight to the camp, but that's not quite accurate. They flew first to Canada, to the reserve where Sandra's son and his wife and their children live, to go to a powwow there. This seemed like a good opportunity, with the helicopter already rented and all. Sandra assured Lyle and Diane that the women were all right and that another day wouldn't make any difference, because the official searchers were looking in the wrong quadrant. The Amazon Scouts had changed their plans as part of their wilderness survival practice.

The pilot, Winona Running Bear (Sandra's niece), whose husband, Lionel Running Bear, works for the highway department, failed to file a flight plan, because Winona doesn't recognize national boundaries. It was a good powwow, Sandra seeing old friends and relatives and dancing in the Ladies Traditional Shawl Dance and even winning a prize; and she found several lost items for people there, including one woman's husband, who was lost in the eighteen-year-old Powwow Princess's bedroom. After the powwow, loaded up with fry bread and venison jerky, they took off, just as the RCMP drove up, and headed for the missing Amazons. A couple of Sandra's grandchildren went along because they had never been in a helicopter, or in the States, for that matter.

Winona Running Bear, a slight, handsome woman with a shag haircut and wire-frame glasses, earrings of porcupine quills, and a space where her right upper bicuspid once was (lost in a bar fight with a biker who grabbed her where she didn't want to be grabbed, the biker afterwards giving up the hearty reunions in Sturgis as a result of the testicular injury sustained in the brawl), guided the helicopter expertly across the treetops and over the lakes, swooping and swerving and giving Lyle's stomach, and the pickerel, fry bread, and venison sausage therein, a bit of an osterizing. Winona said she flew with the guidance not of the flight manual but of the rough-legged hawk, her spirit guide in the realm of the air.

Sandra Flies Far went into a trance and guided Winona by saying "Go right" and "Go left a little," but after awhile Sandra grew impatient with that second-hand navigation. She took over the controls and flew the helicopter with her eyes closed. Diane and Lyle were sitting in the back, with the grandkids. Diane didn't notice that Sandra had her eyes closed. Lyle did, but he didn't say anything.

Finally Sandra Flies Far opened her eyes, each eye peering in a different direction as usual. Winona Running Bear opened her eyes, too. She'd been catching a little shut-eye since she had been up all night at the powwow visiting with relatives. Sandra said, "Down there," and aimed them toward the trees, rather precipitously, Lyle says. Fortunately Winona grabbed the controls. They leveled off and made a more gentle descent. Sandra said it was the Amazons' psychic healing that drew her to them. "It was like a searchlight on a Hollywood opening night, scanning the sky, but pulsing. It was women's energy."

The Amazon women wouldn't let Lyle get out of the helicopter. They had made the area a sacred womanspace, or womynspace, as they spelled it, and they didn't want him to undo their careful work. So they brought the Senator's wife, Judy Jump-Larson, to the helicopter on the litter they'd made of hewed saplings, woven grasses, and vines.

There wasn't room in the helicopter for everyone, so Diane and

Sandra and Sandra's eight-year-old granddaughter stayed with the remaining Amazons. Winona radioed search headquarters with the position of the camp—Lyle gave her a hand with the map reading, which she hadn't covered yet in her helicopter pilot's course, even though it's supposed to be one of the first things a neophyte pilot masters, but the flight school, run by Bud Ostrum's brother, Skip Ostrum, a former crop duster in North Dakota, is not, apparently, actually a licensed flight school. Winona, Lyle, Sandra's ten-year-old grandson, Willy, and Judy Jump-Larson then departed, Sandra having taken all of the fry bread and venison jerky to share with the women, who had been subsisting on wild plants, native tubers, berries, small animals they had caught with snares, and grubs.

It took the official rescuers two days to find Diane, Sandra, Sandra's granddaughter, and the Amazons. Lyle, it turned out, had misread some numbers on the map because he'd accidentally left his reading glasses at the powwow. At least, that's what he thought had happened. Actually, Sandra's granddaughter, Nokomis Flies Far, had borrowed them, and they were under the seat in the helicopter all the time.

The rescuers were grounded the first day anyway. A storm churned up above the reserve—a result of the powwow, Sandra and Winona said, all the singing and drumming and dancing, it always happens—and the tempest whipped south, lightning licking the lakes, thunder rocking the forest, and wanton winds bending the tall trees into huge bows.

DIANE: WILD WOMYN

> Our attitudes towards animals...reveal
> our attitudes towards ourselves.
> —Joyce E. Salisbury, *The Beast Within:*
> *Animals in the Middle Ages*

It's a massive collapse of the heavens. We're soaked before we can move. Sixteen of us, counting little Nokomis, dripping and laughing, squeeze into the lean-to. The bodies are slippery and solid. The voices are loud and musical. The Amazons haven't bathed for days, so the bouquet is vigorous and heady. A feral electricity zaps from woman to woman.

I had expected to find confusion and panic. Instead I am bathed in riotous cheer and lavish camaraderie. Strangers hug and kiss me as if we were long-lost friends, separated for years, and now restored to some royal privilege hidden from us all this time. I try to withdraw into my usual private psychic space, but all I do is smile a silly smile. I surrender to the hot wet skin rubbing against my flesh. I embrace the pulsing muscles, something more than innocent, that crowd my body. A reckless voluptuousness singes the air.

It's a good thing Lyle didn't get out of the helicopter. He would've been scared. These women look like sun-burnished Medusas, their hair matted and flying in all directions, their eyes wild, their exuberance frank and ferocious. Their shirts and jeans are dirty and ripped, their hands scratched and callused, their strides long and sure. Some are barefoot, and their feet plant themselves on the muddy earth like tree roots. Some took off their shirts as soon as the helicopter rose over the tree tops, and their breasts hang and sway with startling insouciance. Hair grows unabashedly from their armpits and legs.

The leaders of the group are Mattie and Leona, two husky, brusque women in their early fifties with crew cuts and many earrings. Mattie has tattoos in unexpected places—a delicate rose on her right breast, below the large brown areola, and a snake that emerges from her navel, circles, then slithers down her stomach until its head disappears into her vulva. I say it must have hurt, but Mattie says, No, that was back in the good old days when she dropped a lot of acid. Leona has scars on her arms where she cut herself in her younger days, when she was married and Catholic and having children and going crazy.

Mattie and Leona are known on this expedition as Squirrel and Skunk. When the group set out, one of the rituals was the taking on of a name from nature. It could be an animal name or a plant name or something else that occurs in nature. I've been introduced to Sunburst (a grandmother and retired kindergarten teacher), Wolf (a thin, shy woman, recently divorced and living on welfare and here on a scholarship because, as nearly as I can make out, she and Skunk are lovers), Poison Ivy (a computer programmer for an actuarial firm), Lightning (a housewife who says she's happily married but looking for adventure), Blackberry (a psychic healer and part-time accountant), Rabbit (a karate instructor, bartender, and snow plow operator), Rock (an actress and hospice worker, living on alimony), Poinsettia (a writer of children's books), Porcupine (a dermatologist), Brook (a former policewoman, fired, suing, now a private investigator), and Loon, who prefers to say nothing about her life before this pilgrimage into the wilderness.

We rescuers are invited to take names, too. Little Nokomis says her name is Mosquito. Sandra says she already has an animal name, it was given to her on a vision quest by the Great Spirit, but it's a secret name. So we call her Secret, because Nature has many secrets, and she says that's just right. Then everybody looks at me.

Suddenly I'm feeling as if I've been air-dropped into a foreign country where everybody knows the language but me. On the other hand, I feel incredibly welcomed, even though they know nothing about me. Loon (whom I discover later is the CEO of a large foundation and gives away millions of dollars a year) eyes me carefully and says, "Dance."

"Dance?"

"Your nature spirit will move your body. Then you'll know."

My body decides for me. I step out of the lean-to into the rain. The women clap a beat. I stand for a moment motionless. I let myself feel the rain on my skin. I forget who I am. My arms extend. My knees rise. My head bobs forward and back. I flap my arms and set my feet in the mud. My voice croaks. My arms swoop in long graceful strokes. My neck stretches. My legs feel long and thin, my skin feathery, my head beakish, my being airy and watery, my spirit searching and flighty. I am Heron.

The women join me, making animal noises, and even plant noises, what they imagine plant noises to be, Poison Ivy clucking and Poinsettia lullabying and Blackberry whistling. We're all moving like our animal or bird, or standing and swaying like our plant, in the pouring rain, with lightning flashing and thunder cracking and wind gusting. I think, These women have been in the woods too long. They've gone bonkers. But I'm doing it too. Maybe it's an escape from the pressure of flying around the country trying to make Lyle famous. Maybe I've given too much of myself to Lyle. Whatever is happening, it feels good. I close my eyes. I fly. When I open my eyes, clothes are flying.

The bodies are bronze and pink and chocolate. They're bony and muscular and fat. They're jumping and hopping and leaping. They're bouncing and jiggling and wobbling. They're all over the place. I'm the only one not naked.

Now I'm naked.

We're dancing in the rain, chorusing to the rain and thunder. Mosquito is buzzing about, pretending to bite people. Rock hunches in the center. Brook wriggles her lithe body and long legs across the ground. Poinsettia weaves back and forth, her wet auburn hair plastered over her face. Skunk makes everybody laugh, sticking her rear out at people.

Now Skunk changes before our eyes. Her body stretches, her arms extend, her eyes blaze. She roars. Someone cries, "Cougar!" She leaps into the woods. Wolf pounces after her.

Three days ago they began their periods, all of them but the older women. Dark splashes stain their thighs. They scoop blood from between their thighs. They paint their stomachs, breasts, and faces, a proud, crimson embellishment to their naked splendor.

And now Secret, on all fours, lumbers up to me, swinging her head from side to side. She stands. She puts her paws on my shoulders. She says, *Whoof!* She licks my face.

Later, when we're all exhausted and hoarse and standing quietly in the rain catching our breath, our ankles sunk in mud, I ask Secret/Sandra, *What hit me? I've never let loose like that.*

You were with friends, she says. *You knew you were safe. You were wound tighter than a spring on a ten-year clock.* She whispers in my ear, her breath tickling my ear, *The heron came to you. You must thank her.*

How? I ask.

Say it in your mind, she says. *The spirits hear what we say in our minds.*

I thank the heron spirit in my mind. I don't stop to think how silly it is.

From now on, Secret/Sandra says, *you can call on the heron spirit to help you out or give you advice. You remember,* she says. *It'll come in handy.*

Something crashes through the brush. Cougar and Wolf run out of the woods, baying and screeching. They're clutching an animal between them. Some of the screeching is the animal. They're tearing it apart with their hands. Other women grab the animal. They tear flesh with their teeth. Blood splashes their breasts.

Not everyone. Not Squirrel, or Poinsettia, or Secret. Not me.

Later, Secret finds dry branches. Poinsettia builds a fire. Squirrel skins what's left of the fawn, and we roast it and eat it.

The fawn is smoky from the fire. The meat is dark and pungent. Everyone moves slowly, as if in a dream. Women slip away into the dark night. They wash themselves in a stream. Mosquito wears the fawn's head on her head, the skin hanging down her back, swinging against her bare buttocks as she runs about. She says her name is Fawn now. The rain stops. The stars climb out of the sky, diamonds hurled from the void.

The women spread their sleeping bags. We lie down, hip to hip, shoulder to shoulder, skin to skin. I lie next to Secret, and Fawn squeezes between us. I think it's Poinsettia on my other side. I can't tell in the dark. It doesn't matter.

LYLE: ROUGHING IT

> The school of life is unplanned and chaotic...
> —Albert Einstein

Judy Jump-Larson cries all the way, until we run out of gas and have to emergency land at the old Makwah Resort, abandoned now for several years since the other resorts, closer to roads and electricity and telephones, went high-tech and old Claes Ostrum died and his boys didn't have the money or the ambition to fix the place up. Winona sets us down on the old dock—quite deftly, I must say—there wasn't any open space with all the trees—and I ease Judy out, her arms around my neck. Judy's crying because she's sorry to leave her sisters. They forged a bond, she says, that will never be broken. But she couldn't take it any longer, eating worms and roots, try as she might.

She says she made a few decisions in the wilderness. She says she's going to run for her husband's Senate seat next year. She says she tells him how to vote on everything anyway, why shouldn't she get the credit; and Loon, whoever she is, promised to raise millions for her run for the office. She'll run as an Independent, she says, because both parties are hopeless, and their members vain, duplicitous, and dumb.

We're bunked in the old lodge, out of the rain. I've swept out the mice nests and spiders and the droppings of sundry animals. I found some dry wood, scraps of newspaper, and a box of matches, and made a fire in the fireplace, after clearing the wood duck nest out of the chimney.

Willy, Sandra's grandson and Winona's nephew, is whining that he's hungry, so I send him outside to look for wild game, let him run off some of his pent-up energy. He's a good kid, even if he is a bit jumpy, with a snub nose, scraggly hair, and large brown eyes that look at everything with a disarming clarity. He comes back a few minutes later, more hyperactive than ever, saying he saw ten bears, two moose, a tiger, and a tyrannosaurus rex. I tell him he'll be a writer some day, or an animal researcher. I send him back out to scavenge the eight run-down cabins and bring back whatever looks useful.

Winona's feeling a little responsible for our layover here, not filling up before we left the reserve, but I remind her that the Mounties were on our heels, she didn't have much choice. It wouldn't be so bad, she says, if the radio hadn't gone on the blink.

What? asks Judy, whom we thought was asleep.

I tell Judy I'll take a look at the radio in the morning, when there's more light. It's probably just a loose connection, I say.

Are you an electrician? she asks.

I say I've had some experience with radio collar transmitters.

Willy comes back with some fishing line, a rusty fish hook, a bobber, two old lures, and a raggedy blanket. He says he's starving, and my stomach's beginning to growl, too. I send him down to the lake and tell him to catch us dinner. He peels out the door and high-tails it for the dock. I don't expect anything. I'm merely getting him out from underfoot.

"He's got Mom's gift," Winona says casually. "Lionel and Willy's dad went hunting last fall, and they took Willy along, and they got two deer." She can tell I'm not that impressed, so she adds, "He found your reading glasses, under the helicopter seat."

Judy's resumed her psychic healing, which consists, she says, of "active imagery." "I see little calcium cells," she says in a dreamy voice, her eyes closed, "tumbling out of a little slot machine, like the ones at the casino, and they're filling up the cracks in the bone." She opens her eyes and looks at me, and I can tell she doesn't care if I believe her or not. Her eyes are cinnamon, and her lips are small and pouty. She's gotten a nice ruddy tan out in the wild, a coppery patina over an initial sunburn, and her brown hair is bleached by the sun. She looks tired, but she looks peaceful, too. She closes her eyes again.

I watch Judy, trying to see the calcium cells tumbling out of the slot machines, but all I see are nickels and dimes, and I wonder if my mental imagery is telling me something about my life and career.

I hear a splash down at the lake. I look out the window. The helicopter has tipped off the narrow dock on which it was balanced so nicely, and the helicopter is settling into about four feet of water and two feet of mud and loon shit. Bubbles rise to the surface.

Dancing with Bears   *129*

"Willy!" Winona cries, and runs out the door.

I run after her. By the time we get to the dock, Willy has swum out of the helicopter and is climbing onto the dock. He's crying a little from the scare but trying not to cry. He was in the helicopter, he says, pretending to fly, playing with the controls and pedals. Once Willy catches his breath, he points to the live box submerged by the dock, where he's put the four large rock bass he's caught.

The cleaning shack is still standing, although the screen is torn in several places, so the mosquitoes and flies and hornets find us quick enough. I bring a bucket of water from the lake, and Winona Running Bear and I stand shoulder-to-shoulder, beheading and gutting and filleting silently. Sometimes, when we're alone together, the thought pops into my head that we have something to talk about, Lionel Running Bear's wife and I. But, when you think about it, there isn't really anything to say about some things, even if a fellow thinks there might be.

Winona's a matter-of-fact gal, with short dark hair and a serious mien, married young and the bearer of several children. She's impatient with rules and ambitious to get ahead in life—hence the helicopter lessons, which Skip Ostrum is giving to her free, so long as she pays for the fuel, which she does, out of her earnings as waitress at the Lost Duck Cafe and Roadhouse and chambermaid at Ralph's Motel.

(I wondered what inspired Skip's altruism, since he's a pretty tight-fisted fellow. Guilt at the theft of Indian lands by his forebears? Or a connoisseurship of the pregnant female form, which he shares with his brother, Bud, and a consequent indebtedness to Winona's modeling sessions each time she was with child? But enough of that.)

Winona grabs the pan with the fillets, and I dump the heads and bones and guts on the beach, and we hurry inside to escape the mosquitoes. We grill the bass in the fireplace, in a lattice of green branches Winona wove, and the fish tastes excellent. Winona sprinkled the fillets with herbs she gathered but would not identify for me, and they give the bass a heady, slightly licorice taste. She gathered some greens as well, which Willy dubs a "wild weed salad." We also roast wild onions and, something of a rarity, she says, Indian breadroot, gnarled tubers which taste like grumpy yams. Winona says the small onions, which have a kick to them, will clear our sinuses, banish headaches, and, just in case, cure snakebite. The water from the nearby spring, cool and crystalline, tastes like a fresh Pinot Grigio from northern Tuscany.

Willy, wrapped naked in the blanket while his clothes dry, falls asleep curled in front of the fire. Judy, alert and content, apparently taking a break from the little slot machines, sits in a rattan chair, her splinted leg propped on an upright log. Winona is boiling water for bearberry tea, and I'm arranging the leaves and grasses I gathered before the storm hit into a mattress we can all share. Lightning dances across the sky, and thunder rattles the timbers, and rain drips from the ceiling here and there but not where we're huddled.

Winona pours the tea—steeped from both the berries, which turn sugary when boiled, and the bearberry leaves—*Arctostaphylos uva-ursi*—into two cracked cups, for her and Judy. Winona says it's a reliable women's medicine, although I can have some if I want but I'll be up a dozen times during the night and she imagines a fellow my age has to get up a few times as it is without the encouragement of a diuretic.

Winona's worried about the helicopter. Will Skip make her pay for it, which she couldn't do in a million years? I tell her that technically the helicopter is in the service of the Emergency Rescue Office, which is a subdivision of the Division of Forestry, and I'm sure they have funds for these contingencies. She says she's heard that I play fast and loose with government money, and that the Division of Forestry, and maybe the FBI, too, is going to nail my ass before long. I say there are a lot of small-minded, mean-spirited people out there. Judy, who I thought had been back pulling the handle of her little calcium-spitting slot machine, says not to worry, she has friends in high places, and this has been the most important two weeks of her life, including tonight. She says she knows everything happens for a reason, and her mind is clearer than it's ever been.

Winona helps Judy hop to the porch. The lightning has passed but there's still a steady deluge, so no one wants to go to the outhouse down the way, so I think the ladies are simply backing up to the edge of the porch. When they return, I go out and plant my feet on the edge, gazing, a little fretfully, I have to admit, out at the night's raw uncertainty. Won't the radio be useless, soaked in lake water? Will rescuers ever find us? I have faith in Winona's aboriginal wisdom and foraging skills, but can we survive an extended hermitage? Who would even think to check the old Ostrum place, abandoned now so many years? The resort flourished as long as people looked for a little hardship along with their vacation, when city folks thought it was exotic to live for a week or two reading by kerosene lamp, playing checkers for amusement, and shitting in a hole in the ground. Now folks panic if they forget their cell phone or can't plug in their toothbrush.

It gets pretty cool at night. I build up the fire with the last of the dry wood, and Judy and Winona and I pull the blanket over us and spoon together, while little Willy curls on the other side of Winona. Even though we shiver at first, eventually we warm each other.

On the lake, loons warble their plaintive communiqués. They sound lonely and bereft of hope, but I know that's anthropomorphizing. Really they're happy and content and simply sharing some gossip. That's what the loon researchers say, anyway.

In the morning, when I wake, my hand is on Judy's D-cup breast. I believe I can feel her nipple pressing against my thumb.

I can tell by Judy's breathing she's awake, but she's pretending she's asleep. I pretend I'm asleep too, as I breathe in her woodsy odor, the scent of days of sweat, sun, and impetuosity, which kindles in me a primitive arousal. Her hair, matted and tangled and smelling of wildflowers, tickles my nose. I don't move my hand. I'm content to feel the heft of Judy's breast and breathe the dense spoor of her sojourn in the wilderness. (Diane's been gone a lot recently; and, even when she's back home, she's so tired, or tense, or preoccupied, that we fail to enjoy our customary wild entanglements. I think she may not be eating properly.)

Minutes crawl by like caterpillars arching methodically toward a particularly tasty leaf at the tip of a long branch. Morning suffuses the lodge with a leisurely stretch of shadows and sunlight. I'm suspended in a strange ecstasy, wondering if she can feel my arousal pressing against her buttocks. She sighs deeply, and I wonder if she is asleep after all, as she grabs my right hand, which is snuggled under her neck, and pulls my palm down firmly against her other breast. As she breathes, her breasts fill my palms. I can't tell where her breasts stop and my hands begin.

My arm is asleep, the circulation cut off at the shoulder by Judy's head. I have no feeling in my right hand. I wonder what it's worth to hold Judy's heavy breasts a few seconds longer, because I have the feeling this is my only chance to weigh that soft plumpness.

I wonder how long before gangrene sets in.

Finally, as I pull away, Judy takes a deep breath, and stretches, and pretends she's been asleep all this time.

As I roll over and pretend to wake up, Winona's sleepy hand falls limply into my crotch. Then Winona's awake and, without realizing where she's placed her hand, she sits up, using that hand as a lever to push up with.

Judy wants to wash her hair before the rescuers arrive. She knows there'll be photographers, and she wants to look presentable. She says she has some shampoo in her back pack. I know this means hauling water from the lake and heating it over the fire which I'm blowing to life in the fireplace with the dry branches Winona has easily found with her sharp indigenous eye, so I suggest to Judy that maybe it will be better for her Senatorial campaign if she looks like shit, if she looks like she's really endured a lot and made it through, a triumph of will and fortitude, and she agrees and throws away the shampoo.

Later, I see in the cloudy mirror behind the door that I don't look so hot, either, so I salvage the shampoo and wash my hair in the cold water of the lake, since there's no reason for me not to look respectable. Kneeling on the sand, rinsing out the suds, I notice a great blue heron wading in the wild rice. It looks at me, I could swear, in a disapproving manner, its head cocked to the side and its eye flashing, before it gives a raucous croak and lifts off, long wings flapping against the dewy morning air.

On the beach the fish heads and guts are gone. Bear tracks come and go. From the size and indentations, I'd say a male, about 350 pounds, in no hurry. As I head back to the lodge I meet Winona. She gives my combed wet hair a questioning glance, but all she says is "Judy says her leg is healed and she wants to take her splint off."

Judy is sitting on the porch tugging at the vines securing her splint from ankle to hip. I tell her to wait for the X-rays to make sure. She asks me to get her a knife. I say the little calciums from the slot machine might take longer than she thinks; those jackpots don't go on forever, and they need milk and vitamin D to get more chips out of the casino's vault. She stands up, hops inside, and hops back out again with a knife. She hacks at the bindings.

I tell her she's going to cut her leg off like that, and I take the knife out of her hand. She starts crying, saying I'm just like a man, damn it, and she misses her Amazon sisters who taught her to survive in the wild, and she grabs the pole I've been working on to fashion into a crutch for her and hops into the brush to find edible tubers and live by herself until her sisters come and rescue her.

Winona walks up, dripping wet. She and Willy have been in the lake, salvaging things from the helicopter. Willy's still there, swimming around the helicopter. Winona looks at the retreating Judy, smashing into the woods one hop at a time, then at me, as if it's all my fault— Judy hopping away, Judy crying, the helicopter running out of gas, the helicopter falling into the lake, Judy breaking her leg, my reading the map wrong, the hunger in our stomachs, the deer flies diving at us, and her peoples' loss of a hundred million acres of land. She spreads out the things from the helicopter to dry.

I follow Judy into the woods, helping her up when she falls. Every time I help her, it makes her madder, but she can't do anything about it, because she can't get up by herself. We stumble along this way, Judy sobbing and hopping, looking for tubers, I guess, then falling, I lifting her and setting her upright and she hating me for helping her and hating herself that she needs help, and hopping some more, and falling, and so on, until finally, unable to find any edible tubers, she falls face down on the ground and bawls good and hard for awhile. I hunker nearby, not saying anything, because I know a good cry is all a person needs sometimes to release the endorphins and brighten the perspective. When she subsides to a few gasps and sniffles, she sits up, her face dirty and tear-streaked, her eyes red, her cheek scratched, leaves and grass and other forest detritus clinging to her clothes and hair. I go over to her slowly, the way I'd approach a bear who'd had a bad time of it. I sit down beside her, in the dirt and leaves, and I hold her, and she's all right with that, wiping her nose on the back of her wrist.

Then it seems natural what we do, alone in the woods, desperate, lost, and maybe doomed. At first the splint is a hindrance, but we overcome that by doing it like bears, which she says she likes anyway but her husband doesn't. Afterwards, she says she loves her Amazon sisters and will never forget them but, Jesus Almighty, there's nothing like a man shoving it in there like you're the last salvation in the world for his rock-hardness.

Little Willy kills a squirrel with the slingshot Winona made by cutting a belt off the engine. By the time Judy and I hop back, the squirrel is skinned and roasting over the fire Winona built outside because she was feeling claustrophobic in the lodge.

"No tubers?" Winona asks dryly. Judy starts to make excuses, but I know Winona's merely exercising her Native sense of humor, so I say, "You don't want tubers with squirrel, you want a nice green salad, and an aged Carneros Pinot Noir."

We have the salad—more greens Winona finds, these presenting a peppery, earthy taste. Winona finds some wild garlic, too, and we roast the bucket of snails Willy collected.

Judy's long ordeal, despite her recent hormonal release, seems to be taking its toll on her equanimity, because Judy suddenly questions Winona's wilderness gastronomy. These comestibles are not, Judy says, items mentioned by the Amazons as they were living off the land. Winona says you can't learn everything from books. Judy says, But the Amazons took much of their survival know-how from Native informants. Winona says that's the trouble: people *take*. Besides, Winona adds, we don't tell people everything. People have to keep some secrets, Winona goes on, don't they, looking at Judy, then at me.

The Amazons in the rescue helicopter see the smoke from Winona's fire, as well as the "H E L P" Willy spelled out with rocks on the beach, and the pilot radios our position to headquarters. The helicopter is also carrying Sandra Flies Far. The pilot thought he was off course, his compass malfunctioning, whereas he was actually being guided by Sandra's psychic radar. She said later that she didn't know we were here, she just knew she'd lost something down there at the old Makwah— "Bear" in the Ojibway lingo—Resort. Winona was never worried about being found. She knew her mother would find her.

A few of the Amazons, committed to survival on their own terms without the assistance of paternalistic technology, were going to refuse rescue and hike out; but, after watching the others lift blithely off, they decided that they were pretty tired after all, and anyway they had proved themselves beyond what anyone had expected and, besides, they had to get back to jobs and family.

Towards evening a seaplane lands and taxis up to the dock and takes us away. Winona and I and Willy accompany Judy to the hospital, where the doctors (flown in from Minneapolis) cannot believe that her leg, broken only days before, is, as evidenced by the X-rays, almost healed. But the doctors put Judy's leg in a cast anyway, to save face.

By midnight we're standing outside the hospital—nothing but a small clinic, really, with an emergency room, a nurse, a few beds, and a budget deficit—why doesn't Congress care about medical care for the folks in the woods?—waiting for Judy to make her appearance. There are reporters from *Time* and *Newsweek* and *People* and *The New York Times*, and from NBC and CBS and ABC and CNN, and there are stringers for *Vanity Fair* and *Cosmopolitan* and *Good Housekeeping* and *Out.* (They say Dan Rather's on his way, wearing his safari shirt and flak jacket, but I never see him.) Some of the reporters are making jokes about the Amazons and asking if they're a radical lesbian survivalist militia, training to overthrow the government.

Listening to all that irreverent jabber, Diane gets her dander up. She grabs a microphone. She holds an impromptu press conference of her own, and one of the Amazons, Mrs. Arlene Chang, the CEO of some big foundation, joins in, and another Amazon, with a crew cut, who is a Congresswoman from Oregon, backs her up. The Amazons have had a chance to shower and change clothes, so they're not immediately recognizable, except for their burnished complexions and free-wheeling confidence.

They straighten out the reporters in a hurry. They ask those fellas and gals from the East, dressed in their new clothes they bought down the street at Ray Ostrum Outfitters so they'd look cool on camera, if they'd like to try a few raw grubs, and Arlene pulls a handful of the shiny white squigglers from her pocket. Then, just as Diane reminds the press that the women were found by the famous bear expert, gourmet, and media personality, Judy emerges from the hospital.

Judy hobbles into the bright corona of white light. She pauses, blinking, resting her weight on her crutches. Her husband, Senator Mark Larson, tries to shoulder his way into the spotlight and embrace her, as if he's the one who rescued her, but she smacks him with a crutch. Then she decides to hell with the god damn crutches and tosses them away. She says the Amazons healed her leg, the doctors don't know shit. She says she'll be running for ol' Mark's Senate seat. Then, Judy adds, he'll have plenty of time to run around with 20-year-old tootsies wearing bunny ears on their heads. She doesn't pay any attention to me, although she does thank "everyone who gave all they had to rescue and succor me."

About two in the a.m., Diane and I, alone together finally, repair to Celine Ostrum's Browsing Bear Gourmet Restaurant, which Celine has kept open all night for the reporters and TV crews and Dan Rather if he shows up. Celine tells us not to pay any attention to the prices she's printed on the blackboard that lists the specials, they're for the rich media folks. She says business hasn't been this good since the triple murder and suicide five years ago—do I remember that?—when they paroled a sociopath by mistake because he had the same name as a hapless lad in for 20 years for selling a joint.

Celine's a stout, middle-aged woman with long curly gray hair and bright red lipstick, a conspicuous gold tooth that flashes when she laughs, and rhinestone-studded glasses. She wears Birkenstocks winter and summer (wool socks in winter), jeans that bulge in many places, and a blue T-shirt with a picture of a browsing bear on it. Her braless breasts sag in the T-shirt, but she's indifferent to the conventions of appearance.

She's married and divorced several men—I lost count after eight—all of them outsiders who'd show up in early summer, from Minneapolis or Chicago or even New York or Paris, seeking a brief wilderness respite from the turmoils of urban commerce, and they'd fall in love with her, and she'd fall in love with them. She says falling in love is the easiest thing in the world for her to do. It's her curse and her joy. But then the men would leave, sometimes by Labor Day, sometimes by Christmas, but nearly always before Valentine's Day. One man, Arnold Lowenstein, from Dallas, toughed it out until the next spring, when the ice broke up on the lakes, but he left, too, because, he said, Celine got bossy and grumpy and sometimes even delusional in the winter, for lack of sunlight.

Celine admits that's true. Last winter she tried to cure her winter disorder by wearing a headband with a battery-powered light on it, but the light made her homicidal, and she tore it off just as she caught herself spooning rat poison into her famous chocolate mousse. She refuses prescription drugs because, she says, they're not natural and it's the big pharmaceuticals ripping us off anyway. So she's resigned herself to summers of lustful ecstasy and winters of near madness, but I figure we all make compromises, that's Life. The mysterious grim dealer who flips the cards your way works with a stacked deck, full of jokers.

It's slack at three a.m. at the Browsing Bear Gourmet Restaurant. The reporters are off filing their stories or taping their stand-ups, or they're in bed at Ralph's or Fanny Ostrum's Hide-a-Bed (Fanny is Celine's cousin) or Emma's We Won't Tell Travel Lodge. Celine is sitting with us having a glass of her Stags Leap District Cabernet Sauvignon, which I coaxed her to bring out of her secret cellar, a Cab softer than those from other peaks and valleys in California and so more relaxing but nevertheless flexing its muscle as it waltzes after the Duck d'Lyle, a recipe I gave her that employs a stuffing of wild rice, roasted peppers, pine nuts, and rye bread crumbs and a sauce of cranberries, allspice, cloves, cinnamon, and Tawny port. Summer squash roasted with garlic and Balsamic vinegar and steamed garden-fresh French string beans sprinkled with a Thai seasoning round out our menu.

As I'm digging into the mousse, a thick, dark, rich chocolate heady with a dash of bourbon (Bookers, if I don't miss my guess), Celine says casually, tapping her red-nailed forefinger against my knuckle, "Did you hear they found Ben Creswell's headless body?"

LYLE'S WIFE RECEIVES A NEWSPAPER CLIPPING

Saskatoon

Dear Lyle,

    I guess that was you sent me the clipping about Ben Creswell shooting himself and being eaten by bears, but couldn't you at least include a note or a howdeedo? I know Ben was your bête noire, and he was a mean man and he didn't respect the law, but I felt a twinge of regret reading the newspaper article, because it must have been Vietnam that did that to Ben, made him need to live by himself in the woods. He was a casualty of war. Do you think he could have lived with people if someone had loved him? Or had he seen too much in Vietnam and Laos and other places where we were not, supposedly? Had he killed so much that there was no one left to kill, finally, but himself?

    And outside the cabin there was the skeleton of a bear he had killed, which the other bears ate, but bears are hungry in the spring, and they'll eat even rotting meat.

A gal with a heart

William Borden

Saskatoon, near Batoche, where the
French-Indian Métis rebels shot it out
with the government troops in 1885

Dear Lyle,

The follow-up article to Ben's untimely death was enlightening.
But is any death timely, come to think of it? I suppose it is, if you have
cancer and are terminal. But aren't we all terminal? We're born terminal. It's a matter of time, that's all.

Are we terminal, Lyle?

Perhaps that was your appointments secretary who answered your
phone when I called today. I guess I should have given my name, but
I was nonplused to hear a woman's voice. Or does the voice on the
other end of the fiber optic belong to—well, I guess the big question for
me, and maybe I should bring this up at group tonight, is, is there a
permanent replacement in our king-size bed? Or have you been getting
along with temps?

She answered the phone, "Bears, Incorporated."

Are you no longer a person?

Who would have thought Ben was an expert chess player? And
that his PO Box was overflowing with correspondence from people
with whom he was playing chess by mail, two of them grand masters,
and that he was the Creswell of the Creswell Defense, "a defense,"
the article says, "that seems to prefigure the player's defeat but, when
executed properly, tricks the adversary into a suicidal attack."

There's a lot we don't know about people, isn't there? Not only
people like Ben—I saw him in town a couple of times—I wanted to say
hello, I wanted him to feel like he could have a friend, but he was so
jumpy I was afraid to—but also people close to us whom we've known

for almost thirty years, people we think we know everything about, but they're strangers like everybody else.

When the sheriff said it looked like a couple of bears had broken into Ben's shack and shot him and eaten him, what did he mean?

Isn't it strange that Ben would poach a bear and then kill himself?

And why would the Ben-eating bears drag off the skin of the poached bear so it was never found?

Your wife, bearing up

BEAR HOSPITALITY

If hungry people come, give them food. If thirsty
people come, give water. If suffering people come,
help them. That is our job—life after life, just
continue to help all beings.

—Seung Sahn

Judy Jump-Larson has stopped by to thank Lyle for saving and suc-
coring her. Judy has a few extra days before she meets with the campaign
contributors Arlene Chang is lining up. Lyle has invited her to relax
in the rustic comfort and gourmet ambiance of his lodge/research sta-
tion/home, and Judy, her hair cut and styled since her rescue (a shag,
with highlights of platinum), and wearing a white summer frock that is
transparent when she stands a certain way in the sun, has accepted.

(Diane is in L.A., meetings scheduled with Eisner, Spielberg, How-
ard, and Reiner.)

Judy seems to think I'm Lyle's hired hand, because I'm ripping
weeds out of the garden that's run wild in the far corner of the property and Lyle, without thinking, I'm sure, yells at me to carry in her
bags and bring a champagne up from the cellar.

I ignore Lyle and go back to weeding. Last summer the garden
must have been in pretty good shape, but now it's an emblem of the
struggle between civilization and the wild, with the reminder that ulti-
mately, and often sooner than we think, the wild eats up the civilized,
the savage crowds out the tamed, and chaos runs roughshod over the
linearity of rows and boundaries. The second law of thermodynamics
runs amok in Lyle's wife's garden.

Oh, there are some perennials, like the mint, the basil, and the
arugula; and there are the iris and daffodils, which I cut and brought

into the lodge to add some color and fragrance to our lives, which Diane commented favorably on but which Lyle didn't seem to notice. And now there are roses and carnations (sweet cinnamon scent!) and tiger lilies and daisies, and soon there will be gladiolas, and here and there I can spot, amidst the weeds, various volunteers (onions, radishes, potatoes, lettuce, a watermelon vine, and an intrepid zucchini).

I attack a patch of particularly arrogant thistles, reflecting, as I wipe the sweat from my eyes, that actually a weed is not any particular plant or genus of plants. A weed is simply something we don't like, a hapless growth we want to uproot, get rid of, exterminate. In truth it's no more ignoble than a radish or a rutabaga, but we don't want it mingling with our radishes and rutabagas. A weed, as far as that goes, is simply a plant we're prejudiced against.

Some "weeds," I contemplate, jerking them from the earth and tossing them in a pile, are in fact edible. Some are medicinal. Some are even flowers. Is it because weeds come without our inviting them, I ask myself, that we're hostile to them? Illegal immigrants, uninvited house guests, unnamed gate-crashers arrogantly flashing their green cards, are they repugnant merely because they're strange, because they speak another language, because they have unseemly habits, smell rankly, and steal the livelihoods of more familiar legumes and herbs? Or is it, honestly, that they are evil border-crossers, nefarious interlopers, rapacious invaders, sucking up the moisture and nutrients needed by the nasturtiums and the cauliflower (building its brain-like head from nitrogen and the rotted compost of our winter's banquets), the bully weeds shading the tiny sprouts of peas, crowding out the tender shoots of lettuce?

It's a battle, an unremitting struggle, between the civilizing efforts of the gardener and the indefatigable invasions of the wild. And, without vigilance and thought, without dedication, sacrifice, and persistence, the order and calm purposefulness, the logic, reason, and Platonic harmony so aptly represented by a neat row of peas (small green bullets in their bulging cartridge belts, Mexican revolutionaries ready to ride) would be overcome by rampant savagery, selfish willfulness, and runaway chaos.

But then, I wonder, pausing at the end of the row, my hands smarting, the smell of dirt in my nostrils, sweat cascading into my eyes, where would we be without the wild? Where do our ideas come from if not from some spontaneous sprouting? And what is more spontaneous than a weed? Wasn't a radish once considered a weed? The potato noxious? The tomato a bad joke?

Wasn't democracy a weed in the garden of monarchy? Aren't the bureaucrats weeds in the fertile soil of creativity? Don't we go wild—say on New Year's Eve or after a hard day at the office—in order to recover something, revive ourselves, become, really, human again? Can we be human without the wild? Isn't some savagery necessary, even at a formal table? Isn't a weed Nature's way of telling us to dance, not march, when we hear the music of the wind in the leaves, the symphony of the waves, the sonata of the lark, the polka of the spheres?

Without rushing, I shower and put on clean clothes and—only then!—lug in the six suitcases, which seem excessive for a short stay in the woods, although I learn later that I needn't have brought them all in because all but one are for the rest of her trip.

Lyle, coming out of the bedroom in his blue boxer shorts with the little red bears on them—a gift from an admirer, he said—looks at me impatiently, wondering if the champagne is chilled yet. I don't have to say anything. He knows I'm thinking, *I'm not your servant get your fucking champagne yourself,* so he gives a shrug and pads barefoot down to the wine cellar.

While he's down there, and I'm standing in the living room, Judy comes to the bedroom doorway wondering where Lyle has gone. She looks surprised to see me. She obviously doesn't associate me with the dirty lout in the garden. She asks, "Are you Lyle's secretary?" Then, not receiving an immediate reply, she adds, "Or his biographer he was telling me about?"

Her questions throw me into my usual existential quandary. (*Who am I, really? And Even if I'm thinking, am I? And Am I thinking, or is this noise in my head merely God whistling through Her teeth?*)

Judy doesn't have much patience for thoughtfulness. She wanders back into the bedroom to wait for Lyle, her plump fanny jiggling, unabashed by its dimples, her stomach unashamed of the scar from Cesareans, and Judy herself oblivious to the provocative asymmetry of her robust breasts and the imperturbability of her raspberry nipples. Lyle reappears carrying a bottle and saunters into the kitchen for ice. "Lyle?" she calls from the bedroom. "Lyle, honey?" He can't hear her, banging ice cube trays in the kitchen. She emerges from the doorway.

"In the kitchen," I say. "Getting ice. For the champagne." I try not to stare at the dark inverted triangle, wild and woolly and turbulent.

"Oh," she says plaintively, one plump hand on the door jamb, her weight on her right foot, her fingernails and toenails the color of the roses I arranged on the dining table, "I thought that gardener was going to get it."

"The gardener is the gardener," I say. "He doesn't do domestic service."

"Oh," she says, disappointed by a disturbance in what she thought was the order of things. Lyle enters, bucket in hand, the champagne pocketed in ice cubes—I'd better fill the trays if we're going to have any ice for the gin and tonics he and I usually imbibe before our evening meal. He gives me a querulous look, put out, I can tell, by my being a witness to Judy's frank nudity but unable to say anything since she placed herself in front of me of her own volition. He closes the bedroom door behind them.

Later, Lyle makes it clear without saying anything directly that we won't be having our customary gin and tonics this evening and that I will not be included in the dinner plans. I take his pickup and drive to the Lost Duck Cafe and Roadhouse, where Winona, in her starched pink and white uniform, serves me a plate of roast pork, mashed potatoes, gravy, creamed corn, and lime jello. She doesn't have much to say. In fact, I don't think she even knows who I am.

I leave her a large tip, which she doesn't acknowledge, and I hang back to let her husband come in, a good-looking fellow filling out in the chest, with a smell of tar and creosote clinging to him like a relentless cologne. She's just getting off, and he's come to drive her home.

William Borden

BEARS ON THE EDGE

The next day Lyle takes Judy out into the woods to see bears. She could as well have come with me since I have to slap on my D of F cap with its well-rolled bill and pick up Barry, who's rolling in a lady's laundry; Sally, who's denting a picnicker's car to get at the peanut butter and jelly sandwiches in the back seat; and Rudy, who's up to his usual tricks of stopping cars by sitting calmly by the highway and jumping inside the car if anyone opens a door to get a closer look.

When I get back, it's dark, and, since the lights are on in the lodge, I figure Lyle and Judy are up, playing cribbage, maybe. There is the alluvium of their dinner on the stove and table: bones from a rack of lamb, two sections of lamb remaining; a potato roasted, it looks like, in a glaze of caramelized onion and sprinkled with fresh basil, accompanied by roasted carrots, garlic cloves, and baby beets (from my garden? the beets ripped prematurely from their womb to sate Lyle's greedy maw?); and an empty bottle that once held a rugged Merlot from the Alexander Valley.

I decide that a Carneros Valley Cabernet, or possibly a Napa Syrah, would go like gangbusters with this late night repast. I ease into the living room and toward the stairs to the cellar. I pass the open door to Lyle's bedroom, from which comes Judy's desperate command, "Again! Harder!" and then the shocking smack of palm on butt.

When it gets quiet, except for the bounce of the bed springs, I descend to the cellar. I bring up a sassy Syrah. Treading lightly past Lyle's door I hear Judy's voice coo, "Now the Big Bear has to lick the Little Bear right *here!*" And then a whimpering, which, much to my surprise, does in fact remind me of Sally as she was lapping the oatmeal and honey with which I lured her into the live trap this afternoon.

A couple of hours later I'm still in the kitchen, sitting at the rustic wooden table, finishing the Syrah, which doesn't properly follow the rice pudding with dates and Calvados I found in the refrigerator, but I'm too tired to find the Armagnac that might have been the thing and, besides, I don't really want to pass before the bedroom door again, when Lyle, naked, sits down and takes a desultory bite of the pudding and pours the remainder of the Syrah into a tumbler. He doesn't seem surprised to see me.

He examines the palm of his hand, rubbing the fleshy part as if to ease a smarting. He says, "She wanted me to use a belt, but I have to draw the line somewhere." He looks at me. "She'll make a good Senator. She knows what she wants, and she goes after it." He gulps the Syrah. "I'll vote for her. You like the pudding? I should've put a little more vanilla in it, don't you think?"

"Touch of cinnamon?"

"Nutmeg?"

I consider it, a gustatory fantasy on my tongue. Lyle's tongue seems to hang limply, dog-like, from his mouth, a tired tongue. "I don't think so."

"You're right."

"A little B&B?"

"That'd be good."

"Not too much," I caution.

We stare together at the empty bowl, remnants of the pudding crusting the sides, imagining this Platonic rice pudding. He says, "She's worn me down, jocko. She's got an insatiability that won't quit. Overactive hypothalamus. I try every trick in the book, rare recipes from the esoteric oral tradition, the Kabbalah of erotomania. I get her right to the brink, she's teetering on the edge, she's hanging by her teeth, a thread, a wish, but she can't get over. I can't shove her over, drag her over, nudge her over. So she's ravenous again, like a bear in springtime." He sounds defeated, bewildered, at his wit's end. And he doesn't like to give up on a problem.

Then she's in the kitchen, a silent materialization, stealing across the bright rag rug on her bare, plump feet. She stands expectantly at Lyle's shoulder, across the table from me, in her pink nakedness, hardly aware of my presence. "I think I know how I can come," she says, as one might say, I think I know how to find those keys I've lost. "I think I can come if we do it in public."

She waits for Lyle to respond, to start up his truck, maybe, and drive them to town to do it in the middle of the high school football field, if only it was half-time and the stands full. But Lyle has a frightened look on his face, an expression I've never seen before. He looks at me. For sympathy? For advice?

For help?

BEARS ON THE HIGH ROAD OF LIFE

 As to pleasure with women, if you do indulge in it, do it in the way which is conformable to custom. Do not, however, be disagreeable to those who indulge in these pleasures, or reprove them; and do not often boast that you do not indulge in them yourself.

—Epictetus

Splashed by the pickup's pasty headlights, Lyle's white skin and Judy's bronze limbs writhe atop the rumpled sleeping bag in the middle of the highway. The boom box blares the maniacal cheering at a Beatles concert, from a cassette of sound effects. I stand on the asphalt, spread no doubt one hot day by Lionel Running Bear and other county road maintenance workers. I gaze down at Lyle's and Judy's fervid pulsings, their carnal gropings transfigured by Lyle's insatiable good will, by his inexhaustible patience, and by his relentless resolve when it comes to wild things and their hunger. Judy's eyes are shut tight, her lips pressed firmly together. She's trying hard. Maybe too hard.

The tape jumps from frenzied hoopla to roaring engines. It must be the Indy 500, the thunder and zoom so real I can smell the oil and exhaust. The high-pitched metallic whine, as if something huge were about to fly apart, notches Judy to a faster throb, to a louder bleat, to a new quivering of sweaty flesh. In the distance, out of the indifferent craw of the night, headlights toss their pale white glimmer. The headlights are high, as on a truck, a logging truck, that hurtles down the highway at seventy miles an hour weighted with hundred-foot logs two feet in diameter.

I'll have to drag them, coupled, to the side of the road, out of the path of the oncoming behemoth. I clutch the edge of the sleeping bag.

Judy seizes my wrist.

Headlights, twin eyes of dieseled doom, shimmering disks of cruel calamity, hurl themselves closer. Her fingers flutter against my groin.

"For god's sake, give us a hand here!" Lyle cries.

I let her grab what she wants. I let her put it where she likes.

Lyle pumps. Judy gobbles. She's not racing as fast as the truck.

Lyle hauls her onto her knees and elbows. Her teeth give me a nasty abrasion.

Lyle whips the belt from his trousers. Lyle gives her what for, not because he's aroused but because he's mad, mad at all the trouble she's causing.

The headlights loom.

I purse my lips the way I played trumpet in grade school. I buzz Judy's juicer, toot Judy's horn, tweak Judy's tickler, teeter Judy's totter—

Horns wail, brakes shriek, rubber burns, tires skid—

It's that small extra nudge that Judy needs, that she's needed for so long, the whisper that starts the avalanche, the crack that breaks the dike, the tilt of the axis that sends the planet spinning—as the tires slide into the gravel, as the klaxon caterwauls, as the truck shimmies to a halt, as the driver jumps out, as Judy clutches me to her, as the driver runs toward us, as Judy expels an exultant ululation of heavenly release, release from the pent-up tensions of a lifetime or maybe several lifetimes, a cry so unremitting and chthonic that the trucker halts in his tracks. When it fades, lingering like a tired memory among the branches above, the trucker turns around. He walks back to his truck with unsteady, giddy strides. He drives away, engine coughing, gravel spitting, tires whimpering. He's witnessed a scene so primeval he will not even talk about it at the Cenex where he'll gas up and have breakfast, but he'll remember it all his days like an archetypal dream come roaring out of the collective unconscious to smack him in the eyes and blind him, like Paul on the road to Damascus, until he admits there's a life larger than any he'd ever imagined. That's what I think, anyway.

Lyle and I carry Judy to the pickup and slide her into the back. She's out like a light, and we're pretty tired ourselves.

So tired, back at the lodge, we leave her in the truck, cover her with another sleeping bag, and Lyle lies down beside her, so when she wakes up she won't feel abandoned. I stumble back to my cot in my shack near the sauna, my clothes still on the highway, troubled only by the pawings of a curious raccoon.

Late in the morning, when I enter the lodge to check on the bear nuisance reports, Judy's packed and dressed in a stylish but conservative suit, proper as a Presbyterian. But there's a dazed look in her eyes, as if she can't quite focus anywhere, and a flush on her cheeks, and a limpness to her whole body, as if a terrible pressure had been discharged, and while she feels a lot better, she isn't quite used to her new equanimity. She seems to have trouble walking, and stumbles over nothing, and she looks around vaguely as if she's forgotten something, but maybe she's only leaving behind a bad memory, like a piece of wiring you thought you needed but was getting in the way of a direct circuit after all.

Lyle carries her suitcases to her car and nestles them neatly into the trunk. We stand by the car, the three of us. "You have so many people around, but they never come back," she says in a wondering voice. He looks around for the people. "The gardener, the secretary, the cook," she explains, still looking around, as if they would appear, one by one, summoned by her words, "the wine steward, the biographer, the creature from the woods who was here last night, a faun, a satyr...?" Her voice drifts off, and her eyes narrow and her brow furrows, as if she's trying to remember a dream. She looks at me. I think finally she's going to recognize me. That all of those lackeys she has assembled in her head will come together before her now, in me.

But instead she asks, with a tremor of fatigue in her voice, "But who are you? You look like Lyle. Are you Lyle's brother?"

We watch her car disappear down the driveway, and we stand for awhile in silence, mesmerized by the inevitable improbability of life's little adventures.

Then I make french toast with Lyle's oatmeal-ricotta bread, Lyle washes the sheets, I wash the dishes, and we're off to find the mysterious silver-coated black bear.

WHERE DO WE COME FROM? WHAT ARE WE? WHERE ARE WE GOING?

> Everything you can imagine is real.
> —Pablo Picasso

Lyle's pretty excited by the prospect of seeing this silver-coated black bear. It's a real anomaly in this region, but not uncommon in the western states. Could one have traveled all the way from Montana? Or Saskatchewan? Or is this a local genetic aberration? It was sighted by campers near Lac de la Grande Vulve Lake (named by the early trapper-explorer, Ourson de Bière, a name some believe to have been the alias of a minor anarchist and premature eco-terrorist, Guillaume Vicaire, who fled Quebec after trying unsuccessfully to blow up the first steam locomotive in Montreal).

We've driven a hundred miles and left the pickup at the dead end of a Forestry service road, and we've followed a deer trail until it petered out, and now we're tromping cross country, following some mystical internal radar of Lyle's, which he thinks he has from his years of kinship with bears and which will lead us unfailingly to the silver-coated black bear. I'm backpacking a tent and sleeping bags and assorted supplies, while Lyle's packing the videocam, videotape, extra batteries, the tranquilizing rifle, a radio collar to put on the silver-coated bear, and two extra radio collars just in case. I'm using a staff to help me over the rough terrain, although I must admit, with all my recent activity, my leg seems stronger. I don't tell Lyle this, however, because it's handy to fall back on a little lameness when I get tired. Lyle seems always indefatigable.

There was even some speculation in the weekly newspaper about this bear, not to mention the report that went out over the wire and resulted in the phone calls from the Minneapolis and St. Paul papers, wanting Lyle's expert opinion. At first Lyle made light of the report and said he imagined it was an ordinary black bear that had gotten into somebody's flour; but then, after an unidentified Native American suggested that this was a spirit bear, predicted ages ago to be a harbinger of the end of the world, Lyle updated his response to wonder if this might be an albino black bear, albinism being a rare but known phenomenon among bears, as among humans. One observer, however, a backpacker with some experience in the woods, swore the bear had a black nose and dark eyes, which would rule out the albinism, although not, Lyle added, partial albinism, also a known phenomenon but not one heretofore reported in Minnesota.

When the call came from *The New York Times* and Lyle wasn't here—he was supposedly showing Judy some of his bears but I wonder how interested she really was in bears because there was evidence of non-research activities, in particular yellow panties, bright as a sunburst, abandoned beneath the sleeping bag in the back of the pickup—I thought it was simpler to answer the questions myself, allowing the reporter to assume that I was Lyle, the famous bear expert and culinary guru.

I had, after all, been doing a little research of my own, digging through Lyle's prodigious files. I said that it was unlikely that a brown bear, or a western black bear, both of which could be quite light in color, had traveled across Montana and North Dakota, or across Alberta and Manitoba, without anyone noticing. Nor would a bear travel that far unless he had heard there was a hell of a fine berry crop in Minnesota, or he had been removed from Minnesota and was simply coming home—such instances of long-distance return were not unknown. Nor was this likely to be a grizzly, as some scare-mongers had warned, since the sightings had described a bear smaller than a grizzly, a bear in fact the size of a black bear, and a bear without the grizzly's characteristic hump between its shoulders.

"Then would you say," the reporter asked, "as a scientist, that it could be a ghost bear, a spirit, as the Indians say?" I said that as a scientist I could say no such thing, because scientists do not admit ghosts or spirits into their world of observation and classification. I said that if a scientist saw a ghost, a scientist would not say he saw ghost; he would say he had a visual hallucination.

But, I added, it is possible that northern Minnesota bears are beginning to experience a genetic anomaly similar to that which characterizes the black bears of Princess Royal Island, where one out of every nine black bears is white. These are known as Kermode bears, I went on, scanning Lyle's files as I talked, named after Francis Kermode, who studied the bear but never, sad to say, had the privilege of seeing one in the wild. "Have you?" the reporter, her name was Margot, asked, "ever seen a Kermode bear?"

"Of course," I answered, "and they are beautiful." I explained that the Kermode bear is merely another of Nature's little genetic tangos, that a Kermode bear is simply a black bear with white, or yellowish-white, fur, that a mother bear might be black and have a white cub or, as I had seen (here I was looking at photos in Lyle's "Kermode bear" file), both a black and a white cub, or a white sow could have two black cubs, or a black and a white, or two white, take your pick, isn't Nature wonderful? I went on as I discovered another, unlabeled, folder stuck into the "Kermode bear" file, and that folder contained photos of women in carnal congress with various animals, including a donkey, an orangutan, and a Great Dane. "If it could happen in Canada," I said to Margot, "it could happen here."

Later, when I mentioned my Kermode bear hypothesis to Lyle (having returned the file, including the unlabeled folder, to its place in the overflowing file drawer), he dismissed it peremptorily, saying genetics do not work that way and did any newspapers call while he was gone and I said No.

We've been plunging cross country now for four hours, except for a break we took by a stream to rest and eat the chicken salad sandwiches I packed (mayo, chopped onion, capers, sage, a spot of Balsamic vinegar, freshly ground white pepper, on thick slices of home-made seven-grain-oatmeal bread), a Kosher dill, a ripe pear apiece, and a chunk of Asiago with the pear. We cooled the white Bordeaux (grassy, sinewy, recondite) in the stream.

I'm glad I secretly left the message with the D of F office that we were heading out, and gave them some coordinates—although it turned out Lyle drove farther north and west than he said he was going to, but still they should be able to find us after we get lost, that is, if they're not pissed off after the Amazon rescue and decide to teach Lyle a lesson, which is possible. Of course, we're not supposed to be looking for bears, and I'm supposed to be back in the home region trapping the nuisance bears. But Diane's due back today or tomorrow. She'll surely send out rescuers if we don't return. Unless she's pissed that Lyle's not there to greet her, as she specifically asked him to be, in the message she left on the machine and which I hope I relayed to Lyle but can't remember now if I did, what with all our concern over Judy's suscitational problem.

Lyle's kneeling on the mossy earth atop a knoll when I catch up to him. He's opened a jar of honey and is pouring it on a log. "I'm hoping he might come to us," he says, "now that we've made this effort to come to him."

I look at the honey oozing into the bark, and the flies and wasps beginning to gather, and I blow the mosquitoes away from my face, and I ask, "How do you know he's around here?"

He gazes awhile at the wasps buzzing around the honey. He licks a little off his finger. "In cases like this, I let my intuition take over."

I hear a squirrel scolding from the branches. "Does it work?"

"I wanted to find a restaurant one night a few years ago in Minneapolis. I was hungry for sea bass prepared in an Asian manner. I had no idea where I might find it. I drove around the city, turning here, there, no idea where I was going, everything totally impulsive."

We move off a little and drop our packs. "Did you find it?"

He checks his tranquilizing rifle. "Even better. I pulled into a parking space. I got out. I looked around. Down the street there was a pizza parlor. I walked in, and damn if they didn't have a calamari pizza with arugula and feta and horse radish and kalamata olives. Run by a Greek fella. It was out of this world."

He leans against a tree and slides down the trunk until he's sitting on the ground. "But you didn't find your Asian sea bass," I remind him.

"That's the beauty of it," he says. "You see, I only thought I wanted that Asian sea bass. But my unconscious knew that what I really wanted was that exotic pizza." He looks out at the honey-smeared log. "Finding that pizza was like having that satellite-based remote sensing equipment that tells you where you are anywhere on the globe and how to get to any other place. Only we have that remote sensing already, always have had it. It's in our brains, and it doesn't need satellites. Sit down. We'll keep a watch here for a spell, see what happens."

We each lean against a tree and watch the clearing. Lyle has his videocam in his lap and his tranquilizer rifle by his side. Then he seems to realize that he can't handle both at the same time, so he hands me the camera.

We sit for a spell.

Lyle takes the camera and hands me the rifle.

He shoots a few seconds of tape. "Establishing shot," he says. "The empty clearing, the quiet woods." He lays the camera in his lap. "Now we're ready." He peers through the trees. He says softly, "Come on, boy, we're ready for you."

I heft the rifle.

"Don't shoot until I tell you," Lyle warns. "I may even grab the rifle and give you the camera, after I've shot a few feet."

"Whatever," I say.

We sit for awhile.

"If it is a genetic wildcard," Lyle says, "like a Kermode bear—"

"I thought you said—"

"If it is a true silver bear here in Minnesota, it will have no relation to a true Kermode bear. It will be indigenous to this region. It will be a new bear. It will need a new name."

"What name?"

"What name do you think, jocko?"

I'm thinking about my name, because I'm here, too, or maybe both our names, like the Michelson-Morley experiment that confirmed Einstein's Special Theory of Relativity, or the musicals by Rogers and Hart, or the Einstein-Rosen-Podolsky thought experiment that proves that every particle in the universe knows exactly where every other particle is, or—

"Which do you think sounds better, *The Gustafson Bear* or *The Lyle Bear?*" Lyle asks. "*The Gustafson Bear* sounds more scientific, but it's a little clumsy tripping off the tongue. *The Lyle Bear* flows smoothly, but is it too nonchalant? Too much like *Teddy Bear?* Would a *Lyle Bear* be taken seriously?"

I say, "You know, Lyle, there are two of us—"

"That's important for verification of this sighting," Lyle says. "But you know, 'Lyle' could be a fella's last name. *The Lyle Bear* could easily fall respectably into the scientific lexicon."

"But we're both going to see—"

"Don't you think?" Lyle throws me a brief glance, but then he looks away, into the trees, up at the cloud-ridden sky, and I can tell he doesn't care what my opinion is, and I hope the bear never shows up, at least not today but sometime when I'm alone, with the videocam, and I'll name the damn bear myself, or, if he shows up today, I might accidentally shoot the tranquilizing dart into Lyle's rear end, which maybe I should do now, before the bear gets here.

I raise the rifle, as if to merely get the feel of it, point it at the log, swing it about—

"Here, stop playing with that thing," Lyle says. He grabs the rifle and lays it on the ground on his other side.

We sit for awhile.

Lyle gets reflective.

"You know, jocko, we're merely animals, after all—animals with a vast, complicated social system, to be sure, a system that embraces an unholy array of technology, most of it unnecessary and irrelevant to any real purpose in life—has the fax machine given one person an improved ethical foundation? Has the Pentium microchip answered the soul's existential yelp?"

I wonder if the silver-coated black bear will be enticed by Lyle's intellectual spoor, but I don't say anything. I just keep a sharp eye on the log and the wasps congregating over it. Lyle continues, "All that complexity and gadgetry doesn't obviate the fact that it's just a bunch of hairless bears running the machinery, bipedal vertebrates driven by primitive instincts of fear, jealousy, hunger, lust, curiosity, and the insatiable desire to be petted and fondled." Lyle aims the rifle at the log. "The only difference between us and the other fauna," he goes on, "is we can take the elevator."

He falls silent for awhile, then he starts up again, like a battery that needed a little rest. "We think we're smart, and animals are dumb. 'He's just a dumb animal,' we say. Okay, maybe a bear, for example, doesn't have the abstract concept in his mind of, say, 'hunting season,' or even the notion of 'hope' or 'despair' or 'justice' or, hell, even 'love.' But let me ask you this. Do we understand bear ideas?"

I listen to the silence awhile, to the breeze rustling the leaves, the croak of a raven, the scold of a blue jay, a rustle somewhere in the dead leaves. There's the smell of afternoon in the air, and of solitude.

"Sometimes," he begins, his voice tentative, lost, "I wonder if I've gone off the track. Judy, for example. My altruism there, my willingness to dedicate myself to her needs. Who could find fault? Yet it led me to the brink of death. And I dragged you along with us. Was that wise?"

I start to say, No, but he ruminates on.

"And the Ben Creswell thing. Not our fault, surely. Got what he deserved. Reaped what he sowed. Certified murderer himself." He pauses. "Still." He stares at the rifle.

"And this cooking show, and the publicity, the fame and everything—it's gathering momentum, I'm a boulder tumbling down a mountainside, accelerating thirty-two feet per second per second—I'm gathering no moss, but there's a quiet beauty to a moss-covered stone, isn't there? Have I lost my compass? I don't know, jocko, I don't know."

We both must have fallen asleep, because the next thing I know there's a crashing in the brush behind us, and Lyle and I jump up. We follow the crashing, Lyle carrying the rifle and I the camera. We pursue the noise down a hill, splash across a creek, and scramble up another hill, through grass unusually high and bushes aggressively thick, brambles and nettles lashing and stinging. Up ahead something silver flashes in the brush, but we can't see enough to get a shot with the rifle and we're moving too erratically to get a record with the camera, so all we can do is thrash through undergrowth and vines, tripping and panting, branches whipping my face as I follow Lyle, the glimmer of silver teasing and the grass rippling as something large and determined races through it.

And then it's gone.

We walk slowly to the last place we saw movement. Lyle holds his rifle ready, loaded with the tranquilizing dart, good for a four-hundred-pounder. I rest the camera on my shoulder. Our boots shush through the grass. My hands are bleeding and raw from the brambles and nettles.

There's a thick grove ahead. We hear something in there. Lyle gives me a look, a nod. We move slowly, carefully, as quietly as we can. We don't want to surprise the silver bear too abruptly and have him turn on us. We want to see him before he sees us.

A loud thump comes from the grove. A log dropped. Looking for grubs under the log. We push through brush, we slide between trees, we creep under foliage. We emerge into a small clearing. Lyle raises the rifle, stock to shoulder.

Two bears. Moving logs. Silver head. Black head. One swings an ax. The other, silver, bent over, stands, turns, a silver shirt, turquoise belt, white hair.

"There you are," Frank Running Bear says, as if he's been expecting us.

A SWEAT IN THE WOODS

> The bear is the supreme model—and therefore
> the guiding spirit—of the theme of renewal.
>
> —*The Sacred Paw*

"Where's the bear?" Lyle asks.

Frank and his son, Lionel Running Bear, look at each other, as if each thinks the other might have the answer. Then they look around the clearing, as if the bear might be lounging nearby but they haven't noticed. Frank says, "We come out to sweat." Lionel goes back to chopping a log.

Frank moves stiffly, and he rubs his hip frequently. He's a short, wiry man, with a brown leathery face and eyes the color of strong coffee that look straight at you and seem to find something missing there. His shirt is a frayed white dress shirt, with ruffles down the front and embroidery on the cuffs. He wears white jeans marred by grass stains, and on his feet are white hand-made moccasins, decorated with flowers fashioned from white and blue and red beads. His silver hair hangs loose down his back.

Lionel wears a Cleveland Indians baseball cap smudged with tar and grease, a blue flannel shirt, the sleeves rolled to his elbows, and jeans and Nikes. His black hair swings in a braid across his shoulders. Lionel's hands are big and callused, yet his fingers are delicate and oddly innocent. An old scar drifts across his cheek.

As Lyle and I scour the woods to gather rocks, Lyle says, "Frank's eighty-some years old. You see how he moves, with his arthritis and that broken leg that never healed right. No way was that him running that fast on all fours. Or Lionel, for that matter, with that pot belly he's put on." I load another rock, the size of a football, onto Lyle's burden.

He's holding six now, clutched against his stomach, like a woman pregnant with a heavy promise of hope. "That's enough," he says. I scoop up three more to cradle in my arms, and we tramp through the undergrowth toward the clearing. "Bear must've snuck away somehow," he goes on. But he doesn't sound convinced. He adds, "They tell stories about old Frank." We're back at the clearing, and Lyle doesn't say anymore.

Frank has planted one end of a sapling in the earth, bent it over into a semicircle, and secured the other end in the ground. He's done the same with the other saplings, forming a frame, an inverted half sphere, and he's tied the saplings where they cross with strips of red cloth. A hole, a foot and a half across and about two feet deep, has been dug in the earth in the center of the frame.

There's a pit a few feet from the frame, and we dump the rocks into the pit. We go back into the woods for more rocks, and Frank comes with us this time, moving now with a sudden suppleness, like a young man, finding stones hidden beneath brush and logs as with a second sight, and loading Lyle and me up before we know what's happening.

Back in the clearing Frank arranges the stones in the pit into some cabalistic formation, and Lionel lays the logs over the stones in regular rows, as if he were building a small log cabin, and then he tosses in some dry brush and throws in a match.

By now it's dark, so we take Lionel's flashlight and follow Frank to retrieve our packs and bring them to the clearing. Frank and Lionel cover the frame of saplings with tarps and blankets, and we open our sleeping bags and lay them over the frame, too, so it's air-tight inside.

Lyle and I sit on a downed tree, and Frank and Lionel sit on a couple of boulders. The night hangs like velvet around our homey encampment. Lionel throws some vines on the coals, and they make a white smoke that keeps the mosquitoes away. Lyle, fidgety and restless at first, calms down after awhile and accepts the evening's contingency as if he'd known it was coming all along. I'm confused, as usual, wondering what invitation passed unspoken between Frank and Lyle, what we're in for, and did we really see the silver bear flashing through the brush, but I know I heard the grass whispering and the branches breaking.

Frank rolls a cigarette and lights it with the tip of a stick he's stuck into the fire. "I should quit smoking," he says, "but I'm afraid I might live too damn long." He gives a raspy laugh. The sky above the trees seems thick somehow. There's no moon. I can't see any stars. An owl trills a wavering call. Lionel looks up. "Some people," Frank says, "think the owl is the messenger of death, so they don't like to hear the owl. Lionel's mother died the day she saw a snowy owl looking in the window at her. But the owl can bring many messages from the spirit world, not all bad."

Lionel stabs the pitchfork at the logs, spraying sparks high into the night. The white-hot logs collapse with a crash. At the bottom of the pit the rocks glow a lustrous crimson. Frank flicks his cigarette into the fire. He limps stiffly to the dark curtain surrounding the clearing. He comes back carrying a duffel bag. He squats before the sweat lodge and unzips the bag. He takes out a small cloth with a geometric design and lays it in front of the lodge. His fingers delicately smooth the cloth. He turns back to the bag and slips both hands into the gaping slit. Carefully, like a doctor removing a baby from its mother's womb, he lifts something from the bag, something chalky and craggy and toothy and luminescent in the flickering fire, something he raises above him as he stands, and then he bends, arms outstretched, and places the skull, its two empty eyeholes black and watchful, on the small rug.

The bear skull rests like an ancient sentinel in front of the sweat lodge, gazing skeptically our way. I hear Lyle suck in his breath. Is this a head Lyle recognizes, a Yorick of youthful research? Lyle told me once that the Ojibway sometimes shoot bears, although Frank maintains the old ways, Lyle said, asking the bear's forgiveness and sprinkling tobacco on the bear after he frees its soul from its furry mobile home.

Frank steps into the darkness again. He returns carrying a battered attaché case, as if he were an elderly businessman going to work. He opens the attaché case and removes a long leather bag, fringed and decorated with beads. From the bag he takes the bowl of a pipe, the bowl carved from the red catlinite from Pipestone, Minnesota, and a foot-long pipe stem fashioned from cedar and decorated with beaded deerskin and feathers. He fits the bowl onto the stem. He takes out a leather bag containing a mixture of tobacco, bark, and kinnickinick, and he fills the bowl of the pipe, tamping the mixture firm with his finger. He takes an eagle feather from the attaché case, and then he closes the case, snapping the latches shut.

Frank takes off his clothes. Lyle and I follow suit. We stand in the feeble light from the coals, the uncharted expanse of the wilderness magnifying our nakedness and advertising our vulnerability to the far reaches of the universe. Frank's haunches are thin and shrunken. Antique scars climb over his arms and chest and back.

With a coal from the fire Frank lights a braid of sweet grass. The eagle feather, in his other hand, whisks the wisp of incense across his chest and down his legs and around his head. He circles the clearing, the aroma purling around us, a soft protective spirit. He circles the sweat lodge, laying down a trail of pungent meditativeness. Then he circles each of us in turn, Lionel, Lyle, and me, the eagle feather caressing the smoke, the smudge washing our bodies. When he taps the top of my head, a pulse of white light flies down my spine. My head comes loose.

Frank crawls into the sweat lodge, pausing at the entrance to say something in Ojibway. Lyle crawls in after him, repeating the words, and I follow Lyle, hoping my mumble approximates the proper greeting.

It's low and cramped inside, with the hole in the center leaving little room for my feet. Lyle and I sit scrunched up, backs bowed, heads bent, feet tucked under our thighs. Frank seems comfortable, however, as he lights the pipe with a branch from the fire. He puffs on the pipe to get it going, then raises it to the four directions and the sky and the earth, praying in Ojibway. He passes it to Lyle, who takes a puff, and Lyle passes it to me, and I put my lips on the wood and draw the hot smoke into my mouth. We pass the pipe around, taking a puff or two, until we smoke it all. Frank passes the pipe out to Lionel, who has not taken off his clothes. Lionel hands in a large white plastic bucket full of water. He hands Frank a dipper carved from a gourd. He hands him a deer antler.

Lionel passes in the white-hot stones, balancing them on the pitchfork, some of the stones so hot they've split apart, and Frank takes the antler and nudges the stones off the tines and into the hole, the heat already warming the enclosure.

"Okay," Frank says, and Lionel pulls down the flap of blanket and tucks it in at the ground, so we see no light from the fire outside. The gourd swishes into the bucket. The rocks hiss. Frank sings, a high-pitched, wavering prayer in his old language. Steam wraps our naked bodies in a sage-scented amniotic fluid, heats us to a pin-point of consciousness. Time stretches into forgetfulness. This is our womb. This is the gestation of the possible future of our flawed and guilt-smeared lives.

Finally Frank calls out something in the old tongue, and Lionel raises the flap. I think we're done, I'm ready to get up and leave, but

Frank doesn't move, and neither does Lyle. It's only a break in the dedication, a rest to renew our fortitude, an acquiescence to human limitation while we breathe in cool air for a couple of minutes and Frank tells a few jokes.

Then Frank says something, and Lionel digs up more red-hot stones from the fire pit and forks them in, and Frank takes the antler and nudges them off the fork and into the hole, seven stones again, and Lionel lowers the flap and tucks it in.

Frank says the first round, as he calls it, was to pray for people far away. He forgot to tell us that, he says, but we can pray this round for them, whomever we might have in mind, as well as for the sick, whom Frank is praying for this second round. "Sick in mind or body," Frank adds, "or spirit." He ladles more water onto the stones and prays for another ten minutes or so. I wonder if I'm sick but don't know it, and I wonder how I'd find out, and I wonder how one prays if one doesn't believe in a god, but Frank, as if reading my thoughts, says, "I just pray to the Great Mystery," and that seems right to me.

We take another break, the cool night air a welcome benison. Frank gives us a drink of water from the gourd. The water is cool, and fresh, with a flinty taste. As Lyle is swallowing, Frank asks, a certain glint in his eyes, what sort of a bear was he looking for out here beyond his usual research territory?

Lyle gets a pained look, as if he knows he's stepping into quicksand but he's got to go this way to get to where he's headed. Lyle says, as scientifically as he can, some hikers had seen a silver-coated black bear up this way. Frank stares a moment at Lyle, as if to make sure Lyle's on the up and up, then Frank calls out, "Lionel, you seen a polar bear around?"

"Not lately," Lionel says, his eyes on the smoldering fire pit.

Frank, deadpan, shakes his head at Lyle.

Lionel shovels in more hot rocks. The rocks clink on the stones below. Lionel closes the flap. I think I hear a chuckle, but later Frank says that was the spirits whispering, because it was a hard sweat, and a good sweat, and the spirits don't always come to a sweat.

During this third round the heat is too intense to think. All I remember is that Frank says, from the darkness, "This round you could forgive anybody you might have bad feelings toward, anybody you think did something to wrong you."

The break seems brief this time, but Frank again offers us water from the pail, and we take turns drinking from the gourd. Lionel takes

William Borden

a drink, too, and I think I see a glance pass between him and Lyle, but I could be wrong, sweat dripping into my eyes and my sight bleary.

Frank says to rub our bodies with the sage that's lying around us, that'll help with the heat, and purify us, too, which is what a sweat is for, healing and cleansing, whether you think you need it or not.

Lionel passes in the rest of the rocks, most of them cracked into smaller pieces from the heat, until the hole is full, the hard heat an inch from my feet. Lionel tucks in the flap. Frank pours the remainder of the water onto the rocks.

The pitch black shovels out my squirming thoughts, the heat sears my quotidian concerns into inconsequence, Frank's pulsing wail collars my earthly troubles and tosses them away. Steam paws my tired skin. It slithers up my nostrils and crawls down my throat like a small animal.

"Now you can ask forgiveness for anything you might have done that's wrong," Frank says, "or an injury to someone, or if you killed someone, even by accident, you could ask forgiveness, and wash away trying to ignore your guilt, and let your regret come to the surface, like the grease in a stew, so it can be skimmed off."

I wonder how he knows, because I'm sure he knows. I'm sure this sweat is for us. I don't understand how or why or what the silver-coated bear has to do with it or with Ben Creswell's ugly decapitation, but suddenly I see, where Frank is sitting—are my eyes open or closed?—I see a silver bear, sitting on his haunches, his long pink tongue lolling from his jaw, his beady black eyes staring at me. I see Lyle beside me, glowing in the luminescence of the bear's fur, Lyle's eyes squeezed shut, his milky skin drenched in sweat, the sweat turning into blood, the blood dripping onto the stones, a crimson mist rising into the air.

My skin melts. My blood bubbles. I stare at my bare white bones. I cry, "I killed him!" My mouth opens but no words fall out. The top of my head lifts off. My brains jelly out, drip down the skull of my face, down the back of my neck, dribble down my spine.

The luminescent bear laughs, a rattling, sizzling guffaw. Sparks fly from his fur. The bear cries, "I killed him! I killed him!" in a growly boisterous sing-song. The bear leans across the hot rocks, he thrusts his shimmering snout in my face, and he spits a steamy breath down my throat. My lungs convulse. I can't breathe. I think the bear has killed me.

The bear's paw knocks me on the head, knocks the top of my skull back in place. Air fills my lungs. A small dark animal, like death, wriggles from between my legs and, darting this way and that, disappears, squeaking shrilly, into the night.

Or is it Frank's high-pitched wailing? The song transports my battered mind to some effortless pure space. I ride the song into oblivion. I don't know where I am. I don't know how long I stay there. My mind is burned to an ember of unknowing.

PILGRIMS' PROGRESS

Bear ritual points to integration of the
personality following a period of dissociation.

—J. L. Henderson, *The Others*

I'm scoured, rinsed, polished, and buffed. I'm bright-eyed, clear-headed, distilled and decanted. I'm tuned up.

We shake hands all around. Frank's palm, soft and paw-like, barely touches mine. Lionel's palm is rough and calloused, more a caress than a squeeze.

"Anybody got anything to eat?" Frank asks.

We eat everything we brought. Frank and Lionel eat ravenously, our three days' provisions consumed with gusto, all but the token portions Frank sets in front of the watchful bear skull, along with a pinch of tobacco.

Frank, sipping the mulligatawny soup stirred up from the packet of dried ingredients and spices, and chewing the chapati, says, "So those other Indians have stew and fry bread, too?" Frank gives the half-eaten chapati the once-over. He says, "I guess it's a good thing Columbus didn't think he was in China. What about you, Lionel? Would you rather be an Indian or a Chinese?"

Lionel favors the penne tossed with sun dried tomatoes, pine nuts, Greek olives, and parmesan, as well as the loaf of garlic-herb bread. Neither Frank nor Lionel cares for the rehydrated asparagus with Hollandaise sauce, however, so Lyle and I eat that, as well as the granola and assorted dried fruits, which Frank and Lionel also spurn.

Frank finishes off his repast with the smoked eelpout on crackers, observing that sometimes in a hard sweat like ours folks see things.

"Some say the heat makes the mind crazy and you see things that aren't there." Lyle picks at the crumbs of trail mix. Frank goes on, "Others say those things you see are spirits, and if you don't take them seriously, you run into a lot of trouble."

I contemplate the bear skull, ghostly and ruminant. I imagine it hearing and seeing everything. I can't see the offerings of food Frank set out for it. If I were not a rational being, I would think the spirit of the bear had eaten them.

Frank asks Lionel, "Lionel, you see anything out here? Anything come running and squeaking out of the sweat lodge?"

Lionel is polishing off the venison jerky and the barbecued sweet potato chips. He nods.

MORNING BREAKS

The Egyptians used the bear to symbolize the man who is born deformed but later acquires his proper shape.
—Beryl Rowland, *Animals with Human Faces: A Guide to Animal Symbolism*

Flickers of sunlight dapple the clearing. Frank and Lionel are asleep, wrapped in the blankets that covered the sweat lodge. Lyle's sleeping bag is empty. He's standing off a ways, in the trees. He's contemplating the morning, it looks like, or life, reflecting, perhaps, on the night's transcendence.

He bends his knees in a time-tested genuflection, turns, and walks towards me, zipping his pants.

Lyle and I roll up our sleeping bags. Frank and Lionel roll up the blankets. Lionel goes off with the bucket and comes back with water, which we drink and splash on our faces. Lionel stirs up the coals, throwing in small kindling and branches, while Frank produces a metal coffee pot from somewhere, fills it with water, tosses in a handful of coffee from a ziplock, and sets the pot on the fire.

We sit around sipping the peckish coffee, breathing its cantankerous aroma and savoring its woodsy integrity. Frank smokes a cigarette. When he's finished, he snubs out the butt and scatters the tobacco to the four directions.

Lionel shovels dirt onto the coals. Frank leaves the frame of the sweat lodge standing, a den to return to.

Frank picks up his attaché case in one hand and, in the other, the duffel bag, the toothy bear skull tenderly wrapped in a silk scarf and secured inside. Lionel balances the pitchfork and shovel and ax on his shoulder, gathers the blankets under an arm, and carries the bucket, which now holds the coffee pot, antler, gourd, and Frank's sweater.

Lyle asks, "You fellas hike in a long ways?"

"Not too far," Frank says.

Lionel heads off up a hill.

"We're back that way," Lyle says, thrusting his head vaguely in the opposite direction. Frank gives him an odd look, then follows Lionel through the trees.

"Maybe we'll look for that bear a little more," Lyle says half-heartedly. Frank and Lionel keep going, their legs shushing through the grass.

"Shit," Lyle mumbles, starting after them. "Come on," he tells me, "maybe they'll give us a ride to where we left the truck."

"What about the bear?" I ask.

"There's no fucking bear." Lyle plunges up the hill, his long legs pumping. I can't tell if he's angry or relieved.

It's about a half mile to the service road. A battered van, rust-splotched and dented, sits in the road, a patina of dust covering it. An eagle feather hangs from the rearview mirror. Bumper stickers announce OFFICIAL INDIAN CAR and FRY BREAD POWER and FREE LEONARD PELTIER. In front of the van, as if magically materialized, sits Lyle's official Division of Forestry pickup.

Did Frank transport it? Telekinesis? Or drive it here? To play a trick? Or help us out?

Lyle stares at the pickup. Frank and Lionel load their gear into their van. Lyle looks around: trees, road, sky. "Shit," he mumbles, tossing his pack and bedroll into the back of the truck, "we've been going in circles."

"The thing about going in circles," Frank says, "is you always know where you're going."

FRANK RUNNING BEAR'S GOURMET CURRIED WILD RICE FRY BREAD

Frank whipped up this recipe after I introduced him to the chapatti, which spurred his interest in possible historical, spiritual, and culinary resonances between the two cultures irredeemably confused by that Italian in the employ of Spain who was rumored to be a Jew and thought he was sailing to Japan. Frank wondered if those pilgrims crossing the antediluvian land bridge might have been not Mongols but long-striding folks from the Punjab, and that coded in their DNA helix was a hankering for fried dough, call it fry bread or chapatti or whatever. So Frank came up with a few innovations, his attempt, I guess, to bridge the two cultures and reunite long-separated kin.

2 cups flour
1 tsp baking powder
1/2 tsp baking soda
3/4 tsp salt
1 cup cooked wild rice
1 cup buttermilk
1/4 cup sautéed chopped onion
1 tsp oregano
1/4 tsp marjoram
2-4 tsp curry, sautéed in ghee
oil for frying

Mix together everything but the oil. Shape the dough into a ball. Pull apart a handful, flatten on a floured board, drop the bread into hot oil, fry quickly until golden.

LYLE'S WIFE WANTS TO FORGET

Saskatoon, which the original teetotaler
settlers were going to call Utopia,
which means Nowhere

Dear Lyle,

I haven't written for some time because I'm trying to forget you. I
hope you understand.

I bought Mother a CD player and headphones, so she won't dis-
turb the other denizens of Marigold Manor, and *The Complete Polkas of
Lawrence Welk*, which I hoped would help her get her bearings in this
strange and fluctuating world we live in, but she said she was listening
to one of the aides' CDs, a young woman with lavender hair wearing a
gold ring in her right eyebrow and four in each ear, and Mother wants
me to buy her a CD by some group called "The Monks," which may
signal a surprising interest in monasticism on Mother's part.

Prudence—that's the young aide's name—seems quite attentive to
the old people, although I don't think she eats enough, and I don't
think her jade green nail polish goes with her lavender hair. Mother
says Prudence showed her her tattoo—Prudence's, not Mother's—but
Mother must be imagining things again, because she said it was a tattoo of Jesus and it was on Prudence's fanny. Mother said it showed that
Prudence was religious, no matter what the nuns think.

Sometimes I wonder if those stories about aliens taking over our
bodies aren't true, and if that wouldn't explain girls like Prudence
more effectively than the socio-psychological theories we hear on television or read in the pseudo-intellectual magazines.

Maybe an alien has entered Mother's body and mind and is simply
confused.

You said you saw a UFO once when you were out in the woods,

that it hovered over you, then zipped away, and you were disappointed. You said it seemed as if they were looking you over but decided you weren't a very good specimen and went on their way, and it put you in the dumps for weeks. You thought the UFOs carried researchers from other planets who were tagging and studying humans the way we were tagging and studying bears and wolves. Maybe an alien presence did enter your body that day, Lyle. Maybe that accounts for your behavior, which is alien to me.

Which would punish you more, my writing you every day, hoping to whip you into a storm of guilt, or not writing you ever again, forcing you by my absence to remember me?

The wife from Arcturus

DIANE MAKES A DISCOVERY

Send word, bear father
Send word, bear father
I'm having a hard time
Send word, bear father
I'm having a bad time
—Lakota

"Whose the hell are these?" Diane asks, holding up Judy's fire-engine-red bikini panties with ruffles.

"Oh, shit," I say, before I can think of anything else to say.

Diane's back from her entrepreneurial jaunts, criss-crossing the country to line up various projects. The next six *Cooking with Lyle* segments have been okayed, to be sponsored by a natural foods outlet. A blender company wants Lyle to host an infomercial showing exotic back-woods gourmet uses for their blender, even though I've never seen Lyle use a blender. And where in the woods would you plug in the blender, anyway? And a new syndicated television news magazine called *The Beautiful and the Bizarre* wants to do a segment on the rescue of the Amazons, featuring Lyle as the rescuer of "the newest pretty face to run for national political office."

Diane stretches the panties out before her, the tips of her thumbs and forefingers pinching the panties at the elastic, as if the panties were contagious, or dangerous, or hot from the oven. I'm wondering if Judy has any panties left, if leaving her panties is a kind of marking behavior on her part, like a bear rubbing the bark off a tree or a wolf peeing on the boundaries of her territory, because I also found, but did not tell Lyle I had found, blue bikini panties, blue the hue of a Minnesota lake on a sunny spring day, in the wine cellar, not to mention the paisley thong panties in the sauna, the sienna bikinis with maroon lace under the rag rug in the living room, or the silver French-cut briefs Bud Ostrum unaccountably found in the mail box by the road and quietly returned to me with a postage due stamp affixed to them.

I'm standing in the doorway to Lyle's bedroom. Diane's standing by the bed. She was getting ready to put the Ralph Lauren sheets with a Fauve motif on the king-size mattress, having pulled off the "Call of the Wild" sheets emblazoned with howling wolves, snarling cougars, and charging grizzlies. She always changes the sheets when she returns from a trip. I'm not sure why. It may be a nesting thing. I know that shortly after she brought a significant portion of her clothes here she also brought three sets of newly purchased sheets and pillow cases and refuses to sleep on any of the sheets Lyle slept on with his wife.

Lyle is on his way to Nymore, a crossroads not far from the source of the Mississippi River, where the Division of Forestry is planning to shoot a mother black bear—and her three cubs, if necessary. The ten or twelve people who live in the metropolis of Nymore say the bears are terrorizing them and their children. In reality, the bears are only looking for a few square meals a day, and they're nosing around Nymore sniffing for Swedish meatballs and apple pie only because the berry crop down that way is as meager as it is up here. She's not one of Lyle's bears, since the Nymore territory is beyond Lyle's domain, but he hopes to save her and the cubs nevertheless—save them from the usual hysteria that is rampant among the confused and uninformed.

"Children are playing with the cubs," local parents complain.

"If that's a problem," Lyle says, climbing into the pickup, "why don't they shoot the children?" and he roars off minutes before Diane pulls wearily into the driveway.

"They were tucked under the mattress, as if for me to find." She gives the crimson tattletale a once-over. "A chunky gal." Her voice is shaking a little as she tries to stay calm. It's as if a gal knew that some day if she stayed away too long a pet was going to make a mess in the house, but she didn't think this would be the day.

Diane looks at me. She expects an answer. I am her eyes and ears when she is gone. I tell her how Lyle is eating and if he's drinking too much and if he's out with his bears because if he is she knows he's happy even if he isn't at home to take her call. She's jet-lagged and hasn't had a lot of sleep. It's a warm day, and she's wearing shorts and sandals and a denim shirt with the ends tied under her breasts and, so far as I can make out, no bra. Her honey hair is tied carelessly in a pony tail. I'm wearing shorts and a tee shirt.

"I'm sorry," I finally say.

The silence seems to wander about the room, resting, finally, on the scarlet silky talisman she holds before me.

"I shouldn't have used yours and Lyle's bed."

The silence bounces on the panties.

"It's not my bed," she says briskly, regret and impatience in her voice—regret and impatience with my presumed imprudent venery or with the fact that it's not legally her bed?

I take the panties. They're satiny and smooth and strangely warm in my hand. "Lyle was gone—." I grin awkwardly. She wipes the tips of her fingers on her shorts. "I met this—well, spur of the moment—my cot out in the shed is so narrow—yes, chunky, but—"

"Spare me the details."

"One of those things—"

"I just don't like finding strange underwear in my—our—Lyle's—bed."

"Of course not."

"I'm sure you can understand that." Her voice is still trembling, and she's standing stiffly as if called to attention before she could get her balance.

I find myself squeezing the panties, rubbing them between my palms. They feel electric, as if there were a tiny nuclear core in the crotch. I wipe the sweat from my face with the panties. A malapert pungency tickles my nostrils. I inhale the impudent elixir. "I can," I manage to say, the aroma scrambling my cognitive faculties, "understand perfectly how you feel."

Diane's face sags, the tautness around her eyes released, the strictus pressing her lips unstrung. "I don't know where I am," she says. "The last three airports I had to look at my ticket to find out what city I was in."

Tears moisten her eyes. "I never get enough sleep. I try to make a great career for Lyle, I dedicate myself to him—to you, too, by the way—I insist that you write any scripts, which always puts a big fat load of cement in my deals because nobody's heard of you, but I stick by you as long as I can and if I sacrifice you to make the deal at the end, you have to understand it's either you or Lyle, and I know you're dedicated to Lyle just as I am—not exactly the same, of course—and when I finally get back—fourteen hours in the air, delays from weather, mechanical difficulties, reroutings, Minneapolis airport at three in the morning,

William Borden

everything closed, and a ten-hour drive up here—I finally get back, I can't wait to see Lyle, I even look forward to seeing you—you're gone, Lyle's gone, the two of you off god knows where looking for a fucking polar bear—"

"Silver-coated black bear."

"And her fucking clothes are still in the closet!"

She sits on the bare mattress and sobs into her hands.

I sit beside her.

The sheets, old and new, are crumpled around us.

She bawls.

I put my arm around her.

Her head falls onto my chest. I put my other arm around her. She lets her anguish burble out. Her heavy spasms of uncertainty rock against my sternum. Her breasts, not hefty like Judy's but pert and pliant, peep from the unbuttoned V of her shirt. Tears wet my shirt, a blue tee shirt with a picture of Rudy on the front.

Without thinking I brush her honey hair from her damp forehead. I smell the faint mossiness of her unwashed hair. I stroke her temple. I feel her pulse throb beneath my fingertips. I notice the dark roots of her golden hair. I caress her wet cheek, soft and delicate, and feel her hot breath in the palm of my hand. Her bare knees are pressed against my bare knees. My hand on her shoulder squeezes Judy's red panties, and I wish I could squeeze the red panties so that when I open my hand a bright red dove would flutter into the air, and its scarlet wings would carry it gaily out the open window and into the clear blue sky.

Diane's sobbing collapses into a few rattling sniffles. "I could never cry like this in front of Lyle," she murmurs into my chest. "He needs to think of me as strong and capable." She rubs her nose against my shirt. "He expects so much of people, himself included." We look down at the arc of mucous above Rudy's head. "Oh my," she says sadly, "what was I thinking?" She pats my chest. "I'm sorry."

"No problem."

Wrong thing to say, maybe, because she absently fingers the hem of my tee shirt and then pulls the fabric to her nose and gives a good honk. "Oh dear," she sighs, "what's wrong with me? I'm using you as a big old handkerchief."

"It's okay." I grab the shirt where she's clutching it so as not to lose anything and pull the shirt over my head. I wad up the shirt, no longer wondering why so often I feel like a handy rag for anyone to use to wipe up their mess.

Diane stares at my naked belly. She threads her fingers through the hair on my chest. "You're hairier than Lyle," she muses.

Her red, wet eyes have trouble finding mine. "You've let your beard grow, haven't you?" She pats my chest again. "I lost my contacts," she says, "and without my glasses, with my eyes all teary and swollen, you look like Lyle."

LYLE'S WIFE WRITES AGAIN ANYWAY

Here

Lyle—

Once I resolved not to think about you anymore, you kept appearing before me like a ghost in a bad movie. Like yesterday when I saw a man downtown with a loping gait like yours and a beard. I opened my mouth to yell, "Lyle!" but then he joined a group of Mennonites, other men with beards and women in nineteenth century frontier smocks and little caps on their tightly bunned hair, and for a second there I wondered if you had a secret life as a Mennonite, but I knew a religious life isn't for you, unless it's the kind Rabelais describes at his Abbey of Thélème where you do whatever you damn please, which sums up your religion in a nutshell.

Or the knock at the door, which I thought insanely was you but it was only a kid selling subscriptions to magazines to buy uniforms for the school band, and now what am I going to do with subscriptions to *American Survival Guide, Au Naturel, Love and Rage: A Revolutionary Anarchist Newspaper,* and *Threads?*

Maybe I'm going nuts, like Mother—who, by the way, is now first chair in the spoon-and-saucepan section of the All-City Kitchen Band, a cooperative venture sponsored by Marigold Manor, The Ukrainian Home for Retired Ladies, and The Vivaldi Society. Prudence, who now has green hair and black fingernails and, I think—it's difficult to keep count—two more rings in her ears, talked Mother into it, which is good, because it gets Mother out under supervised conditions. I go to the concerts, but it's not easy, listening to a tinny "Jingle Bells" in summer, or Beethoven's "Ode to Joy" transfigured by the enthusiasm of the solo accordionist who was once known far and wide as the Polka King of Moose Jaw.

Remember those cassettes of romantic music I bought in the dreary winter when I thought I was missing you, lifetimes ago? They were reminding me of love gone bad and making me want to listen to Country-Western songs, which is a really scary impulse, like thinking about cleaning the oven or buying a prepaid funeral or should I get a pair of sensible walking shoes. So I gave the cassettes to Prudence, hoping the music from a more innocent time might dilute the hopelessness that seems so integral to her generation. On the other hand—I thought as I placed them in her small palm with its tattoo of the eye of Horus—maybe Johnny Ray and Patti Page would only intensify her free-floating fin-de-siècle fatalism, the contrast between a doggie in the window and today's deafening nihilism a source of terror and absolute despair. We never know, do we, the consequences of our actions? Help a blind lady across the street and you only put her in the way of a drive-by shooting she would have avoided if she had stayed a second longer on the curb.

Prudence showed me her tattoo of Jesus. She said her boy friend posed for it. She said her boy friend is actually very religious and plans to become a priest when he's old and not interested in sex anymore, which makes a lot of sense, when you think about it, and might solve the Church's celibacy problems.

Going to Mother's concerts reminds me of our family concerts, when the five of us sat around and jammed, you on your viola, Babette on her clarinet, Bjorn beating his drum, and Bernadette trilling so beautifully on her flute. Those were good times, weren't they?

I have to talk to Prudence, however, because she's encouraging Mother to get a ring in her nose, Mother who never even pierced her ears because she thought only waitresses and prostitutes had pierced ears.

But then I think, Why not? And, Who cares?

And then I wonder if I'm losing all moral orientation, if I've wandered completely off the map of common sense, or if I'm awash in relativism and drowning in the tidal wave of pre-millennial chaos.

Anyway, this time I mean it. I'm not writing anymore. Not until I hear something definite from you. Tell me you want me back. Tell me you never want to see me. Tell me you'd like to see me in five years. Tell me something.

But why, my friends in my group ask, when I read them this letter so far, are you giving Lyle all the power?

Good question, I say to my group.

Do *you* want to go back to Lyle? they ask.

Yes, of course, I say, because why else have I been thinking about the son of a bitch all this time?

But when I imagined going back to the lodge, my stomach twisted into a slipknot of panic. If I went back, what would I find? Strange clothes in my closet? Another perfume bottle on my dresser? Slippers not my size tossed familiarly beside our king-size bed?

When we were together, I felt that I was your conscience. Like any conscience, I was not always paid attention to. But I was there, Jiminy Cricket on your shoulder. But I never stopped you from doing what you wanted because I've always believed in freedom and self-actualization—whereas you, Lyle, are more on the path of Nietzsche (go for it, who cares who it hurts), Schopenhauer (the will is what counts, screw everyone else), and William James (if it works, use it).

Most people think philosophy has nothing to do with everyday life. Most people think that for everyday troubles you need practical people, like Ann Landers, Miss Manners, and the psychic hot line. But I've been thinking about these things since I've been taking this course at the U of Sask, which, even though it's mainly an ag school, pays attention to the liberal arts as well, because even a farmer or rancher needs to know right from wrong and whether the Good is teleological or instrumental.

My father amused himself in the winter reading Epictetus, Marcus Aurelius, and Lucretius. He said he wanted to understand what a Stoic really was, because it seemed as good a way as any to cope with drought, flood, grasshoppers, and loan officers. But to me the Stoics are hard, flinty men, who grin and bear it and don't kick up their heels enough.

Not that Epicurus is the answer. Oh, I'm not against eating, drinking, and being merry. In fact, I could use a little more of each these days and nights. And anyway Epicurus has been misinterpreted as nothing but a good-time Charley, whereas he was actually quite circumspect in many ways. And his student, Lucretius, although an atheist and a true scientist who postulated atoms two millennia before we had any proof, ascribed the movement of things—stars, atoms, groundhogs, my heart—to love. To Venus, goddess of love. It was a strange thing for an atheist to do, but it shows a certain insight, don't you think? Spinoza, on the other hand—but I don't think you're interested in this, I merely wanted to ask, Now that I'm not there, who is your conscience?

Contemplatively yours

Dancing with Bears

HERE COMES THE SHERIFF

> I tell you nothing is permanent in all the world.
>
> —Ovid

I leave Diane to wipe her eyes and blow her nose on her Ralph Lauren sheets. I saunter into the late afternoon doldrum, surprised that there aren't any nuisance bear alarms hanging fire but grateful for the lull in my responsibilities. A sheriff's car slides silently into view, rolls up the driveway, and pulls to an ominously gentle stop, its front bumper sniffing my knees.

Sheriff Irv Nyquist eases his robust frame from the car, tugs his heavy belt, with its pistol and handcuffs and other devices of law enforcement, up around his stomach, then releases the belt to let gravity again exert its ineluctable pull. He's bareheaded, his gray wisps combed sideways in hopeful but useless camouflage of his pink baldness.

My heart beats faster. In some mad flight from reality I had believed that Ben Creswell's body would never be discovered, that any memory of him would vanish from the earth, even as I failed to erase it from the unscheduled movies of my mind. When he was found, his death ruled self-inflicted and blamed on post-traumatic stress syndrome and the unrelieved despair of a long cold winter, I breathed easier.

Irv asked Lyle if Lyle, as a kind of token of forgiveness, would say something at the memorial service, but Lyle declined. Lyle told Irv he wasn't sure he had forgiven Ben, even though Ben was nothing now but tooth-notched bones. Lyle told Irv he didn't want to be a hypocrite.

We debated going to the service, finally settling on a rationale of paying our respects to another human being, never mind that everyone knew he was Lyle's nemesis. But then, just as we were dressed in our clean clothes and ready to step into the pickup, Lyle admitted that he was afraid that at some especially poignant moment, some oration from a one-legged vet praising Ben's sacrifices to keep us free and capitalist, Lyle, in an inexplicable paroxysm of patriotism and guilt, would yell out a confession.

So we didn't go.

I heard later, from Joe Manello, the veterinarian, who was there, only a few fellows remarked at Lyle's absence, as they were drinking to Ben's memory at the Blue Ox Bar and wondering if Lyle hadn't put those bears up to eating Ben, and somebody else saying, A fella should put one of those collars on Irv Nyquist's wife, Eunice, so he'd know whose bed she was in. That was before word had gotten around that Eunice had left Irv for good, after she had promised him she'd go stay with her sister in St. Cloud and join the sexual addiction treatment program there but instead kept driving all the way to Key West where she took up with Irv's brother, Richie, whom she'd always loved and finally could live with, on his fishing boat, now that his wife was dead, having fallen overboard during a storm, a tragic victim of the unpredictability of the high seas.

Irv saunters up to me, breathing stale coffee and breath mints in my face. His law enforcement training has eliminated any need for personal space, so he gets real close to a fellow, an inch or two away, which can be intimidating. I take a step back.

"Lyle here?" Irv asks. I tell him about the bear emergency in Nymore. Irv shakes his head fondly. "Lyle loves those bears, don't he?" he says. Irv rests a hand on the holster of his pistol. He says, in a thoughtful, lazy tone, "You know, there's something about the Creswell thing that's been bothering me."

I wonder if there's room on Richie Nyquist's fishing boat for one more, if Richie would ferry me to Guyana or Cuba. But I take the initiative. I ask, with a Sherlock Holmesian musing, "You mean finding the body outside the cabin?"

"No," Irv says, "it's clear the bears dragged the body out. We even found an arm—the arm bones, anyway—a hundred feet off in the woods. No, those bears had a banquet on old Ben, that's for sure. It's as if they knew who he was and what he'd done to their kin all those years, and they were as unrepentant as the Donner Party folks. No, what's been puzzling me—"

"Why he'd take his own life just as he was about to check-mate the chess master he was corresponding with?"

"I considered that, but I figured, once he knew he had check-mated him, he'd finished the game. No, what I couldn't figure out was, why would he poach a hibernating bear, a bear with not much meat on her bones?"

"He was hungry?" I suggest.

Irv gives his head a small shake. He fingers the handcuffs snapped to his wide black belt. "He had half a moose hanging out in his meat house, a deer, rabbits, smoked venison. He had plenty to eat."

Irv clicks his false teeth, a mannerism he has when he's getting ready to spring a trap or tell a punch line. "I've been monitoring his mail, of course. Not much comes anymore. Out of courtesy we sent a notice of his passing to the chess magazines and the chess partners. But a few days ago he received a letter from San Francisco, from an herbalist in Chinatown. The fellow was wondering why the promised shipment was so late."

Irv clicks his teeth, hitches up his belt, and narrows his eyes. He says, "Ben was shooting those bears for their innards, the liver and heart and kidneys and balls and so on, that the Chinks use in their medicines and aphrodisiacs." Irv lines his belt buckle up with his shirt button. "I let the feds know, and they broke up a ring that stretched all the way to Hong Kong." Irv smoothes his hair over his bald spot. "They gave me a commendation."

"Congratulations."

"Nothing I can brag about, line of duty and all that."

"You cracked that case wide open."

"I'm thinking it might be something they could portray on one of those TV shows, don't you know, *Unsolved Mysteries* or *Crime Stoppers.* What do you think?"

"It's a solved mystery."

"Well, they do those, too, don't they?"

"It might be just the thing for *Sixty Minutes*. Morley Safer, wearing a flannel shirt and hiking boots, following you around Ben's cabin as you describe the crime."

"I was hoping for Lesley Stahl."

"She's pretty."

"I've been lonely."

"Life's hard," I agree.

Irv clicks his teeth again, something he does also when he's too sad to think of anything to say. But then he comes back to the present. "There was still one question, though. *Why* did he trade in bear organs? He didn't need the money. He lived cheaply, and his veteran's checks covered his necessities." Irv chews his lip thoughtfully. He eases his belt off one hip, scratches, lets the belt slide back. He looks around the yard—lodge, woodpile, sauna, storehouse, gas tank, the two snowmobiles covered with tarps, the garden with its flowers flourishing, the luxuriant forest surrounding everything. He pushes his bifocals up his nose with his thumb. He sighs through pursed lips, a raspy heave fraught with professional suspicion. "I still have a mystery to solve." He eyes me, waiting for me to suggest a wrong answer so he can show he's smarter than I am.

"Salting away a nest egg?" I speculate.

"No sign of a savings account, mutual funds, or IRA."

"An adherence to Chinese medicine after his experiences in the Far East?"

"No sign of that as a hobby."

Irv jingles the keys on his belt.

"Ben wasn't all bad," I muse.

"None of us is perfect." He hitches up his belt. He moseys to his car. He starts to get in, then pauses. He looks shyly across the top of the door. "Say. You write things for Lyle, for his TV appearances and things, don't you?"

"I scribble a few lines."

"I hear you might write a movie about Lyle."

"We've had some inquiries."

"But you've got some contacts, you and the gal Lyle's shacked up with now, don't you?" I nod. "Well, I was wondering, if you was to write up something, you know, about me cracking this case. Don't you think that would make a movie? Or would it be a TV thing? And I was wondering, too, if it might be a human interest thing for a talk show, maybe Maury or Sally Jessie or Geraldo—Geraldo likes that grisly stuff—and the talk show would churn up interest in a movie. Isn't that how it works? Or would that cheapen it? Should I hold out for *Dateline*? What do you think?"

DIANE: SHE PUTS HER HOUSE IN ORDER

 Relationships are easier with animals than with men.
—Franz Kafka

Lyle thinks I didn't hear his pickup rattle in at two-thirty in the morning, or hear him bang on the writer's shed, or watch them from the dark kitchen window parade naked to the sauna for some male bonding bullshit, like the damn writer is more of a companion to him now than I am. I woke up on the bare mattress, the sheets pulled over me by the writer after I blew my nose on his shirt.

Now Lyle comes sneaking in, and I switch on the lamp. I know I'll say things I'll wish I hadn't said, but I can't help myself. I rant on about how I've knocked myself out for him and he can't even bother to be here when I get home, and we need some privacy—does the writer have to hang around all the time, doesn't the writer have a life, a home, a family, of his own?

I glare at the starry ceiling, which I hate.

Lyle says he'll get the writer a room at Ralph's Motel or Fanny Ostrum's Hide-a-Bed.

I say, Never mind, I'm just frazzled from my traveling.

No, no, Lyle says, we could use some privacy.

I say I had hoped we might enjoy a little privacy tonight.

He says, Well, we've gotten a little out of synch recently, with you gone so much.

I tell him I'm gone so much because I'm making his fame and fortune, does he think I enjoy those narrow airplane seats and long rental car lines?

He says it's not his fault there wasn't enough rain and there are no berries and the bears are starving.

I ask him why the hell he painted stars on the ceiling, who wants to sleep in a god damn planetarium?

He says he has enough hysterical women to put up with when he picks up the bears without having one at home.

I don't say what I suddenly realize, that I'm mad at the writer because I opened up to him, never mind smearing my snot all over his shirt. Who bangs some fat chippy in my bed while I'm gone.

Lyle asks me if I'm premenstrual.

I grab the nearest thing and throw it at him. It's the ceramic image of a bear the Tibetan monks gave him, which he cherishes and says is a thousand years old and was blessed by the Dalai Lama.

I start crying.

Lyle looks at the shards around his feet.

I blubber that I'm sorry.

He gathers the shards in his hands.

I sit on the braided rug with its bright colors, and I weep.

Lyle says by the time he got to Nymore they'd already shot the mother bear and one cub. The children were gathered around the carcasses crying.

BORDERS

You can't run away forever
But there's nothing wrong with
getting a good head start
                                    —Meatloaf

When I was a kid, our dentist was Dr. Borders. His office was around the corner from our house. Next to Dr. Borders' office, with its reassuring odor of antiseptic, was Dan Anderson's Grocery where, at the cash register, Dan kept the charge slips for a few dozen neighbors; the slips were clipped into green metal drawers, and everybody paid at the end of the month. There was a drug store at the corner, where I sipped chocolate ice cream sodas at the fountain and read comic books with benign stories—Captain Marvel, Superman, Wonder Woman.

I found Wonder Woman enticing in indescribable ways, her proud bust and bare legs evoking stirrings in my preadolescent imagination I could not articulate. It was an age of innocence, of shooting Japs and Nazis from my front porch airplane, of Arthur Godfrey playing his ukulele every morning and of Guy Lombardo playing "Auld Lang Syne" on New Year's Eve. There were no gangs, no rock and roll, no drugs. I had never heard of rape, masturbation, or homosexuality.

Years later, one summer when I was home from college and I had heard of all of those things, I went to Dr. Borders again, although we no longer lived in that neighborhood, and Dan Anderson's Grocery with its easy credit was now a run-down antique store and the drug store was boarded up. I went to get my teeth cleaned. Dr. Borders, by now past retirement age but too restless to retire although his hands trembled, had a new dental hygienist, a sturdy young woman about my age in a starched white uniform whose full breasts pressed against my

William Borden

pounding chest as she scraped and polished my incisors, bicuspids, and molars.

We dated all summer. I became more familiar with those breasts, although with nothing else. I didn't think about Wonder Woman at the time, but now, in retrospect, I can see that she was like Wonder Woman, and that perhaps I have been looking all my life for that bare-shouldered, high-booted, high-flying amazon.

I'm thinking of all this as I approach the border. It's a desolate, lonely, half-hearted border station, on the left a small white-painted wooden structure flying an American flag and, a hundred feet further, on the right, another white-painted wooden structure flying the maple leaf. The two-lane road is empty. The border station closes at midnight. It's evening. I pull up under the wooden canopy in front of the station on the right. After a minute or so—is the wait a test to make contra-band-runners nervous, or is the customs inspector merely a Type B per-sonality?—the Canadian guard saunters out of the station, little more than a shack, with a unisex privy outside, and leans his elbows on my window ledge. He asks where I'm going, and I tell him. He steps back and eyeballs the pickup and the Division of Forestry logo on the door. "Official business?" he asks suspiciously.

I give the rolled bill of my D of F cap a tug. "It's a new partner-ship," I say. "Cooperative wildlife management." He tips his official cap, rather like a policeman's cap but not as threatening, as he scratch-es his head. I can tell he's trying to decide whether to relieve his bore-dom by making something of this or to simply go back to his television inside and save himself from a bureaucratic labyrinth he might not be able to find his way out of. "NAFTA," I explain.

An incipient glimmer appears in his eyes—of understanding? Or resentment? What does NAFTA mean to him? Yankee imperialism? More traffic at his kiosk by the lonely highway? (To energize his day, make his existence more meaningful? Or keep him from his soaps on the telly?) "North American Free Trade Agreement," I add impulsive-ly, wishing I hadn't, because now he'll think I think he's dumb, and there's nothing worse than an official who wants to show you that although he may not be smarter than you he can screw up your life without even working up a sweat.

He adjusts his cap, which has a white cloth top and a black plastic bill. "What's your take on NAFTA?" I ask quickly. "More work? The politicians never ask the little guy, do they? Well, I suppose it'll be good for some, bad for others. I'm not sure what will happen with this wildlife deal. We're only testing the waters right now."

He's a young fellow, trying to grow a mustache. I wonder if his life might not be an enviable one, solitary, independent, unfettered by supervision, a job for a writer, maybe. I wonder if he and the American guard ever amble toward each other and stand, one foot apart, each on his own side of the invisible line that divides their countries, their allegiances, their lives, and talk—show one another family photos, eye the sky for weather, tell jokes ("Did you hear the one about the Canadian...?" "Did you hear about the American who...?"). Somehow I don't think they do, and I think that's a shame.

"You have some official papers?" he asks. "To authorize taking the truck across the border?"

"Oh, sure," I say, too quickly, adding stupidly, "you bet," popping Pandora's glove compartment, everything vomiting forth—maps (torn, badly folded), tissue, flashlight, plastic spoon, condom (Lyle's? Judy's? Diane's?) in its foil wrapper, pencil with no point, screwdriver, padlock, a brightly-colored rag—no, by golly, another pair of Judy's panties, orange, bright as a Florida sunrise—more maps, a bear collar—I show him the bear collar as a token of my authenticity, but he doesn't seem impressed, so I dig further—a pen, one work glove with teeth marks, a breath freshener, a tampon (super absorbent), scraps of paper with cryptic notes written on them (some mine, some Lyle's), a pair of sunglasses missing one green lens, a rolled cigarette—no, good god, a joint!—which I slip casually beneath the disordered pile on the seat—just as the guard straightens himself, getting in that mode of Thorough Search Never Mind the Program on the Telly, when I exclaim, "Hell, what am I thinking?" and pull out the envelope I have folded in my shirt pocket and show him the return address, official print job, canceled Canadian stamp. I raise the flap on the envelope. "This is the agenda, protocols, meetings, seminars, what-have-you," I say, bored as can be, implying he would be bored looking at it. "The boss said, take the truck, it's easier, because if I took my own car they'd have to reimburse me, mileage and everything, and those funds are long gone, even though the year's only half over—well, the fiscal year just started, but the legislature cut everything, we don't know what the hell we're going to do, but international cooperation is a top priority come hell or high water—"

He gives me a wave of his hand. "Go on," he says, and heads back to the little guardhouse.

LYLE'S WIFE HAS A VISITOR

Where Saskatoonberry pancakes
make a scrumptious breakfast

Dear Lyle,

I opened the door, and I said to myself, Oh, Lyle's trimmed his beard, and he's come all this way to show me and maybe make love to me—these spontaneous warm thoughts surprising me, considering my recent ultimatum to you. Then, as I stood in the doorway looking at a man who might be you, the eyes seemed sad, and not so blue. It was evening, when the light seems to retreat from objects, as if it's being pulled away by some invisible languor, and faces lose their edges.

No, I reasoned, not Lyle, someone lost, or a man selling something—Tupperware, vacuums, salvation. But he looked at me as if he had come in answer to an ad I'd put in the paper, as if I were the one wanting something.

Finally I said, "Yes?" the way you ask someone politely to get on with it, state your business, quit wasting my time. He stared some more, his lips spreading into a grin that edged close to idiocy. I thought, I've got a crazy man on my front step, a dolt, a pervert, can I get the door shut fast and call the police—when he says my name. He says it like we're old buddies.

Did you give him my address?

He brought vegetables from my garden, which he said he was trying to rescue from chaos and neglect, no thanks to you, but things had gotten away from him recently, although he salvaged what he could because he thought I might like a little green reminder of home, which was very thoughtful, I thought.

And flowers from the garden, carnations with their fragrance of reckless cinnamon, amorous thorny roses, insouciant daisies, and stargazer lilies, aristocratic and imperious, which he kept in a cooler, freshened by ice he'd buy every few hundred miles, or as we say here in Canada, kilometers.

He showed me clippings about Ben Creswell's demise and digestion, as well as the article in *Soldier of Fortune* by a Guillaume Vicaire, *petitfils*. If Ben had received such recognition while alive, he might not have grown so despondent only a few miles from us. If only he could have held on a little longer.

That's the way I feel: if only I can hold on a little longer. I don't mean to life, our time here is short enough. I mean, hold on to hope, to expectations ground to dust by the inexorable Future that steamrolls blindly toward us. Or to the past—well, holding on to the past is like walking toward somebody in a dream but your feet are sinking in a quagmire of indifference.

He says he's working on this book, about bears and everything, and I wondered, am I Everything?

Since Mother isn't here anymore, I told him he could sleep in her room while he does his research.

Your, as always, dutiful wife

P.S. I ask him what he's published, but he's evasive, mumbling something about an early novel that went nowhere and complaining about the vagaries of free-lancing. I say a free-lancer is a knight who is no longer in the employ of his prince. I remember later that they also have a knack for rescuing maidens.

HOW BEARS COME CLEAN

If the guest is wanted, fling the door open.
—*Old Kalevala*

Can I wash my dirty clothes? I ask. I'll do it, she says, taking the bundle out of my arms. I protest, but by the time I catch her she's in the small utility room at the back of the house, pulling the clothes apart from the tangle into which I'd twisted them. I'm embarrassed, watching her handle my socks, stiff from dried sweat, and my undershirts, never mind the shirts rank under the arms. She holds up a shirt. I wonder if it's the one I dribbled gravy on in Dauphin, where the A&W advertised "POUTINE AND ROOT BEER SHAKE" and poutine turned out to be french fries and cheese curds smothered in heavy brown gravy. She presses her face into the sleeve, the collar, the armpit.

"I haven't smelled a man for so long," is all she says. She pushes the shirt under the billowing suds. Suddenly she seems frail. I want to put my arms around her. But she keeps a reserve about her, like a thin glass shell that she's not even aware is there but which I'm afraid to touch for fear it will shatter and expose her to some hurt she knows is waiting nearby.

Later, at supper, she says, "We forget to smell. Smell is our oldest sense. The olfactory nerves in the nose plug directly into the brain. We're not as good at smelling as we used to be, a million years ago. Nevertheless..." I wait a moment. "Nevertheless, we can follow a trail sometimes, if we concentrate. I followed a bear once by her smell."

Still later: "Rudy slept on an old sweater of mine when he was a cub. One day I washed the sweater, it had gotten so grungy. When I gave it back to him, he was really upset. It wasn't his any more. And it wasn't mine, either, so far as he was concerned. It was Tide's. Finally I took off the shirt I was wearing and gave it to him. He sniffed it, like I did yours a while ago. He smelled me. He was happy."

I'm drying the dishes. She prepared no-nonsense down-home macaroni and cheese, muscular with sharp cheddar and thickened with flour and milk, reminding me of the honest midwestern fare of my youth. I sliced the zucchini I had rescued from her garden and fried the stalwart discs in olive oil rambunctious with garlic. We had a lettuce salad with radishes, carrots, and cucumber, all salvaged from her garden. And we imbibed the insolent but beguiling Chardonnay from Washington I had stowed, along with a few other volunteers from Lyle's cellar.

She says, "Lyle wanted me to nurse Rudy. He thought it would be, I don't know, mythic or some damn thing. He'd read that a woman could start producing milk by taking a hormone and stimulating her breast. He'd even gotten the pills from Joe Manello, the veterinarian." She hands me a plate, off-white with little red berries decorating it, to dry. "When we made love, Lyle would squeeze my breasts and suck at them. He pretended it was foreplay, but he'd never paid attention to my mammaries before. Finally I told him, If you want somebody to nurse Rudy, take the hormones yourself."

I slide the dry plate on top of the others and take the forks she hands me. She concentrates on the dishpan. "He didn't make love to me for weeks after that. He was off fucking the woman ranger." She dumps the dishwater as if chucking a fetid memory.

"I nursed my children. My breasts filling up, leaking, the baby greedy and then grateful—it seemed a miracle and the most natural thing in the world." She dries her hands. "Sure, Rudy was cute. But he was a stranger. Would I let a strange man nurse at my breast?"

The furniture in the living room has the dusty odor of time. Antimacassars garnish the chairs, and the velvet hassock is concave, where feet have rested for decades. Lace curtains, yellowed by age and distraction, hang at the windows. Old family portraits in sepia watch from the walls. "I'd get excited nursing my kids. They'd suck away, and by the time they were full and had fallen asleep—"

The room has grown dark.

"—I'd get in bed and masturbate," she says finally. "I was ashamed at first, but then I thought, heck, it's only the nervous system, stimulus-response, what do you expect? Would a bear feel guilty? By the time I was pregnant with Bjorn, I couldn't wait to nurse him."

I stroke the antimacassar's filigree.

"I don't know why I'm telling you this. Well, you never say anything. One of us has to talk, doesn't one?"

From time to time a car drives past, the headlights sweeping across the wall, her silhouette floating past like a chancy enigma. "I might be giving you the wrong impression, prattling on about nipples and sex. I haven't had anybody to talk to is all."

Silence fills the room like water. Thoughts, like fish, swim mutely between us but never touch us.

BEAR MUSIC

> O, she will sing the savageness out of a bear!
> —William Shakespeare

Some of her mother's clothes still hang in the closet. Knickknacks crowd the dresser. The drawers are full of miscellaneous clothing. The bed sinks in the middle. "I know she's not coming back," she sighs, "but I haven't had the courage or the resignation to throw things away. It smells like an old woman in here, but I've left the windows open, and it's a warm night, so I hope it won't be too bad."

I tell her it will be fine. She says good night. I hear her in the bathroom. Then the house is quiet. I think it will take me a long time to get to sleep, but that's the last thing I'm aware of.

Until 2:20 in the morning, when I'm roused by a soulful, lonely harmonica. I think Lyle's wife is watching an old western on TV, and the cowboys are gathered around the campfire after their dinner of beans and biscuits, and Andy Devine is holding his harmonica—the only musical instrument you can put in your pocket—to his lips, and the other cowboys rest their heads on their saddles and pull their Stetsons over their faces to keep the moonlight out of their eyes, for there's a full moon, surely, high in the sky, and a coyote will howl in a moment—but the TV is dark, and the music wafts like the scent of an exotic flower through the old house, and I don't think to put anything over my nakedness as I pursue the haunting melody to a door half open from where I see the silvery moonlight caressing the window and illuminating, with the same softness and delicacy that infuses the harmonica's plaintive call, Lyle's wife, cupping her mouth, as if the sound were coming from her pale thin hands, and her hair is a shimmer in the moonlight, her gown black, eating up light and music.

I listen until the music floats away into the moonlight like a dream you want to relive, and her hands fall to her lap, her face still turned toward the window. The night, lonelier and sweeter than before, seems suspended in time. She rises and, without looking at me, glides to the bed and disappears into its darkness.

My knees are stiff from standing, and I hobble quietly to my room.

THE LETTER GOES ON

Chez moi

Dear Lyle,

I haven't mailed my last letter. I've been busy showing the writer around Saskatoon, which is larger than he had imagined, "a real city," he says. At first I assumed you had sent him, but he rarely mentions you, as if your name might be an embarrassment, like an untoward flatulence or a booger hanging on one's nose. I wonder if you even know he's here.

He says his book started out about you but became bigger than you, and now he wants to know something about me. I was offended because, once again, it seemed that I was merely an appendage to you, even though he assured me that I'm important for my own sake. I don't believe him, but I'm giving him a chance anyway, as I've given you, Lyle, so many chances lo these many years.

What puzzles me is that he doesn't interview me or even ask me much of anything. But maybe that's his technique. Because in his unformed silence I find myself babbling. But whom have I had to talk to these last few months? There's my group, but I have to let others talk, too; and the others' stories are so interesting—Elaine's multiple personalities come out, Rhoda remembers her abuse, Louise tells about when she was a professional wrestler but she never got to be champion because she refused to sleep with the promoter—I hate to fill the precious time with my minor tragedies.

There's my Advanced Philosophy class at the U, but there I'm engaged in a dialectic of the mind, trying to unravel the spindles of Spinoza's axioms and the insanely intricate knots of Hegel's gargantuan obscurity and the warp and woof of Whitehead's ever-changing woolly carpet of speculation. Some of the students think I talk too much in class; but they never say anything, they're young, they haven't experienced Life, or Love, or Heartbreak. Besides, Professor Dangaard, who's young and good-looking and an apostle of the Frankfurt School but currently reassessing that allegiance in the light of Richard Rorty's neopragmatism, encourages me to speak up and, I can tell, finds me a welcome, if somewhat waggish, interlocutor. He was dubious of my proposed term paper, in which I hypothesized that Whitehead and Spinoza, despite superficial differences, were actually barking up the same tree, but he finally said, Okay, he was turning me loose. He gave me a B+ on my paper, which I thought was unfair, but an A in the course, because of my lively class discussion. It's a different me in his class, one I scarcely recognize.

Yet I recall our occasional philosophical jaunts, Lyle. You were not immune to dialectical excursions, such as, Do bears have a sense of self? Are voles, the ready victims of dozens of predators, a paradigm for the precariousness of human existence? And, Could bear growls and whuffs be reduced to symbolic language?

Did you tire of those questions? Decide they were unanswerable and hence ho-hum? Step out of the tangled woods of cognitive disputation and into the placid meadows of giddy unknowing? It's true, I too put aside speculation for many years, immersed as I was in the pragmatics of children, career (yours), and homemaking. Still, I remember fugitive speculations as I brushed down spider webs (was Spinoza's delight in watching spiders fight a defect in his character or an embrace of Nature's, and therefore God's, profound indifference to pain?), sudsed dishes (if cleanliness is next to Godliness, why are there dust bunnies?), split wood (if we can split matter infinitely—atoms, electrons, quarks, strings, where will it end?), and knitted sweaters (does religion knit for us a scratchy turtleneck to keep out the chill wind of Nothingness but by so doing leave us sweating, fearful of that hot flash of eternity?).

So here I am blabbing away to this bearded stranger, who, an unwitting pneumonic device on two legs, at first made me think about you, but whose presence lately tends to mop your muddy paw prints from the windows of my mind and let in fresh air and the scent of flowers. Even as I'm writing this letter to you, I'm actually thinking about him.

I took him to meet Mother. "I should visit my mother," I said.

"I'd like to come," he said.

"Is my mother part of your research?" I asked.

"Everything is my research," he said.

"Even now?" I asked. "This conversation?"

"*Research* isn't the best word," he said. "*Research* suggests to *search again.* I haven't searched the first time yet."

"You're doing *search?*"

I was driving on Broadway, through Friday morning traffic, about to cross the river. "What are you searching for?" I asked, hanging a right onto Second Avenue and hitting the brake at the stop light. He looked out his window, as if what he was searching for might be the Garfield suctioned to the window of the car in the next lane. I had a flash, one of those psychic teleprompters you don't know is accurate or a bubbling from your fantasy, that he was about to say, "You. I've been searching for you." His lips—his lips are full and sensual—were parting. I imagined I could see "You" coming out of them, like a cartoon balloon. His pale blue eyes seemed to get deeper, as if something were sliding open and I were about to look into the inconceivable spectacle of his soul—I, who had not believed in the soul since Sister Marguerite laid me across her black-robed thighs and pulled down my white cotton underwear and snapped her ruler across my buttocks—and my father said that night that I would start public school next morning, he hadn't wanted to send me anyway to the papist school even if it was supposed to be the best, how could it be any good if it hurt people, it being an on-going debate between Mother and Dad whether life is, as she always said, inherently painful and that's how we achieve salvation, and he arguing that any god who thought pain was good for us was a god damn sadist, he preferred the motley crew on Olympus who might be capricious but at least were never downright mean.

So I stared into the writer's lapis lazuli eyes, and his full lips were opening to tell me what he was searching for, and he was saying—but I couldn't hear what he was saying because car horns were blaring all around me.

"What?" I yelled above the cacophony.

He breathed into my ear, "The light's green."

I swung right onto College, forgetting I was in the center lane. Tires screeched. I yelled above the brassy threats behind me, "You're searching for the green light?"

He nodded.

Mother was outdoors with a few other inmates, guarded by an aide who was trying to engage them in a game of Throw Me The Stupid Beach Ball. Mother was wandering off—wanting another peek at the movies, I suppose—so I said we'd watch her, and we ambled with her a hundred feet or so, she ignoring us as if we weren't there, until she turned to the writer and asked, "Where are your bears?"

He hesitated only a second. He said, "They're in the woods."

"Good," Mother said. "That's where they belong."

"She thinks you're Lyle," I said.

"I know who he is," Mother said.

We came to a bench, and she sat down. I sat on one side of her, and he sat on the other. She stared at him. She asked, "Am I in Minnesota, or are you in Saskatchewan?"

He said, "We're here."

She said, "I can't tell you how confused the people around here are." She patted his hand. "You should come see me more often."

"I will," he said.

"But where's your wife?" she asked. "She never comes."

He said, "She's right there."

She looked at me for several seconds as if she were trying to bring me into epistemological focus. "That's a woman," she said. "My daughter's a little girl."

"That was a long time ago," he said gently.

"Yes," she said, "but was it that long?"

She looked away, into the distance. Her mind seemed to follow her gaze.

STILL LIFE WITH FLOWERS

Here, near my hut, in total silence, I dream of
violent harmonies amid the natural perfumes
that intoxicate me.

—Paul Gaugin

The heady bouquet suffuses the house as she arranges once again
the flowers I brought from her garden. She arranges them for the bril-
liance and the complementarities of their colors. She selects them for
the luxuriant blending of their fragrances, as if she were inventing
perfumes. She mixes them according to unspoken intuitions, esoteric
alchemies, and daring improvisations. I find a single scarlet rose beside
my bed, an ambush of pink carnations in the bathroom, an attack of
stargazer lilies in the hallway. A lascivious tiger lily flaunts itself by my
chair in the living room. A coalition of gay blossoms clamors in her
bedroom. Pink and yellow roses float sweetly past me, on their way to
the dining room table.

"I can't believe you went to all the trouble to bring me these flowers."

"I thought you might miss them."

I sauté greens in peanut oil and dress them with hard-boiled egg,
onion, balsamic vinegar, and croutons, and we steam small new potatoes from the farmer's market and slap them with butter and toss
them with tarragon and freshly ground pepper, and we broil the fresh
sockeye salmon without embellishments, its natural flavor pure and
impeccable. As we eat, she reminds me that the grizzlies at this very moment are flipping the spawning sockeye from the streams of Canada's
west coast. Her fingers idly rearrange the saucy roses.

She says, "I don't know how you got everything through customs.
The guard didn't notice anything?"

I tell her I was cutting the flowers in her garden, was going to take a few into my shack to brighten my pitiful life, when a voice in my head said, *Wouldn't she like these flowers?*

"It was my voice. It was telepathy."

"Were you thinking about your flowers a few days ago?"

"I'm sure I was."

I go on to say that I found myself cutting every flower in the garden, and I thought, hell, might as well get the veggies, too, and I threw my clothes in my bag and drove the pickup to town and bought the coolers and the ice, and I headed out. I was feeling giddy, I say, and scared, as if I were doing something wrong.

"You were stealing a state pickup truck," she says, her turquoise eyes amused, her teeth munching the salmon's pink succulence.

"Not stealing, really," I say, "because it's come to seem like my own truck—and as I'm barreling through the woods, all of a sudden the silver bear we were looking for is loping across the road. I hit the brakes, jump out, plunge into the woods. Nothing. I tromp back to my truck. Then this van pulls up behind me, and Frank Running Bear climbs out, his silver hair pulled back and the braid hanging to his waist, saying, *I didn't think I was going to catch you. Here, you take these things to her.* And he gives me the bag of wild rice, which he said he and Lionel gathered last fall and roasted in the old way, and the jug of maple syrup he and his family tapped this spring and boiled down in big iron kettles in the woods. *This batch is heavy and earthy, the way you like it,* he said.

"I asked him how he knew where I was going, but he acted like he didn't hear me. He said to say hello, and that these porcupine quill earrings are for you, from Winona, she made them"—and I take out the earrings and she puts them on— "and he gave me this"—and I unbutton my shirt to show her the bear tooth on the rawhide string around my neck.

"And they let you through customs with all that?"

I say I worried about that, too, after I got back in the truck, when Frank pulled alongside me as if he'd read my mind—

"Like you read mine, when I wanted my flowers."

And he yelled across, *Don't worry about customs, they won't see a thing,* and he swung a U-turn and roared off.

"That explains it," she says, her euclase eyes serious. "He made it invisible to the guard. Old shaman trick. He does that all the time. One time we drove in, Lyle and I, and the lodge was gone. Whole damn lodge. We thought we'd turned in the wrong driveway. Drove out. Saw our sign. Drove back in. Lodge was there. I knew then it must have been Frank. That was when Lyle was going to arrest Frank for shooting deer out of season. Lyle never bothered Frank after that."

She took a bite, went on as she chewed. "Lionel could do that sometimes. Lyle would come home, wouldn't even see Lionel. But Lionel's not as expert as Frank. Frank could make you disappear, right now, even while he's in northern Minnesota." The sockeye gives a jerk in my stomach. "You wouldn't really disappear." Her melanite eyes sparkle. "I just wouldn't see you. Or the salmon on your plate might disappear."

The salmon's gone. I blink. The salmon's back. It seems smaller, however, as if someone in a parallel universe took a bite. I stare into her chalcedony eyes. She smiles. "I'm not very good at it. You barely missed it, right?" I eat the salmon, quickly, before it goes away.

I pour the Caymus Conundrum, a blend of whites that rocks and rolls across the tongue and pirouettes down the throat. She eyes the label. "I can't believe Lyle would let that out of his cellar." I don't say anything. Our glasses clink. "You were nice to Mother today. She's nothing to you, after all."

"She's your mother."

"But I'm only your research."

"You're my search. You're what I'm searching for."

"Pass the lemon."

She squeezes the lemon wedge. Juice squirts in my eye.

"Does Lyle give you my letters? Or do you steal them?"

I examine the sockeye for hidden bones.

She says, "I found the letter I wrote him from the Saskatchewan Wildlife Management Office."

"You went through my things?"

"I didn't find much."

"That official Saskatchewan Animal Management envelope got me through customs."

"Did the guard read the letter? Might have made his day." She quaffs the Conundrum. "Did it make your day?"

STROLLING WITH BEARS

Love will enter cloaked in friendship's name.
—Ovid

We stroll the quiet neighborhood, the houses old but trying to keep their pride. Tall trees canopy the street. Through a window we see a black family watching television. Aboriginal teenagers cluster at a corner, then run off, the girls laughing and the boys whooping, their long black hair flying in the breeze.

"They fired me, you know."

"Animal Management?"

"I destroyed the applications for bear hunting permits."

Across the street, a sitar ripples an evening raga.

"It was a temporary job, something to do outside my own pathetic life of Mother, group, philosophy class, and wondering where everything was going to end up. It was nothing but opening envelopes, sealing envelopes."

"I was supposed to write scripts for the cooking shows," I say, "but Lyle ad-libs. I was supposed to write scripts for the wildlife features, but they insisted on experienced wildlife-script writers. At least that's what Diane said."

There's a sudden rupture in the vespertine equanimity. I blurt, "She's sort of an agent—"

"I know who she is. The one in the video. Fellini." An electric wheelchair, steered by a young man with a twitching hand, creeps down the middle of the street. "You were in it!" she says, turning to me. "That was you!"

"Only a couple of seconds. She cut the rest of the footage I was in. Time constraints. So she said." The aroma of Chinese food wafts on the air.

"So she's been there ever since?"

A dog, frantic to tear us to shreds with sharp, slavering teeth, hurls himself at the fence beside us.

"Comes and goes."

"Where does love go?" she asks.

I look up through the high leaves at the pale evening sky.

"Sometimes," she says, "I have no more feeling for him than I have for a lamp post." I watch my scuffed, stained hiking boots reach out for the sidewalk, then disappear under me. "Other times I feel barbed wire wrapped around my heart and squeezed tight." The sidewalk rises where tree roots have nudged it upward, nature's slow persistence disturbing human attempts to determine our paths. "Love hurts," she concludes.

I say, "Betrayal's what hurts."

The back of her hand brushes the back of my hand, our arms swinging loosely as we walk.

"I forgot to go to my group tonight," she says.

Somehow the palms of our hands find each other.

"I'm going to quit," she decides. "Everybody in there's unhappy. Besides, I have you to talk to now." Our hands swing as we walk, fingers gripping tentatively. "What'll I do when you go?"

William Borden

MORE OF THE SAME LETTER

Well, Lyle,

I keep writing this same letter in the odd moments when my guest is away, driving about the city in his, or I should say the Division of Forestry's, pickup, or taking a solitary stroll around the neighborhood, because we recognize that we each need, the writer and I, some private time, even though we get along quite well and spend considerable time together—which is understandable, considering that I am his single, for the time being, source of information for whatever it is he's writing, if he is actually writing something, which I wonder about since he never takes notes. Maybe he has a prodigious memory, but I wonder about that, too, because he forgets his way around the city, or he walks into the kitchen and asks, with a wry look on his bushy face, why he's there, and then remembers that he wanted a glass of water or would I like to eat supper out.

Speaking of writing, my mind keeps circling back, like a raven over a road kill, to those articles I wrote for which you received such glory and renown. I thought I had washed away those globs of resentment.

Oh, sure, you said I should put my name on those articles, but I said, No, you're the one with a career, making a name for yourself following the bears, living like a bear, which no researcher before you had done. And I felt a visceral satisfaction correlating facts, discovering patterns in the spontaneity of behavior, fleshing out paragraphs from the cryptology of field notes, and stitching together a tapestry of enlightenment out of the confusion of irreconcilable data.

At the same time I raised three children.

As when Bernadette ran off to Minneapolis with Kenny Sees Far when she was 13, to join a punk band. Or Bjorn was picked up by the sheriff for copping the 22 rifle from Ostrum's Guns and Gizmos. Or Babette's abortion at 17.

Where the hell were you all those times, Lyle? Or Bjorn—while I'm on the subject—or Bjorn knocking up Katie Nelson, even if he said it could have been three other guys. It was I who made him take responsibility and work another year for Guy Ostrum to pay not only for the rifle and not only for the surgical procedure, but also counseling for Katie, even if it didn't seem to do much good, since she ran off with that logging truck driver, eventually appearing on New York talk shows as the Truck Driver's Fantasy Whore, describing her travels to South America as far as Tierra del Fuego. On the other hand, she's now an editor for *Travel and Leisure*, so maybe my making Bjorn pay for her counseling set her on the right track eventually, and helped Bjorn learn responsibility, too, because it's sometimes a torturous and uncanny path from despair and aimlessness to amounting to something and doing something with your life.

And it was I who dealt with the pot I found in Babette's room, along with her diaphragm.

And Babette's gulping a bottle of vitamin C, thinking, in her tears, they were aspirin, in her wayward attempt at suicide after Freddy Bernstein left for Tacoma without saying goodbye and she was 12 and in the maelstrom of confused adolescent hormones, but she didn't have a cold all winter, even though vitamin C is secreted from the system within 24 hours, but it seemed like something worth looking into, and I wrote Dr. Linus Pauling, but he never answered, and she hasn't had a cold since, either.

And what was always so difficult about writing those articles, Lyle, I don't think you ever appreciated this, was to rein in my natural rambling and organize the multivalent threads of my thoughts and funnel the natural wandering exuberance of my prose into the lifeless technicalities science wanted and the flippant vacuity the popular magazines paid for.

So where, Lyle, would you have found anyone to take care of those messy Details of Life and cook and do housework and keep a garden and festoon the house with aromatic fresh flowers and fuck you almost as often as you wanted and even let you take photos of her?

I guess it's the writer being here, a guy who gets credit and money for his own work, which has brought to the surface my petty rancor about all that.

What's the story with your writer, anyway? Is he married? Divorced?

A widower with a secret anguish? I try to bring up these things, but it's like stepping into a fetid swamp of evasive silence. My guess is that he's been unlucky in love, betrayed perhaps by a fickle woman who did not appreciate his qualities. Or he has suffered some unspeakable tragedy too heart-wrenching to confess. Or has he, on the other hand, remained solitary all his life, dedicated to his writing, married to his Muse, a secular monk in the service of Art?

Well, I guess a writer is really a faceless entity, when you think about it, a medium, dictated to by you, by me, by the Muse or the babbling in the alleys of his own dark mind. Maybe a writer doesn't really have a life of his own.

If he has a life, it's irrelevant. If he has a past, it's forgettable. A writer lives in the present, experiencing and writing. His life is a piece of paper. His future consists of words marching across the page, of the pages blowing in the wind. When the paper's gone, he's gone. Shakespeare says his poem will outlast marble; but where are all the beautiful marble statues sculpted by Phidias? Where's the roof to the Parthenon? And where the hell are the ninety lost plays of Sophocles, Euripides, and Aeschylus?

WHAT BEARS THINK ABOUT WHEN THEY THINK ABOUT LOSING IT

> Which way shall I take my guest
> Which way convey my darling?
> —Karelian Bear Song

The gray-haired woman in the ticket booth gives us a suspicious once-over as I buy our tickets, but she doesn't say anything, and I lead Lyle's wife and her mother into the Lysol-pungent darkness. The flickering colors on the screen illuminate the scattering of men, old, young, middle-aged, sitting separately, absorbed by the thrashings and moanings.

I said, Why don't we take your mother to a movie, get her out for awhile. I was thinking of one of the feel-good movies of the summer, but Lyle's wife said she'd tried that and her mother got bored and started asking questions, like Why do they keep shooting each other? and What do their children think? in a loud voice. But there is one movie house that seems to keep her attention, she added.

We got a bit of a jolt when we picked Mother up. She was sporting a little gold ring in the lobe of her right nostril. She said it bothers her when she picks out a booger, but she thinks she'll get used to that. She said her daughter gave her the ring. Her daughter is a nurse, she said, did we know that?

Just then Prudence, in her starched white miniskirt and white stockings and rings sprouting from her ears and eyebrows and nose, like tiny brassy flowers sprung from her sunny *joie de vivre*, peeked around the door to hope we weren't mad but Mrs. Chambreau insisted, and shouldn't even old ladies have a right to decorate themselves as they please?

And is this Mr. Gustafson, come to visit, finally? Prudence asks, stepping into the room and extending her hand.

I say, Just a friend, hi, Prudence, wondering if she'll show me the tattoo I've heard about, but the purple teardrop beneath her right eye is all I see, and it seems ironic for that permanently needled weeping to cloud the cheer of such a vivacious young woman, but perhaps it is the manifestation of some unspoken despair.

So, what do you think, eh, Mrs. G? Prudence asks, nodding to Mother's nose ring.

Mrs. G appears speechless, so I say to Mother, "You look very smart. You could play in a rock band."

Mother says curtly, "I play in a band. I play the two-quart Revere ware and soup ladle. I play first chair. It's a heavy metal band."

Prudence says, "I'm going to book them into the Groaty Goat. That's a club I go to. If we mike the pans and the washboard, we'll have an awesome sound."

I look at Lyle's wife to see how she's taking this. To me, it's nothing but fun and amusement, but she's watching a mother she thought she knew metamorphose before her eyes into someone who might open for a group called Frothing Vomit or Satan's Tits.

Prudence goes on, "I know, Mrs. G, it's awful, she thinks I'm her daughter, and I corrected her a few times, but, well, you know how she is. Besides, I've never really had a mother. Mine was alcoholic and slept around, and I ran away when I was 13. By the way, I used a sterile needle and anesthetic on her nose, so it didn't hurt, and I'm keeping an eye on it so it doesn't get infected. There is one favor, though, Mrs. G. Could you tell the floor supervisor that you okayed it? Because if you don't, I'll get fired. See, the supervisor thinks you should give approval, but I believe Mrs. C has a right to make some decisions on her own, otherwise what dignity do these ladies have?"

"Maybe I'll get one," Lyle's wife says, and walks out the door.

Prudence and I get Mother ready to go out, get her walking shoes on and a nice dress. Prudence chatters away about how Mrs. G has seemed happier these last couple of times, it must be because I'm visiting, am I an old friend?

Not so old, I say.

You like her, don't you? Prudence says in her chipper, matter-of-fact manner. I can tell, the way you look at her. But she's not sure about you. Are you moving in on Mr. G, or is he out of the picture?

I ask her if she has a lot of tattoos.

Did she tell you about Jesus?

I nod.

I'm going to get the Virgin on my other fanny, Prudence says, when I have enough money. Or Mary Magdalene. What do you think?

I say, You see pictures of Mom Mary all the time, but Mary M gets short shrift.

Prudence says that's what she thinks.

Mother pulls me toward the door. She says, "Come on, Lyle, let's blow this joint." She hooks her arm in mine and drags me down a corridor lined with people in wheelchairs staring into the past, or into that inscrutable darkness ahead of them, who can tell, and Prudence waves goodbye.

Mother watches all three features with a steady attentiveness and leaves only to go to the bathroom.

She wants to watch the cycle all over again. I say, It's the same movie. She says, Maybe it'll be different this time.

Finally we get her to leave, after we convince her she's hungry, which we are, and take her to a small restaurant that boasts HOME COOKING. After dinner we treat Mother to a drive around Saskatoon. She falls asleep, but we drive anyway. Then the head nurse, a husky, bitter harridan with a mustache, bawls us out for keeping Mother out past bedtime and asks why in heaven's name we let Mother put a ring in her nose. She could report us for abuse, the head nurse says. Lyle's wife says her mother can put bells on her fingers and rings on her toes if she wants, she's loony tunes anyway, so if it makes her happy, who the fuck cares?

After we leave, we're sitting in the car, and Lyle's wife says, "If I lose my marbles, I'd rather they shoot me than put me in a home." She drives home in silence.

When she pulls up in front of her house and switches off the motor, she says, "Maybe someday I'll come get her and say I'm moving her to Vancouver Island, and I'll take her out to the woods and let her curl up in a hole like a bear and go to sleep. Would that be mean?"

"Does she like the woods?"

"No. I do. That's what I'd like someone to do for me, if I was out of it. Take me to the woods, on a fall day, and there's an excitement in the air, chickadees flitting, squirrels scurrying, animals burrowing—everything's getting ready for winter and dying, but everything's kind of excited by the prospect. And I'd squiggle into a soft place under a tree, and I'd sleep, like a bear, all winter."

Her beryline eyes picture a tellurian repose. "I'd like to crawl in

210   *William Borden*

with a bear," she muses, "hibernate with the bear. You could probably do that, you know, once the bear was sleepy, if you crawled in quietly and you had rolled around where the bear had been so you'd have a bear scent, because there's some evidence that the bear doesn't smell as keenly during hibernation, since you can introduce a strange cub into the den and the mother will let him nurse and think he's her own, whereas later, in the spring, once they're out of hibernation, if you introduce another cub, the mother will eat it. And the bear could eat me in the spring, the way the bears ate Ben Creswell, except I would be a willing gift.

"Why shouldn't we let the animals eat us?" she asks. "I can't see the point of rotting inside a metal crate, or burning until you're a shoebox full of ashes. Even if I was senile like Mother, I'd remember enough to like sleeping with a bear and dying with a bear, if somebody would come get me from the nursing home, or, better yet, never put me there in the first place. Would you do that?"

"Put you in a nursing home?"

"Take me out and leave me in the woods."

"If that's what you wanted."

"Can I count on you?"

"I need to think about it," I say. "It's a commitment."

"You might have to take me off the life-support machines, fight the hospital authorities, break the law."

"If it's what you really wanted, I'd do it."

"They might view it as murder."

"Letting you hibernate with a bear?"

"If it was in Canada, you wouldn't get the chair. There's no death penalty."

"We'll do it in Canada, then."

"Take me up to the mountains around Banff, no one would know."

"Banff it is."

"Don't promise unless you're certain."

"You can count on me."

"I can't rely on Lyle. He might say he'd do it, but then, when the time came, he'd be off cooking on television or collaring bears or fucking Diane."

"I'll do it," I say. "I'll take you into the woods, find a denning bear, and shove you in."

"But can you find a denning bear?"

I straighten up, preen a little, answer, "I've taken over some of Lyle's duties. I've gotten to know bear ways." She eyes me doubtfully. "I've been handling the nuisance bears. That's how I got the truck. And the cap."

"What if you go first?" she asks suddenly. "If you're nuts, but I still have my wits, do you want to sleep with a bear?"

"Let her eat me in the spring?"

"That's the idea."

"I haven't really made plans, one way or the other."

"But what if, in five minutes, say, you keel over? Heart attack, fast-growing cancer, meteor falls on you? Do you have family I should contact?" Her euclase eyes bore into mine. "Don't dilly dally. Any second—who knows?"

I remember firing up Lyle's self-cleaning oven after an experimental pudding went volcanically awry, and the sediment of ash in the oven afterwards. I envision a coffee can, Folgers or Butternut, containing my ashes. Maybe Chock Full o' Nuts.

"We might not have all day, buddy-o."

"Take me to the woods."

"If you're already dead?"

"If I'm already dead."

"But you're undecided, as of now, concerning the let-the-bear-eat-you-if-you're-cuckoo question?"

"I need some time on that. But I'll keep tabs on you. If in thirty or forty years you're like your mother was today, I'll snuggle you in with a bear. I'll know that's what you want."

"Except, did you notice, although she seems out of it in the usual sense, she seems actually with it in a deeper sense?"

"I noticed."

"Do you think she's really with it in a deeper sense? Or is she just bonkers?"

"It's hard to tell."

"What if I still have a few good years left?"

"If you resist as I try to shove you into the den, I'll take you back to the nursing home."

"I don't want to go back to the nursing home."

"You don't know it's a nursing home. You're out of it."

"As you take me back, I'll struggle."

"Then I'll drive you back to the god damn woods, and the god-damn bears, and leave you!"

"But I'm not ready!"

"What do you want?" I shout.

"I want to live with you!"

"You can't take care of yourself!"

"I want you to take care of me! Feed me gruel, wipe my chin, change my Depends." Her chalcedony eyes fix me, like a nail through a board.

"I hardly know you."

Her eyes, deep as jade, flutter like wings over my face. Her hair, a burnished henna with a few strands of ash-gray along her temples, caresses her shoulders. Her voice grows huskier, as if she had swallowed honey and it's purring in her throat. "You know me very well, buddy-o. My letters? Lyle's files? Lyle's videos? Who knows what else? You've ransacked my life, buddy-o. You've shoveled up my past. You've crawled into my dreams and rearranged the furniture."

> *Hunters examining a den in Russia's Okhinsky district were startled to discover a wanted criminal snoozing in a warm embrace with a hibernating bear. The Itar-Tass news agency reported that the awakened fugitive was incoherent and could not explain why he had taken up winter residence with the bruin near Lake Baykal. It was also unclear why the bear had not reacted to the man's intrusion.*
>
> *—Earthweek: A Diary of the Planet, April 7, 1995.*

DIANE: LYLE HAS A VISITOR

> The female knows from the scents on marked
> trees that...males in the area are on the prowl.
> —*The Great American Bear*

Lyle, I say, simply because a woman has camped in your yard doesn't mean you have to let her stay. I don't care if it is technically state property, and therefore she has a constitutional right to be on it, it doesn't mean she can pee in the yard whenever she feels like it. But Lyle is soft-hearted and, sometimes, soft-headed.

She was there one afternoon when we came back from getting groceries. She was pounding stakes for her pup tent. She asked, "Are you Lyle Gustafson?" Like an idiot he had to say Yes. "I'm here to be your disciple," she said. He told her he was suspended and couldn't do any bear research, not legally, but she just threw her sleeping bag into her tent. He said he couldn't afford to hire her, either, but she just lifted her Coleman stove out of her station wagon. I told her she couldn't stay, but she ignored me. All she said was, she had come to see Lyle, not me, whoever the hell I was, she knew I wasn't his wife.

So now he takes her with him when he goes to check on his bears. He says it's a law of the universe and bad karma if a guru doesn't welcome a devotee. I say, your wife may have put up with this sort of thing, but I won't. He tells me, Come with us, I've got nothing to hide. But he knows I can't, with all the phone calls and faxes and everything to take care of now that the writer is gone.

I wanted to report the pickup stolen, but Lyle says he's sure the writer's on official business somewhere. The Division of Forestry wants to know where the truck is, too, because no one's picking up the nuisance bears. So now Lyle goes out and gets the bears.

One woman swore a bear opened her screen door by hooking his

William Borden

claw in the handle, strolled into her kitchen, stood on its hind legs, opened the upright freezer, removed three pints of Ben and Jerry's (Wavy Gravy, Rain Forest Crunch, and Cherry Garcia, ignoring the raspberry-banana sherbet and the pineapple ice milk) and ate the Ben and Jerry's there in her kitchen.

The bear was gone by the time Lyle got there. The three cartons were on the linoleum, all right, he said. What really got her, the woman said, was when the bear, Cherry Garcia smeared on his snout, got to the screen door he stopped, sauntered back to the freezer, and closed the freezer door.

Lyle types up the reports and signs the writer's name to them. He wrote that the woman's children had eaten the ice cream and blamed it on a bear. When I pressed him, he admitted that he had taught Rudy to open doors, including freezer doors, and that Ben and Jerry's was in the freezer at the time and was employed as positive reinforcement. But he said it was the writer who taught Rudy to close the door when he was through.

The woman camping in the yard, who says her name is Pepper, short for Peppermint, Volkensky, is beginning to get on Lyle's nerves, but he's afraid to call the sheriff because he doesn't want to draw attention to himself, or to the absent pickup, or to anything else.

We'll have to get rid of her ourselves, he says.

We stand at the kitchen window. In one fluid motion she lowers her shorts and squats. I turn away. Lyle stays, observing.

LICKING

Bear play is characterized by a lack of vocalizations and by spread ears. It can include restrained biting.

—*The Great American Bear*

We sit in the living room, letting her fried chicken (dipped in cream and rolled in flour, onion salt, garlic powder, pepper, and rosemary), mashed Yukon potatoes cloaked in thick white gravy, fresh green beans sautéed in peanut oil and garnished with pimento and chopped cashews, and a cole slaw prepared from an old Chambreau family recipe, digest. She's tapping her foot, impatient with something—her digestive juices, the phases of the moon, the expansion of the universe? No. She's impatient with me. "I don't know what to do with you," she says. "You're here, but you don't do anything. You just hang around."

"I took your mother to the movies. We went swimming. Walks along the river. The art gallery. Wanuskewan Heritage Park, where the Cree guy did the hoop dance and spread the hoops along his arms and legs so he looked like a butterfly and then an eagle."

"But are you getting what you want? For your book," she adds, "or whatever it is you're doing?"

I look out the window at the street, empty as my excuse for loitering around her life, which seems happy enough, even if the victim of unpredictable mood swings, and as fulfilled as one might expect at the tail end of the twentieth century, when the only problems left seem to be insoluble, and so not worth thinking about.

"You just seem to be..." She glances about the room, trying to find what I seem to be. "Waiting," she concludes. "What are you waiting for?"

I should leave. What madness is this, anyway? Can one live like this, suspended between lives? "Do you," I finally ask, "want me to leave?"

Her verdelite tourmaline eyes assess me—cynically? Amusedly? Challengingly?

"Dessert?" she asks, rising.

The chocolate chip bars cool on the red and white checkerboard oilcloth faded from earnest cleansings with Comet. I watched her stir extra chocolate chips and extra butter into the batter, and crushed walnuts, and she set the timer to slightly under bake, so that the bars, carved into generous, paw-sized squares, are heavy and rich and oozy, suggestive of excess and sin. We sit at the kitchen table, the plate of warm indulgence between us.

The loamy sweetness fills my mouth, sticks to my teeth, clings to my gums, slides like concupiscence down my throat. Specks of chocolate tremble on her rosy lips, and when she finishes the bar her lips purse around each of her fingers and her thumb in turn, her malachite eyes surveying me, the sugar careening to our brains. I stare at my fingers, the succulent chocolate clinging in globs like the afterthoughts of vivid sweaty dreams. She grabs my hand. She licks the chocolate off my fingers. She gnaws my knuckles. Her tongue curls between my fingers. A velvety current slithers up my arm. It slaloms into my chest, knocking my heart to one side. It knots my stomach and toboggans into my groin. My erection, quick as lightning, punches my trousers.

"Milk?" Her voice purrs dark and creamy.

She fills two glasses. She bites into another bar. She holds the bar to my lips. We watch each other chew. Her nephrite eyes are playful. I discover my hand holding her wrist. I discover her fingers in my mouth. I lick and nibble. She closes her eyes. A whimper escapes her throat. Her fingers taste tempestuous, tenacious, tendentious.

We say goodnight. She kisses me, briefly, chastely—well, almost chastely. Her hand lingers on my shoulder. Her wedding ring is thin, gold, and worn. Her hand drops to her side. She turns and steps softly to her room.

I lie in bed awake.

Later, when I get up to go to the bathroom, I pass her door, half open—or half closed, depending, I guess, like the glass of water, whether one is an optimist or a pessimist. I pause, because to listen to her sleep-drugged breathing seems forbiddingly intimate. I hear the rattling of a snore, like Rudy's snuffling not long ago as he napped in my shack, following me in and refusing to leave until dawn.

I hobble to the bathroom. Returning, I pause again by her door, but her breathing has lightened, and I wonder if she knows I'm standing outside her door, and I wonder if she's wondering if I'm going to come in, and, if I did, I wonder what she would do, and I wonder if she's wondering what she would do, and what, I ask myself, does the door half open (or is it half closed?) mean? Is half-way a sign of indecision? Of half trust? Of half interest?

I enter my room, her mother's room, which still smells like an old lady's room, a lingering powdery perfume, a brittle dustiness, a sad forgetfulness. I ease into the bed, the springs whimpering.

I leave my door half open.

WILD

> In a love affair, as in a poem or a film, there are always crises, significant disjunctions in which meaning appears to be collected.
>
> —Harold Bloom

The next morning we breakfast on wild rice pancakes lounging in Frank Running Bear's maple syrup, alongside Frank's spicy venison sausage and a growly Costa Rican coffee. We're luxuriating in the snappy earthiness contributed by the wild rice, the indulgent sweetness of the syrup, the reckless bravery of the sausage, the intrepidity of the coffee. The indeterminateness of half-openness remains, but a fellow, like an atom, has to learn to live with uncertainty is the way I see it. Lyle's wife, however, may be a mite off balance, herself uncertain of the distinctions between half-open and half closed, which may account for her silence this morning, a certain tentativeness in her movements, a puffiness, fetching as it is, under her eyes, as if she hadn't slept soundly, and a thoughtful perplexity on her brow. I'm hoping the matutinal refreshment I prepared will prove bracing.

The phone splinters the silence.

It hasn't rung since I arrived. Why do I think it's for me? No doubt she has friends. Someone from her therapy group reaching out, a philosophy classmate puzzling over Wittgensteinian puns, Prudence with a request from her mother for toiletries. She grabs the receiver off the wall as if the shrill clanging were a personal attack. She swivels on her heel to face me. "How interesting to hear from you," she says. Her tone is dry, camouflaging surprise. "The writer?" she asks innocently. "Here?"

She leans a shoulder into the wall. "Why would he be here?" She flips hair from her face, positions it behind her ear. "He might be unstable?" She throws me a suspicious glance. "What truck?" I pick up my cup of coffee. "The Mounties?" I put the cup back on the table.

She turns her back to me and talks to the wall. "Why would I think of you?" I wonder if I should leave and give her some privacy. "Why would you think of me?" She walks in a small circle, the cord tying her up. "No," she says, "if he comes to see me, I won't tell you." I take a step toward the doorway. She gestures for me to stay.

"I don't care about the truck." She turns counterclockwise, unwrapping the cord. "That's their problem." She reaches for her cup of coffee. "That's your problem." She takes a swallow. "What makes you think he's dangerous?" She eyes me dangerously. "What makes you think he's here now?" She puts the cup down. "You mean, you think he might be standing here in the kitchen, maple syrup dripping down his beard from the wild rice pancakes we might be eating?"

She snatches a napkin, wets a corner in a glass of water, and scrubs my hairy chin. "No," she says, "I wouldn't tell you if he was here." She twangs the cord like a bowstring. "Because." She grabs her Tequila Sunrise. "Just because." She drinks. "Tequila Sunrise." The back of her hand wipes her lips. "For the hell of it."

She tugs impatiently at the cord. "I have to go."

She twirls the cord like a lasso. "None of your business."

She hammers the receiver into the hook.

"Why"—she swivels to face me— "does he call, for the first time in months"—she holds up the cracked receiver—is she going to call someone?— "looking not for me"—she clubs the phone box— "but for *you!*" She bludgeons it. She beats it senseless. Pieces scatter on the floor. Bells tinkle on the linoleum. She rips the cord from the wall.

"Did he call because you took the truck?" she asks, I think, rhetorically. "No." It *is* rhetorical. "He doesn't care about the truck." She raps the cord against the wall. "He called to find *you.*" She whips the table leg. "*Because,*" she says, dioptase eyes flaring, "*you're buddies.*" I feel a nick at my knee. "*You're fucking buddies!*"

I marvel at her malachite eyes, blazing like gangbusters. "But we're buddies," I say. "*You* and *I* are *buddies.*" She raises the cord above her head. "He didn't call," I say, "to find a buddy. He called to see if another bear was sniffing around his den."

She whips the cord against the table, spilling the coffee. I find the *smack* of the cord strangely provocative. She says, "This is *my* den."

William Borden

LYLE: HOW TO HANDLE A NUISANCE

Exit, pursued by bear.
—William Shakespeare

So I walk her into the woods a little ways, and I tell her, if she keeps peeing in my yard, all the big boar bears for miles around will smell it and come galloping in and fuck her, because they'll think she's marking her territory as an invitation. I tell her I can't be responsible for what happens.

But now she looks intrigued. She asks what would happen if they tried to have intercourse with her.

I say bears don't have intercourse. I say, "Bears fuck, Pepper. From behind."

I can see maybe that was a mistake, maybe my psychology isn't working, maybe I misjudged Pepper Volkensky's predilections, because she's looking even more fascinated. I try again. "A bear can do it forever," I say. "He's got a bone down there, keeps it hard as long as he wants."

Oh, hell, now she's really interested.

"He'll tear you up," I say. "It'll be like getting fucked by a baseball bat. A baseball bat with warts on it. It'll go on for days, without pause or rest."

She's breathing heavy now. She wants to know how soon the bears will come. Should she pee now, right here?

I say, "Pepper, you'll give birth to bears."

She says she doesn't care. She says she came all this way to be with me, why am I trying to get rid of her? She wears a black tee shirt, one of the tee shirts with a picture of me and Rudy that we sell by mail-order. She doesn't wear a bra. "Haven't I helped you, looking for the bears?" she asks plaintively. She wears new hiking boots. They hurt her feet, and I've had to give her medicine for her blisters. She scratches a mosquito bite on her knee. "I thought, if I was with you, everything would be all right."

I suppose a few fellows have heard that said to them, Jesus and Gandhi and Elvis, for instance.

"You understand me," she says.

I see her reading sometimes, wearing granny glasses, sitting in one of my lawn chairs, reading true confession magazines and exposé weeklies. Sometimes I'll saunter over and pass the time, ask her what's going on with the dog who has Jerry Garcia's reincarnated soul and can play the guitar, and how the President's wife is doing now that she's pregnant with the space alien twins. I keep thinking maybe if she feels more normal she'll feel like moving on.

"I was counting on you," she says.

I tell her I have enough problems already, she should be able to see that.

"You mean that woman," Pepper says. "She doesn't like me."

I don't have to say anything.

Then I say, Besides, Pepper, my yard is beginning to smell.

There's an old scar on her forehead and scars on her arms, and I think she's had a rough life, and a troubled one. But, just as you come across nuisance bears, bears that can't seem to understand they've gone too far, so sometimes you run into nuisance people, and you have to either remove them or shoot them.

"You were kidding about the bears fucking me, weren't you?"

I nod.

"There's no future for me here, is there?" she says.

I shake my head.

"Could you give me some money to get on my way?"

I pull out my billfold and give her all that's in it, a hundred and twenty-six dollars. She wads up the bills and squeezes them into her shorts pocket. "Would you do one more thing for me?" She sounds small and pitiful. I say, Yes. "Would you pee for me?"

Her eyes are lonely. I pull it out. At my age it takes a minute to get up some pressure. Finally the stream crinkles in the earth, kicking up leaves and bits of soil. A small sudsy pool forms. "Can I hold it?"

I take my hand away. She moves it about, directing the stream. She describes circles, squares, and other non-Euclidean designs. It dribbles to a stop. "You have to shake it," I say. She shakes it. "Harder," I say.

She gets a good grip and shakes it hard. A few more drops sprinkle out. She squeezes Things begin to firm up. We look at each other. Should I bow to nature's synoptic demands? Or let common sense prevail for once? My autonomic nerves answer for me, shrinking that momentary bravado from her slackening fingers.

She walks back toward the house. I zip up.

I stay in the woods a while longer. I feel like I need to get my bearings. I feel like that when I encounter unexpected phenomena in the domain of animal behavior, a world that will constantly surprise us if we let it.

When I get to the yard, the pup tent is gone and she's starting the station wagon. I lean my elbows on her rolled-down window. I tell her how to get to Emma's We Won't Tell Travel Lodge and that I'll call Emma and tell her to put the room on my credit card because I can show her more about bears but this isn't the place.

She pulls away without saying anything, and I don't know if I'll ever see her again. I think it's better if I don't ever see her again. I amble toward the house, certain without looking that Diane is watching. I skirt the muddy spot in the yard, the ammonia odor an unsettling prickling in my mind.

A PRUDENT PARTY

> Our life should be lived as tenderly and
> daintily as one would pluck a flower.
> —Henry David Thoreau

We have a strange invitation from Prudence.

She tried—unsuccessfully, of course—to phone. Then showed up, invitation in hand. Would we bring Mother? You can sign her out, Prudence says, for the night.

Lyle's wife looks at me. Mother's room...?

Prudence gets the picture.

She can crash with me, Prudence assures us. Her lavender-lacquered fingernail taps the invitation card. The fingernail next to it is blood red. Next is aqua.

At eight o'clock the Groaty Goat is packed. Mother is on stage, her two-quart Revere ware pan miked and connected to a reverb machine piloted by Athelbert, Prudence's boy friend, who has long blond dreadlocks and an easygoing manner. Mother is accompanied by Terrell Longtemps on amplified washboard. Terrell is a large man in a wheelchair who lost both legs to diabetes and is blind and is part Assiniboine. He's 90 years old. Prudence signed him out. He has no family to witness this event, so we tell him we'll be his family tonight, to which he seems indifferent. Charles Bloody Tooth is playing drums. Charles, who is 54, lives in a group home where Prudence worked before she started at the rest home. Charles has cerebral palsy, which gives his drumming a Cagean randomness which, Prudence says, is exactly the effect she wants.

Prudence has decided to become a performance artist, and she's getting her right buttock tattooed tonight in front of two hundred people with pierced body parts and hair of kaleidoscopic colors. We are the oldest couple in the audience.

Prudence has also, since we saw her this morning, shaved her head.

Mother calls her Yul Brynner.

Prudence whispered in my ear, as we entered the Groaty Goat, that she owed this evening to me, that my inquiries regarding her still bare buttock had catapulted her thinking into warp speed, and, like falling into a wormhole, everything had crystallized for her. Prudence wears an ankle-length translucent gown, and she works the audience, going from table to table, greeting friends. Lyle's wife and I are honored with a front row table, and our drinks are on the house, or maybe on Prudence. I wonder if we should have brought Prudence a gift, since the event seems to be as much a coming out as a performance piece, more like a bat mitzvah than an evening of pure theater.

Suddenly Charles Bloody Tooth gives a roll on his snare drum. Apparently Charles' improvisation is involuntary, due to the spasms in his arms. But Prudence holds to a deep trust in the rightness of chance events and decides it is time for her performance to begin. She glides like a ballerina to the stage. Mother takes her cue from Charles and begins beating her pan, and Terrell, who must rely on his hearing and whatever second sight he might have, rasps a polished stone over the ridges of the washboard held, like a precious mistress, on his lap.

As Prudence dances lightly up the steps onto the stage, from stage right enters a stocky, muscular woman sporting a peroxided crew cut and large hoop earrings and wearing black leather pants, black leather jacket, and black leather boots. Her face is tattooed like a Maori warrior's, and she wheels out a tattooing machine. Prudence introduces her as Yvonne Grabowski, who has been honored in numerous body art magazines, and she has come expressly for this event all the way from Toronto.

Athelbert leaves the soundboard in someone else's hands and moves to the stage with a minicam to immortalize the evening.

A massage table stands stage center. A satin pillow rests on the table.

Prudence, her back to us, stands before the table. She raises her arms, expanding the diaphanous wrap as if she were a butterfly unfolding her lustrous fragile wings. She holds that pose, and the instruments fall silent, as if the musicians had suddenly become part of something larger, as if Terrell could see, and Charles had Gene Krupa's coordination, and Mother were perfectly aware of what was going on. In the silence, in the cavernous expectation of the audience and the hush of the congregated psyches, Prudence arches forward. Her torso rests on the pillow. Her butterfly wings quiver and flutter as the gauzy wrap undulates up her thin pale legs and up her thighs and up over the twin creamy orbs of her buttocks.

The crowd applauds. Yvonne raises her needle. The musical trio plunges into a raucous tumult, something Charles Ives would have been proud of.

It's not a fast-paced performance, but then a lot of performance art is like that. Yvonne is graceful but careful, a deliberate Rembrandt rather than an impetuous Pollock. The band seems to bother her at first, but, like any good artist, she summons reserves of concentration, and soon she seems deaf to the ever-more-frightening amplified cacophony.

We are not, however. And the youth around us no doubt have already had their hearing damaged, so the decibels that pound our ears are maybe mere whispers to them, which is why Athelbert's assistant keeps cranking up the volume. Finally we thread our way through the ever more boisterous crowd, the fascination with Prudence's ass and the intricate swirls of Yvonne's electric pen losing their fascination as the young people, in their grunge and leather, their studs and rings, their chains and self mutilation, move about and talk and drink and smoke.

In the alley we lean against the brick wall, the concert still audible but diminished, as if the notes had grown small and the percussion were tiny pulses in the bricks, the muted static of quarks breaking loose from their gluey prisons to tickle our eardrums. I light the joint I scored on the way out, and we pass it back and forth. It's a strange weed and it hits us before we know it. She says we'd better not smoke it all, because she has already levitated several inches off the ground, and the only person she ever saw do that was Frank Running Bear, and he did it for only a few seconds, just long enough to prove it wasn't merely a jump. I lean over to look at her feet to see if she really is levitating, but I find myself on my back looking up at her, a giant towering above me.

She rests her foot on my chest. She's wearing high heels. My hand encircles her ankle. Encased in a lavender stocking, the flesh and bone throb with the music, and the petulant fabric feels alive beneath my fingers. My fingers glide up the calf of her leg, drawn as if by reverse gravity higher and higher, beneath the billowy folds of her lavender skirt.

The heel of her shoe enters my chest. It pierces my heart.

She lies beside me.

I can see into her mind. It's a dark cavern illuminated by candles, a cozy primeval abode smelling of musk and patchouli. Her thoughts are written on long ticker tape that weaves down the corridors. It moves too fast for me to read.

"Go slower," I say.

She says she can't.

"Can you see into my mind?" I ask.

I see in her mind a big banner. It reads, *I've always been able to see into your mind.*

I say, "I was afraid of that."

A policeman looms over us. He says, "It's over now."

When we get to our feet the policeman has become Athelbert. Athelbert wearing a military cap.

Have we missed the show? Who is on Prudence's ass, the virgin or the whore?

We float back into the Groaty Goat, Mrs. G hanging heavily on my arm, the atmosphere viscous, the floor a trampoline.

When you decide that something should be done, never avoid being seen doing it, though many will form an unfavorable opinion about it.
—Epictetus

At Prudence's and Athelbert's pad, where we've been invited for the after-performance party, Athelbert passes out coffee and is solicitous about our health. He says he could've given us some sensible ganja, but the best thing for us right now is to relax. We're feeling better, actually, lounging on the sagging couch, and Mother seems content on the beanbag chair in the corner talking to Terrell. Terrell has lowered himself from his wheelchair to sit beside her on the beanbag, and Yvonne, the Raphael of the tattoo needle, is rolling hypnotically back and forth in Terrell's wheelchair, while an androgynous waiflike young person with short azure hair sits on Yvonne's lap. Charles the drummer had to go back to the group home. He has to get up early to go to work.

A few young people sit around the small room. They haven't taken off their leather jackets or their chains. Athelbert moves about with his videocam, documenting this party, as well as the performance, for posterity. I wonder whatever happened to what's-his-name, was it Red? Fred? Jed? But Athelbert is a much calmer cameraman, slow and steady and without pretensions, which says something for the intuitive talent of amateurs.

Ned! It was Ned!

I start to tell Lyle's wife about Ned, but I realize that Ned will bring up Diane, so I keep my mouth shut. Then I wonder if Lyle's wife can still read my mind, even though I can no longer read hers.

Athelbert hands me the camera and asks me to shoot a minute or so with him in the picture, so he's part of the documentation, and I do. But soon I find myself possessed by the spirit of Ned, going after fancy shots and weird angles, until Athelbert calms me down. I realize a kinship with poor Ned I hadn't suspected before. When I hand the camera back to Athelbert and sit next to Mrs. G, she asks, "Who's Ned?"

Before I can figure out if I'm hallucinating again Prudence comes out of the kitchen carrying a tray of hors d'oeuvres like any suburban housewife and bends over to offer me some. She's still wearing her diaphanous gown, and, as she bends over, her small breasts appear within the gauzy folds. Her breasts are pear-shaped, with tiny rosebud nipples. Her breasts have a sweet innocence, a pink freshness. "Have one," she says.

I'm reaching out my hand when she points to the arrangement on the tray: "Cream cheese with chipolte peppers on blue cornmeal taco chips, jalapeños stuffed with goat cheese then rolled in red cornmeal and deep-fried, mushrooms stuffed with Saskatoonberry salsa. I used to work at a Mexican restaurant. Did you get a good look at my tattoo?" She turns, still holding the tray of Mexicali delights. "Lift my gown." We lift together, Mrs. G and I. There's Athelbert/Jesus, on the right. And there's—

It's difficult to make out, so elaborately looped and swirled is the visage, that I have to lean my head back and pull out my glasses before everything becomes clear. "Do you recognize it?" Prudence asks.

"But it's—" I stutter, "it looks like—"

"It does, doesn't it?" Prudence says. "You look just like Einstein!"

"With a beard?" Mrs. G asks.

"He should've had a beard," Prudence says, offering the hors d'oeuvres again.

"But Mary...?" I ask.

"I decided a woman's face is going to unbalance me. I needed another strong, charismatic, earth-shaking man's face. And I told Yvonne to add the beard because, well, because a beard just belongs there. Don't you think?"

Yvonne appears, a cigarette in one hand and a Moosehead beer in the other. "If you look close," Yvonne says, "you can find my name entwined in the beard. Like the guy who draws the theater caricatures in *The New York Times*, he puts his niece's name in every drawing." Prudence turns her back to us. Yvonne lifts the wrap. "Look close,"

Yvonne says.

I have to search awhile, running the tip of my finger over the warm quivering convexity of Albert Einstein's beard. "You found it," Yvonne affirms, as my finger swirls the loops and curls. "Do you see it?" Yvonne asks Mrs. G. "Poor dear," Yvonne says, "she's fallen asleep."

"Listen," I say to Prudence, "I have something for you. A gift. In recognition of the importance of tonight."

"Oh, no—"

"Really. I haven't known who should have it, but I think you're the one. It's in my truck. I'll get it."

When I return, Prudence looks frightened at first, but Athelbert is quite excited by the gift.

"Really," Prudence says, "this is too—"

Mrs. G has awakened. She says sleepily, "It looks like Holly," then nods off again.

Mother has fallen asleep in the arms of Terrell, whose large hands are squeezing Mrs. C's breasts.

When we awake, Prudence and Athelbert are asleep on Holly's bearskin, Prudence sprawled on her stomach, her bruised buttock bare to the healing air.

We take Mother and Terrell to breakfast, where Mother has steak, fried eggs, and a huge plate of lumberman's flapjacks, and I wonder if that was only a cigarette she and Terrell were smoking last night. Terrell has bacon and scrambled eggs and biscuits with sausage gravy. Mrs. G has a mushroom and Swiss cheese omelet. I have Saskatoonberry pancakes and Canadian bacon.

Terrell and Mother are holding hands.

We cross the South Saskatchewan River about sixty kilometers northeast of Saskatoon on a four-vehicle ferry. The ferryman wears heavy workman's gloves and a cap and a blue shirt with a Saskatchewan provincial patch on the sleeve. His brown walrus mustache droops around his mouth. He's sun-burned and jolly, and he wonders what I'm doing all the way up here in an official pickup wearing my official cap. I say I'm looking for bear.

"I see bears," he says.

He watches me make a note in my pocket spiral notebook. "These are Canadian bears," he reminds me.

"Bilingual?"

"Could be."

There are several of these ferries along the South Saskatchewan, each at the terminus of a winding dirt road that descends into a quiet verdant valley. In winter the ferry is hauled up on land; then a fellow can drive across on the ice.

He says he's been a ferryman for nineteen years. "Meet people from all over the world," he says. I think of the ferryman in Hesse's *Siddhartha*. I wonder if it would be a satisfying job. His gloved hand adjusts the control, and the ferry slows. The forward edge nudges the shore. He says he doesn't always know whether he's coming or going. I say I know what he means. He unhooks the chain across the end of the ferry and walks it to the side. We climb into the truck. The ferryman gives me a casual salute, which I return. I drive slowly onto shore, past two cars waiting to board. Lyle's wife says that's life exactly: Are we coming or going?

"Are we coming from somewhere," she asks, "a previous life, a spiritual realm, or are we going somewhere, heaven, hell, a different dimension? Or is life a ferry, a stepping on from nothingness and then an exit into a void? We fret and grieve that we won't live forever into the future. Why don't we regret the infinite amnesia that precedes our birth? Do you ever think about these things?"

I ease the pickup past a field of golden wheat. A couple of horses graze in a pasture. We pass a meadow of mint, green and luxuriant. Cows sun themselves in a clearing. At Fish Creek she says, "Here," and I pull to the side of the road and turn off the engine. Across the road I can see, amidst some trees, an untended graveyard. The path to the graveyard has grown over.

We walk through the whispering grass, still wet from the morning dew, mosquitoes swarming around our legs. She walks purposefully, with long, relaxed strides. The hem of her skirt floats around her bare ankles. Her sky blue skirt is tie-dyed, emblazoned with silver stars and moons and planets, a universe flapping and caressing her slim, freckled legs. Her narrow feet are laced in leather sandals, the thongs criss-crossing halfway to her knees, the kind of sandals Greek goddesses wear when they descend from Mount Olympus to dally with poor mortals.

We reach the graveyard, surrounded by a fence of metal bars, to find the gate secured by a rusty padlock. She grips the bars of the gate with both hands, looking in at the crosses and headstones half hidden by the grass gone wild. "Hi, Dad," she says, then leads me back to the truck, hurrying through the clouds of insects.

She points to a field. I make out the stones that were once the foundation of a house. The ruins of a fireplace and the remnant of a chimney rise from the grass. "That's where we lived," she says. Her arm sweeps the area. "This was our farm. This is where I grew up. I played here. I rode my horse here. Saw my first bear here. This was my Arcadia."

"It's beautiful," I say.

"All gone now."

We drive a few kilometers, the pickup trailing dust along the deserted road, then bump cross-country through a pasture. I pull up under tall cottonwood trees. We carry the picnic basket past wild raspberry bushes and rose hips to a grassy bluff overlooking the lazily winding South Saskatchewan River.

"Swift water," she says, pointing to the river, which doesn't look swift. "That's what 'Saskatchewan' means in Cree." She spreads the red and white checked tablecloth over the grass. Mosquitoes are miraculously absent.

"A hundred and ten years ago," she says, lifting the potato salad out of the basket, "the Canadian feds sent out soldiers to claim this region which the Métis, the French-Indian mixed-bloods, had already settled."

She divides the potato salad between us, plopping a mound on each china plate. "I hate plastic," she says. "I think picnics should be elegant. Don't you?"

I pass out the tuna salad sandwiches I made, the curry-flavored tuna salad slathered between thick slices of potato bread.

"The Métis," she continues, "declared themselves an independent country, just like Jefferson and Franklin and those Yankee rabble rousers, and called in Louis Real, who'd led an insurrection for an independent Métis state in Manitoba a few years earlier. They fought off the federal army for several days."

The dills are crisp and cranky.

"Right here, where we're sitting, bullets were whistling."

The deviled eggs are flecked with parsley and teased with mustard and a dash of Tabasco.

"Over there was the town, Batoche. It's all gone now, but some of those families are still here, you can see their names on the mailboxes. Poor Louis thought God would deliver the final blow, so instead of attacking the soldiers, when they were off balance, as he should have, Louis waited for the Lord to intervene. While he was waiting, the soldiers attacked, and the Métis were defeated."

I pour the crystal glasses half full. The feisty Carmignano, a smooth Tuscan brigand famous since the Middle Ages, glows like rubies in the sunlight. The bouquet slithers up our nostrils. The liquid rolls perspicaciously across our tongues.

She slips off her sandals and plants her bare feet in the grass. Her feet are straight and strong, delicious and delicate, arching at the instep like the curve in a statue, a balance of grace and muscle. Her porcupine quill earrings brush her bare shoulders. Her shoulders are freckled and tanned. The Saskatoonberry pie sits between us.

I take off my shoes and socks and let the cool grass grow between my toes. I wear my D of F cap with its rolled bill to keep the sun out of my eyes. We eat from opposite sides of the pie pan. I pour espresso from the thermos into demitasse cups.

She lies back in the grass. She falls asleep, her face beatified by the afternoon sun. I observe the outline of her nipples under her sleeveless cotton top, it too festooned by stars and comets, suns and planets. A breeze caresses her hair. A lithesome curve of thigh peeks from a reckless skirt. A thread of white encircles her finger where her wedding ring used to be.

There are many ways of being lost, and this is one of them. The grace of her foot, the gentle slope of her calf, the smooth articulation of her knee, the pale vulnerability of her thigh heave my heart into my ribs. Something like a paw pushes against my chest. Tears come to my eyes, as if an inexplicable sadness has come over me.

"Have I been asleep?"

"Snoring."

"No!"

"Demurely."

"Of course."

She leaps to her feet. She smoothes her skirt around her hips. She looks around the horizon: grassy fields, woods, the calm winding river. We could be the only people in the world. "When I was a teenager, my two girl friends and I would come out here in the summer. There'd be nobody around. We'd take off our clothes. I felt free."

I push myself vertical, my knees creaking. "That's what we're here for," I say.

"To feel free?"

I unbutton my shirt.

"That was a long time ago," she sighs.

I hobble out of my pants.

"We were just girls."

I kick off my shorts.

"You're very strange."

She pulls her top over her head. It floats to the grass. She slides her skirt to her feet. She slips her panties down her long trim legs. She takes off running.

Her buttocks are smaller than I'd imagined, or remember from the photos in Lyle's files, although I'm not thinking of Lyle's files now or Lyle. I start to run after her, the bear tooth, which Frank said would help me chew life and taste love and swallow danger, dancing against my chest, but I fall, and all I can do is watch her race across the meadow and spin, arms outstretched, hair swinging, inhibition abandoned.

William Borden

She lopes back, panting and laughing, and falls to her knees beside me. Her hair smells like berries. Her skin glistens with perspiration. Her breasts sway stylishly. She says, "I was afraid of this."

"What?"

"You. Me." She brushes damp hair from her forehead. "I wasn't going to let this happen."

"But the other night, when we licked chocolate off each other's fingers—?"

"Oh, then I was flirting."

I brush a few strands of hair from her cheek.

"Now?"

Her fingertips flicker up my chest. She palms the bear tooth, yellowed and primordial, and contemplates its curvy mana.

She jumps up. She throws me my clothes. She pulls on her skirt. She pulls her top over her head and tugs it around her waist. "Get dressed!"

I hobble into my under shorts. I hop into my pants. I throw myself into my shirt. She's pacing back and forth. "Where are my panties?" She pulls up the tablecloth to look. "They must be somewhere." I button my shirt. "Have you seen them?"

"No." Next to my ribs, something soft and silky nestles.

We cross again on the ferry. The ferryman waves, but we don't get out of the truck, because she has her skirt pulled up to tease me as she gazes serenely out the window.

We bounce over deserted washboard roads. She pulls up her top to expose her breasts. Her breasts bounce with the truck. She says, "Keep your eyes on the road."

As we make our roundabout way home, evening slides in like Destiny smoothing a gauze coverlet over the earth. We pass through small towns, through St. Isidore de Belleview, Blaine Lake, Radisson, Duck Lake, and Borden, the last a quiet village of wide deserted streets, tidy houses, and trim yards, with not a soul in sight, moms and dads and children and grandparents no doubt inside eating wholesome suppers of roast beef and mashed potatoes and white bread spread thick with butter. At one silent intersection cluster white frame buildings, each identified by its sign—the Borden Lodge, the Borden Senior Citizens Center, the Borden Town Meeting Hall. All are closed, including the small wooden house that is a replica of the childhood home of John Diefenbaker, prime minister in the late 1950's.

We walk along the grass to the tiny pub, which is open but empty, except for the owner, a tired middle-aged woman not given to casual conversation but eager to sell the pub and the seven-room hotel above the pub, the rooms no doubt dim and shabby like the pub but which, she says, are often occupied by tourists and truckers. She's lived in Borden fifteen years, married a fellow who farms nearby, but she's weary of the seven-days-a-week business, and she doesn't know why the Diefenbaker house is here, since Diefenbaker was born not here but in Ontario, although he did attend the University of Saskatchewan, and she doesn't know how the town got its name, and she clearly doesn't care. Then an old guy hobbles in, leaning on a gnarled cane, his white gravy-stained beard brushing his belt, to say that the hamlet was called Baltimore until the railroad came through in 1906; then it was named for the Minister of the Militia at the time, Frederick William Borden, a country doctor who took a Militia disarrayed by political appointments and whipped it into shape in time for the First World War. The old guy raps his cane on the bar for a beer, but the woman tells him to go back upstairs and stop bothering people.

LYLE: APRÈS LE DÉLUGE

> Everyone observes with admiration and delight in animals the very things which he detests and regards with aversion in men.
> —Baruch Spinoza

They've got Rudy, god damn it.

They weren't even going to tell me.

"He's not *your* bear, Lyle. He's a research bear. He's so to speak a ward of the Division of Forestry. You have no say-so anymore." Sheriff Irv Nyquist is a patient man for an officer of the law. He prefers explaining to arresting. It's his patience that's gotten him re-elected all these years.

I'm at the jail, bailing Pepper out again, explaining to her that even if she has seen dogs and horses and even a bear pee in the street or on the sidewalk, people can't.

She asks why not.

"Because we're not animals," I explain.

"You always say we are."

"Well," I say, "we're social animals. We have rules."

"If dogs can do it I don't see why I can't."

I look at her a moment, figuring what tack to take. Irv was amused the first time he brought her in, and she told him I was her friend and he called me and he let me take her away, but this is the third time he's had to bring her in, people complaining how she squatted in front of Fran Makosky's Taxidermy & Freeze-Drying. Fran, a strapping woman in her forties with a loud voice but a soft touch, will give a fellow a good time in her back room on a bearskin rug she keeps next to the freeze dryer, where an otter or a beaver might be undergoing a treatment, although they say she's gotten rather pricey after she watched the

Mayflower Madam on TV and learned what the gals in New York were charging. But she gives discounts to lumberjacks, because her first husband was a lumberjack, killed by a tree jackknifing on him some years ago. Fran was wrapping up a big deal with a wealthy fisherman from San Francisco who had landed a record walleye, or so they told him, and she had just sold him on a gold-plated mounting board, when he looked out her picture window to see Pepper watering the daisies along the sidewalk.

A few days earlier she peed in the parking lot of the Wolf Center outside town, where they supposedly educate people about wolves with a display of stuffed wolves gnawing a bloody stuffed deer, and a young gal in a red cape pretends to be Little Red You Know Who and gives a talk about how no one's ever really been eaten by a wolf. They keep four wolves penned up and pretend they're wild, poor fellas. Someone at the Center reported Pepper's open-air micturation that time, while a busload of Japanese tourists took photos.

Virgil Ostrum turned her in a day or two before that when she relieved herself in his store by the pool and lawn equipment. She was standing, leaning backwards, trying to get a masculine arc. She'd been practicing in the woods behind Emma's, and she wanted to show folks what she could do. Virgil, Fanny's adopted brother, said she needed a good spanking, and he'd be the one to give it to her if Irv would give him the go-ahead. I promised Irv I'd keep an eye on her.

But I couldn't stay with her 24 hours a day, with Diane getting suspicious about my being gone so much, which left Pepper unsupervised the night she caused a commotion at the Blue Ox Bar, a pretty rough place frequented by bikers and woodsmen, stump-jumpers as we call the odd-jobs fellows up here, chaps who have migrated to the north woods to escape wives, child support payments, and the tatters of any superego they might once have had.

Pepper wandered in about ten that night with a posse of bikers. She loves to hitch rides with bikers, loves to wrap her arms around their great bellies bursting from their black Harley-Davidson tee shirts and feel the bristles of their Tolstoyan beards on her arms and the grease of their shaggy hair in her face. The bikers, who had first-hand acquaintance with her urinary euphorias because the rumble and the ramble of the big black hogs agitated her bladder, spread word of her predilection throughout the Blue Ox, prompting the locals, as well as the raucous bikers, to ply her with beers—in spite of the dissuasions of Joe Manello, the veterinarian, a biker himself and, in the winter, a champion bowler in the Oddfellows League and, in the summer, a coach for the Little League. But the bedlam was too great, the boozy anticipation too breathless for anyone to listen to Joe.

Pepper was trying to go straight. She started for the ladies room several times, but the fellows dragged her back, saying, Just one more, Pepper, we've got a bet going how much you can hold. And in fact there was a lot of money piling up on the bar, and the guys were stuffing bills into her braless tank top.

(I got the blow-by-blow the next day from Joe Manello. I'd dropped by to get a few vials of tranquilizer in case I needed to quiet one of the bears. The bears are still raiding cabins and scaring campers, and the D of F is shooting the poor starved creatures just to get them out of the way, labeling them "incorrigible.")

Pepper—her face red, red splotches on her neck and arms, her hair flying in all directions, reckless now and in even more of an altered state than usual—was reaching for another beer when it sprayed out before even Pepper knew what was happening. She didn't have time to squat. She didn't even have a chance to pull down her hiking shorts she likes to wear in the woods, never mind the mosquito bites and scratches on her bare sturdy legs. The guys were taken by surprise, the waterfall splashing off the old wooden floor full of nicks and scuffs. Pepper stood there, the foam-capped mug in her hand, a far-off, glassy look in her brown eyes, her lips parted, sweating, the flow gushing and splattering, her bare legs glistening, her hiking boots darkening, and a pool spreading remorselessly from her feet in all directions like the relentless largess of God's love to the deserving and the undeserving alike. The circle of men spread out, back stepping, the way you skip backwards at the beach when a wave rushes in faster than you'd expected. Their cheers melted into awed silence. They were witnessing nature at her most awesome, most elemental, most bounteous.

Pepper closed her eyes. She was in a transcendent state, the dim yellow light of the bar casting a hazy halo around her head. She seemed transformed, Joe said. He's a Catholic, and he thinks in religious terms. He claims to have witnessed several appearances by the Virgin Mother, not to mention manifestations of over a hundred saints, some major, some minor, not all of the emanations, he swears, while he was under the influence of controlled substances. Pepper, Joe claimed, was transfigured.

The stream was unending.

Then Bobby Kincaid, who shouldn't have been in the bar anyway, not simply because he's only nineteen but because he's required by the terms of his probation to abstain from alcohol and drugs and to stay away from sheep, cows, and large dogs like the Newfoundland he was caught with—Bobby gives a tortured groan from the ring of men poised on the edge of the advancing tide of Pepper's expulsion, and Bobby sort of swims to her, his sneakers sloshing, his arms windmilling, like he's doing the crawl there in the smoky air of the Blue Ox, until he reaches Pepper, whose eyes are still closed, whose face is still splotched but beatific, and Bobby Kincaid hurls himself to the floor and lies face up between her boots, arms outstretched in a crucifixion of ecstasy, sprinkled in a baptism of hot hallucinatory profligacy.

That's when the spring goes dry.

Pepper gives a shiver. A few more drops dribble out, much to Bobby's satisfaction. She opens her eyes. She looks around, a wonderment on her face, and an amnesia of the past few golden minutes.

She sees Bobby's upturned face. She asks him what the heck he's doing down there, she's not the kind of girl who lets guys beaver-spot her. So Bobby stumbles to his feet, all wet and smelly and not sure what to do.

But now the guys are getting wild and ornery. The scent has juiced some primitive synapses in what passes for their brains. They grab Pepper and feel her up.

Joe can see that things are getting out of hand, so he wades in and punches a few fellows, who don't fight back because they're not so drunk they can't see that Joe will mop the floor with them. He toured a couple of years as a professional wrestler and was even on TV once, until he got tired of having to lose to bohunks he could easily beat just because he was the Mad Mauler from Milano and the other guy was blond and got to win.

Joe took Pepper back to her motel and held her head while she threw up and gave her a bath and put her to bed and sat in the chair all night to make sure nobody bothered her.

So now, at the jail, with Pepper in Cell B of the two-cell hoosegow, Sheriff Irv wants me to get her out of town for good or he'll shackle her and drive her to Brainerd to the loony house there, and they'll keep her indefinitely for sure because she's nuts no doubt about it. Clicking his false teeth like a telegraph key, he saunters to his desk and pulls out a set of shackles. They clank with a terrible brutality.

I say she's not nuts, she's a free spirit. And sometimes a little bewildered by life, like all of us.

Irv slides his bifocals up his nose with his thumb and says he guesses they'll decide that at Brainerd. He brushes his hair with his fingers, crossways, to hide his baldness. He wears a Masonic ring on his third finger. In the spring, when the Shrine circus tours the north country, he takes off for Duluth to wear his red fez and drive a little motorcycle in the parade.

Diane says either I quit trying to rescue bears and wayward women and come with her to Hollywood so we can get my career off the ground or she's leaving. She says she didn't move up here to sit around by herself while I save every creature four-legged and two-legged that doesn't know how to take a leak in private. Diane says she, Diane, is a lonesome wayward animal, too, who needs help and companionship. Where am I when *she* needs me, she asks, and why don't I rescue *her*?

Irv gives me his official look, jangling the shackles in his hand.

I've never been able to let innocent animals be tortured and harassed by unfeeling humans. I think, Diane is a rational creature, Pepper is not. Pepper's like a bear, who needs care, not thorazine. Diane can understand logic.

I hope.

I tell Irv I'll take Pepper, and I'll take her far away.

I don't know where I'll take her. She's not a danger to anybody. She just needs to learn a little impulse control.

Irv leads me back to the cell. Pepper looks woeful and forsaken. She looks like she doesn't understand why all this is happening to her. When I've asked her if she's done this kind of thing before, back in Saskatchewan where she's from, she says, No, pretty much when nobody was around, but I'm 35, she says, and I think I should be able to do what makes me happy, don't you? Don't we deserve that? she asks. To be happy?

Irv unlocks the cell door with a clank. I say, Come on, Pepper, let's go. She doesn't move. I take her hand. I say, It's okay, I'll take care of you. Finally she stirs and steps out of the cell. She holds my hand tightly, as if afraid she'll float away. I look over her shoulder at the puddle in the middle of the gray cement floor. Irv's busy with the key and doesn't look into the cell, so I hurry Pepper outside onto the sidewalk, which is when I see the D of F truck go by pulling the live trap. I run into the street to see who they've incarcerated this time, and it's Rudy, his nose still in the carton of Ben and Jerry's.

LA PÉTAUDIÈRE

Pétaudière: Disorderly, noisy assembly;
bear garden; bedlam broken loose.
—*The Concise Oxford French Dictionary*

Pale moonlight paints our naked bodies. She swallows the Vouvray from the glass beside her bed. The bed is firm as lifelong love, and the crisp sheets, perky with pictures of yellow daisies and garlands of ivy, smell of summer breezes, sunshine, and indolence.

I sniff the chocolatey autumn of her breath, the raspberryish shampooness of her hair, and the raffish cinnamon in the hollow of her throat. I taste the vinegary sultriness of her right ear and the vanilla assertiveness of her left. I breathe the amaryllis cologne pulsing from her neck, the shyness of tulips lounging along her wrists, the musky juniper wafting from her shoulders. Under her arms there's a sweet pungency of thyme, lemon, and freshly baked bread.

I put my ear to her chest and hear the tremulous throbbing of her heart. I listen to her stomach growl. Her bowels squeak and rumble, gurgle, pop, hiss.

Her nipples, sassy and persimmony, solicit elaborate, lingering attention.

I slither my tongue between her toes. She screams a delicious desperation. She twists and beats the bed with her fists, but I don't stop, because she doesn't want me to stop.

And then I stop, because I'm nibbling her ankle. Licking behind her knee. Kissing the inside of her thigh.

I turn her over, my fingers squeezing the firm plumpness. I ease the resilient mounds apart. I breathe the lingering perfume of apricot soap. I nuzzle a heady bouquet reminiscent of a savage Nebbiolo from the right bank of the Tanaro in the Piedmont region of Italy. I sniff the stirring scent of a mature ticklish Syrah. I follow the spoor of a conceited Amontillado until I taste the tincture of a muscular, oak-aged Merlot, the frantic flavor of a Cabernet Franc from Anjou-Touraine in the Loire Valley, the startling smokiness of an aged Lagavulin, and, finally, the stylish anarchy and the cataclysmic confusion of Ethiopian coffee beans fresh from the roaster.

When I come up for air, she rolls on her back, grabs my hair, opens her legs, and hauls me into a wild swampy invitation to passionate redemption.

I swoop into salubrious syncopations of dark lubricity, into nutty, malty beers, raffish ales, and perturbed porters, into pungent cascades of Chambolle-Musigny, Chasselas, and Champagne, into dizzying rivers of Gewurztraminer, Pinot Gris, Camembert, and cherries, into soundings of salty insouciance, peckish promises, and savory stillnesses, into salutatory suavities of saffron, nutmeg, cedar, and cloves, into bounteous liquefactions graveolent of ginger, allspice, artichokes, marjoram, sarsaparilla, and somnolence.

My tongue slips here and there, *largo*.

Her fingers stroke my temples, *legato*.

I flick sideways, dolce. Crossways, *animato*. Clever ways, *subito*.

Her fingertips tap, *staccato*.

I sniffle, snuffle, *rubato*.

She growls, honey over gravel.

Rinforzando I slide. Sostenuto I swash. *Andantino* I sluice.

She moans, an ache finding voice.

My lips pucker, *adagissimo*, pluck, *accelerando*, purse, *ritardando*, pulsate, *affetuoso*, palpitate, *appassionato*.

Her fingers flutter, *agitato*.

I slurp, tremolo, swab, scherzo, swallow, *obbligato*.

Her fingers scratch, *con spirito*.

My tongue, *glissando*.

Her fingertips, *pizzicato*.

I lap, maestoso. I lollop, *giocoso*. I loll, *grazioso*. I lave, *morendo*.

Her heels drum the sheet, *allegro*.

I whisk and whirr and whiffle and whoof. *Vivace!*

She clutches. *Assai!*

I stroke, I stipple, I stir, I stoke. *Con brio!*

Her hands jerk. *Vibrato!*

Da Capo! Repeat from beginning!

Her hips rise! *Volare!*

Doppio movimento! Twice as fast!

Teeth rattle! Knees knock! Spine shivers! Ears warp! Skin sparkles! Fingernails fry! Tarsals tremble!

Crescendo!

Bones melt, brains crack, toes tintintabulate! The sympathetic nervous system sympathizes! Time takes a breather, space hiccups, galaxies stumble!

She's in a delectable delabialized delative delirium. She's gladly grandly gallimaufried. She's swimming in a satisfied swoon.

My tongue's a tuckered tuber.

We take a breather.

Champagne pops. Asiago crumbles. Strawberries are sequestered in fervid dens. Champagne fizzes from bellybuttons. Strawberries are munched from their hiding places. Ice cubes are secreted, melt, tantalize.

Fingernails, suggestive, unsettling, compose arpeggios on the pianoforté of my skin.

She hovers, a carnivore, above me. Her hair brushes my thighs. Animal breath provokes me. Wet lips enfold the flower of my dreams like grace sweetly absorbing the soul's sundry sins.

Nefarious nibblings, nocturnal gnawings, piquant puckerings, charmed chewings. Tiny nippings up and down, teeth teasingly tormenting.

Lengthened?

Impossible!

Lips osculate, a soft tropical flower, insatiate, tremulous, tenderly tyrannical.

Widened? Broadened?

Secret ministrations, astral positionings, occult oscillations, sacerdotal thrummings, transcendental agitations, esoteric tremblings, cabalistic spasms.

Stalwart, sturdy, stony, adamantine!

Bounce boulders, tiddlywink mountains, hoist mainsails, swat home runs, balance for hours on it, eighth wonder of the world!

Primal, persistent, polymorphously perverse primordial penetration!

I'm stewed, slobbered, slithered, sloughed, slimed, smeared, samsonized, sanitized, empowered, embraced, embodied, endowed, entered, entertained, entailed, ensconced, waltzed, tangoed, flamencoed, mamboed, polkaed, cachuchaed, sarabanded, cancanned, limboed, cakewalked, legonged, beguined, gopaked, pavaned, bossa novaed, hakaed, rumbaed, galliarded, saltarelloed, sicilianoed, carmagnoled, tarantellaed.

She shivers me timbers and scuttles me butt. Syncopates, scintillates, strategizes my scrotum. Bamboozles my balls. Bullies my ballocks. Jazzes my jism. Jimmies my joint. Jacks my John Thomas. Gerrymanders my geography.

She fingers my jewels and jostles my flanges. She rubs my rascally rabbit and elmers my fudd. Tessellates my testicles, verifies my vas deferens, counts down to blast off but backs off, leaving me barmy, beaming, balmy, blinking, and brimming.

She decalvinizes my caution. Masters my fate. Captains my soul. Lassoes my lunger, lactates my louie, lubricates my libido, lavages my limbic lobes. She fumigates my fundament, vandalizes my vesicle, vivifies my viscera. Pulverizes, vulcanizes, canonizes my prostate. Pummels, prods, possesses me. Pickles me, pleats me, plumps me, prunes me, pities me.

I'm stupefied, simonized, sanctified. Wonked, winded, wrinkled, waffled. I wallow, whistle, and wobble. I'm sideswiped, blindsided, slipped a mickey, milled, mulled, and mopped. I'm drummed, dabbled, diddled, and dunked. Dessicated, debilitated, differentiated, discombobulated, diffractioned, deconditioned, deconstructed, debunked, derridaed, dunced, doodled, dipped, drunk. I shiver, I shudder, I shout, I shimmy. I sweat and scent and suffer and spout. Splash, stutter, slobber, sink. My forehead flowers. My flippers flap. My perineum is promulgated. My platitudes are pondered. My personality is peppered. My psyche is stymied, my heels are hung, my neck is wrung, I'm sent around the bend and hung out to dry. I go through the wringer and wind up a wild whizzing wommera. I'm shipped out and swabbed down.

Man overboard!

I'm slammed into a black hole, squeezed to infinite mass, shot out, warped, woofed, wrapped, walloped, whipped, whooped, whapped, tumbled, transitioned, transformed, transcended, transected, transported, teleported, and taken to the cleaners.

Whee! Whoopee! Way to go!

LYLE: TO THE RESCUE

> Tales of bears kidnapping and raping women and
> of bears becoming secret paramours of willing
> wives are widely disseminated in European folklore.
> —Beryl Rowland, *Animals with Human Faces:*
> *A Guide to Animal Symbolism*

I catch up to the truck at the Division of Forestry Office, but
there's a padlock on the cage, they've never padlocked the live trap before, what the hell's coming down? I storm into the office to straighten
things out.

It's a new guy, a young fellow I've never seen before. He says he
was sent up from St. Paul. They're getting calls of bears biting heads
off children, bears ransacking houses and shitting on fine Persian rugs,
bears going to the movie theater, bears demanding soft serve swirl at
the Dairy Queen, bears crashing wedding dances, smoking pot, chas-
ing women, and stopping traffic. He says he's been sent here to shake
things up, weed out the incompetent, and straighten out this sorry
mess.

I say if they hadn't relieved me of my duties—out of jealousy, enmi-
ty, incompetence, and power-seeking—I'd've had everything under control—as I've had for years past, as well as bringing fame and recognition
to the Division of Forestry, through my research and advocacy—and all
they had to do was give me a free hand, let's put out some garbage away
from people, the bears'll be happy, the people'll feel safe, I've been trying to tell you knuckleheads in St. Paul that's the way to handle these
situations.

"We're not paid to feed bears," the young whippersnapper says.
"We're paid to control them."

I tell him he and all those bureaucrats in St. Paul are fascists.

He says You must be Lyle.

I say Fuckin' A.

He says if this bear—he gestures to the cage outside—was only eating garbage it might not be so bad, but this bear's broken into three houses today, ripped the doors off three freezers, given an eighty-year-old man a heart attack, made sexual advances to a woman with one leg, and stolen four gallons of ice cream. The woman, the young ranger adds, even wet her pants.

Pepper, who has followed me into the office, gets a sudden spark in her eyes, but she doesn't say anything.

"Why did you padlock the live trap?" I demand.

He says evenly, "Because they warned me about you."

I say, "I'll tell you what. You're busy. You're new. I'll take this bear. I'll take him far away."

The kid smears a superior smile across his pimply face. He says, "I know which bear this is."

I say, "This bear is an indispensable research bear."

He says, "This bear is on the Most Wanted List."

I say, "This bear is a television star, and if anything happens to him, millions of children will weep into their cheerios and sob themselves to sleep, and your name will be Mud."

"This bear," the kid says, "is going to the Minnesota Zoo." He straightens his ranger hat and stiffens his backbone. His steely eyes glint with determination. "I have my orders."

LA PÉTAUDIÈRE, PART TWO

> Delight of men and gods, life-giving Venus
> ...you pierce our hearts with hot love.
>
> —Lucretius, *On the Nature of the Universe*

I tickle her fancy.
She fancies my tickler.
She tweaks my twanger.
I twiddle her twat.
I'm the catalyst for her clitoris.
I energize her estrogen and pilot her progesterone.
I organize her orgasms and eventuate her ecstasies.
I jam her jelly. She jowls my berries.
She musters my marbles. She lobs my lozenges. I ream her rim and she rims my reamer. She wets my whiskers. She resuscitates my rectum.

I apotheosize her pert petunia. She buggers my begonia. I adore her dreamy delphiniums. Her pansy perfumes my pistil. My passionflower permeates her pennyroyal. She cranks my columbine and torques my trillium. I diddle her daisy and she do-wops my dandelion. I irrigate her iris. I please particularly piquantly her petulant pouty petals. She festoons my famous falal with flowers from the florist, a felicitous farrago of feracious fictile fiddling. I fall for the fortuitous folly of far-fetched flings following frumptuous farts. She fondles my firming flinger.

I compromise her contentiousness. She dishes the detritus from my dour demeanor and dumps my despair. I define her dimple. She decorates my decorum. I doubt her dubious disdain. I blow on her bum and bump her balloons. I bite her bippies and teeth her titties.

She confabulates my connies and I congratulate her cunny. She pinches my prepuce and palmolives my pickherupper. She jiffies my jouster. She's loamy. I'm livid. Liminally I laugh. She luffs my looper, and I lip her loofta. I shower in her spume and splash in her suds. I mouth her mucous and munch her muff. I infiltrate her filament and flatter her firmament. I irrigate her canals and fertilize her fallow furrows. I swoon in her sweat and sit in her slat. I follow her into the darkness of delight and catch opportunity by the tail. I yang her yin and she yarovizes my younker. She yerks my yam. Yippee! Yodelaydee-yo!

She banks my billiards and chalks my cue. She's behind my eightball and sucking it. We're sauced in serotonin. We're cupid's kids.

She changes my oil, rotates my tires, lubricates my joints, balances my ball bearings, calibrates my timing, loosens my lugs, tightens my tappets, reams my cylinders, adjusts my carburetor, speeds my choke, slows my idle, dunks my dipstick, lights my brights, flushes my radiator, rams my rods, redesigns my chassis, polishes my bumpers, fans my fenders, jump-starts my battery, blows my gasket, thumbs my thermostat, belts my alternator, grinds my valves, twirls my phillips, and tightens my nuts.

I bogey her breasts, birdie her behind, and blast from her sand trap. I'm lost in her rough. She raises my flag. Hole-in-one!

She makes my software hard and my hardware soft. I download her dreams. She upgrades my hard drive. I access her database. She runs my program. We network. We surf shimmery skin.

I flip her switch, blow her circuits, peak her outage, surge her amps, up her voltage, and readjust her rheostat.

She grabs my gatling, rubs my remington, wanks my winchester, manhandles my magnum, lards my luger, packs my powder, cocks my carbine, aims my musket, muffs my muzzle, lights my fuse, offs my safety, and bites my bullet.

She funnels my flimflam into her funhouse. She fingers my fuming flapdoodle. My fizzer foams. Her quim quakes. My wacky wooer wets her. She deluges my darter with dripping delight. I liquefy her lap. I'm the cream in her coffee, the icing on her cake, the cat's pajamas, the last straw, the end of the road, the road not taken, the lollapalooza.

We're watchful, waiting for the wherewithal to continue. We wonder why we're here and where we are and why anything and everything. Answers? We dally in the delirium of dubiety. We wallow in whoopie. We're winsome.

We soap our skins, silence our censors, superannuate our sancti-
monious stern superegos, and suspend the rules. She slaps my seat and
I smack her sitter. I kiss her keester and burrow her bung. I bivouac on
her bonny bush. She moulin rouges my can can.

She pities. She primps. She plucks. She pumps. She pulls. She
pushes. She kneads and knots, wobbles and wiggles. She fibrillates my
flabby flower. It nods hello. She jostles and jiggles, jangles and joggles.
It jives, jaded. My foregone foreskin, forgotten and forlorn, would
freak. Fortunately five fingers flail my fillerupper. My frenum frolics.
Phrenology phails. There's plenty of plenum to palliate. Perhaps, she
says, we should coordinate.

She bites my bologna and mangles my masher. She bruises my
bratwurst. She gallimaufries my gazongas. I lick her lima, french her
bean, lip her lentil. She nuzzles my nuts. I ravish her radish. She makes
my zucchini zoom. Her turnip turns turbulent. I bouillabaisse her boo-
bies. I suckle her milky ways. I grope her grapefruits. She picks my pa-
paya. I kiss her kiwi. She puckers my prunes. She guzzles my garbonzas.
My chingus? Chow down!

Nosing her nymphae, I sniff Neufchâtel, a frisson of fennel, a whiff
of whey, and a tease of tarragon. I chomp her champignon, suck her
shitake, masticate her morel.

I lap her lo mein. She fries my wonton. I scarf her pot sticker. She
engorges my egg roll. I salivate her sprout. She Szechuans my sausage.
I dote on her dumpling. She shells my shrimp. I open her cookie and
read her fortune. It's the thirty-first hexagram of the I Ching, "Hsien,
Love-making."

I bite her bagel, bounce her bannocks, flip her flapjack. She scram-
bles my eggs, fries my bacon, broils my banger, and butters my pumper-
nickel. My loaf rises.

I nestle in her naughty nookie. She knocks on my knockwurst and
kneads my knaidel. My knose knuzzles her knee. She dips me in her
guacamole. I fondle her fajita. She jalepenoes my habanero. I sip her
savory sangria. She tastes my tamale. I tongue her tostada. My tortilla
tickles her taco. She enchantingly encinctures my encomiastic enchi-
lada.

My cannelloni is *al dente*, her manicotti is *caliente*. She parmigianes
my veal. I munch her marscopone. Her minestrone murmurs. Her tira-
misu, flavored with rum, brandy, espresso, and talent, is triumphant.

I chomp her chapati. She pats my pakora. I nab her naan. She
tastes my tandoori. I pepper her papadam. She pummels my paratha.

I moan into her mulligatawny. She paddles my poori. I slip my samosa into her sambal. I chart her chakras and curry her climax. I kindle her kundalini. She licks my lingam. I yum her yoni. I savor her sutra. Kama, kama, she says, kama na ina my house.

I enter her entrée. She plants my plantain and milks my coconuts. Her quiche quivers. Her consommé contracts. Her borscht bubbles. I cream her callalloo. I guzzle her gazpacho. She calls me Gaucho. Or is it Groucho?

I'm zonked, zapped, zoomed, unzipped. Astrally projected. Shot to the stars, socked to the moon, whacked to twenty-six dimensions, enlightened, illuminated, elucidated. Rebirthed, reincarnated, primal screamed, cathexised, actualized, peak experienced. Chewed up, spit out, bound for glory. See God, say Hi, coming and going.

We die our little deaths, diving through all the rooms of the Bardo. A billion buddhas cheer.

Our heads press against one another, the bones of our skulls hum together, the whirrings of our brains and the snappings of our neurons and the pumping of our blood the same, undivided, indistinguishable.

LYLE: DESPERATE TIMES

The beast in me is caged by frail and fragile bars.... God help the beast in me.
—Johnny Cash

There's the rifle in the cabinet on the wall. I know it isn't loaded, but maybe the young fascist doesn't. I smash the glass with the paperweight on the desk—a stone carving of a bear—grab the rifle, and point it at him.

He says, You're in big trouble, Mister.

I say, Give me the key to the padlock.

He says, I know that rifle's not loaded.

Pepper slips behind him.

He takes a step toward me.

Pepper grabs the mounted northern pike, all shiny and expertly preserved by the hyperhormonal Fran Makosky, off the wall.

I shift the rifle, grab the barrel, and poise as a batter, ready to swing.

"Listen, you old fart," the young fellow says, grabbing for the bat.

Pepper brings the pike down on his head, crushing his cute boy scout hat.

He swerves.

I bring the rifle butt down on his head.

He crumples.

I hope I haven't killed him.

He's breathing. He's stirring, in fact.

I've got a vial of tranquilizer in my pocket and a hypodermic dart.

The kid—Arnie Westhall, it says on his shiny new nametag—slumps peacefully onto the floor.

William Borden

I get the key to the padlock out of the kid's pocket. Still, I'm thinking, this is going to be bad. Arnie knows who I am. I could escape to Canada, sure, get a boat, head through the lakes—but what about my career as a television host, chef, and world-renowned bon vivant?

Pepper looks clear-eyed and ready for anything, as if this emergency has kicked into gear some wheel that had been stuck for awhile. "You know that Joe," she says, "who took care of me? He was telling me he has all kinds of drugs, drugs that can make you seem crazy."

I give Joe a call and he says he'll be right over, as soon as he examines Vera Ostrum's sick emu. I say we don't have time for that, we've got a red alert here, me and Pepper. Joe says, Oh, Pepper's there? I'm on my way.

While we wait for Joe, I ransack the D of F filing cabinets, ripping out the false and scurrilous and maliciously motivated complaints made about me going back several years and feeding them into the shredder. Meanwhile the telephone rings like it's announcing the Second Coming or maybe the long-promised arrival of the exotic dancers at Vern Afinizy's Lots-a-Lakes Lounge and Supper Club, just outside the city limits, a dozen nude dancers from the Wet and Wild Club in Minneapolis. Vern, an ambitious immigrant from somewhere in the Middle East—he's always vague about a specific country—has promised the dancers for over a year now.

Once Joe arrives on his rumbling Harley, his black leather chaps flaring like rugged wings from his legs, his bare torso wind-burned, his goggles bug-splattered, his long hair and frantic beard tantalizingly terrible, he assesses the situation and opens his satchel full of pharmaceuticals, psychotropics, and high quality street drugs. He administers a spectrum to Arnie and, for good measure, hypnotizes him, planting certain suggestions deeply into his unconscious.

Joe says he doesn't have time to wait to see how the drugs and the suggestions work. He has to get to Vera's emu before it infects the rest of the herd. She's sure emu meat will become the thing soon in New York restaurants; it tastes like veal but has less cholesterol than beef, pork, or chicken. But before Joe rushes away he gives Pepper a long look and she him. They stand immobilized for a moment, and then he's out the door and Pepper's whimpering.

I figure action is the best cure for Pepper's sniffling, so I haul her out the door, spring Rudy from the cage, and persuade Pepper to drive him back to my place while I take the truck and the cage to round up the other errant bears.

But Rudy's been confined too long. He ignores the Volvo and races down the street. I run after him, yelling to Pepper to head to Ernie LaFolle's Bottle Shop and get a bottle of their best imported dark brew.

LA BELLE DAME SANS MERCI

> Wretched excess is barely enough.
> —Shirley Corriher, *Gourmet*

She aspirates my amorous armature. I bedazzle her bosom. She comforts my cantankerous comer, dials my dandy dunker, and elongates my excited emergence to an eleemosynary emission. I fandango her fantastic fibrillator. She garnishes my gonads, gladhands my geezer, gooses my gander, and galvanizes my gumption. She hoodoos my hooligan and homogenizes my homunculi. I investigate intimately her improper imbroglios. She jacuzzies my jumping joe. I ken her kalathos. I loosen her lucidity. I murmur, "Mammary, mammary." She nibbles my nefarious nimble noodler. I ogle her omphalos. She provokes my plums, palms my privates, pampers my possum, plumbs my possibilities, pinches my plunger, and pockets my plugger. I quaff her quivering quintessence. She ruminates my rowdy rump. I stunningly stodge her succulent sticky sucker. She tabulates my testosterone, tests my tolerance, and trifles with my tachycardia. I uxoriously ululate her unique uterus. I voraciously verify her various vaginal vibrations, verily. My whistling wad waltzes her whimsical walnut. She xamines my xiphoid. My zany zoomer zaps her zesty zaftig zipper.

We're dancing cheeks to cheeks. Our bellies banter. Her foot's in my mouth. My chin's on her chine. Our thighs throb, calves cleave, toes tickle, shoulders shudder, clavicles clatter, knuckles nudge, wrists wrangle, stomachs stick, hips hop. She finds my fingers facilely frothing the fiery fluids of her formidable furry firmerupper. She fingers my flatulator and foresees my fellation. She jaws my jones. I gamahuche her gamelon. My gamester glows from ganosis. I grease her gams. She shakes my shaft. She shines my shillelagh. She doesn't shilly shally. She shimmers, shudders, shivers, shakes, and shouts. She pre-empts my prematurity, prolongs my performance, permutates my possibilities, percolates my potential, and permeates my pretenses.

She lubes my laggard liquidizer. She lengthens my lounger. She levitates my labarum. She lustrates my lollipop. I query her quirky quim and question her intentions. She yearns to yank my yonny. Yo, Yolanda! I yump for yoy!

She trepidates my tush. She hickeys my heinie. I cosset her cooze. I pet her pelt. I fan her fern. She buries my bone. I wag her tail. I taste a fine stiltson, sniff peach, recognize the suggestion of portobello mushrooms, follow the spoor of pine woods after rain. I'm a cunning linguist.

She pokes my plumbing, palliates my popper, and probes my pooper. I clep her clapper. My vagrant vibrator volleys her vagina. My wily willy winks. I'm elongated by her libidinal longing, restored by her resourcefully rough but refined, rational but reckless, runaway rimming. My firmness ferments. I gulp her guinness. She blows my berries, my bubble, my bugle, my bagpipe, my fortune, my savings, my fuse, my mind.

I bach her breasts. She vibratos my vivaldi. I touch her tchaikovsky. She straddles my stravinsky. I rimsky her korsakov. She bites my beethoven. I scratch her scriabin. She wrinkles my waller. I viggle her wagner. She crunches my coltrane. I meddle with her mingus. She swallows my schoenberg. I buzz her berlioz. She rubs my ravel. She shocks my shostakovich. She chaffs my chopin. My ocherina aches. I mumble into her muff, "Mozart, Mozart." She orchestrates the cunctation of my emission.

She hums my hume and busses my berkeley. I give her whitehead. She arouses my aristotle. I voltaire her vulva. She deweys my doohickey. I sartre her beauvoir. She nectarizes my nietzsche, a gay science. I shave her legs with occam's razor. She showers my schopenhauer, willfully, representatively. She's worldly that way. She libates my leibniz. Our monads mutually masturbate. She wittgensteins that pal o' mine. Pragmatically, this is a variety of religious experience in a pluralistic universe.

I'm the beast in her jungle. She's my golden bowl. We're ambassadors of love. She turns my screw. I wing her dove. She's the madonna of the future. I'm an American, a passionate pilgrim, the last puritan. She's my princess case-my-joint. I roderick her hudson, dripping and pulsing. I'm within the rim. We're no Bostonians. We're an international episode. I'm her reverberator, her sacred fount, the real thing. We're off the wheel of time. We're what Maisie knew. I'm William Wetmore, his story, a small boy, a son and brother, in his middle years.

She mobies my dick. I scarlet her letter. I'm the last of the Mohicans, the deerslayer, the pathfinder. I'm a sinner in the hands of an ardent god. I cotton her mather. She madames my bovary. She tilts my windmill, quixotically. I'm gargantuan. I pant on her gruel. She chatterleys my mellors. She shakes my spear. I fletch her beaumont. I kyd her marlow. I caress her congreve. It's the way of the world, it's important, it's earnest. To the lighthouse, Finnegan!

I boomerang her bazooms, bazooka her begosh. I batten her hatch and snaggle her snatch. I rumple her rump. She holds my hoser. I pump her hooters. She hoovers this hoosier. She shakes my six-shooter. Serious spumer! My humpback sings! My spiracle spouts! Steady as she blows!

Godot comes!

Her warm breasts, bursting with yummy contemplation, headphone my ears. I hear the planets' patient partitas, the moans of the moons, the silvery stars' siren songs, sea chanties flying from far constellations, waltzes of wayward conflagrations, bebop boogies from black holes, gravity's grave galloping corralling of the night's glistenings, merry meteors meandering through the milky beltways of the echoes of the big bang, the great guffaw, the galactic gangbusters, the primal pellucid climax, the universal rapture, the ejaculation of gazillions of galaxies from nothing, the giddy spurt of stars seeding the dark void, sucked to ecstasy by the dark universe pulsing, welcoming, receiving, enticing, a vulva of eternal space welcoming the infinite mass exploding, the first, biggest, best orgasm of them all. We're still spinning, flying, shaking, shuddering, shivering, gasping from that big cosmic come twenty billion years ago.

LYLE: DEFIANT DESPERADOES

Take a bear out to lynch today.
—Lyle Lovett

Rudy's gallomping in overdrive, and I can't keep up with him. I run through back yards until I have to stop to catch my breath. As I'm bent over, huffing and puffing, Pepper pulls up with several six-packs on the seat beside her, saying she couldn't decide which one to buy so she bought them all, and Ernie put them on my charge card because Pepper remembered the number from my charging her room at Emma's We Won't Tell Travel Lodge.

We cruise down the alley in the direction Rudy gallomped, the car cell phone beeping hysterically but I can't take time to answer it now, and there's still no sign of Rudy. Finally Pepper asks, What about your antenna? So I have her pull over, and I get out my antenna to try to lock onto the signal from Rudy's radio collar. I'm not having much luck until I hear a burst of screams a few houses away. I jump in the car, and Pepper lays rubber. We find Rudy in a back yard chowing down on some steaks from the grill while several elderly people crowd into the back door and a woman in a wheelchair, abandoned by her fleeing friends and relatives, screams without mercy.

A white-haired man comes out of the house with a pistol in his hand. I yell at him not to shoot, but he can't hear me above the woman's screaming. He starts to take aim. I give the wheelchair a shove and send her rolling toward the assassin. She hits the man just as he's drawing a bead, the gun goes off, leaves fly overhead, and Rudy takes off down the alley. The man and the woman are on the ground. The woman's holding the man tight, yelling she's always loved him, even though he is her brother-in-law, loved him ever since their hasty, mad

William Borden

affair forty years ago. Another woman bursts from the house, her sister no doubt, and grabs for the pistol, but I take advantage of the familial contretemps to take the gun for safekeeping and hightail it after Rudy, Pepper following in the car.

Rudy's sniffing some hamburgers on the grill a few houses down. Five or six children are playing on the swing set. There are no adults around. Pepper stops in the alley. I get a six-pack and walk over to Rudy to tempt him into the car once he's polished off the hamburgers, which are his first priority. But these are foreign beers that need an opener, so I go to the back door to ask for a church key as a bald guy in an undershirt comes out toting an assault rifle.

I aim the pistol at him and tell him all I need is a bottle opener and I'll get the bear out of his way. What bear, he says, I was only going to scare those kids they're always peeing in my yard. I wonder if Pepper's brought some exotic virus that's spreading through the town. Then he sees Rudy and he sees no more hamburgers. I say I'm an official bear researcher and this is an official research bear who mustn't be harmed. Rudy is on his back, the catsup bottle between his paws, guzzling the catsup. The kids are crowded around Rudy, petting him and pulling his hair. I take the man's rifle, and he brings me a bottle opener.

But goddamn it, Rudy's off again, over fences and across yards. He knows he's giving me a merry chase. He blames me, I think, for letting him get captured. Or he's mad, like Diane, because I haven't paid much attention to him lately. And now the kids are running after him, yelling and screaming, and Pepper's squatting, and the man's yelling there's no decency anymore it's the end of civilization.

Pepper and I get in the car and follow the kids, the cell phone bleating, I wetting my whistle with the beer, and I open two more, so I'm ready for when we catch up to Rudy. We pull onto a wide residential street shaded by large maple trees. We spot Rudy cantering down the middle of the street. More kids are after him now, maybe twenty or thirty. They're not laughing anymore. They're screaming a high-pitched, feral howl. They're fired up by the chase. Some ancient blood lust has kicked in, some fever for the hunt coded since Australopithecus. Rudy recognizes it. His DNA has been coded for a million years, too, to run like gangbusters to escape the inchoate hunting frenzy of *homo sanguinarius*.

I hear sirens howling, coming closer, and I'm thinking, shit, I'm done for, and Rudy, too. That's what I get for trying to save the world, sirens.

THE NAKED TRUTH

> It's only by thinking even more crazily than
> philosophers do that you can solve their problems.
> —Ludwig Wittgenstein

"If we hear sirens," she says, walking naked as eternal truth into her bedroom, "it'll be the police." She's carrying a newspaper and a couple of envelopes. "I stepped onto the porch like this. Do you see what you've done? You've taken away my shame. If I'm arrested, will you bail me out?"

She drops the newspaper and mail on the sheet and falls into bed beside me. "Do you think love dies?" she asks.

I say I don't know much about love.

She says she knows that, but what happens to it? "Is it like dew, evaporating in the noontime heat of practicality? Or like wine in a bottle with a faulty cork—a little air from the outside world and all that richness and complexity collapse into a tongue-turning vinegar? Is it like the news"—she shakes open the newspaper— "interesting only for a moment—a headline today, an obituary tomorrow? Like a letter"—she picks up an envelope— "you think is from a friend but it turns out to be"—she tosses it on the floor— "junk mail?"

I say, *In my experience—*

"You must have had a lot of experience," she interjects. "Based on last night's adventures."

You seemed excited, I acknowledge.

"You didn't learn that from books."

Our souls, I say, *were one.*

"Do you believe in the soul?"

An animating principle?

"An essence, a self, immaterial, that might or might not survive death or exist before birth. What do you think?"

I think that's too speculative for me.

"Spinoza says everything's God: you, me, sun, mind, algebra, Saskatoonberry—the whole ball of wax: God. What do you think?"

I can entertain that idea.

"Some say that's just pantheism, as if they were saying, 'Oh, that's just orange juice.' But what's wrong with pantheism?"

Exactly.

"Pantheism," she goes on, "is a hot, steamy cassoulet." I watch her mind whirling, the juices snapping in neuronal adventurousness. "It's full of chicken and pork and sausage and beans and herbs, onions and garlic and celery and carrots." She paces beside the bed, her bare legs lean and sturdy, her pale breasts bouncing with the stridings of her thought, her unbrushed hair wild as unfettered dialectic.

"Pantheism"—she takes a deep breath, building up momentum for her next syllogistic volley—"is a bouillabaisse. A paella." She sits on the bed, curling her legs under her. "A jambalaya." Her stomach bulges endearingly when she sits. Her stretch marks are maps of experience, small highways to visceral luminosity, a configuration bespeaking resilience, survival, intrepidity.

"Monotheists"—she places her palm on my stomach—"think they're so smart, like they've invented dentures or suspenders, as if choosing one deity above all others was an act of genius rather than an inability to concentrate on more than one thing at a time.

"But monotheism"—she rubs my tummy, massaging her ideas into my guts— "*abdicates responsibility*. Monotheism says that everything holy is *up there*, and everything *down here* is shit. No wonder monotheists suffer low self esteem. Or, they think God is their main man and they've got the sole scoop (soul scoop?), so they think they're not only *shit*, they think they're *hot shit*. And everybody else is cold potatoes. Are you following this?"

I am, adoringly.

"Now shallow-minded people think that pantheism is merely cool, like, 'Groovy, we're all God.'" She leans over me, her warm breasts caressing my chest. "But they don't understand what pantheism really means. Pantheism"—she taps my nose with her finger— "carries heavy responsibility." I comb her auburn tresses with my fingers. "Because, buddy-o, if everything is God, we have to treat everything—bears, berries, shit, boogers—as if it were God. If *we're* all God, we have to treat *each other* like God." She falls on her back beside me. "We have to be nice to each other."

"It means," she rearm, lets her hand fall, grasps, *prima facie*, what it happens to fall on, and begins, *a priori*, to rhythmically knead it.

She opens her eyes. "But then, Spinoza said it wasn't easy."

Liking monotheists?

"Pursuing the path of clear and ruthless thinking." She tugs, a posteriori, at my *raison d'être*.

"I think it was Spinoza." She squeezes my *Ding-an-sich*. "Maybe somebody else said that." She diddles my *Dasein*. "Maybe I said that." She apodictically rubs my *res extensa*.

She recalls, "I told Frank Running Bear about Spinoza once. About old Baruch saying that everything's God. Frank said Spinoza must have been an Indian. I said, Baruch was Jewish. Frank asked, Did he live on the ghetto rez? I said, Well, the Jews kicked him out, said he wasn't a good Jew. Frank said, We Indians know about diaspora."

She sits up and, practicing *epoché*, eyes my little eye. She opens her mouth, *ad hominem*. She lowers her head, *a fortiori*. Her teeth, ad hoc, circumvolve my categorical imperative. Her cyrenaic cutting edge presses *de re* my *élan vital*. Her mouth full, she mumbles something.

What?

She lifts her head. "Did you know that to circumcise means to purify spiritually?"

I didn't.

Her eyes sparkle pyrrhonistically. Her hand clasps my entelechy, pour-soi. My cimelium circumnutates. Her white teeth gleam enthymematically. Her incisors insinuate hylozically. "Are you afraid?" she asks aporiacally.

Her hair falls, en-soi, over my blossoming apeiron. "Priapus was a god," she murmurs. Her moist breath warms my priapus. Her *meshuga* teeth munch lightly, like mice, like memories, like mortality. "All religions eat their god," she croons. Her teeth close.

Ignoratio elenchi, I don't move. *Salva veritate*, I'm hers. She has me, apocatastatic. Ataraxic, I can be consumed. *Risus sophisticus*, she licks her lips. "Are you trusting," she asks, "or just foolish?"

I'm a trusting fool.

"Maybe love simply goes," she sighs. "Like summer. Like youth." She sits back, lost in thought. "Maybe it's Nature's way of scattering the species. Of turning over new leaves." She leaves my moistened *modus ponens* to dry in the breeze. "Maybe dead love is merely the natural compost of the emotions."

Maybe dead love helps new love to grow.

"Then where does love come from?" she asks.

LYLE: WHAT BEARS LOVE

No truth appears to me more evident, than that beasts are endow'd with thought and reason as well as men.

—David Hume

Rudy's frightened by the sirens, and he's surrounded by the screaming kids, maybe forty or fifty of them by now, and two fire engines, and an ambulance, and Sheriff Irv in his car, red light flashing, and he's not going to be happy, blaming every little disturbance in the county on me, as he's gotten into the habit of doing, although thank goodness he hasn't pinned the terribly unfortunate Ben Creswell thing on me although when Ben is mentioned Irv looks at me with a troubled wrinkle on his brow. And even the state patrol is pulling up now, all colors of lights flashing, blue, green, red, phosphorous, the car looks like a Christmas tree gone nuclear, and the trooper, it's Freddy Garfield, whose patrol car is often parked in the rear of Fran Makosky's Taxidermy, is climbing languidly out of his car and putting his trooper hat on and bringing a shotgun with him. And Irv's unholstering his revolver.

But the kids are whooping it up around Rudy, so nobody's going to shoot yet, giving me a chance to wade in, a beer in each hand, and knee the little brats out of the way. I don't know how Rudy knows they're only innocent children despite their bloodlust, but he does, and although he's getting pretty antsy and whoofing, he's not biting, but he is beginning to scare them, so I've got a path now, and I waft the bottles under Rudy's nose. As soon as he gets a clear gander at the Volvo he races to it. All Pepper has to do is get out of the way.

I don't say anything to Sheriff Irv or Trooper Freddy.

We drive to the D of F panel truck parked in front of the D of F office. I climb into the truck and pull away, the live box attached. Pepper, with Rudy in the rear leaning on the front seatback to keep an eye on everything, follows in the Volvo.

We find Abercrombie at the Browsing Bear Gourmet Restaurant where Celine Ostrum is smacking him with a broom, trying to drive him out of her kitchen, a half-fried walleye in his mouth. Abercrombie surveys the stove, sniffing the other menu items, the large pan of Pork Chops de Lyle (sauté strips of onion and red pepper in olive oil, dredge the pork chops in flour and black pepper, brown the pork chops, add chopped tomato, Portobello mushrooms, a bay leaf, and a pinch of thyme, dowse with a generous splash of an ebullient bourbon, and simmer for an hour), the pot of Cream of Broccoli and Wild Rice Soup (too complicated to go into here), and the kettle of mashed potatoes with roasted garlic and chives.

I remember the writer fella telling me that Abercrombie had been behaving strangely, the consequence possibly—the writer was a bit elusive here—of some experimental potential-enhancing medication Joe Manello had employed, prompting Abercrombie to promenade extraordinary (for a bear) distances on his two hind feet. Abercrombie was seen entering the old Corinthian-columned Carnegie Public Library, waddling to the magazine section and riffling through *Cooking Light, Bon Appetit,* and *New Age Journal* (Edna Dancing Loon, the thirty-something Assistant Librarian, made careful notes), and finally carrying off—it had to be mere happenstance—a copy of The Human Nature of Bears, a dusty relic from the nineteenth century by the deservedly obscure fabulist Willy Bulleback, said to be a pen name for the infamous explorer-naturalist-anarchist, Guillaume Vicaire.

As Abercrombie debates the merits of the menu steaming before him, I grab the large bowl of Celine's Creamy Homemade Tapioca Pudding (tinctured with well-aged cognac) from the waitress, a sprightly college student wearing hot pants and hiking boots who has, despite my better judgment, caught my eye. I waft the tapioca's heady aroma under Abercrombie's scarred nose. I back toward the door, holding the bowl out before me. Celine yells, "Not my Tapioca!"

I back all the way to the live trap, slide the bowl inside, and step aside. Abercrombie inhales the pudding's flirtatious beguilement. He scrutinizes the live box, an enclosure he's inhabited before. Bears have impeccable memories, so he knows what awaits him. Will Celine's seductive tapioca overcome his cautious ruminations?

He lowers himself to all fours. He grunts as he descends, as if he's having trouble with his hips—a malady I can identify with. I think he's going to enter the box. But he doesn't. He pads with solemn deliberation to the passenger door on the truck. He rests his paws on the windowsill, silent and stoic, as if contemplating The Contingencies of Life.

Celine has brought her broom outside and watches from the doorstep. The young gal takes a few admiring steps in my direction. Before I can help myself I give her a wink and a smile. Celine swats her with the broom. Swats her because she can't reach me, but she's looking at me. The click of a latch draws our attention to the truck. The door is open, and Abercrombie is crawling onto the seat. I place the bowl of tapioca in Abercrombie's lap and shut the door.

The waitress brings me a fresh salmon and a walleye and a coconut cream pie for bait for the other bears, and I drive off, old Ab beside me, gulping the tapioca, his butt on the seat, his front paws cradling the bowl, and his hind feet perched indolently on the dash. Pepper follows in the Volvo.

We drive to Dunkin' Donuts, run by Polly Kincaid, née Ostrum, the beleaguered mother of Bobby Kincaid, idolater of Pepper's pungent stream, where Londonderry and Yardley are rummaging through the dumpster. Neither the cajolery of my voice nor the blandishments of Celine's food are tempting them from their investigation of the dumpster. It's their curiosity, insatiable as a scientist's, that's motivating them. They need a temptation more elemental than food to entice them into the box.

Here's where I can finally put Pepper's talents to good use.

She shakes her head. "I'm not a performer," she says.

"I know that, Pepper, and I respect that. But this isn't a performance."

"I had a bad experience the other night."

"I heard about that."

"I drank too much."

I say, "We all over-indulge from time to time. How else are we going to embrace life to the fullest?"

The bears topple the dumpster, scattering garbage all over the parking lot. Customers are beginning to gather. It's situations like this that I try to avoid—spectacles and crowd scenes, where the naturalist's job is compromised by undesired publicity and the spontaneous intrusions of over-eager animal lovers.

"I wonder if I'm an addictive personality," Pepper muses.

Abercrombie's licking up the last of the tapioca and Rudy's eyeing the dumpster debris with some interest, and the crowd is drawing nearer, some friendly, some self-appointed bear-baiters, and I've got to do something soon before matters get completely out of hand. I say, "Please, Pepper. You've wanted to help me. Now you can."

"If I help you," Pepper says, "will you get rid of that other woman and let me live with you?"

I wonder how I get myself into these messes. I watch Abercrombie paw at the door handle of the truck. I watch Rudy try to squeeze out through the half-open window of the Volvo. And now the pretty waitress shows up. Maybe someday she'll be a renowned animal researcher like me, and don't I have an obligation to mentor these young people?

And now, standing in the doorway of Dunkin' with her arms crossed, is Polly Kincaid, a weathered woman wearing too much lipstick and too high a beehive, a hairstyle she's kept with more fidelity than she's kept husbands these many decades.

Pepper waits sullenly for an answer, one hand on her hip, an assertiveness sprouting suddenly that I haven't seen before. Has Joe been injecting her with mind-altering chemicals? Or has my altruistic nurturing merely brought her self-confidence to the fore?

I ask her, "What about Joe? I thought you and Joe—?"

She tears up. "Joe doesn't like me."

"What makes you think that?"

"He doesn't try to take advantage of me."

I see we've got a long-term therapy situation here, one even I can't solve in a few seconds, so I say, "Let's talk to Joe about it, what do you say?"

Londonderry charges a cluster of onlookers who've pressed too close, and they go running and screaming and yelling for guns. It's a mock charge, of course, with the usual *Whoof!* and slapping of paws on the ground, but some vigilante is getting his rifle from the rack in his pickup, and now Londonderry's charge has agitated Yardley, who's foaming at the mouth, a sign of stress, not anger or rabies, and Rudy's rolling down the window in the Volvo, and Polly is striding closer. I say, "Pepper, we've got to put personal desires aside for the moment and save these bears." I say, "I need you, Pepper."

"I love Joe!" she bawls.

I say, "I know that," and lead her to the live trap. She drops her shorts, and I circle behind Londonderry and Yardley, herding them toward the trap.

The man with the rifle is creeping nearer.

The splatter catches Yardley's attention. He raises his nose, catching the scent even I can smell. Polly yells, "Is that the whore who got my Bobby sent back to jail?"

Yardley hops into the trap. Pepper pulls up her shorts and slips past Yardley, leaving Yardley to nose the puddle. Yardley's getting an erection. Pepper drops the barred door on the trap. Polly screams into Pepper's innocent face, "Pissing bitch!" Pepper decks her. A roundhouse to the jaw.

The student gal has Londonderry interested in the coconut cream pie and, a quick learner, draws him into the back of the panel truck. She asks me, "Should I pee, too?" Her hands are on her shorts. I say that's not always a necessary element in bear management, only an emergency measure. But, I add, there might be an occasion when it would be providential, and we could explore that at a future time.

Sheriff Irv and Trooper Freddy pull up, but they turn their attention to the guy with the rifle, who's running for his pickup, whom they quickly disarm and arrest, Irv recognizing him, I later learn, as wanted for murder in several states.

And now everybody's distracted by Arnie Westhall, the young ranger we left comatose on the floor of the D of F office sedated by Joe Manello's drugs, who's running on all fours down the middle of the street, *whoofing* and *whuffing*, proving that Joe's post-hypnotic suggestion is working.

WHERE LOVE COMES FROM

> Sex is a battle against metaphysics.
> —Rebecca Goldstein,
> *The Mind-Body Problem*

I spread Saskatoonberry jam over her right breast. I position one blood-red Saskatoonberry atop her nipple. It keeps falling off, so I have to balance it carefully.

"Is this your breakfast?" she asks.

I lick in concentric circles, starting from the outside and spiraling in. I lip the sides of the nipple, which quivers. Finally there is the Saskatoonberry, perched on top. I suck up the berry, succulent and tangy. She twitches. I press the berry between my teeth. It pops.

"It's not a balanced breakfast," she says.

I daub jam on her left breast. I lap it up, *modus tollens*. When I reach the berry atop her nipple, the berry falls off. "You'll have to do it again," she says. I do. She says, maieutically, "I think you should do it again," and I do. She says, "Bite it gently," and I do. Finally she nestles my head against her sticky breast and pets me.

I'm not sure about the honey, but, *petitio principii*, she insists. She guides me in, and I think the stickiness is going to impede and the gooiness is going to make friction, not ease it, but after a few tentative pushes the honey is warmed, and, *mutatis mutandis*, I move forward and back as in a viscous dream, and I taste the opulent sweetness through my honey plunger, as if it had sprouted taste buds, and she says she can taste the honey inside too, and a tingling embraces our skins, like tiny bees coyly stinging, and as my honey dipper darts and dollops, dibbles and dabbles, her mouth honeys mine, and I dive faster and she levitates higher, and I hear a buzz in my ears and I see bees swarming and a hammer hits the top of my head and another hits the base of my spine, and, QED, gobs of apodosic honey pulse phenomenologically into her hot hive of foaming Feuerbachian hope.

"There," I gasp, "that's where love comes from."

LYLE: HOME SWEET HOME

 It is then part of my happiness that many others should understand as I do, and that their understanding and desire should be entirely in harmony with my understanding and desire...
—Baruch Spinoza

I pull up to the lodge in the D of F panel truck, Abercrombie on the seat beside me, pawing at the wheel and slapping the gear shift, wanting to drive. Towley has joined Londonderry in the back of the truck, and Barry and Kerry are crammed into the live trap with Yardley. For Cranberry and her cubs I requisitioned an unattended house trailer parked along the street and hitched the house trailer to the Volvo. Diane is standing in the driveway, and she looks ready, as they say, to eat bear. It occurs to me that maybe it's she who's been calling all afternoon on the cell phone.

I kill the engine and climb out. Pepper pulls up beside me, Rudy in the back seat, the house trailer dragging behind. She shuts off the motor. She stays in the Volvo, leaving this reunion moment to Diane and me.

Diane asks, "What's the use of a cell phone if nobody answers it?" It seems to be a rhetorical inquiry. "We can be in constant communication with anyone around the globe and even in space, but I can't raise a middle-aged, bushy-bearded bear nut a few miles down the blacktop road."

I'm not sure to whom she's speaking. An audience of judges loafing in the trees? She does that when she gets mad—refers to me in the third person and appeals to some unnamed Board of Review that always seems to be on her side. "And then," she goes on, gathering steam, "she pulls up driving my Volvo?"

Now Pepper gets out, as if to deny her culpability, and walks a little ways away. Diane looks inside the driver's window. She's checking the seat to see if Pepper has restrained herself, and she has. "And poor Rudy's cowering in the backseat—" but no, she's mistaken, he's sleeping, and empty bottles of Bass and Beck's clutter the footwell, and there's an empty tub of Schwann's double chocolate chocolate chunk, and the backseat's a mess I'll never clean up she's going to kill me.

She looks in the live trap, where Yardley, Kerry, and Barry have put aside their customary jockeying for dominance and are stretched out, snoring, stupefied on ice cream and beer.

"It'd be better," I admit, "if they liked plain old Bud or Pabst, but I always thought they should have the best, and they've gotten used to the imported lagers and bocks, ales and Guinnesses. Trouble is, they each have their individual preferences. Barry thinks he's Bob Marley and wants Red Stripe; Towley thinks he's Yeats and heads for the Harp; and on it goes. The ice cream's even worse. Kerry likes the Schwann's vanilla—we captured her at the picnic grounds, we heard the screams and figured somebody had left their fried chicken upwind—and Barry goes for Haagen-Das, strawberry especially but he'll nose after a lemon-lime as a close second. He was climbing through Mrs. Wiloughby's kitchen window but was stuck, poor guy, wailing and woofing after her caramel rolls—here, I brought you a dozen, she was nice enough to give them to me in gratitude—Towley, on the other hand, will eat any ice cream at all; he's a gourmand rather than a gourmet. We netted Towley loitering in the alley behind Mel's Supermarket, where he is every evening, I'm told, waiting for them to put out the spoiled produce, only he must've passed the good news on to Cranberry because she was there, too, with her cubs, Raspberry and Quince. Well, I was out of tranquilizer, so I commandeered the Schwann's truck, which was pulled up in the shade on Main Street, and I made Cal Simonson, the Schwann's man, donate his ice cream to preserve the safety and tranquility of the town. But the bears, crowded so close together and invading each other's space, are not going to be happy once the euphoria from the beer and ice cream wear off."

I've talked more than I usually do, but then I figure I owe Diane an explanation.

"We've got to get the fellas far away from here, honey," I go on. "The bad guys are after them with rifles and have no more patience for inter-species cooperation than a Moslem has for pork chops marinated in brandy. As far as most people are concerned, when push comes to shove, it's humans first every time."

BANFF BOP

Banff in early autumn is a quiet village of hotels and restaurants
and boutiques, the sidewalks trod by retirees in plaid trousers and rain
hats and youths wearing shorts and hiking boots and backpacks. In
one of the boutiques I find a leather miniskirt that smells wild and
mammalian, and between my thumb and fingers it feels alive and impatient.

"I can't wear that."

"Try it on."

"It's too short."

"When I look at your long, creamy thighs, warm and wanton, lithe
and lascivious, I want to fall on my knees and praise God." She gives
me an agnostic look. A passing clerk, a good-looking lad, bouncy and
cologned, makes a sudden swerve to adjust the sweaters on a nearby
table. I drop to my knees. "PRAISE GOD!" An amused smile flickers
across her lips. "FOR THESE BEAUTIFUL LEGS!"

"Now you're embarrassing me."

The clerk rests a hand on my shoulder. He says to her, "It's you."

"I'm too old."

An elderly woman comes over to ask if I'm all right. I climb to
my feet. I've done something to my back. The elderly woman advises,
"You're never too old, honey," and shuffles toward the Victoria's Secret lingerie.

"I'm a mother of grown children."

"*Experience*," the clerk sighs. "You can buy almost everything with money—food, clothes, looks, sex, even love. But experience?" He massages my shoulder. "It's one thing money can't buy."

"I don't know," she sighs.

He says to me, "You can see her in it, can't you?" I nod. "What do you see?" I search for words. "What do you feel?"

She's waiting, skeptical, challenging, saucy.

I say, "It's giving me a hard on."

She snatches the skirt and disappears into the dressing room. The clerk says, "She reminds me of my aunt. She taught me everything about sex. Well, almost everything. I was sixteen; she was thirty-five." He closes his eyes, remembering. "You're a lucky man," he whispers.

A pain arcs down one leg. "What?" he asks. I mumble, *back, pain.* "Bend over." He pushes me until I'm looking at my knees. "Relax," he says, "I'm a certified acupuncturist." He kneads my sacral vertebrae. He hums, I don't know if it's a show tune or a mantra. A breeze slips down my legs. The pain's gone. He pulls me erect.

I try on a leather vest. I imagine it's from the same animal as her skirt. An animal taken in the midst of rut, sacrificed in the cataclysm of climax, the lust in the blood suffusing the vibrant hide. The clerk gives it a tug at the back, an adjustment at the shoulders, a straightening of the front. "*It's your destiny,*" he says.

She comes out, long legs swinging. She gives my vest a yank, says she likes it. I hand the clerk my VISA. His name is Phil. "*Phil* means *love,*" he confides. "*Philosophy? Philanthropy? Philadelphia?*"

"*Philodendron?*" I ask.

William Borden

LYLE: FIRST THE BAD NEWS

> In heraldry the bear denoted the man of power or
> nobility attacked by underlings...
> —Beryl Rowland, *Animals with Human
> Faces: A Guide to Animal Symbolism*

A moving van labors up the drive, swerves around the live trap and the Volvo, rolls onto the grass, and jerks to a stop. The air whooshes out of the brakes. I imagine they're lost and they've come to ask for directions, but Diane's strolling over as if she's expecting them.

I say, What eviction notice, and she says, I was trying to call you on the cell phone, if you'd stick around I might have a chance to tell you. It's the Division of Forestry, demanding their lodge back. Judge Michaels' restraining order was lifted by a higher court, and Judge Michaels is being investigated for exceeding his limit of game fish. So we have to move, because Sheriff Irv's due out here tomorrow and that's the last you'll see of that wine cellar.

"Where are we going?"

"Hollywood," she says. The movers are climbing out of the cab—they're in no hurry, they're being paid by the hour—and saunter into the house.

Diane says, "There's good news, too."

I say, "What's that?"

"Ben and Jerry want to use Rudy in a commercial for their ice cream."

I say, "Ben and Jerry called you?"

She says, "Ben."

I say, "Is he the fat one?"

She says she thinks they both have ample girths.

I say, "Commercial?"

"They'll send a crew to film him breaking into houses, opening freezers, eating the ice cream. There was a story on the wire service."

"About Rudy?"

"And the Cherry Garcia."

"But only you and I know about that." Diane has a pinched look on her face, as if she's determined to hold something in, the kind of look Pepper gets.

"Rudy'll love it," she says. "It's not exploiting him. It's no different than what you do! Why not Rudy?"

The van guys, as if they lived here, god damn it, have perused the frig and they come out, one sipping a Sapporo, the other a Dos Equis, and sit on the two-person wooden swing hand-crafted years ago by Abe Frankenheimer, an old recluse and gifted carpenter until he was killed one night at the Peacock Lounge, which is what the Blue Ox used to be called when Irv's father, Roscoe, owned it—shot and killed by Pastor Swenson, the Lutheran minister who preached hellfire and late one Saturday night while he was writing an especially brimstoney sermon got it into his head that Abe Frankenheimer was humping his, Swenson's, wife, Monica. Then Pastor Swenson, standing over Abe as Abe's blood spread dark and sticky across the Peacock's wooden floor—the stain's still visible after all these years of Clorox scrubbings—put the shotgun to his own sternum and destroyed forever the heart that had been so broken. But poor Abe was an innocent victim of excessive Biblical fervor and a bad guess, because Monica was actually having carnal knowledge of Rosemary Ostrum, Virgil's first wife and Fran Makosky's sister. Not many people know that.

Anyway, that old wooden two-person swing resonates with memories of me and the little woman passing cool summer evenings swinging back and forth, the little ones playing in the grass at our feet, and then, years later, me sitting in it alone, she mad at me and not speaking, and then, sometimes, she sitting in it by herself, even in winter, in her parka, breathing frost, the snow up to her knees so she couldn't even swing, I watching from the kitchen window wondering what I could do this time to make things right, but now I wonder if there hasn't been too much water over the dam, whether I should take my chances with Diane, even if Diane does seem edgy and unforgiving at times. Maybe she's my only hope now, for comfort and companionship, and Diane and I have had a few memorable moments in that swing, like the time earlier in the summer when she stood in front of it, her back to me as I sat in it, and she bent forward, and I was supposed to swing forward and insert myself with precision accuracy, but my aim was not exactly marksmanlike and my tumescence was faltering so we wound up on the grass, finishing just before the writer fella came back from some secret rendezvous of his own, before he took off without a say-so.

Well, I was taking him for granted, I can see that now, and a friend-ship has to be nurtured like a marriage, nothing happens from inertia except moss and lichens, but didn't he by the same token owe me a goodbye note at least, leaving me with these bears to corral, as well as everything else?

"May I use your bathroom?" Pepper's twisting her legs this way and that.

"Of course."

Pepper hurries, with short steps, knees together, to the door, bump-ing into one of the van guys going in for another beer. He blocks her way for a moment, a good-time fellow, barrel-chested, balding, needing a shave, wants to pass the time of day. She tries to get past him. He sees, then, she's in no mood for chit chat and steps aside. I say to Diane, "I can choose to be exploited. Rudy can't."

"Rudy likes Ben and Jerry's. Rudy would want to endorse their ice cream."

I look at Rudy snoring innocently, paws twitching in some bear dream, in the back of the Volvo, ice cream and beer stains on the leather.

"If he could talk," Diane says, "he'd say he wanted to be in a Ben and Jerry's commercial. He'd sign on the dotted line." Rudy whimpers at something in his dream, as if in his dream some mean guy was taking away his ice cream. "Rudy will get a life-time supply of Cherry Garcia." I lean on the Volvo, a kind of wailing wall for my moral convolutions. "And we'll get a hundred thousand dollars." I can see some scratches and rust spots on the car. Maybe it's time she traded it in. "If they use it for more than six months, we get another hundred thousand." Rudy gives a little yelp in his sleep.

No, it's not Rudy, it's Pepper, inside the screen door, asking where a mop is. "I tried," she says plaintively.

I tell her the mop's in the closet in the corner of the kitchen.

"The other good news," Diane goes on, as if the ice cream matter were settled, "is Steven Spielberg's people are interested in my idea."

I hear the mop and broom and buckets clanking in the kitchen.

The moving guy comes out holding a bottle of the French beer, the liter bottle. This guy's African American, a slim but muscular tall fellow, and his partner's white, and I'm feeling good about this multiculturalism and maybe we're getting someplace in this country after all. But I think the least he could do is help Pepper mop up. I ask Diane, "What idea?"

"My idea about the murder mystery at a public television station."

"I thought you were going to write a novel about that."

"With a novel you have to think about adjectives and chapters and describe the wallpaper in a room. I don't have the patience for that. I mentioned the idea to our writer friend—do you suppose he's dead? Should we worry?—and he wrote up a treatment, and I showed it to this woman I met in the ladies' room at Spago's—there was no more toilet paper in her stall—whose sister is a receptionist at Spielberg's outfit, that new company he's formed, and they want the writer to sign an option—where the hell do you think he went?"

BUTTERFLY BEARS

> Good girls go to heaven
> But the bad girls go everywhere
> —Meatloaf

Driving through peaceful forest over the gracefully winding road from Banff to Lake Louise, she rests her hand on my crotch as if she's afraid something might get loose there. Or she teases me by exposing her pertinacious pink nipple. Or she escorts my hand under her leather skirt to moisten my fingers in the wings of her dewy delectation.

And then she unhouses me altogether, exposed to the wind and her flickering fingers, while a long line of cars builds up behind us, unable to pass on the hills and curves, until I swerve onto a pullout, and the cars speed past, frustration and anger in their exhaust, and her silky hair falls like a fragrant shower over my innocent bud.

I say, I'm not sure how many times I can—

The delicate wings of a butterfly, a Two-Tailed Tiger Swallowtail or a Great Purple Hairstreak or an Aphrodite, or a rare variety known only to Vladimir Nabokov, flutters around my nectar-squirter. RVs and trailers whoosh past us on their breakneck search for the thrills of the Canadian wilderness.

My perky pistil metamorphoses, teased by the velvety petals of a rose, a Taboo or Timeless or maybe a Stainless Steel. I'm absorbed by a carnivorous blossom, a succulent suctioning that yanks apocalyptic cataclysms from my heels. The Vesuvius of my doubts erupts. Second thoughts spurt. Doubt ejaculates, a dubious drunk ejected from the express bus of bliss.

A ravenous flower presses my lips apart. A saucy salutation slides down my tongue. A yeasty brew tickles my throat. "Nothing will disgust you," she says. "You'd never shame me, no matter what I did." Her hand grabs my wilted weathervane. For assurance? As a threat? "Would you?"

LYLE: MEANWHILE, BACK AT THE LODGE

> A confession has to be a part of your new life.
> —Ludwig Wittgenstein

The moving guys—Jamal's the tall one, Gill's the short one—have finished their beers and have to quit for the night, union rules, they'll be back in the morning and really get down to work, could I suggest a motel? I'm about to mention Fanny Ostrum's Hide-a-Bed or Ralph's when Pepper pipes up that she's been staying at Emma's We Won't Tell.

Of course Diane gives me a look. Did *I* get Pepper a room at Emma's? I see the question in a tightening at the corners of her eyes and a thinning of her lips.

I tell the guys how to get to Ralph's, and then I say, casually, to Diane, as the guys are firing up their diesel, that I sent Pepper to Emma's *precisely because it was in the woods*, so Pepper would have that easy access to the outdoors that she enjoys so much, and she wouldn't get herself into trouble at the less rustic motels.

I don't know if Diane buys it, but she seems willing to let further discussion pass because a fight is breaking out in the live trap. The trap is shaking, the bears are banging the sides, there are wails and growls, and it's getting Rudy riled up, too, in the Volvo. He's lunging at the window trying to get out and see what the commotion's about.

And now the phone's ringing.

Ordinarily I'd open the door and let them loose, but they'll only get into trouble again, and the D of F will shoot them.

Diane comes out of the house, cordless phone in her hand, saying, "It's the sheriff."

I take the phone. I tell her to open a few bottles of beer and slide

Dancing with Bears   *281*

them into the cage. "That's what's wrong with them now," she says. "They're like men. They get mean when they're drunk."

I say, "Now you're the bear expert?"

"Fuck you," she says, and slams the screen door.

I say, "Irv?"

Irv says he's always been my friend and he's gone out of his way to give me the benefit of the doubt, cut me slack, turn the other way, close his eyes, and so on, but there comes a time when even he can't—

I say, "Cut to the chase, Irv, I've got nine bears and two women in close quarters here and the fur is flying."

Irv says he got a call—well, it's on his machine, so he can stall a little—from the D of F in Duluth, where they had a big meeting—did I know that young D of F fellow was in restraints at the hospital? The doctor thinks he's been drugged with exotic psychotropics and wonders if the CIA is up here doing clandestine testing again. Why do they always try that stuff up here? Do they think we're all rubes?

I ask what about the call from Duluth.

Irv says, "Oh, right, they're faxing an order for me to seize all your files and evict you immediately and seal the house until the state investigative crime unit gets here sometime tomorrow—wait a minute, today's Saturday, they won't be here until Monday. But I have these orders. As soon as I listen to my answering machine. And as soon as my fax machine comes back on line."

I ask if these orders are in addition to the eviction notice Diane told me about.

"They are," Irv says. "The eviction notice was about having a private residence in a state-owned research facility. These new orders are from the State Attorney General's Office and are premised on the probability of several crimes having been committed."

"Crimes?" I ask.

"Oh," Irv sighs, "you know, misappropriation of funds, stuff like that."

"But you won't have to do anything until your fax machine comes back on line?"

Irv says, well, he guesses somebody must have accidentally tripped on the wire and unplugged it. It won't be able to receive anything for awhile.

I ask how long.

He says he supposes he'd better get on home to supper—well, no, they might call him at home—maybe he'll have a bite at the diner—but really, if he's out of touch too long those urban tight-asses'll report him, too, and we'll both have our titties in a wringer.

I say maybe there's something more serious wrong with the fax machine, a more fundamental mechanical or electrical breakdown.

Well, maybe.

That couldn't be repaired until Monday.

"But hell, Lyle," he says, "they can drive the order here before Monday. They might drive it here tonight. Do we really want to throw them out of their customary lethargy?"

I say there's no point in that.

He says, if the fax comes back on-line in a couple of hours, he could imagine the order getting misplaced by Flo, who cleans at night, and he not coming across it until tomorrow morning.

I ask if he wouldn't be going to church in the morning.

He says he's sure that would be beneficial for his chances in the hereafter, but that would mean that a deputy might find the order and enforce it. "There's a limit, Lyle," he says, "to what we can do here."

I say those files by rights are mine, not the D of F's.

He says he has to follow orders, never mind the Nuremberg Trials. He says, "Oh by the way, did I tell you the Mounties found that missing D of F pickup?"

"No."

"Outside your wife's place, her mother's place, up there in Canada, in Saskatoon, don't you know."

"Really."

"She wasn't home."

"Well," I say, "I think her mother's in a nursing home now."

"No, your wife."

"Wasn't home."

"I wouldn't be surprised if the RCMP doesn't ask her a few questions when she gets back. Unless she's back here now, with you."

I watch Diane carry six-packs of my best ales, porters, and lagers and hand them out to the bears. "No," I say to Irv, "not here."

He says, with a wink in his voice, he didn't think so.

Then he says, "Did I tell you I found out why Ben Creswell was selling those bear parts to the Chinese herbalists, what he was doing with all that money?"

"No."

"He was putting his daughter through college. She's a senior at Harvard. She's majoring in art history. She didn't know where the money was coming from. He sent it through a bank. She thought it was a trust fund. She didn't know what had happened to her father."

"A daughter," I say, my skin going cold.

"Art history," Irv says.

"You never know, do you," I say.

"Ben loved his daughter," Irv says.

I say, without thinking, "Listen, Irv—"

"The feds didn't find that out about the daughter," Irv says, "I did."

I say, "About Ben's death—"

"Old fashioned police work," Irv says.

I say, "I have to tell you something."

Irv says, "Don't."

"What?"

He says, "The case is closed."

I say, "But maybe you should know—"

"The law knows everything it needs to know," he says. He says nobody wants to go back and rehash something like that. He says if anybody has anything more to say about Ben Creswell's death, they should tell a priest or a psychiatrist, not an officer of the law. He says my attention should be focused now on securing my files and getting my bears and my women and my ass out of town. He says he can give me until tomorrow noon, he can't do any better than that without losing his job.

I say, "I guess I owe you."

He says, "I guess you do."

WHAT BEARS REMEMBER

> What a place to live, what a
> place to die and be buried in!
> —Henry David Thoreau

We're returning to Banff from Lake Louise, taking the wilderness road with signs that say *Danger d'ours*. She pulls off at a sign that warns *No Admittance* and eases beneath shady pines. We step out of the car. We saunter deeper into gothic shadows and other-worldly silence.

She kisses my eyelids. I clean her teeth with my tongue. She chews my chin. I slip my tongue up her nostril, tasting cardamom, cinnamon, basil. My fingers float under her leather skirt. Her wild nest drips. She kisses hard, hands at my neck. I hear the squish of my fingers. Her breath comes fast. We fall on the spongy moss. We grapple, two blind animals maddened by some edaphic edacity. We tangle and groan, paw and growl, lick and whimper. Her thighs squeeze my ears. My tongue tastes her stiffening sobriquet. A cry flies from her throat. She drinks the nectar from my mouth.

We lie on the moss, catching our breath. She sniffs the air. She crawls to the base of a large tree. She holds up a black plug, like a chunk of old tobacco. "Bear shit," she says. "From last winter. The bear leaves a small plug in the spring. They used to think the bear plugged himself up when he went into the den." She sniffs the dark cavity under the thick roots. "Here. If I'm old and out of it, drag me here. To sleep with the bear."

"So he'll eat you in the spring?"

"You can eat me first. Like you just did."

"You won't know who I am."

"Then we'll be two strangers, in the woods of Alberta, fucking our brains out at ninety years of age."

"Would you want a stranger to eat you?"

"Listen, buddy-o. Just slip my drawers down, nuzzle your beak in there, and give my old shriveled gumdrop a few flicks of your tongue. I may not recognize your face, but my little love lozenge'll recognize your licker-lapper. The mind may go, but the clitoris remembers."

DIANE: IN HER ELEMENT

 Basically it's none of our business how somebody manages to grow, if only he does grow, if only we're on the trail of the law of our own growth...
—Rainer Maria Rilke

It's in these times of crisis that I'm happiest.

Lyle can do better in smaller crises, as happened last fall when four drunk hunters with assault rifles wanted to slaughter Rudy in his pen, at which point Lyle calmly reminded them that to even threaten an official research bear like Rudy they were looking at mandatory jail terms during which they would find themselves cheek to cheek with icy-veined murderers and weight-lifting butt-fuckers.

But in large crises, like this one, calling for visionary planning, multi-tasking, and improvisational chaos management, like others born under the sign of Aries, I shine, instantly and effortlessly solving problems of timing and people power. Lyle's eyes follow me with adoration and respect. Lyle sees that he needs me. He knows life was not like this before me.

Before me, his life was aimless and haphazard. Oh yes, he was a famous researcher, and he had the ambition to be to bear research what Vesalius was to anatomy and Pasteur to smallpox. But he wasn't a household name. His was not a name that had actually passed the lips of Michael Ovitz, Michael Eisener, and Colin Powell ("Lyle has a recipe for barbecued chitterlings followed by a sweet potato pie augmented with sour mash whiskey and walnuts? Can you fax that to me?").

Oh, I know, you'll say, life can't be one long crisis. Life is a sine wave, ups and downs. Or for most people life is steady, like a life support machine monitor after the patient folds it in and the green line goes flat. That's ordinary life, you'll say, a straight line, no heartbeat. But we can make our crises. We can keep our life exciting.

I have Pepper call the motels to find the moving men. I'll tell them I'll make it worth their while to forget their time-wasting union rules. Lyle meanwhile calls Joe Manello, to have him bring his potions to sedate the bears.

But there's no huge van parked at Ralph's or Fanny's or Emma's, and I wonder what the hell happened to the movers, who work for a reputedly reliable national company. It's only later that I find out they had driven to Vern Afinizy's to see the exotic dancers and, they hoped, bring a couple back to their cab with its bunk.

So I flip through the yellow pages and call the first number I see under MOVERS: *Aboriginal Drayage—We're On the Move.* But the message on the answering machine is in a strange language, and there's drumming and wailing in the background.

I look in the yellow pages again. I start to dial the next listing, OSTRUM HAULING, *You Call It, We'll Haul It,* when I hear the rattle of three beat-up trucks pulling into the yard: one a milk delivery truck, from back when they had home delivery of milk, the guy in his white uniform and cap bounding up your front steps swinging his metal carrier full of bottles of milk with the cream risen to the top—weren't those the days!—another a retired U.S. Postal Service truck, and one a cast-off rental truck, all three announcing ABORIGINAL DRAYAGE—WE'VE BEEN ON THE MOVE SINCE 1492.

How did they know?

An ancient Indian with long silver hair, his face lined with the valleys of experience and sun, steps out of the first truck, and Lyle introduces me to Frank Running Bear. More Indians get out of the other two trucks—Winona Running Bear, whom I know already, of course, and Winona's husband, Lionel Running Bear; Winona's brother, Albert Smith; Frank's nephew, Bertram Runs Slow; and a fellow who so far as I can tell isn't related to any of them named Arthur Fish. Irv the Sheriff was eating dinner at the Lost Duck and mentioned to Winona that Lyle might need help moving tonight, just a hunch, know what I mean?

Arthur and Bertram and Albert roll the file cabinets out on dollies until Frank, wise not only in the ways of the woods but savvy to the labyrinths of bureaucracy— "I've played hide and seek with the Bureau of Indian Affairs long enough to know a thing or two"—suggests we leave a few filing cabinets and papers not crucial to Lyle's research so the Division of Forestry cannot claim that Lyle stole official Division of Forestry documents.

"Damn good idea," Lyle says, and sends the filing cabinets back inside. "I'm not going to need articles in Danish and Russian on bear habitat," he laughs, "or the origins of circumpolar bear myths and all that shit. I'm beyond that now. And the raw notes in that filing cabinet—they were transcribed and published long ago. And those videotapes? Do we need those?"

Frank Running Bear has a special rapport with the bears. Frank hunkers for a few minutes, until the bear gets curious and nuzzles him. Then Frank whispers into the bear's ear. He might talk to the bear for a long time. Then the bear does whatever Frank wants the bear to do. Frank says that long ago the bear gave his people their ancient language, the words they still use to pray with.

Lyle leads the pitifully drunk, vomiting, Abercrombie into the outbuilding with the sauna. We turn the shower on, and Abercrombie sprawls on his back, letting the spray wash over him, opening his jaws and gulping the cool stream. Towley is in the garden, which is fenced to keep the deer and raccoons and woodchucks out. We put Yardley in the shack where the writer was staying—I wonder what he'll think when he comes back, the entire place abandoned like a village in a war zone—if he does come back. We lodge Kerry in the pen by the lodge where Lyle kept Rudy during hunting season. Cranberry and her cubs we leave in the house trailer. They've already destroyed it, so there's no point in putting them elsewhere. Londonderry is in the wine cellar sleeping it off. Barry, generally a playful, easy-going bear, is belligerent when drunk and has been left in the live trap. Rudy is in our bedroom asleep on our king-size bed, all tuckered out from his big day on the town.

Bertram Runs Slow, a chubby teenager with an infectious smile, wearing cutoffs and a Rudy tee shirt and tennis shoes with no socks, hauls out his boom box and slides in a cassette of drumming and high-pitched wailing from a powwow. Soon everybody is getting things done smartly and gracefully, and nobody breaks anything.

Cal Simonson pulls up in his Schwann's truck. Lyle located him in Fran Makosky's back room, with its Liebfraumilch on ice and its furry bearskin rug, scented candles, and year-round blinking Christmas lights. Before he joined the Schwann's team he was a logger out in Oregon, but he had to quit when he slipped a disc in his back. Cal's a young fellow, with sandy hair and a handlebar mustache, unconcerned that Fran has a good twenty years on him. We're loading Lyle's frozen food into the Schwann's truck.

Fran hot-wired Mel's Supermarket's refrigerator truck, and we're loading the wine into it. Fran carries the cases with ease, her muscled arms tireless, her logger's boots clomping up and down the stairs. She's something of a clothes stylist. Even in this warm weather she's wearing a velvet skirt, and under the skirt she wears jeans, and she wears a man's checked lumberjack shirt with the sleeves rolled up, but the shirt is unbuttoned to reveal a black lacy bra and a fulsome bosom.

Winona's brother, Albert, hasn't said a word and seems rather sullen, but he works with steady efficiency. Albert is short and stocky and much darker than Winona. Lyle says they had different fathers. Lyle says Albert was shifted for years from foster home to foster home, ran away, hustled on the streets of Los Angeles and nearly died of drugs until he finally made his way home a couple of years ago and, with Frank's help, has straightened himself out. Albert sings and drums in the Wounded Warriors Drum Group—that's their cassette that's playing—and Albert was told in a vision to keep silent for five years, using his voice only in prayer and singing, and that's why he doesn't speak.

Now Lyle says it's time for a break. I say it's only the middle of the night, we can't stop yet, we're not half done, what if the sheriff or the D of F militia arrive before dawn? Lyle says those short-sighted candy asses have never seen the sun rise in their miserable lives. I say, No, we have to keep working, I know what I'm doing, I have everything under control. He says, You're hysterical. I tell him, Go fuck yourself. He says, There, that just goes to show, we all need a little something to eat.

　　　　　　　　　　　　　　　　　　　　　William Borden

UNE BILLET BELLE DE BANFF

L'AUBERGE DE L'AMOURETTE
423 Big Horn Lane
Banff, Alberta

Dear Lyle,

Well, you see where I am, what a surprise, eh? (As we say in Canada—"eh?") The air is clear here, and my mind feels clear, too, about us, anyway. Our kids are grown, and they know things aren't hunky dory between us. Bernadette even asked recently if we were getting a divorce. She seemed to expect it. Babette's talking about dropping out of school and joining the Air Force, so she's still on shaky mental ground, but I think she would be whatever we were doing. I don't think a more definitive definition of our relationship will make her any more flighty than she is. It may in fact have a stabilizing effect, giving some permanence to your and my relationship, or absence thereof.

Bjorn'll be busy studying—did he tell you he got accepted at the U of Minn School of Nutrition? He says that even though there's big money to be made working for the conglomerates developing expensive non-nutritious food, he's going to remain true to his principles and use his knowledge to make a granola with raisins that don't get dry and hard.

We I haven't seen any bears, although they do abound up here, both grizzlies and black, as you know, but we I haven't ventured into the back country to see them, preferring to relax among the human creature comforts here in this resort village sprinkled with retired couples, sinewy-limbed young back packers, and camera-brandishing folks of the Japanese persuasion.

I have a new skirt, leather, very short, that makes me feel sexy.

While I'm on the subject, what were you thinking, walking in there to Ben Creswell's with the writer? What were you going to do? Shoot him? I don't think so. Scare him? Is that likely, a man who killed hundreds with sharpened bamboo and piano wire? Good lord, what if Holly hadn't miraculously revived and attacked him, causing him to blow his own head off?

Well, I wanted to let you know I'm OK, if you care anymore, since I'm not home and my phone is broken because the last time you called I smashed the shit out of it.

I'm calmer now.

Time flies.

So does love.

LYLE: A BEAR CONUNDRUM

> Wild thing
> You make my heart sing
> —The Troggs

We're sitting around the kitchen table. We may have to leave the table behind, even though a lot of memories are stained and scratched into its wooden surface, but there's not enough room in the trucks for everything. Diane's frying up venison sausage heavily flavored with garlic and sage, while Bertram Runs Slow flips buttermilk pancakes. Arthur Fish is making sandwiches for later, when we're on the road: chunky peanut butter and sweet pickles, creamy peanut butter and strawberry jam, chunky peanut butter and honey, chunky and sliced banana, creamy and sliced avocado. Arthur, a whimsical lad in his twenties and a pal of Bertram's, slathers the peanut butter an inch thick on my oatmeal-cracked-wheat bread we pulled from the freezer. Arthur played basketball on the reservation high school team that went to the state finals a few years ago. He's been in the movies, too, playing an Iroquois in one and a Comanche in another, but he's actually part Anishinabe, or 'Shinob, as he says, and part Lakota. He wears a goldfinch yellow Rudy cap backwards. Winona is mixing up fry bread dough, which the silent Albert is frying in my expensive extra virgin first pressing Tuscan olive oil, but what the hell, they've sacrificed for me.

We're trying to figure out what to do with the bears. Even at this moment I hear Abercrombie howling in the sauna and Barry moaning from the live trap. "Maybe you should leave the bears," Diane says, "just let them go. They wouldn't shoot research bears, would they?"

I say some folks would shoot me, never mind those bears dedicated to the advancement of science. I say it would be a bear massacre, those bears murdered by government agents in the name of public safety or by a homeowner in the name of the Second Amendment. Bertram pours more batter on the griddle and asks why don't we barrel down the back roads as deep into the forest as we can go and then release them? I shake my beleaguered head at my maple syrup-sogged flapjacks. Problem is, now that they've binged on beer and ice cream, damn it, I've given them the idea that town's the place to go for treats. Even if we take them a hundred miles away, they'll be back, knocking on Ernie LaFolle's Bottle Shop growling for more St. Pauli Girl.

"Take them up to Canada," Arthur proposes, "like the war resisters during Vietnam. Maybe they'll get amnesty."

Diane, turning the sausage, asks, if we take the bears far away, where does that leave the research project? Won't the D of F want to continue the bear research, even if I'm gone and in disgrace, perhaps even a fugitive? I ask her who the heck she thinks could do the research if I'm not here. I'm the only bear researcher in the state. One of a mere handful of top flight researchers in the whole world. This is a complicated, multi-variable, NASA-quality scientific project. They'd have to find somebody with experience. With a track record. With a sound intuitive grasp of the subtle workings of ursine psychology. They can't bring in just any fellow off the street.

"It's a conundrum," Bertram says, seeing how high he can toss a pancake and still have it land on the big griddle—the answer being about three feet, since the four-footer landed on the floor, where Rudy gobbled it up. "To save the research bears, you have to remove them. But if the bears are gone, there's no more research—the research you've invested your life and soul in."

I butter my pancakes liberally and douse them with warm syrup. I slide my sausage patty to the rim of my plate to help it escape the spreading sweetness. I contemplate my conundrums and wonder if I'm going to be a fugitive for life, and am I sacrificing everything for a bunch of mutinous ice cream fanatics and happy-go-lucky furry bohemians.

Just then we hear a truck drive up. We freeze, all except Bertram, who has a rhythm going and a practiced eye for flipping the pancake at the precise moment so each side is speckled the color of ripe wheat in the morning sun.

Are these jack pine savages, random vigilantes come to cause havoc and bear carnage? Because I know I've made enemies, despite my genial manner and convivial ways, with my relentless commitment to bear research.

We hear a truck door slam. The door to the kitchen is open, so we keep our eyes on the opening. Rudy stands on his hind legs to nose Winona's fry bread. She smacks him smartly on the nose, and he drops to all fours, whimpering. Bertram flips a pancake his way. Footsteps fall on the wooden floor of the entryway. Only Frank looks at ease. Frank doesn't even look at the doorway.

It's Joe Manello leaning against the doorjamb. Joe looks as if he hasn't had any sleep. Lionel hooks an extra chair and slides it into the space next to him. "Any you fellas had any experience with German gals?" Joe asks. It turns out Joe took in the entertainment at Vern Afinizy's. The ladies were not, as had been expected, from Minneapolis. They were from Germany, and they were adepts at practices too arcane for the Minneapolis gals. Some of the lumberjacks were repulsed by the ladies' once-weekly bathing and hirsute legs and armpits, but Joe is accustomed to running his blunt fingers through fur of all textures and odors. "This one gal," Joe says, "named Wilda—well, and there was Clotilde—" Winona slides a clean plate in front of him. Bertram flips three pancakes directly from the griddle to Joe's plate, landing only one in Joe's lap.

Joe continues, "Couple truck drivers went in together on Clotilde, and she did them both in less than five minutes and was challenging any fella in the place. Two out of three."

Diane removes the last of the sausage from the frying pan and looks for a chair so she can take a turn eating. Lionel stands up, holding his plate with one hand and his fork with the other, and nods Diane into his chair.

"Five minutes?" asks Arthur, sealing a sandwich in a plastic bag.

"Two out of three?" Bertram asks, popping a sausage into his mouth.

Joe skips the butter—he's watching his cholesterol—and pours on the syrup, submerging the pancakes. "Wrestling," Joe says. "The gals took us on wrestling." His burly biceps bulge from his black Rudy tee shirt. "Those movers got beat time and again." Joe cuts the stack in half with his knife and fork. He pinions the stacked halves, swirls the set in the syrup, and rams them into his mouth.

"Why'd they keep going back?" Diane asks.

"'Cause," Joe says. He chews, eyeing Diane, eyeing the rest of us, nodding his head as he chews, asking us to be patient, we wouldn't want him to talk with his mouth full. But then he forks a sausage into his mouth, to season the pancakes and let the meaty spiciness complement the sweetness of the syrup. "They were naked." He looks for a coffee. Lionel fills a mug and sets it beside Joe's plate. Joe gulps the steaming brew. "They're all big gals," Joe resumes. "Except Vibeka, who's a tiny thing, with long blond hair. She was the referee."

The mug was an experiment, putting Rudy's picture on one side and mine on the other. They never took off the way the T-shirts and caps did. I think it was mainly a marketing problem.

"The other gals, Wilda, Clotilde, and Armina, all have short black hair. And hair on their legs and arms and in their armpits. Wilda has hair all over. Like a bear." Joe plunges his fork into the other half-stack. He gives a whistle of amazed recollection. "That Wilda." He stuffs his mouth, swallows. "I got Wilda because I beat her at wrestling. I was the only one. You had to pay a hundred dollars to wrestle a gal. If you lost, that was it. You'd have to pay more, later, for a bit of her time. If you won your match, you got your half hour free." He takes another sausage. "Well, not free exactly, since you'd already paid to wrestle her." Bertram flips him three more pancakes. "Then I wrestled Clotilde, and I pinned her, too. So I had them both." He empties the pitcher of syrup. "I wrestled Armina next, but I was tired by then." He cuts the stack in half. "Two was a handful anyway." He spears the half. "Those gals put up a good fight." He spears the sausage under the pancakes and lifts the morsel into the air. "Wilda said she hadn't been pinned in years." The fork starts toward his mouth, then pauses. "After the dry wrestling, they had the oil wrestling, with Mazola, for three hundred a match. Those gals can pick a fella's wallet clean as a goose in a French restaurant."

His head is bare, and it's the first time I've seen him without his mangled, stained Boston Bruins cap—later he confesses that he gave the cap to Wilda as a keepsake. Joe's bald and has a tan line across his forehead, so the top of his head is stark white, giving him, this morning, the look of a farmer in church.

Joe's ready to shove the forkful into his mouth when I notice Pepper standing in the doorway, and I can tell by the stricken look on her face she's been standing there for awhile and has heard the whole account of the shaggy Wilda and hispidulous Clotilde. Joe sees the look of concern, or it could be doom, on my face, and he turns, and he sees Pepper, and Pepper gives a choked cry, like a puppy that's been kicked, and she runs out of the house into the early morning gloom.

I think Pepper's poured more into this unspoken relationship than Joe has, which is Pepper's way, I've found, investing a lot more into something than the other person is aware of, much to Pepper's disappointment and the other person's bewilderment.

Joe pokes the pancakes and sausage into his mouth, the syrup dripping down his beard in sticky droplets, grabs a swig of coffee as he rises, and heads out the door, calling, "Pepper! Pepper honey! Hey now, Pepper!"

Around the table we fall into a respectful hush, even Bertram pausing to bow his head as if he were praying to the pancakes bubbling on the griddle, and we chew silently, digesting emotions as well as food, as we hear, in the dark distance, Joe bellowing plaintively, "You're the only gal for me, Pepper Honey!"

SWEET SWEAT

> If any problem arises while bathing, say to yourself, I didn't come merely to bathe but to be in harmony with nature.
>
> —Epictetus

"I've never before lived so much in the moment," she says.

The aroma of hot wood and old water, of historic sweat and desiccated dreams, seems to dim the already decadent light. She rests on my thighs, her back to me, as our hands roam lazily, as if we aren't really interested in what we're doing. We're naked in the sauna at one in the morning.

"I'm not myself," she says.

She flips my floppy Dali sausage from side to side.

"Who am I?"

I weigh the genial bounce of her breasts.

"Is this the *I* I've wanted to be all along?"

I tune the pert dials of her nipples.

"Or Ms. Hyde, sprung from a hedonistic confusion of menopausal delirium, loneliness, and total disregard for the proprieties of middle age?"

The heat from her naked body inflames my mind, the freckles on her shoulders confuse my eyes, the rosy tips of her nipples short-circuit my perspicacity. "Looking back on my life as a responsible mother and a dutiful—well, sometimes dutiful—wife, I wonder if I wasn't being a stoic after all, ignoring my suffering and hanging in there." My palms caress her stomach, her intestines, her pancreas and liver, her gall bladder and kidneys. I imagine them all there, under her skin, doing their jobs, my squishy friends.

She rolls my languid loaf between her palms as if she were kneading a bread stick. "At the same time," she ruminates, "I knew there was the Epicurean in me. But I wonder, you know? Is Epicureanism purely an embracing of pleasure, or is it a frantic flight from the certainty of death?" She tugs, as if trying to pluck an answer from my Cyclopean Epicurean.

"My father had a book of Ovid. Once I realized Ovid was writing about love, I took a new interest in the classics."

My squirmy tongue jams the whorls of her ear. I taste abalone and hops.

"I was fourteen. I was discovering my body and the things it could do."

The hot line from her ear awakens her nether flower.

"I discovered Ovid is saying that love is about transformation."

I flutter its petals, dewy and perfumed.

"Metamorphosis."

Our hands work together. I can't tell whose fingers are doing what.

"That's what's been happening with you, buddy-o."

My fingers feel her bud pop up.

"Since you stumbled up my front steps"—she laces her fingers with mine—"everything's been changing." We buff her burgeoning bulb. "I change." Her hands firm me up. "You change." We crank my contentious creamer. "There's no end to it."

She guides me in. She rocks forward and backward. I breathe her shampoo. She tests how small her movements can be. I gnaw the perfume of her neck. She Kegels me tight. My peccadillo is hers, snug in the night of her purse. She'll carry me with her everywhere—as she fries bacon, runs marathons, rocks in her favorite chair at night. Our eyes closed, our sweat an ethereal membrane, we conjugate an infinitesimal rhythm, careless of quotidian reality.

I'm not sure how long the door to the sauna has been open, but when we open our eyes, feeling maybe a waft of cool air, the man and woman withdraw, silently closing the door. We go on rocking, but they've broken the spell. I go limp, and she's tired. We wrap the towels around us and leave the sauna, passing as we do a man and a woman in the hot tub. I can't tell if they're the same couple, my glimpse was so brief, but they give us a strange look, and their swim suits are thrown onto the edge of the hot tub, and their bodies are pressed together.

I dream we're in a surrealistic New York with narrow, twisting streets and bazaars on every side, and we're holding hands and walking naked, but no one pays any attention to us. Lyle comes up, and Lyle is naked, too, and his wanger is six feet long. He whips me with it, but he doesn't seem angry, he seems to be playing, but she pays no attention to him, she walks away to look at something in the bazaar. Lyle's yelling at me but I can't hear anything, and I'm getting a hard on.

William Borden

DIANE: SWEET MYSTERIES

> Abandon yesterday, and tomorrow, and
> today. Cross over to the farther shore,
> beyond life and death.
>
> —*The Dhammapada*

I watch Lionel go directly to where her clothes are, and I wonder how he knows. I suppose it's an Indian thing, like Sandra Flies Far finding lost objects, and in a sense these garments have been lost to her, to Lyle's wife, and I'm even feeling sorry for her, alone up there in the Canadian tundra, nobody to see her wear these silky unmentionables Lionel is gently removing from their drawers and sensitively folding and delicately placing in the boxes for UPS.

I'm grateful for Lionel's companionship in the bedroom. It was going to be a lonely job, I thought, soaked with ambivalence, as I packed my things and their memories for an uncertain tomorrow and packed her possessions with a cloudy past and an unspoken future. But Lionel, as if he sensed my ambivalence, or even somehow mysteriously shared it, followed me into the bedroom where Rudy's sleeping soundly on the bed, his tummy packed with pancakes and the fry bread he sneaked when Winona turned her back.

Lionel tells me he worked for Lyle— "and the Missus," as he puts it—back when he was a teenager. He says he helped with the garden, too.

I open a suitcase and gather my belongings from a drawer.

"It's sad," he says, "the way the garden's gone wild, although it looks like somebody's been pulling a weed here and there." There's a trueness to wildness, Lionel observes, but, he adds, pulling open, with a shy familiarity, a drawer I once opened, "there's also a need for order and cultivation." We survey the dismantled room, drawers hanging open like hungry mouths and clothes spilled in embarrassed confusion. "Even wild animals have a social etiquette, certain rules they follow. Here's my territory, here's my fish, these are my cubs, that's my"—he hesitates— "mate. Sometimes an animal ignores those rules and there's a scuffle. Sometimes an animal will go crazy. But not often."

Lionel folds the stockings and lays them neatly atop the lavender garter belt and lavender bikini panties you can see through and the matching lavender bra that lifts and reveals. "We aboriginal people, you know, in the old times, we didn't have any schizophrenics or borderline personalities, nobody going nuts and shooting everybody in sight with arrows because they'd lost their job at the Smoke Signal Office or their woman ran off with another warrior."

His voice is soft, and there's a tenderness to it that I wouldn't expect in a man so bulky and rugged. He holds her lavender stockings before him, a strange wistfulness in his eyes. He shows no embarrassment, unusual for a man, no hesitation handling this intimate attire of a woman he only worked for.

"Oh, there was a fellow who wounded Crazy Horse because the fellow's wife crawled into Crazy Horse's teepee, but nobody went to extremes. If you heard voices, you went to a spiritual leader and asked him who was talking to you. Madness is caused by civilization."

We work silently, I wrapping some knickknacks in newspaper, Lionel arranging a skirt atop the lingerie. He looks at the carton a moment, the palms of his hands resting on either side of the box, his blunt fingers trembling a little. Finally he closes the flaps. He wraps the strapping tape securely around the container. He peels off an address label and affixes it firmly. He takes out a pen and prints in block letters a name and address, no hesitation, numbers and letters absolute in his mind.

"I can't believe how well prepared you are," I blurt out, "all of you, here with the trucks when we need them and address labels, as if you had known all along..." He doesn't look at me. I get a funny feeling in my stomach, and I don't think it's the venison sausage.

Before I know what's happening, he's taking my lingerie out of my suitcase, where I had thrown it in disarray. He folds my panties, my bras, my slips, my teddies, and the saucy things Lyle bought me, fitting them neatly in the suitcase, with absolute naturalness. "This way you'll have more room," he says. "Sometimes when you hurry, you wind up

William Borden

taking more time than you would if you didn't hurry."

I want to snatch these silky under things from his big hands, hands scoured clean but the bronze skin ineradicably scored with creosote from blacktopping the roads. I'm afraid he's seeing into my fantasies, as if he could look at that black teddy and see what I did with Lyle when I wore it, as if Lionel's fingers were clairvoyant. But Lionel calmly shakes and folds and tucks, as if he were packing handkerchiefs or shirts. I don't know whether to feel violated or cared for. I don't know why I can't tell the difference. "There," he says, straightening up. "Now you've got room for more things."

"Thank you," I say.

I look around the room at the dark rectangles on the walls where the pictures and mirror had been. I smell the faint dust of potpourri. I say, suddenly tired and bewildered, "I don't know what to pack next."

Lionel opens a drawer. He takes out Lyle's long underwear. He folds it—not as carefully—and tucks it next to my delicate lingerie, until the drawer is empty, the suitcase is full, and there's an angry emptiness in the room.

I ask, "Do you think we're mad? Leaving like this? Escaping?" He looks down at the colorful mosaic of a rag rug we're standing on, a small bright island in a sea of dismal dispersion.

"Lionel?" Winona stands in the doorway. She looks tired. Her shirt is smudged with dirt. "Are you finished in here?" He looks questioningly at me. I say it looks like we're about done. "Are you taking the bed?" she asks me. I say I guess so, it's Lyle's. "I don't know if we've got room," she says. We look at Rudy sleeping on the bed, his paws covering his eyes. "Come help with the books," she says to Lionel. "My back's hurting." Lionel grabs the suitcase and heads for the door. "You want a soda?" she asks him as he reaches the door.

I remain in the empty room. It has the feel of a battlefield littered with corpses and spent ammunition. It seems smaller, desolate, already a stranger. It's the only place in all my life where I've felt at home. Even though it wasn't my room, my furniture, my house, and even though for a long time I felt like an intruder, I felt I belonged. I check the drawers again to be sure they're empty. I abandon the sock, the torn shirt, the hairclip—but the hairclip's not mine.

In the corner of the drawer my fingers close around a soft leather bag decorated with blue and yellow and white beads. It too must be hers. She put it in that drawer, and for some unaccountable reason I wonder if Lionel gave it to her long ago, and I realize that his scent and her scent have been mingling with mine, and with Lyle's, and that we can't free ourselves of each other no matter how hard we might try.

Lionel appears in the doorway again, a box of books in his arms. "I never answered your question," he says.

I've forgotten what question.

"Are you crazy," he reminds me. "Running away like this."

Oh, that question.

"Well?" I ask.

He seems to have to think it over some more. Finally he says, "After the Battle of the Greasy Grass—what you folks call the Little Big Horn—when Sitting Bull knew the army was going to be pretty mad about them wiping out Custer and his soldiers, Sitting Bull took his people up into Canada for safety. We Indians have always liked a good fight, but we never saw an advantage to letting ourselves be wiped out."

He shifts the heavy box in his arms. "And a bear, when he smells a hunter on his trail, he'll get out of the way." He sets the box down on the bed to give his arms a rest. Rudy snuffs and turns over but keeps on sleeping.

"We Indians have had a lot of experience with government. More than most people. The government's always treated us like children, bad children, children they wished they didn't have to take care of, but at the same time they get a certain satisfaction in having to put up with us. From this experience, I can tell you that the government is of the nature of a wild beast."

I realize I still have the small beaded bag clutched in my hand. Lionel continues, "Or rather of the nature of a caged wild beast, one in a zoo, that gives the impression of being tame. But the beast is still wild. And it's unhappy at being caged. And so, if it thinks you're teasing it, or even if you're late with dinner, or you wander into the cage at the wrong time, it's liable to turn on you. It's liable to trample you and maul you and eat you up."

The sachet feels as if it's pulsing, as if it's a heart beating. But I know it's only my own pulse, my own heart pumping.

"So the best thing is to keep the government caged. Keep it fed, keep it happy. But if you do rile it, as happens, even without your intending it, like you and Lyle now, like Sitting Bull at the Battle of the Little Big Horn, and it gets out of its cage, as is happening now, why, the only sane thing to do is take your teepee to another campsite. Find another verdant valley in which to hunt and fish and make love." He rubs his palms against his jeans. He gets ready to pick up the box.

I hold out my hand. The aged packet of scent and memory rests in my palm.

"Lionel?" It's Winona calling.

He takes it, and he gently slips it into his pocket. He picks up the box of books. He disappears.

I turn out the lights. I look up at the ceiling sparkling with the constellations and the galaxies of the night sky. It's the last time I'll see this sky, this sky that Lyle brought inside, so that even in this room he could see, anyone sleeping here could see, the mystery of infinity, and we would never forget the wildness that lies a few feet away, or within the palm of one's hand.

LYLE: BEAR MYSTERIES

> It requires a very unusual mind to undertake the analysis of the obvious.
> — Alfred North Whitehead

Lionel and Albert and Arthur are slamming the truck panels and locking the latches, and Winona and Fran Makosky are stowing the sandwiches and fry bread and the thermoses of coffee, and Cal Simonson is checking the oil in his Schwann's truck, and Bertram Runs Slow is looking up at the clear morning sky and already chowing down a fry bread wrapped around a gob of chunky peanut butter. I look around the yard, the arena of so much love and turmoil in my life.

I still haven't figured out what to do with the bears.

I guess I was hoping for a last-minute inspiration.

They never come, do they?

I mosey toward the garden. Diane slips her arm inside mine, as if we're strolling a Parisian boulevard. "Taking a last look?" she asks.

The fence around the garden is broken. Towley has escaped. Towley has also squeezed his head out of his transmitter collar, which hangs, like an unfulfilled wish, on a twisted wire-end of fence. It's irresponsible, I know, but I'm relieved. There's one less bear to make a decision about.

"We should get going," Diane says. "I gave Lionel a map. He seems responsible."

"Map?"

"To Los Angeles. We'll meet them there. I made some inquiries when I was there last. There's a house on the beach we can sublet. I called last night, put down a deposit. One of the new credit cards I got for you. It's pricey, but if the movie deal comes through..."

"Beach?" I'm trying to casually scan for Pepper and Joe. Not to mention Towley. Earlier, momentarily crazed by her incarceration, Cranberry tore the door off the house trailer and led her cubs into the woods and a precarious freedom. I don't see any sign of them.

"Malibu. The owner's in jail for possession, so the sublease is actually a steal."

Maybe if we leave enough food around here, the bears will hang around and not stray into trouble. I recover the collar and pick off a few of the bristly hairs.

"Maybe they'll bring you back. Once everything gets sorted out."

I feel the tough strength of the leather.

She says, "They're committed to the bear research. They have to be."

I slip the collar over my head. It rests heavily on my collarbone and presses against my ears. For the first time I worry about how comfortable these collars are, and do the results of research outweigh the discomfort of this equipment. But then my research goes to improve the lot of the bears. It proves how much wilderness they need and what trees and berries they need, and how they fit impeccably into the ecosystem, and how without forests and bears and everything else we're all goners for sure, and why the lumber companies shouldn't clear cut and why they should keep the noisy snowmobiles out and why the developers shouldn't build those big resorts.

"Are you going to wear that from now on?" Diane asks whimsically. "So I can find you whenever I want?"

The trucks begin to roll out the driveway, gears grinding, Lionel and Winona in the lead in the converted mail truck, Winona the trusted keeper of Diane's credit card to finance the long journey to the Pacific. Arthur Fish and Bertram Runs Slow pilot the second truck. They're buddies from way back, and they'll listen to rock and roll on their boom box. Cal Simonson commands his Schwann's truck, and Fran Makosky follows him in the refrigerated truck which Mel, of Mel's Supermarket, will no doubt soon notice is gone. I'd better give him a call to explain things. We couldn't find Fran or Cal for breakfast. Turns out they were in the sauna. They had more on their minds than pancakes and sausage. They accidentally let Abercrombie loose when they opened the door. One less bear to feel responsible for, I thought, but with a nudge of guilt.

Frank and Albert will bring up the rear, both of them content with silence, or they'll sing their songs in the ancient syllables, Arthur beating his knees for a drum and Frank tapping the steering wheel. Frank said it was like the old days, when they followed the buffalo, pulling their belongings on travois, although Lionel reminded him that those were the Sioux that did that, but Frank said he believed there was Lakota Sioux in their background, that one of their Anishinabe ancestors had not driven the Sioux westward as he was supposed to but had grabbed a Sioux gal and kept her here in the woods to love and have babies.

The four trucks disappear around the bend, and a whiff of exhaust hangs in the cool morning air. Albert stands beside the ancient milk truck waiting patiently for Frank, whom I don't see, but Frank has a gift for sudden absences and rematerializations.

Joe Manello's panel truck still stands in the grass. No sign of him or Pepper. But there's only so much I can worry about and take care of and manage. Besides, Joe's good with skittish animals.

That leaves Diane and me in the empty yard, and I find that I don't want to go back into the house. All of a sudden it seems like a stranger's house. It seems as if I never lived there.

Then I notice that the pen by the house, where Kerry was secured, is empty. Did Kerry thoughtfully close the gate behind her? And why didn't I notice earlier that she was gone?

I open the door to the shack where the writer stayed, where I put Yardley. Yardley's gone.

The live trap is empty. Barry's nowhere in sight.

I run into the house, down to the wine cellar to find Londonderry. He's vanished, too.

What the heck is coming down, I'm thinking, feeling shivers up my back, because it's looking like some mystery kidnapping going on. Or did the bears let each other out?

Frank Running Bear strolls casually out of the woods, tying up his long silver hair into a pony tail.

I start off toward the woods to look for the bears, but Diane grabs my arm. "You're right," I say, "I should get the antenna. I can track them that way." I start for the house.

She pulls me back. "We don't have time," she says.

"They're my bears!" I cry, delirious with accountability, with honor, with possessiveness.

"Shhh," she says, "shhh," as if I'm a kid panicking.

"Where are my bears?"

The forest surrounds us, silent and serene.

"What'll I do without my bears?"

Frank Running Bear stands before me sipping the last of his coffee. He muses softly, "When you think about it, Lyle, bears need to be free to make their own mistakes, just like human animals."

WHAT BEARS DO WHEN THEY NEED HELP

Nothing, I am convinced, can be the same forever.

—Ovid

She's naked except for the quill earrings that brush her bare shoulders, and I'm in the altogether except for the bear tooth that swings across my chest like a scratchy reminder of a distant life. After so much raucous rumpus here in the hotel room she's voracious. "Let's have a picnic," she proposes. "Eat in the woods. In the dark. It'll be scary."

There's a knock on the door. She cracks it open. A yellow envelope appears. She takes it, inspects it, pulls a five from my billfold, hands it out, and closes the door.

DEAR JOCKO. FORT ATTACKED. BEARS IN DANGER. ALL HELL BREAKING LOOSE. NEED YOUR HELP. YOUR BUDDY.

The telegram is crisp and brittle, like an autumn leaf, between my fingers.

"Well," she says brightly, "it couldn't last, we knew that." She pulls on a skirt. "That's what freed me up." The mellifluous frock swirls around her ankles. "I can be crazy, sexy, wanton. I can be someone I've never been before." The sinuous garment is patterned in brave flowers and somber ferns. "You gave me the chance of a lifetime, buddy-o." She slips on a white blouse that teases out a cleavage. "A fantasy to relive when I'm ancient and confused."

She hands me my pink bikini briefs. "Did you expect it to last?" she asks. "You didn't even think about it, did you?" She bought them for me yesterday. "For you it was like catching a train." She picked out buff, ivy, and plum. "Get off when the engine runs out of steam." A yellow-and-blue striped pair of Calvin Kleins, as well. "But that's okay." They were recommended by Phil. "I hopped the train, too." I pull the bikinis around my hips. "Difference is, I thought about it." She hands me a tee shirt. It says something about saving the rain forest. "I thought, this is a train." I pull on the shirt. "He'll get off." A jaguar leaps from my chest. "I'll ride on." I pull on jeans. "Down the clickety-clackety tracks of my future." Button. "That's life." Buckle. "My eyes are open." Zip. "I'm no Cinderella." Left sock. "My fairy godmother's in an old folks' home." Right sock. "Doesn't know her name." Left shoe. "I'm not worrying about tomorrow." Right shoe. "I know what tomorrow brings." Shoe string breaks. "Tomorrow brings toodleoo." She kneels. "Tomorrow brings getting bored with each other." She splices. "Tomorrow brings lackluster performance." She ties. "Tomorrow brings VISA bills." She stands. "Tomorrow brings a telegram." She hands me my feral leather vest. "Tomorrow brings tomorrow." I slip it on. "You came out of nowhere." She tugs the vest smartly. "Where are you going?" She adjusts the shoulders. "Same place." She slips on a sandal. "*Je ne regret rien.*" She slips on the other. "Edith Piaf." She throws my clothes in my bag. "Your buddy needs you."

"You and I are buddies."

"We're lovers." She pulls at my shirt. "Lovers are temporary." She straightens the jaguar. "Hit the road, jack. You're free."

I don't move.

"We're not kids. I have hot flashes. You take a long time to pee. We know life is short, brutish, and something I can't remember. We know we have to snatch happiness out of the jaws of decrepitude and folly. We know death's hanging around the corner like a mugger in an alley."

"*You're* the only buddy I have."

"I'll stay here in Banff awhile. I'll wear that leather miniskirt. I'll pick up young guys. I'll fuck 'em till they drop. I'll wander into the woods, scout more hibernation spots, get to know the bears, make a map for you, for when I call, thirty years from now, because that contract's still in effect, you're not getting out of that deal." She rummages through a drawer. "I can't find my panties. Did you take them again?"

"Buddies are forever," I say.

"I'm going to wear your bikinis, the lavender ones."

"*I don't have any buddy but you.*"

She whips my lavender bikinis up her legs, a blur of plum vanishing beneath the jungle extravagance of her skirt.

"*I don't owe Lyle anything.*"

"You owe him *everything!*" Her dioptase eyes flash. "Without Lyle, you would never have found me."

"Yes, but—"

"You fucked Lyle's wife's brains out. You think you don't owe him something?"

`   "I don't see the connection."

"*Everything's connected.*"

"We're atoms, bouncing off each other."

"You, me, Lyle, Frank, Rudy, even that blond bitch sleeping in my bed."

"We're alone."

"There are my panties."

"We're isolated by skin, space, time, death."

"In your suitcase."

"We grab what we can, when we can."

"Keep them."

She sprays me with her perfume.

"We rage against it all our lives," I say.

She mists herself with my cologne.

"We've swapped scents," she says. She puts my cologne in her suitcase. "We'll be able to find each other." She tucks her perfume in my bag. "We've become each other."

"I'm not going back."

"The bears need you."

"I don't care about bears."

"I do."

Her beryline eyes fix me in a categorical imperative.

The phone rings.

She says, "It's Skip Ostrum. He's at the helicopter pad outside town. He's here to take you home."

LYLE: HONEY BEARS

> Bear, apple of the forest, handsome chubby fellow of the forest...It will be nice for you there, lovely to pass your time there.
>
> —*Old Kalevala*

Diane sits in the back, suitcases piled beside her. We drive deep into the woods, into the maze of lakes. We go to the end of the road.

I pull the flat-bottom boat off the roof of the Volvo. I slide it into the water.

Like all the research bears, Rudy has a small metal tag in his ear, a bear earring, with a number on it. I pull out my wire cutters. Diane wants to leave the tag on him, so if someone comes upon him, or kills him, we might know about it. I say ignorance is occasionally, well, not bliss, exactly, but why should we ask for bad news?

I slip the tag in my pocket as a keepsake.

I cut off his radio collar.

He scratches his neck. Diane says maybe we should have left it on him. Maybe he'll feel unnatural without it, she says, since he's worn it all his life. I say he'll forget about it. I say he'll feel free. He just won't know why. I tell her I know what I'm talking about.

He doesn't want to get into the flat-bottom boat, but Diane entices him with a jar of honey, and it's all I can do to keep the boat from turning over. Rudy goes nuts licking the honey off Diane's hands, then the jar spills and the honey is all over her, and by the time we get across the lake and climb onto the island where I don't think any human has ever been and I hope will never go, she's laughing and stripping off her clothes and smearing honey over her body, so tan and smooth after the summer, and I take my clothes off and she smears honey over me, and Rudy's licking us and we're laughing and it's afternoon and a great blue heron is flying overhead and the water is sniffing at the rocks on the shore, and finally Rudy wanders off into the woods, into his new home, and Diane and I lie in the cool grass slowly licking each other, while somewhere in the blue pure sky there's the far-off thump-a-thump of a helicopter, and then we come together, holding each other tight, and we're sticking together.

ONE MORE LETTER

The bear will devour all your flesh and make you a skeleton, and you will die. But you will recover your flesh, you will awaken, and your clothes will come rushing to you.

—Inuit

Dear Lyle,

Thanks for sending the clothes. UPS forwarded the boxes hither and yon until they caught up with me, back here where they started, but I guess that's life, isn't it? You travel far enough, you wind up where you started, only you arrive from the other direction. It's the same whether you circumambulate the globe or zoom into space—you meet yourself coming back, Einstein said, when you reach the outskirts of the universe.

Of course you seem to keep moving on, restless and footloose like a good American, and maybe you're where you want to be, out there under palm trees and smog.

Who packed them? It couldn't have been you, everything so neatly folded. If it was she—did you tell her everything about us? But then I guess secrets are merely the lacy pretensions of a bourgeois shame we can do without.

The clothes and the naughty things had a faint strange scent. I'm sniffing it again, now, as I write, because my curiosity is nagging—a slight rankness, as of tar, accompanied by a sweetness, like a teasing smudge of sweet grass...?

I received the brochure about you taking New Agers into the California redwoods to commune with the three or four grizzlies left there and to discover their "True Bear Nature," which I suppose is a good thing, but it does seem a little flimflammy, and not an optimum use of your true talents and bear knowledge. It must be profitable, however, people paying thousands of dollars to sleep on the ground and eat grubs. Frank Running Bear says you wanted him to help you guide those rich seekers on their "journeys into the bear unconscious, forays into the wilderness within our tamed hearts," but he wasn't about to reveal his sacred lore to anybody who put more trust in a crystal than in their common sense.

Frank's hale and hearty as ever, a new father again, doing what he can, he says, to repopulate the aboriginal world after the genocide of 500 years.

Winona was able to quit her waitress job. In the summer she flies fishermen to their remote cabins and walleye lakes, and in the fall she flies hunters, and in the winter ice fishermen, which leaves her free in the spring to help with the maple sugaring.

Arnie Westhall, the young ranger who was found wandering the streets on all fours in the belief that he was a bear, going through garbage and rolling onto his back wanting his stomach rubbed, turns out to be Senator Judy Jump's nephew. It looked as if Arnie had been abusing drugs—there were needle marks in his arms—and that he had gotten hold of some unknown substance which sent him around the bend. He had trashed the Division of Forestry office, smashing the firearms cabinet. He's at the state hospital in Brainerd, where it was thought the effect of the drugs would wear off eventually, but the delusion that he's a bear seems implacable and deep-seated.

Arnie will enjoy a kind of fame as the subject of a documentary being shot about transformation and evolution. A young independent producer, Ned or Ted something, videotapes Arnie in all his bearish mimicry. He's videotaping others, too—a man who believes he's a cocker spaniel and a woman who perches on tables convinced she's an owl.

I feel brutish and peckish sometimes, too, or growly, but I don't let it go to my head.

The Vietnam Vets have made a shrine of Ben Creswell's cabin, spruced it up and hung the heads of dead animals on the walls and erected a bear stuffed by Bud Ostrum, Bud's first venture into large-animal taxidermy, his new hobby since retiring from the Postal Service. It was poor Towley who was shot in season by one of the vets. I can't bear to think of him out there full of sawdust, even if he is an honorary Green Beret.

The Minnesota Chess Club installed a chess display in the cabin that recreates the last game Ben played. It all seems maudlin and sentimental to me, but Ben did fight to keep us free, that's what he believed anyway, for a while, anyway, and there's something noble in any sacrifice. His daughter came for the dedication but didn't seem to know what to make of it all. She's teaching at Berkeley and writing a book on Images of War and Suffering with a chapter on Goya already published in a scholarly journal.

Emma's is boarded up and abandoned, no use for it and no inclination to raze it. That would just cost money. So it will slowly crumble into the earth, the way we all will someday.

We bought Billy Ostrum's old place, the big A-frame overlooking Lost Heart Lake with the eagle nest close by. You and I went to a party there, remember, in our younger days, when Billy was President of the Community College. He was the intellectual Ostrum, I guess. He's Dean of Liberal Arts at Ezekiel College, now that he's found Jesus.

Of course they tried to pay me less because I'm a woman, but Senator Judy Jump pulled her strings and even browbeat the Legislature into establishing a world-class bear research center, library, museum (no stuffed bears, thank you!), and conference center, the Rudy Center, there in our old Home-Sweet-Home.

I'm trying to find time to write the bear book, *Bear with Me*, you were supposed to write but which the publisher wants me to write, which makes sense, since you were merely patching together the articles I had already written. But those days of my ghost writing are over, which I'm sure you'll agree is just as well, everything finally on the up and up.

I told the editor that I was sure you'd pay back the advance you'd received.

He liked my idea for *Bear with Me*, which is to forget about the old articles and start fresh, weaving together personal reminiscences and mythic bear lore with scientific facts, a warp and woof of female grit and bearish wit.

My buddy-o is working on a screenplay about a man and a woman who turn into bears at night and fight crime. He's pitching it as The Werewolf Meets The Avengers, or Batman Meets Beauty and the Beast. He worries that he's selling out, wonders if he should write a tender love story instead, but I tell him love's the same everywhere, high-concept or art house, it's madness and tumult and then a few years by the fire in your furry slippers forgetting what you had for lunch.

Oh, speaking of memory, Mother married a blind musician with no legs. We went to the wedding, which was officiated by a young woman with tattoos who works at the nursing home and is a minister in The Church of the Lonely and Forgotten, based in California, one of those mail-order ordinations but legal as any other, and Mother and Terrell share a small apartment in an assisted living complex. Mother is Terrell's eyes and legs, and he remembers things for her. She had an infection where she had pierced her eyebrow, but it cleared up, so she put another ring beside the first. Where it will end I don't know, but she's happy, and can we ask for more than that at any age?

And speaking of marriage—well, Pepper and Joe Manello are not married, but they are living happily together. Joe had a lonely life after his wife left him for that insurance adjuster in town for only three days assessing the damage to Ostrum's Outfitting when it burned down and determining if it was arson, but he couldn't prove anything even though Ostrum had moved all the expensive equipment out the day before the fire and then used the insurance money to build his new expanded store. Joe's wife was developing allergies to animals, so maybe it worked out for the best, after all.

So Pepper lives with Joe, secure in his big hairy arms, and she doesn't mind the stray dogs and cats he takes in yelping and wailing, or the bald eagle with the broken wing screeching, or the three-legged wolf howling, or the various animals, wild and domestic, in their recuperating pens whimpering and snarling and growling. She cleans up their pens, and she cares for the animals in Joe's ICU—at the moment one of Vera Ostrum's emus and a blue jay a little girl brought in. Joe has acres of land, plenty of room for all the creatures to run and play, and they can pee wherever they want. Isn't it marvelous how God, whoever She is, works in mysterious ways?

We arrived to a lodge dusty and silent, abandoned and deserted, emptied of furnishings and hope, a habitation already surrendering to the rhythms of Nature, cobwebs in the rafters and mice nests in the corners, the house plants dead of despair, dust buried in the grease on the stove, assorted remnants still in the refrigerator molding and festering like alien protoplasms seeking a higher life form.

I'm amazed the rag rugs are still here, all three of them: The medium-size one I made first, after the children went off to school, which lay beside our bed, woven with your tux from our wedding and my nightgown from our honeymoon and the old brown overcoat you wore after it was no longer a fashion statement and my maternity clothes I couldn't sell at the yard sale. The large rag rug in the living room, brightly colored with the clothes discarded by teenagers and my dresses from a colorful period and your red long johns and my green spangled toreador pants that had such a short fashion span and your Nehru jacket that had an even briefer moment at the haberdasher's. And the smaller rug in the kitchen that lay between the stove and the table, the absorber of spilled milk I cried over and beer that foamed over like frustration, a more somber rug from a darker time, yet it too impudent with the white of Lionel Running Bear's torn T-shirt and my ripped summer skirt with bright flowers, memories of a clumsy chaotic summer twisted into the corduroy trousers you wore that winter you had the assistant with long brown hair—each rug a tattered mosaic of memories stripped to ribbons and braided into concentric whorls of love, heartbreak, and abandoned dreams, a pathway to a center, a trail out of despair.

I wondered if I should throw them out, discard a mottled past. I even rolled them up and dragged them outdoors. But I ran into the clothesline, the one I hung to air the sheets in summer, and I hung the rugs on the line, and I beat the dust and detritus out of them. I put my back into it, and the dust flew, and so did my anger and sadness.

We had Joe and Pepper over to the lodge for a quiet re-opening celebration. Pepper, who has a training in astrology, had offered to do my chart, and I said, Why not, even though, Spinozean rationalist that I am, I don't place any reliance on that maltreated forerunner of NASA. It wasn't her predictions that startled me—I don't really believe that I'll get involved in politics (although, come to think of it, Celine Ostrum did ask me if I'd consider running for Manhattan Township Supervisor. I'd forgotten about that!)—nor do I understand what it means when she predicts that I'll be taking care of a baby soon (unless that's what Babette was hinting at when she said she'd been feeling sick to her stomach recently, which I thought was disappointment at being rejected by the Marines and having to work at a restaurant on Cape Cod, where she said the cook had taken an interest in her after learning her father was a famous chef). No, it wasn't Pepper's predictions which startled me, prescient as they may turn out to be, or even her pretty accurate recounting of my life up until now (love, broken heart, travel, new love, job—but she knew all that anyway).

It was what she said when we went into the room that used to be our bedroom, which is now a small museum schoolchildren visit, with pictures of bears on the walls, and here and there assorted artifacts you left behind in your frantic flight, and a TV where they can watch videos of animals in the wild (your video library that was abandoned), and they can look through your forsaken notes and files to see how real research is done, the raw and the uncensored, as it were, from which come the cogent expositions of the research paper. (The files have proved to be surprisingly popular. You wouldn't think adolescents would be interested in scholarship, but they head straight for the filing cabinet, and they spend hours going over those old notes and articles of yours, whispering and giggling, proving, I guess, that true scholarship, if approached in the right way, can be fun and exciting.)

But I was speaking of Pepper, and when I showed her the room and turned off the lights so she could see the stars, she looked at them a long time, which I assumed was due to her interest in astrology, but when I turned the lights back on she showed me my star chart, the one she had consulted to investigate my destiny—for her birthday Joe bought her software that does it all on a computer, spits out the sky at the exact moment you were born, right above where you were born—and she said, Take a good look, then turn out the lights.

And, by golly, you never told me, Lyle, all those days you spent putting those thousands of tiny stars on our ceiling, recreating the visible universe so we would have it to contemplate even on wintry nights when we had to stay indoors, and you never told me lo those many years we were married, neither in times of joy or nights of trouble, that you had made the sky above us the exact same sky that looked down on my birth. It was a secret you carried in your heart, and I guess you were waiting for me to discover it, or ask, but I never did, not when it might have counted.

The rugs are back in the lodge. My buddy says that's all we have behind us, the past, and if we walk on it every day it means our soles (souls?) are warmed by memories of dutifulness, resolve, tenderness, and forgiveness, as well as the less comforting things that are a part of us, things we think are unnecessary and painful, like scabs and mosquitoes and shit, but a scab means a wound is healing, and if we didn't have mosquitoes we wouldn't have dragonflies or bats or swallows flying their graceful swoops, and shit may be smelly but it's a way of getting rid of what we don't need anymore, and there's a beauty in that, too.

Love,
Ursula

"William Borden is a novelist, playwright, poet, and essayist. His novel *Superstoe*, first published by Harper & Row in the U.S. and by Victor Gollancz in England, was recently reissued by Orloff Press. The film adaptation of his play *The Last Prostitute*, starring Sonia Braga, was shown on Lifetime Television and in Europe. His short stories have won the PEN Syndicated Fiction Prize and The Writers Voice Fiction Competition and have been published in over 50 magazines and anthologies. His plays have won over 100 playwriting competitions and have had over 300 productions throughout the world. A Core Alumnus Playwright at The Playwrights' Center in Minneapolis, he was Fiction Editor of The North Dakota Quarterly 1986-2002 and is Chester Fritz Distinguished Professor of English Emeritus at The University of North Dakota. He has an A.B. from Columbia University and an M.A. from the University of California at Berkeley. Born in Indianapolis, he has lived on the windswept plains of North Dakota, on the sun-splashed Greek island of Paros, on a pine-shaded lake in northern Minnesota, and, since 2004, within howling distance of several coyotes 30 miles east of Dallas. He and Nancy Lee-Borden, his wife of 48 years, have 3 adult children and 7 grandchildren."